D0251928

SWEET A

"That's one of my favorite sounds," she said absently.

"What, deer hooves?"

"Yep."

"It's a good one. Flapping's good, too."

"Flapping?"

"Wings, flags, sails, the ears of dogs and cats when they shake their heads," he said easily.

As though this was the most ordinary thing in the world to say. And not, for some strange reason, the most perfect thing she'd ever heard.

She looked at him, and all at once she had an epiphany about what it meant to be "enchanted." As though the stars were in her veins as well as in the sky.

The few inches separating them in the twilight of his truck's cab all but pulsed. She'd never been more acutely aware of another human. Or of her own skin, of her own heart beating, sending the blood singing into her ears. And they seemed so bound together, suddenly, it seemed patently absurd not to touch him.

By Julie Anne Long

Hot in Hellcat Canyon
The Legend of Lyon Redmond
It Started with a Scandal
Between the Devil and Ian Eversea
It Happened One Midnight
A Notorious Countess Confesses
How the Marquess Was Won
What I Did for a Duke
I Kissed an Earl
Since the Surrender
Like No Other Lover
The Perils of Pleasure

Coming Soon

Wild at Whiskey Creek

ATTENTION: ORGANIZATIONS AND CORPORATIONS
HarperCollins books may be purchased for educational, business, or sales promotional use. For information, please e-mail the Special Markets Department at SPsales@harpercollins.com.

JULIE ANNE LONG

HOT IN HELLCAT CANYON

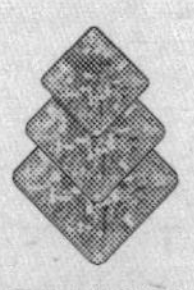

AVONBOOKS
An Imprint of HarperCollins*Publishers*

This is a work of fiction. Names, characters, places, and incidents are products of the author's imagination or are used fictitiously and are not to be construed as real. Any resemblance to actual events, locales, organizations, or persons, living or dead, is entirely coincidental.

AVON BOOKS
An Imprint of HarperCollins*Publishers*
195 Broadway
New York, New York 10007

Copyright © 2016 by Julie Anne Long
ISBN 978-0-06-239761-4
www.avonromance.com

All rights reserved. No part of this book may be used or reproduced in any manner whatsoever without written permission, except in the case of brief quotations embodied in critical articles and reviews. For information address Avon Books, an Imprint of HarperCollins Publishers.

First Avon Books mass market printing: June 2016

Avon Trademark Reg. U.S. Pat. Off. and in Other Countries, Marca Registrada, Hecho en U.S.A.
Avon, Avon Books, and the Avon logo are trademarks of HarperCollins Publishers.
HarperCollins® is a registered trademark of HarperCollins Publishers.

Printed in the U.S.A.

10 9 8 7 6 5 4 3 2 1

If you purchased this book without a cover, you should be aware that this book is stolen property. It was reported as "unsold and destroyed" to the publisher, and neither the author nor the publisher has received any payment for this "stripped book."

HOT IN HELLCAT CANYON

CHAPTER 1

Britt burst out her front door, stag-leaped her sagging front step, scattered three deer and that blue jay whose hobby was harassing her cat, and finished yanking her blue camisole down over her head before she hit the ground.

"Don't eat my roses!" she implored the deer over her shoulder. In vain, probably.

She was going to have to run to make it to work on time, and the merciful morning cool was already beginning to give way to merciless summer heat.

A half mile down the dirt road Roy and Willa Boyd's dog Jet exploded off his porch to chase her, *yapyapyapping* and out of his head with excitement, but then he felt that way about nearly every moving creature. He was the love child of a basset hound and a standard poodle and frankly looked more like a caterpillar than a dog. Britt slowed down a little just to give him hope that he might one day catch up to her on his four-inch legs and bite an ankle. Because everyone needed hope.

He gave up after about a hundred yards, satisfied he'd acquitted himself well in defense of his porch.

Which was her cue to pause and catch her breath.

She tilted her head back and rested her hands on her

hips as she gulped in air. A red-tailed hawk was circling lazily above in the empty, dazzling blue sky, looking for breakfast.

Behind her the hills rose up and up in a glorious tangle of every kind of green: pines, redwoods, oaks, manzanita, Indian paintbrush. Off to the east, scattered along the canyon's edge and overlooking the Hellcat River, the windows of the rustic palaces belonging to tech billionaires and other people who had money up the wazoo glinted like diamonds in the rising morning sun.

She got moving again.

A few feet later the tamped dirt road turned into pavement and became the main road into town.

She jogged down the gently winding main street, past long rows of Victorian storefronts faded to muted butter mint shades by weather, time, and dust. She held her hand up to her face like a horse blinder when she passed Kayla Benoit's boutique so she wouldn't have to see that white dress in the window. Kayla was opening up and thought she was waving, so she waved gaily back.

The Misty Cat Cavern looked like a saloon because it had always been a saloon, and its placement at the end of Main Street was strategic, or so legend had it: inebriated miners who stumbled (or were thrown) out the door only had a short distance to roll right back down to the main gold mining camp. Some of its long, lurid history lingered in the décor and the alleged ghost of a prostitute named Nimble Nellie, shot by a jealous miner. She was the *original* Hellcat, or so it was said. Britt was grateful she hadn't yet met Nellie. She certainly sympathized with her, though.

She swung around back and jabbed her key into the lock in the back door, and wove her way through the kitchen into the main restaurant.

A row of windows set high in the wall showed the

tops of pines and fragments of blue sky. A kindly, dusty, golden, tree-filtered light poured through them early in the morning, but by late afternoon the summer sun was as brutal as an X-ray. A collective howl of torment rose in the Cavern if anyone dared crack the blinds then.

The spinning blades of the ceiling fan casually slaughtered flies, which plummeted to the floor and tables below to be swept up or wiped away by bar rags, to be replaced by intrepid new flies slipping in the door with customers. It was the circle of life in the Misty Cat Cavern. Britt pulled all the chairs down and grabbed a soapy rag and pushed a few little carcasses off tables, then grabbed a broom to do a quick sweep, called "Hey Giorgio!" when she heard rustling in the back room, and got a grunt in reply.

Giorgio was dragging the cover off the pool table and plugging in Glenn's prized vintage beer signs, which lent a luridly cheery glow to the murk. When the sheriff was in for lunch Giorgio surreptitiously disconnected the old Hamm's sign, a signal to put the kibosh on any obvious betting. Britt was positive the sheriff wasn't that unobservant. He probably just picked his battles. There were plenty to choose from in Hellcat Canyon.

Giorgio hailed from way up in the hills in the Coyote Creek settlement, which is where any trouble seemed to originate, and he was small and wiry and dark, as if he'd been grown in the shade and in secret. His mother had named him for perfume she'd shoplifted from a Walgreens back in the eighties. She was in jail, along with nearly his entire family for crimes ranging from petty to grand, and everyone had decided that only sheer contrariness had kept Giorgio out of it. He possessed a certain charisma, if you liked your men saturnine and taciturn (two of Britt's favorite words, because they sounded exactly like what they were, and two words Giorgio had never uttered in his life). But he was a veritable savant with the grill.

"It's gonna be a hot one," she called, mostly for the pleasure of hearing her voice echo in the place, because she knew Giorgio wouldn't honor such obviousness with even a grunt. The acoustics were close to magical, thanks to some alchemy involving the height of the ceiling and the aged redwood floors and walls, and it was the reason touring college bands occasionally detoured here as they made their way through to big California cities or up to Oregon or Nevada. The tiny stage was tucked all the way in the back and flanked the single restroom. There was a small round window up high in the bathroom door, and if a drummer was tall enough, they could gaily wave to anyone sitting on the toilet. Fortunately most drummers never figured this out.

The various locks on the back clunked open and Sherrie at last rushed through the kitchen, her red hair a torch in the soft light. She and her husband, Glenn, the owners of the Misty Cat, were, if Britt had to guess, well north of fifty years old, gone soft in some parts, harder in others, their complexions cured identically brown by decades of scorching mountain summers.

"Sorry, hon. Glenn and I got a late start this morning. I ended up in emergency room last night in Black Oak." She held up a splinted wrist. "We were doing mermaid and fisherman and I fell off the bed."

"I'm sor . . . you were . . . mer . . . *what*?"

Talking to Sherrie was often like taking a stroll along the edge of a cliff—one minute everything was peaceful and easy, even dull, the next you could be hurtling into space, scrambling for a handhold on reality. Sherrie had no filter. Whereas Britt had become someone who filtered nearly everything.

"I dress up as a mermaid and he dresses up like a fisherman, and we pretend the bed is a rock and I'm stranded on it, and then a fisherman comes along to rescue me. But I have to do 'favors'"—she performed air quotes with her good hand—"for him in return."

She said this as matter-of-factly as some people might recite the ingredients for banana bread.

Britt froze, assaulted by questions. Did Glenn wear hip waders? Was a net involved?

Then again, knowing might be worse than not knowing.

"How did you make the tail?" Britt finally whispered. She couldn't help it. Both she and Sherrie loved crafts.

Sherrie leaned in and laid a hand on Britt's arm confidingly. "Listen, hon, there was nothing to it. I cut up an old pair of leggings and sewed them back to—"

The front door swung open, and in came a gust of hot air and a whoosh of that early-morning, pine-and-sage-and-crushed-leaves perfume of the California foothills.

And a man.

They all went silent.

He was lean and tall—his head brushed the top of the door frame—and something about his posture made Britt glance at his hips. She wouldn't have been surprised to see a holster slung there, as if they'd all been transported back to the Wild West and he was the fastest gun. He had that sort of presence.

He stood in the doorway a moment, adjusting to the cool dark.

"Any chance you folks serving lunch yet?"

His boots echoed on the floor as he slowly stepped forward into the light. Longish dark hair, nearly to his shoulders, pushed back behind his ears. Pale blue chambray shirt open at the throat and rolled to his elbows, worn loose over faded jeans. Something about the way his clothes fit his body told her he hadn't bought any of them at Walmart. His stubble-darkened jaw could have been drawn with a protractor, so precise and severe were its lines. It was a face straight out of a daguerreotype. He had a sort of elemental beauty that smacked her in the solar plexus the way her first glimpse of Hellcat Canyon had.

"Maybe." Giorgio had sized him up as *not one of us, and better-looking than me*, and defaulted to surly.

Britt shot Giorgio a quelling look.

A crashing sound and an oath in the kitchen heralded Glenn's arrival.

"We serve it all day," Britt corrected, as Sherrie slipped into the kitchen to see what her husband had knocked over.

The stranger came closer, tilting his head back to study the menu chalked on the board hanging horizontally behind Giorgio. TRY THE GLENNBURGER! the sign always said. EIGHT SECRET INGREDIENTS!

She and Giorgio watched him in uncertain silence, as if a bear had wandered in. Weeks could go by before someone they didn't know by at least their first name crossed the threshold of the Misty Cat.

"Can you give me just a hint about the secret ingredients in a Glennburger?"

Giorgio slowly mopped beneath his armpit with a handkerchief. Britt had never seen anyone mop an armpit threateningly before, but it was happening before her eyes.

"Sweat," he finally answered.

The stranger was regarding Giorgio with mild but unblinking curiosity that made the hair prickle on the back of Britt's neck. As if nothing anyone did could surprise him, but if they tried, boy, would he be ready.

"That's funny," he said. "I was going to guess 'love.'"

It was a masterpiece of irony.

"It has onions," Britt volunteered hurriedly. "Spices. Nothing . . . bodily."

"Guess it's one of those things where you have to know the Masonic handshake to get the recipe."

It was meant to be a joke, but it fell into the vacuum of Giorgio's hostility.

She suspected the stranger anticipated that it would. And didn't care.

Britt shot Giorgio another look. She mostly understood his instinct to attempt to drive off interlopers, the way Jet the dog did. Most of the people who lived in Hellcat Canyon liked it the way it was, and strangers were reminders that if things were different elsewhere, they could change here, too.

But unkindness always got her back up.

Sherrie emerged from the kitchen—Glenn behind her—accurately assessed the situation and the stranger with wide, appreciative eyes, and then gave him a little pat, part pity, part motherliness.

"Why don't you have a seat right over here, hon, and we'll get the grill going. Britt will bring you something cold or something hot, whatever you need. If you try the Glennburger, you'll never forget it."

Enveloped in warm, easy Sherrie-ness, he did what he was told and settled himself beneath a window.

Britt was inclined to like people who flung things like "Masonic handshakes" into jokes. They were few and far between in a small town like Hellcat Canyon, though people here would surprise you. Everyone had their own reason for living here, often very personal or, even, like her own, as secret as the ingredients in a Glennburger. When she'd arrived she'd burrowed into the place like it was a blanket fort, deciding she'd found safety at last.

Though she was smart enough to know that safety was an illusion and that just calling it safety didn't make it so.

He sat down, leaned back with a sigh, and stretched out those long legs as though he'd been walking on them for miles. His boots were dusty and a bit creased, but gorgeous in their simplicity. They looked as though he'd owned them forever and had probably cost more than the land the Misty Cat Cavern sat on.

He plucked up the menu wedged between the napkin holder and the little Tabasco bottle and fanned it open.

"What can I get for you?" she said briskly.

"Well, I think I've already had the something cold," he said in a confiding, lowered voice to Britt, with a tilt of his head in the direction of Giorgio. "And I guess that would make you the something . . ."

He trailed off again at whatever he saw in her face.

"Well, I've been driving all night, and it feels like lunchtime, so I think I'll have a beer," he said. Sounding amused. "A Sierra Nevada. The Stout."

"Sierra Nevada Stout." She didn't write it down.

"And I'll try the hamburger. Excuse me, the Glenn-burger. With all of the ingredients, secret and otherwise. Medium rare."

"Do you want cheese?" she asked.

"The cheese isn't secret?"

"No. A bit enigmatic, maybe."

He smiled at that, slowly, with genuine pleasure, and held her gaze a little longer than necessary. His eyes were a startling crystalline blue. She was reminded of rivers dashed into foam over rocks, and just like that, she was as breathless as if she'd dived into the icy snowmelt runoff of the Hellcat.

She mentally smacked away a surge of want as if it were a fanged predator. That kind of want hadn't breached her defenses in a long, long time.

She steeled her gaze to impassivity.

His gaze turned quizzical and then faintly amused; then he dropped his eyes casually to the menu again. Which she was happy about, because then she could stare at him unguarded. His shirtsleeves were rolled nearly to his elbows. His forearms were tanned gold and corded and dusted in coppery hair. His fingers were long and elegant but the hands looked well used; an old pale scar traversed one. A musician, or a carpenter, maybe. A narrow streak of silver threaded up through his black hair where he'd pushed it behind his ear.

A circlet of tiny, neat black words was tattooed on his wrist: "It has been a beautiful fight."

He closed the menu. "I'll have cheddar on it, then. And I have another question."

"Ask away!" she chirped.

He leaned casually back then, arms folded across his chest, and looked up at her for a moment without speaking. Then his mouth quirked wryly, as if to say, *Now, we both know chirpiness isn't your real personality.*

She gave him her blankly bright waitress face.

"Why is this place called the Misty Cat Cavern?" He said this with great gravity.

His voice was a visceral pleasure: deep, almost lazy, a bow drawn at leisure across a cello string. She thought she detected something Southern in the way he took his time with the vowels. It was a little too easy to imagine how he might sound right after he opened his eyes in the morning, when his sheets were still warm and the sun still just a suggestion of light at the top of Whiplash Peak.

"Well, from what I understand, the previous owner—Earl Holloway?—was falling-down drunk when he ordered the sign over the phone about thirty years ago. Apparently the guy on the other end swore Earl had said 'Misty Cat Cavern' and refused to make him a new one. Earl couldn't afford another sign. He about threw a fit but he hung it. It's the only neon sign on the whole street."

"What did he mean to call it?"

"The Aristocrat Tavern."

The stranger laughed, sounding surprised and genuinely delighted.

What a great laugh. She wanted to dive into that, too.

"I'll be back with your beer," she said, and spun like someone fleeing.

She scribbled his order on a tag and handed it over to Giorgio.

"Did you see his sweet little butt?" Sherrie murmured happily, as she smiled warmly at a swelling tide of incoming customers. "It was as neat as two eight balls sitting in his jeans."

Behind her, Glenn, tying on his apron, gave a short laugh and shook his head and sighed. "Sherrie. Eight balls!" Thirty years of marriage and four kids later, Glenn still thought Sherrie hung the moon, and she sailed through life on the calm sea of his unconditional admiration. She was still capable of embarrassing him, though.

Giorgio was still glowering, his spatula clanging and scraping the grill with more fervor than usual. He sounded like a German industrial band. He already had a row of customers lined up on stools in front of him, eggs and muffin halves and sausage sizzling away side by side in a geometry he understood. He never got an order wrong.

Britt had indeed seen the stranger's ass. "Eight balls" didn't quite capture it metaphorically, but it was as perfect as anything she'd ever seen. A veritable Fabergé egg of an ass, rare and compelling. She could all too easily imagine sliding her hands down over it, but this had more to do with the entirety of him: the denim, the eyes, that barely noticeable silver streak in his hair, that whiff of sandalwood she'd caught, the leanness.

It had been years since thoughts that wanton had sneaked past her ramparts. Most men in town were too polite, or maybe too lazy, to continue attempting to scale the slippery wall of her reserve. Mostly that was okay with her.

She'd learned at a young age how dangerous it could be to see men in terms of their component parts. A man showed you who he was inside pretty quickly if you were willing to pay attention, but even then, sometimes it was too late.

"Last we see of him," Giorgio predicted, gesturing with his chin. Which might be his longest sentence of the day.

God, she hoped so.

God, she hoped not.

"I don't know. Glenn's hamburgers really are the best," Britt said. "He may not be able to help himself."

Glenn beamed at her, his magnificent brush of a mustache twitching in pride.

She smiled back. She was reminded that making someone else happy was always the quickest, best way to get a little hit of happiness when she needed some.

She exhaled. Simplicity, contentment, love. She liked being near it. It was like a refreshing vast ocean she could dip a toe into, even though she'd grown afraid to wade on in.

CHAPTER 2

Not from here.

He could practically hear everyone drawing that conclusion with a single glance. He'd been born in an even smaller town, if you could even call that collection of shacks stuffed full of poor and bitter people a town, and he'd assessed people in just that way, too. He was an island amid the customers eddying around him and filling in all the tables while he devoured his hamburger, which was surprisingly as exceptional as advertised.

He glanced back and his view was butts on stools arrayed before the surly cook, mostly clad in Wranglers. Clearly a popular spot, the Misty Cat. He intercepted a few searching looks—a lingering one from a guy with a badge, to whom he nodded politely, a hard one from a good-looking red-faced blockhead, which he met with utter disinterest—and other kinder, more curious ones. Over the years he'd grown accustomed to every imaginable kind of stare, but no one here seemed to precisely recognize him. These days this was mostly a relief.

He'd learned over the years that some people just needed to classify the whole world as "better than me" or "not as good as me" or "just like me."

He wasn't one of them. He'd simply waited for his first

opportunity to get the hell out of Sorry, Tennessee, and grabbed it in both hands. He hadn't looked back.

As it turned out, however, you could never quite take the country out of the boy.

A lot had happened since then. A wedding. The army. Triumphs. Failures. A long stretch during which he'd done nothing much but suffer the whipsaws of his ego, drink, philosophize, read, fight, and seduce. Every last thing that had happened to him had somehow become useful.

And nobody with any sense fucked with him anymore.

While the diner watched him, he watched the waitress. Not overtly. More the way you'd rest tired eyes on something lovely, a bird flitting from tree to tree, maybe.

He left a big but not obnoxiously big tip, writing "This is for saying 'enigmatic'" on the bill, and slipped out, daydreaming about her eyes. A clear pale green with tawny flecks floating in them, they made him think of panning for gold in Sierra Nevada rivers. He'd liked her delicate nerviness, the fine shoulder blades exposed by skinny straps of her camisole, the tiny tattoo on one of them he couldn't quite make out because she'd been darting like a hummingbird among the customers. She had streaky gold-brown hair twisted and fastened up off her neck with a filigree barrette and a soft mouth at odds with that hard expression she'd clearly perfected in order to shut down men. He'd wanted to lay a hand on her arm and say, *Shhh, honey. It will all be okay*, but he didn't know why, and he suspected she'd deck him if he did. He smiled. Wouldn't be the first time a woman had decked him.

But there was a sweet jolt when their eyes met. A kind of recognition. He'd known a lot of women, in nearly every sense of that word. The jolt was pretty rare.

Bachman Turner Overdrive's "Taking Care of Business" erupted from his phone. It was his agent's ringtone, though lately he thought the funeral march might be more appropriate.

"And?" was how he answered it.

"They went with someone else for the *House of Cards* guest spot. It was close, though. They told me to tell you that."

J. T. went silent. Damn.

He had just turned forty. He knew how to take a "no."

He was just too much of a fighter to ever like it.

He knew better than to ask the next question, but that had seldom stopped him from doing anything. "Who'd they go with?"

Don't say Franco Francone Don't say Franco Francone Don't say Franco Francone.

"Franco Francone."

J. T. said nothing.

His agent laughed. "It's a testament to your acting skill, J. T., that you didn't say a word but I heard 'fuck' loud and clear."

"Pardon my language," J. T. said dryly.

"Ah, shake it off. They loved you and et cetera. It's not a big deal. Francone doesn't have your chops. He isn't going to head up a cable series, for God's sake, and *The Rush* is going to be fantastic. And other agently stuff I always say to you. Did I miss anything?"

"I think that about covers it. And yeah. I know *The Rush* will be great."

"Where are you, by the way?"

"Hellcat Canyon, apparently. Truck started making noises. I got hungry. I stopped."

"Where the hell is Hellcat Canyon? I thought California had two cities. L.A. and San Francisco."

"California Gold Country. Where *The Rush* will be filmed. Had a few weeks before my schedule starts winding up again and it's more or less on the way to Napa.

Thought I'd get a sense of the place, maybe find a place to stay. Gorgeous here," he said absently. "Long way from L.A."

He didn't tell Al he'd got in the truck last night and just started driving because waiting on news of *Last Call in Purgatory* was going to make him crazy and he couldn't stay cooped up in a house. He couldn't remember the last time he'd cared this much about a role.

He didn't ask about it. If there was news, Al would tell him.

"All right, then. If you can't be good, be newsworthy," Al said dryly. "See you at Nicasio's wedding in Napa?"

"Yeah. Thanks, Al." J. T. was supposed to give a toast there, and for many reasons, he still had no idea what he was going to say.

"You bet, J. T."

J. T. ended the call and was just about to stuff his phone back into his pocket when a text chimed in.

He sighed gustily. He knew exactly who it was from.

Better Luck Next Time, McCord.

Franco must have fist-pumped when he thought of that. It was a brilliantly horrible thing to say for a lot of reasons. J. T. almost laughed.

He did what he always did whenever Franco sent him a text about anything.

He sent back a photo of one of his Emmys.

It made Franco *nuts*.

It was just one of the things J. T. had that Franco claimed J. T. had stolen from him.

Franco was wrong on every count, of course. But it wasn't as though J. T. was entirely innocent.

He finally put his phone away.

He got a few feet closer to his truck and paused to

crouch and scratch a black-and-white cat drowsing in front of a florist's shop.

It arched and stretched to greet him, then ecstatically rotated its head so he could reach under its chin.

A little girl, nine, ten years old, peachy skinned, hair bound in two ruthlessly symmetrical strawberry-blonde braids, pushed open the door of the shop and paused to stare at him.

"Isn't my cat soft? His name is Peace and Love."

"Peace and Love, huh? Why Peace and Love?"

"Because he has a paisley on his side."

"So he does." J. T. scratched the black paisley shape.

"And my grandma is kind of a hippie and she wishes my mama was one, too. She thinks my mama needs to loosen up."

"What's a hippie?" he asked gravely and wholly mischievously.

"Oh, you know, they have long hair and their houses smell good. It's the sense."

"The . . . incense?"

"Yeah! It's nice!"

He laughed. Peace and Love the cat rolled over shamelessly so he could scratch the white bib on his chest.

He looked up at the girl and then past her. He'd parked his truck down the street, across from what appeared to be a palm reader, judging from the huge painted hand swinging from two chains over the sidewalk. He was worried about that god-awful sound the truck was making. He had a hunch about what it was, because he'd fixed it before. He could have bought fifteen trucks just like it, if he wanted. Instead, he'd fixed nearly everything on that truck twice.

Suddenly the little girl's eyes went huge, her jaw dropped, and he watched her face go brilliant with astonished elation.

J. T. knew exactly what was going to happen next.

"WOOOoow," she exhaled.

Damn.

And then she threw her head back.

"MOOOOOOM!" she screamed.

Foof! The cat shot straight up in the air, every hair erect, and it disappeared in a blur of scrambling legs, like a cartoon. J. T. staggered backward, blinking, his eardrums shriveling.

The little girl began pogoing excitedly all around him, her pigtails flapping. "MOM MOM MOM MOM OH MY GOSH MOM YOU WON'T BELIEVE WHO'S PETTING PEACE AND LOVE MOM HURRY COME SEE!"

Hurry? Now that was funny. As if he'd bolt, or evaporate in this heat if her mother didn't get there fast enough.

A woman hurtled out of the shop, the bells on the door jangling frantically.

"For the love of God, Annalise, what on—"

She stopped short.

He straightened slowly to his entire height, as unthreateningly as possible, as if he'd been caught in the act of something.

Which he had, in a way. He'd been caught in the act of being himself.

The woman's dark red hair was bundled up on her head in a big ponytail, and he could see where her daughter got her eyes. Same color, same shape, and they got big and round and awestruck in just the same way when she saw him.

She spoke wonderingly. "Good heavens. Is it really you? Mr. John Tennessee *McCord*? What brings you to our little town?"

He liked the "Mr." Women who were about to get hysterical didn't often add a "Mr."

"About to start filming a new series about the California Gold Rush on location nearby. Called *The Rush.* Thought I'd get a sense of the place. Pretty town, Hellcat Canyon. Just ate the best burger of my life at the Misty Cat."

He knew that would be all over town in a heartbeat.

She glowed. "My parents own that place. Glenn and Sherrie Harwood. I'm Eden Harwood."

Ah, small towns. "You should be proud."

She tore her eyes from him briefly.

"Hush, you. I know you're excited, Annalise, but you're being very rude. Apologize to Mr. McCord for screaming. He has ears, just like you do, and you're going to deafen him. And stop pointing. I can see him."

"Enthusiasm is good for my career, ma'am." His ears were still ringing. He resisted an impulse to twist a finger in one to see whether the eardrum was intact.

"I'm sorry for screaming, Mr. McCord," said young Annalise.

"*What?*" he teased, cupping his ear.

Mother and daughter laughed. Albeit a little giddily.

"We often watch repeats in the afternoon of your show, Mr. McCord. That's how Annalise knows you."

It was how nearly everybody knew him, if they did. Repeats of a show that lasted seven outrageously popular years and had ended a decade ago but lived on in quite a few markets at various times of day. He thought he looked quite a bit different now; but then again, when millions of people had stared at you week after week for quite a few years, anonymity was kind of out of the question. His eyes, anyone would tell him, were unmistakable. An indie band out of Minneapolis had even scored a minor hit with "Eyes Like Tennessee."

"Say the thing you always said on TV, Mr. McCord. Will you please please *pleeeeease*?" Annalise folded her hands and implored him.

"Sorry, sweetie, I'll get in trouble from my bosses for saying *that word* outside the television." He winked.

He invented new reasons not to say "that thing" every time he was asked.

He would die happy if he never had to say that word again. For so many reasons.

Annalise was apparently satisfied with this explanation. Kids always related to getting in trouble for saying the wrong thing.

"Would it be rude to trouble you for an autograph?" her mother asked. "It's just that we enjoy your show so much. We'll hang it on the wall in the shop."

"No trouble at all. That is, if I can trouble you for the name of a mechanic, and maybe the name of a local hotel. My truck made some ominous noises on the way and I don't think it'll be smart to drive it."

"Ominous. O-M-I-N-O-U-S," Annalise said triumphantly.

"Wow!" He held out his fist and Annalise bumped it enthusiastically with her own little fist. "Impressive!"

"Impressive. I-M-P-R—"

"That's enough spelling for now, Annalise." But her mother was glowing. "Um, Ernie Di Giulio is probably your best bet for a mechanic. He's way out on Kilburn Road, but the bus goes right by his garage and service station." The woman squinted and pointed down the street; near the swinging palm of the palm reader was a pretty little bench and a post with a sign on it, which was clearly the bus stop. "And the Angel's Nest is the only bed and breakfast in town. It's actually just a block away from Ernie's, straight up the hill from it."

The hill she meant was apparent; the street wound up and up into the mountains—if he squinted, he could make out the rectangle of a white highway billboard. A guy was clambering over it in preparation of changing its message. Heaven forbid a moment should pass without advertising.

"I don't suppose this town has a taxi service?"

He was pretty sure he knew the answer. He was just curious about what she'd say.

"Of course we do!" she said. "But I think he's taking Mrs. Gordimer to the grocery store right now. There's a sale on chicken thighs. She doesn't have a car and she just got her Social Security check."

This was pretty much the answer he'd expected. He smiled. "Guess I timed it wrong."

"I don't know if they're full up at the Angel's Nest, but I'm afraid that's your only option right in town. If you intend to stay awhile."

He followed the direction of her pointing finger, still aimed toward the hills, but his eye was drawn up and beyond it, up past the canyon woolly and dark with pines and redwoods and oaks and manzanita and other California trees he intended to learn the names of, and several rugged peaks. He knew, he could almost *smell*, the way country boys could, that all of that was threaded through with the Hellcat River and creeks and streams.

He could imagine hidden swimming holes and magical clearings and vistas that were nearly impossible to hike to but were worth it, because when you stood there to watch the sunset it was better than church.

A broken truck, a pair of green eyes and a waitress who used the word "enigmatic"—J. T. had never needed much of a rationalization to check out a gut feeling about a beautiful woman, but it was all starting to feel a little portentous to him.

A man, even a man like him, could probably still get lost up there in the hills of Hellcat Canyon.

"I might just stay awhile, at that," he told Eden Harwood.

When J. T. reached the bus stop, a pair of women sporting the sleek, glossy tresses of the freshly blow-dried were waiting there and chattering in Spanish. Across the street a sign featuring a single, huge flirty eye fringed in luxurious sparkly gold eyelashes swung on chains. The Truth and Beauty must be a beauty salon.

They went abruptly silent when he appeared and turned big, admiring, wary eyes on him.

He knew that expression well. It translated roughly to, "Haven't I seen you somewhere before?"

He offered them an unthreatening "I'm not a vagrant" smile and stood at a polite distance.

"*Cuánto es la tarifa de autobús?*" he asked.

Thanks to movie tours and the army and all the various foreign versions of *Blood Brothers*, he'd picked up a hodgepodge of languages, and he'd wrestled a few of those into fluency during his downtime.

They beamed at him like indulgent aunts. They looked like sisters in town for a day of beauty, maybe. "One dollar fifty," one of them told him.

"*Gracias.*"

They picked up their conversation again. "Oh! Louisa!" One of them grabbed her friend's arm and turned her. "Look, Look! *Mi actriz favorita! Ella es muy hermosa!*" She pointed at the advertisement on the bus bench.

The day someone said, "Look at that beautiful woman," in any language and he didn't look was the day J. T. was in his coffin.

So he looked.

A famous actress was ecstatically clutching a new handbag with both hands and her knees were bent in what looked like the beginning of a jump for joy. "Spring into savings with Macy's!"

Oh. Hell.

He could have told them he'd heard that woman fart in

her sleep and he'd held her while she sobbed over losing a part she wanted, and that he'd ducked when she'd hurled a shoe at him during their first big fight but she'd still managed to wing his cheekbone. And millions of other little things, because J. T. was a guy who paid attention. Including the very last words she'd said to him. Which were, "Don't wait up."

Which had been a warning, but he hadn't known it at the time.

"*Mi película favorita es* Better Luck Next Time!"

He knew that she'd hated the script for *Better Luck Next Time*, but it was the movie that turned her from star into mega star.

Or to put it another way, from someone who had struggled to get a mention in any sort of press, let alone *People*, who'd suffered torments that he soothed her out of when some other actress got a mention, into someone so ubiquitous she was practically like the weather. Someone he couldn't avoid, even here in Hellcat Canyon. A town she would definitely consider beneath her notice.

He turned his back coldly on the advertisement and stared straight down the street as if the sheer force of will could urge the bus to arrive faster.

The bus didn't come.

And he imagined he could feel Rebecca Corday's eyes on his back.

Look at you, J. T., with your broken truck and your broken career. You should just get a Bentley, for God's sake. Now you're going to have to walk. Nobody who's anybody walks in Los Angeles.

Oh, Rebecca, he thought silently. You never did really get me.

He decided he was going to walk the rest of the way to Angel's Nest, and like it.

Britt finally allowed herself to stare fully and unabashedly at the stranger when he got up to walk out the door.

She watched him go, panic and relief duking it out in her gut.

Because from the moment he'd walked in, it was as if someone had dialed the universe up a notch: all of the colors were just a little brighter, and everything seemed more distinct and more beautiful, and her very blood seemed to buzz.

She'd once gone out with a guy who drove an ancient VW van with insulated walls. She could put her hand on the side of it and *feel* how loud the music was inside, from how it thumped and vibrated. And when she'd opened the door to get in, the music had burst out, echoing all over the street, setting off car alarms and prompting her dad to poke his head out the door and shout, "Turn that crap down!"

That's a bit how she felt right now. Like a VW van secretly bursting with music.

She knew that as she moved from diner to diner, giving and exchanging smiles, delivering plates, scooping up her tips—the machinery of the Misty Cat was well-oiled and nearly balletic—

He'd watched her the entire time.

She might be a little rusty at whatever this was, but she just somehow knew she hadn't seen the last of that man.

She was just pocketing the tip—*twenty bucks*!—and plucking up his bill when Casey Carson swept into the Misty Cat like a Valkyrie—which was basically how she swept in anywhere—for a to-go order. She was blonde and golden, a big-framed girl who was loud and funny and had gorgeous skin and preternatural confidence, which is how she'd successfully run the Truth and Beauty salon—where you could get anything on your body trimmed, dyed or waxed—since the age of twenty. She was almost thirty now.

She slowed down a bit when she saw Truck Donegal eating a burger.

Then she gave her hair a haughty flip to show she could care less.

Kayla Benoit rushed in right behind her. She was small and slinky and brunette, a piquant blend of the best genes her American dad and Japanese mom had to offer, and she'd named her boutique after herself, which, some people in Hellcat Canyon said, was pretty much all you needed to know about Kayla Benoit. She had a lock on the local wedding and maternity business, two events that didn't necessarily follow sequentially in Hellcat Canyon. But her heart was in the designer dresses. She didn't move a lot of them, given their price tags. Sometimes Britt thought Kayla stocked a few just to torment her.

When Kayla saw Truck she came to a full stop and her face went utterly expressionless.

Then she gave her own hair a dramatic toss and pivoted away from him.

Kayla and Casey ignored each other pointedly and entirely.

Truck hunched his shoulders and ducked his head and applied himself to his hamburger like a wood chipper, eager to get out of there.

And then Eden Harwood and her daughter Annalise burst through the door.

"Grandma! Grandpa! You'll never guess what happened!"

Sherrie rushed toward them, wiping her hands on her apron. "What are all you girls carrying on about? You win the lottery? Did Peace and Love turn out to be a girl and have kittens?"

"You're so funny, Grandma!"

Britt knew that what Sherrie was really dying to say was, *You finally met your daddy?* Because *no one* but Eden knew who Annalise's daddy was, and Eden Harwood, who was a petite woman but stubborn as a rock and almost regal, had been closemouthed on the subject since before Annalise was born. People mostly shrugged when girls in Hellcat Canyon had babies before they got married.

But Eden had been bound for bigger things, and bigger cities, like her brothers. Annalise had kept her in Hellcat Canyon.

And Britt knew, even though they tried never to show it, that her silence on the subject hurt Glenn's and Sherrie's feelings.

"I swear I saw—" Kayla blurted.

While at the same time Casey said, "Let me tell you who—"

"No, no, let me tell, let me tell!" Annalise begged all of them, with limpid eyes.

Casey and Kayla could compete with each other but they could hardly compete with a limpid-eyed ten-year-old.

They clapped their mouths shut, albeit reluctantly.

Eden put her hand on Annalise's shoulder and said, "Go on, baby. Tell everyone."

"Grandma, John Tennessee McCord ate a hamburger in here and he said it was the best ever and stopped to pet Peace and Love and he gave Mama his autograph and I spelled for him!"

"I *thought* I saw him walk by my store!" Kayla crowed.

"I thought I *saw* him walk by my store!" Casey said, as if Kayla hadn't said a word.

"I *thought* I recognized him from somewhere!" Sherrie was all radiant satisfaction. "He's that actor from *Blood Brothers*! That boy is *beautiful*. Didn't you think so, Glenn?"

"Ah, Sherrie, I wish you wouldn't ask me questions like that," Glenn was pained. "He's a good-lookin' kid, sure."

John Tennessee McCord . . . John Tennessee McCord . . . John Tennessee McCord.

Britt was sure she'd heard that name before. It seemed significant. It was a very actory name, that was for sure.

She just couldn't remember ever seeing his show.

She knew what she'd be doing tonight after work, though.

"He's probably stopping by on his way to Felix Nicasio's wedding in Napa, at the end of August," Casey said knowledgeably. "He was the director of *Blood Brothers.* All the A-listers are going. They're meeting at a secret location and going there on a *bus.* And his ex is supposed to be there, too." Casey got all the gossip mags in her salon, and she supplemented these with TMZ.

That wedding was more than a month away.

"Baby girl, let me see that autograph," Sherrie commanded Annalise. "Britt, did you know he wrote something on your tag?"

Britt hadn't noticed yet.

All the women clustered around to read it.

That's for saying "enigmatic."

Britt felt a slow flush paint her all the way to her hairline.

"Oooohhhh . . ." the women collectively sighed.

"And see? The handwriting is the same. That's him, all right." Sherrie was satisfied with her sleuthing.

"Did you really say 'enigmatic' to him?" Casey was astonished. "Gosh. I would never have thought to do that, Britt."

She was full of admiration. She and Britt were always just a little diffident around each other. Like two shy kids who think they might want to be friends but didn't quite know how to go about it.

"Wow. I didn't know you had any game, Britt," Kayla said admiringly.

"*Game?*" Britt was astounded. She laughed. "I didn't know saying 'enigmatic' was *game*."

She hadn't known that Kayla gave much thought to her at all. But she'd clearly been walking around thinking Britt couldn't possibly have game.

"He's not going to forget you. And the best game is the kind you don't even know you have," Kayla said sagely.

Which actually sounded sort of wise, once Britt figured out what she was trying to say.

But Casey rolled her eyes so hard it was a wonder they didn't fall out and bounce across the floor.

"I'm gonna let you keep that tag, hon," Sherrie said. She gave Britt a pat on the arm and an enigmatic smile of her own.

Annalise got in the last word. "He's gonna stay here, he said, cuz he's filming here and his truck is broken!"

"Yeah, yeah, he's a miracle," Glenn groused. "Those hamburgers aren't going to deliver themselves to the diners, more's the pity. If *only* I'd thought to hire someone who carried plates to tables . . ."

Britt folded the tag and stuffed it in her jeans, and whirled gracefully to accept hot plates from a glowering Giorgio, who could really hold a grudge if she let something he'd cooked get lukewarm.

CHAPTER 3

There were only three bus benches on J. T.'s long, long, sweaty walk, but it felt a bit like a gauntlet straight of out of some of his more whisky-fueled nightmares: Rebecca Corday frisked with purses; threw her head blissfully back and beamed her signature dazzling smile to show off the gemstone earrings glinting in her ears; or flung her arms out à la Julie Andrews about to perform a twirl on a Swiss mountainside, a long pastel scarf rippling out from her hand. In every image she was absolutely ecstatic to be sporting something from Macy's.

In between the little electric shock of each of those benches, he rather enjoyed what he saw of the town. Main Street was charming and tidy. The genuine Gold Rush-era Victorian storefronts were scrupulously maintained, and doorways were flanked by bright flowers in baskets hung from hooks or spilling out of terra-cotta pots. A feed store sat side by side with the beauty salon and the palm reader, near a bakery, a fishing supply shop, a tobacconist, and a karate dojo, of all things, which he really ought to look into. Little streets fanned off the main drag, too, and when he craned his head he saw more handsome buildings clearly dating back to the first time miners had set foot in this area, and what appeared to be a fountain in front of a grand old domed building, modest in scale but regal in bearing. City or town hall, if he had to guess.

So Hellcat Canyon is a little town in the middle of nowhere, maybe, but an *alive* town, as neat and pretty as any little toy village plopped down under a Christmas tree, sans snow.

Eventually the sidewalks disappeared, and the town proper gave way to a paved road thickly canopied and lined with pines and oaks. The road gradually sloped up and up and up, and apparently that's where he was headed.

At the very crest of the hill an enormous Victorian house painted a pale lavender sat like a frilly crown.

He approached gingerly. A flight of wooden steps led up to an enormous wicker furniture-bestrewn wraparound porch. Every chair on it sported a fat and flowery cushion.

It looked so thoroughly girly, he wouldn't be surprised if he was required to check his testicles at the door. The way you took off your shoes before you entered a Buddhist temple.

He made for the steps like a pole vaulter and took them two at a time.

Which was how he nearly crashed into a great, dangling wind chime. He gave it a startled swat. It retaliated by swinging at him like nunchucks.

He dodged and feinted nimbly just in time, before it took out an eye.

His black belt in karate came in useful at the damnedest times.

The chimes were still clanging together, as were his nerves, as he turned the knob on the door.

The first breath he took inside told him instantly how Dorothy felt in that field of poppies in *The Wizard of Oz*. Only instead of poppies it was potpourri. And he would lie right down here on the purple carpet and die if he was forced to breathe it longer than necessary.

He looked around grimly. The glossy mauve walls terminated in a pale blue ceiling painted in big, creamy clouds. Everywhere his eyes fell, cherubs of one kind or another gazed lovingly back at him from framed prints on the wall, their chubby cheeks perched on their clasped hands, or their little wings outspread as they cavorted through rosy skies, or from the tops of little gewgaw boxes.

And every imaginable depiction of an angel—ceramic, glass, wood, animal, stone, abstract, medieval, Art Nouveau—lined rows of shelves along the walls. It was the UN of angels.

If this was heaven, he really hoped hell had a better decorator.

As if the budget had all been spent on the interior, there wasn't a single superfluous thing about the woman behind the counter, from her haircut (no-nonsense) to her sweatshirt (gray) to her figure (solid) to the reading glasses perched on her nose. One hand was flipping through a ledger, another hand was tapping away at an old adding machine, and her eyes were darting between it and her cell phone lying on the counter next to a big brass bell that said "Ring for Help."

If only there was a big brass bell just like that for every occasion in life that warranted it, he thought.

She was about the same age as the motherly woman at the Misty Cat, and her hair color, the only flamboyant thing about her, was the same flame red. Either they were related or that particular color was on sale at Costco last week.

She glanced up.

She froze in place, one hand on the adding machine, the other on her ledger.

Then she whipped off her reading glasses as if they might be causing her to hallucinate.

She stared a moment longer, then a bemused smile spread all over her face.

"Well, what lucky wind blew *you* off course, hon? Need a room? A wife?" She gave her lashes an exaggerated flap.

He perked up. He did enjoy a big personality. And he could field that line like Babe Ruth.

"Well, that all depends"—he paused for effect—"on whether *you're* single."

"Let me just pack a bag and write a farewell note to my husband."

"Okay, but hurry it on up. Just think of all the time we've wasted up until now."

She clapped a hand over her heart as if Cupid had pierced it then and there.

He grinned. One magazine article had described him as an "Olympic-caliber flirt" and he'd considered it an honor. There was nothing to it, really. You had to like women. A lot. And they had to like you. A lot.

Her cell phone chirped an incoming text and she reflexively flicked her eyes down.

She went absolutely motionless again.

Her eyebrows dove into a puzzled frown.

She jammed her reading glasses back onto her face.

She remained absolutely still.

Then she levered her head up very, very slowly. And stared at him again.

Word certainly does travel fast in small towns, he thought dryly.

"You would probably be Mr. McCord," she said, sounding somewhat subdued.

"I am indeed Mr. McCord," he agreed pleasantly. Sorry that she was subdued.

Her aplomb stuttered for a millisecond as she stared at him and decided how one addresses a movie star, or whatever he was now. Moments like this had never stopped being odd for him. He was exactly the same person now as he was two minutes ago.

"Well, it's an honor, Mr. McCord."

"Pleasure's all mine," he said smoothly.

Another funny little silence went by. He suspected this woman was thrown for the first time in her practical, efficient life.

"I can't say I watched your show," she blurted finally, as if confessing a crime. It was a blend of apology and defensiveness. "*Blood Brothers*, was it?"

"Not everybody did. Not even my own mother." Then again, his mother had died when he was ten.

But she relaxed visibly, as if she'd been excused from a breach in etiquette.

She got brisk again. "As luck would have it, we've got one room left. Real pretty and has a view of the peak."

"Sounds perfect." He didn't ask what peak.

"Has its own bathroom."

"Always a plus." He could predict right now what the soap smelled like here. He had a manly sandalwood-scented or something or other in his overnight bag. Which he might have to use to scrub the potpourri scent out of his hair.

"Right next to the honeymoon suite."

"That'll do just fine." As long as he wasn't *in* the honeymoon suite. He'd enjoyed an unbroken streak of remaining out of honeymoon suites for most of his adult life and that was the way he liked it.

"We do get a lot of young couples in love here," she added proudly.

"It does make the world go round." The "L" word. Probably the only four-letter word J. T. had never willingly uttered in his life, at least to a woman.

She smiled at him. "No smoking, no hijinks, and breakfast buffet is served in the lounge from 7 a.m. to 9 a.m. If you need anything you can just call the front desk. My name is Rosemary."

"Just out of curiosity, if a person had hijinks in mind, where in Hellcat Canyon would he go?"

She licked a finger and swiped a bright pink flyer from a little stack on the counter and handed it to him.

It was a calendar.

"If you're up for a spot of gambling, there's bingo at St. Anne's Church tonight. Open Mic at the Misty Cat Cavern later this week. And if there's a sale on produce at Rumpole's Grocery, sometimes things get pretty competitive—you might see someone thrown down over the last zucchini. If you want to drive twenty or thirty miles in either direction, you'll find some casinos and wineries. But here in town, at least this week, you might have to use your imagination."

"Oh, I never *stop* using it," he assured her, on a purr.

"Honey, if you could see inside mine right now." She winked, and handed over his room key and reached for the ringing phone at the same time.

Britt's summer evening routine was basically her morning routine in reverse: she burst into the house, peeled off her sweaty diner clothes, hopped in the shower, sang at least one song in there, then threw on clean shorts and a tank, eschewing a bra. She paid a quick visit to all her little plant invalids lined up on a baker's rack—this week she had a sad tomato plant, an anemic basil, an African violet that had been languishing at the grocery store, and a coleus left out on the curb downtown when someone had moved. She couldn't help it: When she saw a sad plant, she took pity on it and brought it home, loved it and coached back into health, and then gave it away to anyone she thought could use a little cheering up and probably wouldn't kill it.

She pinched a leaf here, squirted some plant food in there. "You're all doing *great*," she praised.

And then she and Phillip, her cat, strolled out onto her big porch. She skirted a little obstacle course comprising an old wooden chair she'd salvaged and dragged home to scrape and repaint and a thrift-store ottoman she'd just retufted to get to her big lounge chair. She and Phillip liked to savor the cooling evening air and enjoy the familiar evening sounds—crickets tuning up, Jet getting in his last barks at what was probably a falling leaf before he got brought inside, and her neighbor Mrs. Morrison's radio tuned to a religious program. Mrs. Morrison was ninety-two and as vigorous as someone thirty years younger, apart from her bedtime, which was any minute, and all the impromptu naps she took during the day. She lived alone, which was how she liked it, and was as immovable on the subject as the big old redwood tree in her backyard. But her son and daughter were up on alternating weekends, and Britt kept an eye on her, too.

And vice versa.

The topic of the sermon must be juicy tonight. Britt couldn't hear the substance of it, but the preacher kept landing with impassioned emphasis on the word *sin*.

So all Britt heard was, "SIN" . . . *mumble mumble* . . . "SIN" . . . *mumble mumble* . . . "SIN!" . . . *mumble* . . . "SIN . . . SIN!"

All in all, it sounded more like encouragement than an admonishment.

These past few months she'd been taking her sketchbook out onto the porch in the evenings, after packing it away for more than two years. She'd stopped drawing altogether, because nearly everything about her old self had stopped for a time. As it turned out, her stubbornly silent muse was no match for Glenn's mustache. It was just *there*, fluffy and immense. The friction to her imagination was like a burr under a saddle, until she finally sat down and drew him.

As a walrus.

Big and kind and gruff and exquisitely detailed. But a walrus.

She'd been mildly astonished, but it felt right, even though it wasn't close to the sort of thing she used to draw. She had a friend whose long straight hair had fallen out after a bout with a brutal illness, and it had grown back curly, startling everyone. But it was lovely. Maybe it was a bit like that: she'd lost or jettisoned nearly all of the things she thought defined her before she'd found her way to Hellcat Canyon. It made sense that they would return as changed as she was, if and when they returned.

She wasn't going to sketch tonight, though. Something else seemed to be reasserting herself. It started with an *L* and ended with an *O* and had an *ibid* in between.

". . . . SIN!" the radio preacher enthused.

She took in a long breath and exhaled it, but it didn't help. Her heart was hammering the way it had when she'd looked up the phone number of a boy she liked in the first grade. Which was absolutely ridiculous, given that her thirtieth birthday had been two years ago.

Into her browser window she typed: "Tennessee Mc—"

"Britt, are you out there, dear?"

Britt jumped and her hands flew so guiltily from her keyboard she almost smacked her own face. "Yeah, Mrs. Morrison. Everything okay?"

"I just wanted to tell you there's a coyote in the neighborhood. I saw him with a cat in his mouth."

"Holy shi—I mean, yikes!"

"Well, half a cat," Mrs. Morrison clarified placidly.

"Jesus, Mrs. *Morrison*!"

"Britt, honey," she reproached. Coyote snacks she discussed with equanimity, but the Lord's name in vain was something else altogether.

"Sorry. Slipped out. Thanks for the warning. Phillip sleeps inside when he's not out here with me, so we should be okay."

Phillip, her old and enormous, fat orange fluffy cat, was sprawled on a cushion in front of her. He spread his toes happily at the sound of his name.

Britt dropped a hand down on him and he heaved a contented cat sigh.

"You should get married, dear. Then you wouldn't have to give your cat a man's name."

"Good advice, Mrs. Morrison."

"I don't think you have anything to worry about. Your cat is about as big as a deer, anyway."

"And at least as fierce."

Mrs. Morrison chuckled happily. Britt heard the tinkle of ice cubes in a glass. Mrs. Morrison ended all of her days with a little glass of Dr Pepper and a splash of rum on the rocks. She attributed her longevity to this. Britt thought it might have a little something to do with all her naps, too, but the woman was ninety-two. She was entitled to a vice or two.

"You need me to pick up your prescriptions tomorrow, Mrs. Morrison?"

"If you wouldn't mind, dear."

"No trouble at all."

"Well, good night, Britt. You don't let the bedbugs or anything else bite."

"Not if I can help it. Good night. Sweet dreams."

"They always are. They're full of Elwyn." Elwyn was her husband, dead for ten years, alive in her thoughts and dreams every day. "He carved our initials on the Eternity Oak the day we met, did I tell you that, Britt?"

She had. Fifty or sixty times. But this was pretty much how they said good night to each other most nights. It was their little ritual.

Mrs. Morrison tinkled her glass in farewell.

Britt smiled.

Then her smile faded. Poor cat. The woods were home to a number of feral felines, she knew. But then free-range felines had been taking their lives into their own paws for centuries.

She squared her shoulders, took another bracing breath, and typed "c—"

She gave a start again and clapped her hand over her heart when Skype starting beeping and booping.

She answered the call and the beaming face of her little nephew, nine years old and toothy, filled the screen.

"Hi, Auntie Britt!"

"Hi, cookie. What's shakin'?"

His head disappeared from the screen and then his pajama-clad butt appeared. He shook it.

And then his giggling face reappeared.

She rolled her eyes. The word *butt* and anything butt-related still got a gratifyingly easy laugh from Will.

"I want to show you what I did with your drawing, Auntie Britt."

She'd drawn Will as a monkey with a bright lively face, a dimple, wearing a little hat and a Christmas sweater and sporting a long expressive tail. She'd scanned the drawing and e-mailed it to him.

His face vanished from the screen.

To be replaced with an animated version of her monkey Will hopping up and down.

Rudimentary animation, but *darling.*

She clapped, delighted. "That's awesome, Will! You did that on your own? You are so darn clever. Good job!"

His face reappeared, grinning. "Will you send me another drawing, Auntie Britt?"

"Sure thing, monkey-butt. I have one of your mama. I made her a squirrel. Doesn't she seem like a squirrel?"

"She *totally* does!"

She heard her sister's voice raised in the background.

"William, it's your bedtime! What are you still doing on the computer? Oh, hey, is that your aunt? Let me talk to her."

Will noisily smooched the screen. "Good night, Auntie Britt!" He disappeared and her sister Laine's face took his place. She and her nephew had the same sunny smiles and chin dimples.

"Hey! What's new, Bippy?" Bippy was what her nephew Will had called Britt until he was about three years old. "Still have a half dozen jobs?"

"Half a *dozen*? No wonder you only got four hundred on your math SATs."

The curse of siblings: they both knew each other's SAT scores and dozens of other minute details about each other's lives that could be whipped out at a moment's notice, for better or worse.

"I was out late with the quarterback the night before the SAT. Scored much higher then. Can I get a high five?"

They air high-fived each other on the screen.

Laine had married the quarterback, who was a good guy, and now she had everything she wanted, which was a nice family and a cozy home.

Britt had been the hard-core straight-A student, a cheerleader, and competitive to a *fault*, and she'd thrown herself wholeheartedly into everything she did, whether it was the SATs or sneaking into the football stadium over the back fence. She'd very nearly had everything she'd wanted, too.

It hadn't quite worked out the same way for her.

"Nah, I still just have the two jobs, the Misty Cat and Gold Nugget Property Management, but it kind of *feels* like twenty, so I'll let you have that one on a technicality. Mrs. Morrison just told me she saw a coyote with a half a cat in its mouth. So I guess that's new."

"Neighborly of her," her sister said dryly.

For some reason Britt didn't want to mention the presence of a movie star in town. Not yet. Not until she'd at least thoroughly Googled him.

"Hey, Lainie?" Britt ventured.

"Yeah?"

She hesitated. "Did you ever watch *Blood Brothers*?"

"Daaaaaaamn, Britt, everyone watched that show. That's kind of a long time ago now, though. Where the heck were you?"

Laine started her days with TMZ and CNN. She was always in the know.

"I must have actually been *studying* when it was on," she said wonderingly. "But why did you say it like that?"

"Daaaaaamn? That's the thing he says."

"What 'thing'? Which 'he'?"

Her sister rolled her eyes. "Google it. Read TMZ once in a while. Live a little."

"I was just ab . . . all right."

And then Laine went quiet.

Long enough for a little uneasiness to creep into Britt's light mood.

"Listen, Britt I have to tell you something."

Britt froze. She knew that tone. Her sister only ever cushioned words when it came to one person.

And just like that, fear was like a little icepick in her gut.

Even now. After all these years.

"Jeff's mom came by. She was looking for you. She had your wedding band. It was with his . . . effects. She thought you might want it."

For a millisecond Britt couldn't speak. His name brought with it an atavistic sweep of fear that froze her like a rabbit before a wolf.

The fear swept out again. It always did, and faster each time.

It left her feeling ever-so-slightly weaker.

She wondered if it would ever fully leave her.

"I don't want it," she said instantly and a little too abruptly. "Don't tell her where I am."

She wanted nothing of his. He'd left her with one permanent reminder of her time with him, and a few years ago, right before she arrived in Hellcat Canyon, she'd finally turned it into something she could live with. Something beautiful.

She would be damned if that old part of her life would touch her here.

"Sorry. I thought so. I just . . . I just didn't feel free to make that decision for you. I didn't tell her anything about you. Was it okay to tell you about this?" Her sister was clearly suffering a little over this.

"Yeah, of course. I know you had to ask me. Don't worry about it."

Her sister smiled, relieved. "I wish you would come home."

"Lainie, I *am* home." They did this every call.

Laine smiled as if she knew better.

Sheez. Big sisters.

"Come visit me, Laine. Bring Will. He'd love it. It's all wild and foresty and he can pretend he's Robin Hood or a grizzly bear. You'll think it's quaint. Mitch can go fishing or whatever."

Mitch was Laine's husband. They lived in a modest but roomy ranch house in suburban Torrance, which was Laine's idea of heaven. Being surrounded by woods full of things like cat-snatching coyotes was not.

"When we can get away I promise we will. Hey, any men on the horizon since the . . . what was he, a cop?"

"The sheriff."

"Oooooh, the *sheriff*."

"I only went out with him that one time. It felt less like

a date than an interrogation. 'What's your favorite vegetable?' 'Where did you grow up?' Like he'd Googled how to date before he showed up. He's hot enough but he's a little broody."

"Yeah, not your type."

"Nope." She didn't say he'd probably started interrogating her because Britt hadn't really been holding up her end of the conversation. She'd kind of forgotten how to date, too.

"Don't worry. You'll get back up on that horse. There are bound to be other guys!"

Laine was an optimist.

A few other guys had asked Britt out, Truck Donegal included, but even Laine wouldn't have faulted her for turning them down. And most of them were no match for her invisible force field.

"The longer you wait though, the harder it'll be to *get* up on that horse." It wouldn't be Laine if she didn't feel compelled to throw in some unwanted advice.

This wasn't something Britt didn't already know.

"It's not Noah's Ark around here, Laine. We don't *all* have to go around two by two, you know."

"Of course not," Laine humored. "You'll probably be perfectly happy never having sex again."

"If I never wanted to have sex again, I could just get married again and live in the burbs."

"Oh, BURN!" Lainie was delighted.

Which made Britt laugh.

"So what do you do for *fun,* Bippy? You used to be so good at that. Remember when we sneaked into the football stadium over the back fence, and you totally tore your new pants, and Mom threw a fit?"

"I was just thinking about that! I was grounded for a month and I had to give up all my allowance for *weeks* to pay for them. Worth it, though."

Funny to think that she used to look at fences and the tops of cheerleading pyramids and hot guys and think, *I can't wait to conquer that!* As if there had never been any question. But then, she supposed it was down to naïveté. It was easy to be fearless until you learned what real fear and real pain felt like.

"You ever socialize with anyone out there besides Mrs. Morrison and your cat, Bip?"

"Kinda busy. You know, with my twenty-ish jobs."

The real reason was that she'd feel like a liar if she dodged questions about herself, and someone was bound to ask if she got close to them. Everyone in Hellcat Canyon kind of seemed to take her, and like her, at face value. She didn't think anyone had even noticed she might be a bit guarded.

But sometimes feeling ashamed felt like an additional job she had to do, and took up emotional real estate she would otherwise have given over to having or being a friend. She didn't know how to articulate this to Laine, who would only worry.

Mostly Britt was pretty content with the way things were these days. She could probably coast along the way she was forever.

Laine wasn't about to abandon the topic. "I'm just worried that if you only ever socialize with a nine-year-old, a ninety-two-year-old, and me, you're going to forget how to communicate with regular adults, not to mention men. Not every guy wants to talk about butts."

"Are you saying *you're* not an adult, Laine?"

"What I mean is an adult who hasn't known you since you couldn't pronounce your 'f's. How's that puzzy cat of yours?"

When Britt was about three, she'd resourcefully substituted in "p"s for "f"s in all words until she got a handle on the "f"s.

"He's fine. And fat." She had perfect control of them now.

"Give him a scratch for me."

"I will. Lainie, I talk to people at the diner every day. Speaking of which, I have to get some sleep now, or I might drop plates tomorrow."

"Can't have that! Okay sweets, love you. Alley-oop!"

"Love you, too. Alley-oop!"

The thing she used to say to Britt just before she was tossed up to the top of the cheerleading pyramid. Britt had *always* wanted to be on top, risk be damned. The view from there, she claimed, was better.

And the screen went blank.

Britt stood up abruptly. She realized her lungs were moving shallowly. "Jeff." Just the sound of that name could get residual panic circulating in her bloodstream.

She deliberately took deep, long, greedy gulps of warm night air, and tipped her head back to luxuriate in the scenery—yep, trees, stars, mountains, dirt, Hellcat Canyon. Home. Far, far away from Southern California, where she had once been happy and where everything had gone shockingly to pieces.

"Oop!" She gave a start. She'd just remembered it was garbage collection tomorrow.

She opened the latch on Mrs. Morrison's gate and dragged her trash can and recyling bins out to the side of the road, and then she dragged her own bins out, and the physical exertion made her feel a little better.

Then she returned to the deck and with one final bracing breath for courage, typed the rest of what she'd sat down to type almost a half hour ago.

". . . Cord."

She hit return.

Good *God.*

Such a torrent of information appeared, he was actually categorized by *topic.*

She tentatively clicked his Wikipedia entry and scanned the headings:

> **Early Life.**
> ***Blood Brothers.***
> **After *Blood Brothers.***
> **Personal Life.**
> **Controversy.**

Imagine an entire life summed up in a series of categories. Imagine the internet deciding for you what the peak of it was, and arranging everything else as "Before" and "After."

Then again she supposed her life had "Before" and "After" portions, too. Not to mention a "Controversy" part.

She swiftly scrolled through. Born in the Tennessee Mountains. He'd just turned forty. His mom died when he was ten. He married at eighteen, divorced a year later, joined the army at twenty, then settled in Los Angeles.

According to Wikipedia, that was the sum total of his life up until the television program *Blood Brothers.* He was twenty-three when it started.

It was a top-rated drama/comedy for seven years. Wildly popular. Umpteen Emmy nominations and awards for the show, including four nominations and two wins for Tennessee McCord as Best Actor, playing Blue Summerville, a cop. The character's signature phrase ("Daaaaamn!") briefly took over the nation, but was primarily beloved of frat boys. The series had turned both Tennessee McCord and Franco Francone, who played his partner, into big stars. The series finale broke television viewing records. It had ended in 2005.

After one sentence about his first and only wife to date (one Denise Ray), "Personal Life" was devoted to Rebecca Corday.

The whole *world* knew who *she* was.

They were together for about five years. A pretty long time in Hollywood terms. It had ended for good a year ago, and with quite a bang, at least according to Wikipedia.

He hadn't been linked to anyone seriously since.

Rebecca Corday, on the other hand, had been linked to Sir Anthony Underhill ever since.

The "After *Blood Brothers*" section was short, too: he'd been in two types of movies, the kind with explosions and car chases, and one romantic comedy. One had tanked, the other two had limped to a break-even status, all were derided by critics, though his performance wasn't blamed and he was generally considered the best thing about either movie. Several years later his performances in two independent films that almost no one saw were lavishly praised. One of them was shown at Cannes. He was nominated for a Golden Globe for the other one, *Agapé*. Somewhere in his downtime between films he'd acquired a black belt in karate.

A year later he signed on to play the lead role in a series set during the Gold Rush in California, called *The Rush*, due to air on cable television beginning in 2017. It would be filmed in part on location in the Sierra Nevada foothills of California, site of the Gold Rush itself.

Right near Hellcat Canyon, which was why he was here, of course.

On his way to that wedding Casey mentioned.

The "Controversy" section was naturally where all the juicy stuff was.

A playful rivalry between him and his friend, co-star Franco Francone, had gotten genuinely ugly when Rebecca Corday left Francone for Tennessee. There was something about a fistfight in a parking lot, but no photographic evidence of that episode apparently existed.

McCord had once punched a photographer who had allegedly said something unspeakable to Rebecca Corday. He drank a bit too much more than once. Toward the end of the series, he developed a bit of a reputation for being difficult on set, showing up late from time to time.

A few years after his show had ended, he'd demanded, "Do you know who I am?" of a cop who had pulled him over. *Wow.* That one was wince-worthy.

It was nearly full dark outside, and she'd begun to hear the stirring of nocturnal animals—raccoons and possums, probably, but hopefully not a coyote—by the time Britt decided to look at the photos.

She clicked "John Tennessee McCord—'90s."

In photo after photo he was untenably gorgeous, almost dewily young. The girl was different (if equivalently beautiful) in nearly every photo but his expression was about the same: a sort of wicked, mischievous, slightly dazed grin of a man who just *cannot* believe his luck. Her father would have called it a shit-eating grin. But he'd never really looked innocent. Even at that age he'd had the presence of someone who'd *seen* things. A bit of an edge that conferred dignity beyond his years.

There he was sitting with David Letterman, whose head was thrown back laughing. Accepting an Emmy for his role in *Blood Brothers*, slim as an arrow, devastating in a black tuxedo. Beaming and leaning over the red velvet rope cordoning off the stars on the red carpet from the dazzled hoi polloi, a sea of paper and pens and hands thrust out at him. Posing with a state trooper who had pulled him over for speeding. The trooper was grinning as if he'd caught the biggest bass in the lake.

"I'll be damned," she said softly, amused. It was the same red truck in that photo that she'd seen parked on the street today. Circa 1990-something, if she had to guess. Kind of like her own car.

There were the magazine features: "Why John Tennessee McCord Is Kryptonite." "John Tennessee McCord: Serious Actor, Olympic-Caliber Flirt." At least one of those things was very likely true, as far as Britt was concerned.

On YouTube she found something called "The Tennessee McCord 'Daaaamn' Supercut."

It turned out to be a few dozen spliced-together scenes of him delivering his character's signature word in every imaginable inflection. An impressed "Daaaaaamn, son!" A frustrated "Daaaaaamn, Lorelei!" A furious "Daaamn, Lieutenant!" He'd somehow managed to deliver that phrase each time with impressive and convincing nuance.

There was a muttered "Daaamn," bitter and aching, as someone in a coffin was lowered into a grave.

The very last one was a scene of his character in bed next to a woman, the room shadowy, their faces nearly touching.

"Daaaaaamn," he whispered with a sort of tender awe.

"Jesus," Britt whispered in reply, with closed eyes and a silent apology to Mrs. Morrison.

She suddenly felt about ten degrees hotter. The sound of his voice was like a tongue down her spine.

It was like he'd literally been born to murmur.

She read a few of the comments below.

Ha ha he's so funny he was my favorite
Whatever happened to him?
Click here if you want a larger pen1s.

"Who doesn't?" Britt muttered.

Despite what she'd told her sister, it wasn't as though she didn't get lonely. It was just that getting back up on that horse often seemed more daunting than never experiencing another "pen1s" again, and she could live with a bout of loneliness now and again.

There were other videos, too: snippets from talk shows and red carpet interviews. A John Tennessee McCord supercut of some of the dangerous stunts on *Blood Brothers*. She'd take a look at those later.

She flipped back to the photos.

With a peculiar reluctance she hesitated to examine too closely—because it actually felt like jealousy, which was patently ridiculous—she chose the "Tennessee McCord with Rebecca Corday" category.

God, but Rebecca Corday was pretty. Miles of titian hair and a face that was delicately, distinctly chiseled apart from a big soft set of lips. She offered something fascinating and magnificent to the camera no matter what part of her was turned to it. There were posed photos, both of them dressed like royalty, beaming, their arms linked with a sort of triumphant possession, on various red carpets. There were everyday moments caught by some stalking photographer: walking together down some sidewalk, each of them wearing jeans and a T-shirt and carrying a grocery bag. Standing in a park so closely their foreheads touched, each of them wearing a smile.

There was John Tennessee stepping out of swim trunks on a beach in some glamorous tropical locale, clearly nude—a modest black rectangle had been photoshopped over his penis—and there was Rebecca stretched out on a lounge chair, smooth pale perfection in two scraps of cloth some people might call a bikini covering her privates.

Just lots and lots and lots of photos of the two of them. She always seemed to be laughing. He always looked proud and possessive.

The magazine covers: "Rebecca Corday: Why John Tennessee McCord is the perfect man for me." "Everything you wanted to know about Rebeccasee! How they met, their first kiss, and More!" "How Keeping Separate

Pads Keeps Rebeccassee's Romance Piping Hot!" "Why Rebecassee doesn't need to be married to feel committed."

Then there were a couple of paparazzi photos of them stone-faced, walking side by side, in Los Angeles. One of what was clearly an argument, judging from her clenched fists and drawn-taut features and open mouth. She didn't look very pretty, then.

He stood a few feet away from her, his face angled away, hands shoved in his pockets, face thunderous.

The last video of him she could find was one that was almost a year old, courtesy of TMZ.

He was rushing through a busy airport, head down, a knit cap pulled down over his head. Clearly some kind of failed attempt at disguise. When the entire world has seen you walk and talk on screen for nearly a decade, it must be pretty hard to hide.

"Hey, John Tennessee! We hear Rebecca Corday dumped you in Cannes. What did you do to deserve it?"

"Yeah, what was the last straw for her? Your last movie embarrass her?" another reporter chimed.

The assholes were laughing at him.

John Tennessee McCord flashed a single look at the camera lens. His eyes were shocking. Hunted, haunted, hollow, stunned and weary. About a day's worth of stubble covered his grimly set jaw.

Britt's heart lurched.

He said nothing to the jerks with the camera. Kept his head down, kept walking. Faster.

And still the cameras followed him.

"We heard she left with Sir Anthony Underhill. Guess there's no more Rebeccasee, eh? Guess it's Rebeccathy now, eh?"

Britt leaned back in her chair.

Suddenly she was deeply ashamed. She felt no better

than either one of those stalking videographers, poring over the digital artifacts of a man's life.

And she didn't really know anything more about him now than she had before she Googled him.

That made her no better than a voyeur.

The "Olympic-caliber flirt" had scribbled a note on her order tag. But then, his livelihood depended in part on his ability to charm women to their eyeteeth and hypnotize them with his blue eyes.

Perhaps it was no wonder he was the only man she'd seen in probably two years who had all but literally set her blood on fire, and he'd managed to do it with a single glance and a few words.

Still.

She watched that video until the end. She watched as he skillfully slalomed through the crowds and lost those photographers, who kept their cameras on him until he became just another black speck in the airport crowd.

Suddenly she realized her hand was on the screen.

As if she could push those paparazzi parasites away from him.

She pulled it away gently. Feeling faintly foolish.

She decided that she wasn't going to Google him again.

CHAPTER 4

Britt's eyes flew open when her phone erupted into deafening bar chords.

"Mother fu . . ." She clapped a hand over her thundering heart.

Why, why, why had she thought it was funny to make AC/DC Gary's ringtone? She liked "Dirty Deeds Done Dirt Cheap," but she was a grown woman. She'd nearly just wet herself.

She squinted at her phone. Gary was her boss at Gold Nugget Property Management. The quality of light squeezing in through her blinds in the room told her it was a lot earlier than he normally called, and a lot earlier than she wanted to be awake, given that she'd been Googling John Tennessee McCord instead of sleeping last night.

She fumbled for her phone. "G'morning, Gary."

"That's your morning voice, Britt? Jesus, you sound like Bob Dylan after he's smoked six packs. Hey, I'm calling because some guy wants to see the Michaelson place."

She was more alert now, thanks to astonishment.

She cleared her throat noisily. "Really?"

Gary was almost like Charlie from *Charlie's Angels*, in that she hardly ever saw him and he did most of his business on the phone, usually from his car or the golf course, or even, she suspected a little worriedly, from his toilet in the morning. He was a retired investor in his sixties who had a roster of houses and cabins that he managed or owned and rented out in the Hellcat Canyon area, most of them pretty modest, some appalling, a few palatial, and Britt showed them to prospective tenants and did follow-up maintenance inspections and the like for him. It wasn't a hard job, it didn't pay all that well, and it was pretty flexible.

But the Michaelson place was quite the white elephant of a summer home. The Michaelsons had inherited it a long time ago and tried to sell it several times and failed, so they made do with renting it out when they could. Which was rarely.

"Yeah, I know," Gary marveled in agreement. "But it's the only one we've got open today, and this guy says he wanted to see it, because he—and I quote—'can't spend another minute being stared at by cherubs.' So go sell it for all you're worth. But bring your pepper spray, because you never know. That cherub remark is a little worrisome."

"Aww. I'm touched by your concern."

"Yeah, yeah, I'm a saint. The only other option is the Greenleaf place, and it's currently a dump. At least the Michaelson place doesn't have a hole in the roof. Someone from Ernie's Garage is dropping our guy off there at eight a.m., so you've got twenty minutes to get up there."

He hung up without saying good-bye.

"Have fun on the golf course, Gary," she said. Mostly without rancor. A job was a job, and it wasn't like jobs were thick on the ground here in Hellcat Canyon.

She lay flat for a moment, truly uncertain she could manage to get out of bed. Then she resignedly slid one foot out. Phillip resentfully shifted his fluffy bulk off her thighs. It was a little earlier than they normally rose and he had a powerfully ingrained sense of schedule.

She let momentum carry her forward. She reheated yesterday's coffee in the microwave and slurped it down, wincing, threw on her second best shorts, which were denim and at least clean, yanked on a red-striped tank top from her vast tank top collection, added a necklace with a little star dangling from it to make it fancy, then rubbed the sleep out of her eyes and did a rapid-fire brush of her teeth. She chucked her pepper spray into her purse.

Her car started, thankfully; there was always a moment of suspense when she turned that key.

She brushed her hair at the first stop sign on the way up to the Michaelson place, which was a bit of a twisty drive, then roped it up in a barrette in her usual patented summertime hairdo. At the second stop sign, she changed Gary's ringtone to Mozart. At the third, she added some lip gloss, just because.

She saw the man long before she reached the house. He was slim and stark, a compass needle against the white cement of the big circular drive.

Her impulse was to perform a single smooth U-turn and head right back down the mountain, because she knew exactly who that was, and driving up to him suddenly felt akin to driving right into the deep blue sea. Very compelling. Very, very foolish.

Her ramping anticipation made her approach feel almost cinematic. It would have been even more dramatic if her car didn't make coughing noises and give a great shuddering asthmatic lurch when she cut the engine.

She stayed in the car a moment. She could see the color of his eyes even from where she sat. They were, and she could say this truthfully, bluer than the sky, which surely proved he did indeed have superpowers.

And then she got out, and shut the door with some

effort, because it liked to stick. And then she actually had to throw her hip into it. Which really spoiled her entrance.

She hovered by her car as if it were a guard dog.

She saw him straighten, and register who she was with distinct pleasure.

"Well," was all he said, finally.

"Good morning," was what she said.

And then that was all either of them said for a long, ridiculous moment.

He said thoughtfully, "Forgive me, but I was just thinking that the only thing better than one of you is two of you. You'd make my day if you told me you had a twin."

Olympic-caliber flirt, indeed.

"There are actually five of us. So if you see one of us around town and we don't say hi, that's the reason."

That had come out more tersely than she'd intended.

But he didn't even flinch. He was studying her with an expression akin to a YouTube video she'd seen of a Doberman attempting to befriend a cat who was having none of it. Mildly puzzled but absolutely confident his charm would win the day if he could just figure out where to poke his nose.

It made her feel churlish.

Her churlishness was in direct proportion to how alarmingly, circuits-floodingly attractive he was. She could easily get caught in an undertow of testosterone if she wasn't careful. And these days she was always careful.

He was wearing snug jeans and a black T-shirt, and his biceps, like everything else about him, were works of art: brown, hard, and big, and an intriguing tattoo vanished up into one of the sleeves. The shirt clung to his shoulders and was just a little loose at that narrow waist, which, she thought, left a girl plenty of room to get her hands up in there.

"We haven't formally met. I'm John Tennessee McCord,"

he said, as if there were a possibility she didn't actually know.

Given that all of her senses rioted merely by virtue of proximity, his presence was paradoxically calming. He was probably accustomed to mute and staring women. Possibly even accustomed to snappish little women. Once again, she got the sense that nothing could surprise this guy, because he'd seen everything, and he could handle all of it.

He held out his hand.

"You're the talk of the town, Mr. McCord. I'm Britt Langley." She didn't take his hand. Yet.

"Ah, the 'enigmatic' Britt Langley. A pleasure to meet you officially. Call me J. T."

And then she finally put her hand in his, because she could hardly avoid it. She was a grown woman, after all.

He held on to it briefly, just a little longer than necessary. As if he knew exactly how squirrelly she was, or how electric he was.

His hand was warm and a little rough and it engulfed hers. Absurdly, it felt both reassuring and terrifying. As if he were pulling her up a cliff she was about to tumble off.

One that he'd pushed her over.

He let it go.

But not before every cell in her body had risen from some sort of slumber and was zinging like a limb shaken awake after she'd slept all night on it.

He studied her a moment.

Oddly, she could have sworn he wasn't entirely unmoved, either.

There was a refreshing honesty in this quiet, unabashed appraisal. It was very clear he found her attractive and wasn't the least bit worried about disguising it. And he knew damn well she found him attractive. He clearly assumed she could cope.

And then the bastard smiled. Slowly. As if two of them had spoken all of those thoughts aloud.

BAM, just like that, her breath was gone.

"So you work for the property management company and at the Misty Cat?" he wondered.

"Yeah." That word emerged as a squeak. She cleared her throat. "Yeah. You're looking for a place in Hellcat Canyon?"

"Yep. I'll be here off and on to film on location, and I have a little downtime before my schedule really picks up again. I stayed at the Angel's Nest last night. A little surprised I wasn't spontaneously ejected from the place, like Lucifer from heaven."

Every surface of Angel's Nest that could be was scented, frilled, fringed, or embroidered. If it wasn't purple, it was floral. Cherubs and angels gazed sympathetically from frames and pillows.

And she realized she was smiling, imagining him irritably ensconced amid all of that.

"A little hard to picture you there."

He did, on closer inspection, have faint shadows under his eyes. As though he hadn't slept well, or much.

"Yeah? Where do you picture me, Britt?"

Underneath me. Over me. Behind me. In me.

Those dirty little prepositional thoughts surprised her. Maybe it was just his drawl that turned everything into innuendo.

With some difficulty she reassembled her thoughts. She actually had a job to do. "I can picture you right here in the Michaelson place!" she said brightly.

Truthfully, she couldn't picture anyone in the Michaelson place.

"Is that so?" His expression told her that he knew she was lying through her teeth, but he was prepared to be entertained. "When does the tour start?"

"How about now?" She literally threw her shoulders back, the way heroines in novels did, an attempt to bolster her nerve, and strode past him to open the door.

But she betrayed her lack of aplomb by fumbling an inordinate amount of time with the key, as if her hands were newly installed and she was just learning how to use them.

She finally got it in there and cranked it.

Stale air whooshed out when she pushed open the door. They both stepped back as if dodging an escaping entity.

"The owner hasn't used this place in some time," she apologized.

He peered in. He didn't say a word for a moment.

"Since . . . 1972?" he hazarded. Sounding bemused, and as hushed as Indiana Jones entering a tomb.

The carpet was forest green shag, about four inches deep, or so it seemed, and it was everywhere. Like a living thing. It met them at the front door. She wouldn't be surprised if the carpet one day made it all the way into the bathroom and escaped out into the woods to join the wild foliage outside.

She led him inside.

The house comprised two main rooms and two bedrooms. The main room was vast and open with soaring beamed ceilings, bisected only by the long oval Formica counter of the open kitchen. But the whole place was dark, because brown wood paneling covered every inch of the walls, and the single wall of windows was covered in blinds, and the blinds were covered in dust.

"I feel like I ought to be stalking an antelope." He said it on a wondering hush, as he tread over the carpet. "I can't hear my feet."

"This kind of carpet keeps the place warm in winter," she asserted, mindful that her goal was to get the property rented. "It does get cold up here in winter, and we even get snow on occasion, so if you intend to stay that long, it'll cut down on your heating bills."

"Ah, so that's the purpose of shag carpet," he said somberly, like an attentive pupil. "I always wondered."

"And it might seem dark now, but wait until you see the view," she gushed, though her voice was still a little shaky. "Those blinds . . . um . . . apparently we need to use a remote to open them. Let's see . . . it must be around here somewhere . . ."

"It's probably in the rug." He was nudging at the carpet in an exploratory fashion with the toe of his boot, as if hoping to find treasures in it. Or worried something might be lurking.

In any other circumstance she might have found this hilarious.

But she was appalled she had to try to rent this place to John Tennessee McCord, of all people. His own home was probably so huge and spotless that every word and footstep echoed.

As she rummaged through the kitchen drawers for the remote he was watching her as avidly as if he'd bought a ticket to see her.

"Plenty of spatulas already here," she said brightly, "so you don't need to bring your own."

"Well, that's a relief. I hate when I burn my pancakes."

He was both enjoying her show and taking the piss out of her.

"I bet there's a deck of only about forty-three cards in there, too," he added encouragingly. "And maybe one beater from a hand mixer, and one corn on the cob holder."

Like he was prompting a comedian who'd forgotten her next line.

He wasn't far wrong about the cards, but she didn't tell him that.

She pulled open another drawer and found it empty.

And then another drawer, and saw that sad, depleted deck of cards and a bottle opener. And then another drawer.

He finally turned away and tipped his head back and studied the walls. "Just think . . . someone must have said, 'I know what will make this place even better—dark paneling everywhere.'"

"It acts as an extra layer of insulation in the summer and winter."

She had completely made that up.

He slowly lowered his head and studied her for a beat of silence.

"Does it?" He sounded almost intolerably amused and completely disbelieving.

She cleared her throat.

"Er, as you can see, um, J. T.," she narrated like a spokesmodel, as if he hadn't said anything at all, as she yanked another drawer open, "there's plenty of storage for utensils and groceries and—AHA!"

She whipped out the remote for the blinds triumphantly.

She stabbed at it, and miraculously, the window blinds slid up.

He watched, seemingly fascinated. "How lazy do you have to be if you need a remote to . . ."

He couldn't finish the sentence.

Because they were briefly paralyzed by the sunlight roaring through the windows.

"Christ," he muttered, impressed.

After a moment to establish they both still possessed corneas, he braved a step closer and assessed the view.

She'd seen that view before, so she stood where she was.

And surreptitiously watched him.

The gamma ray brilliance of the light delineated faint lines at the corners of his eyes and faint circles beneath them, a little morning stubble, a semicircle of a dimple next to his mouth, visible even when he wasn't smiling, like a sign saying "here is where you should kiss me."

That surge of untenable want roared through her like that first shot of whisky she'd tried when she was eighteen and trying to impress a guy.

Funny, though.

She could have sworn there was something almost melancholy in his stillness right now.

If she had to guess, she would have said he was lonely.

"Don't anthropomorphize the movie star," a little warning voice in her head said. "They aren't like the rest of us."

And yet. She didn't think she'd ever have assembled the collage of information she'd gleaned about the man last night, from the cavalcade of women to the video of him being hunted at the airport, into the wryly funny, down-to-earth, gracious—you'd have to be gracious to endure a tour like the one she was giving him—man standing here.

"And are those little glints across the ridge windows of other houses?" he asked finally.

Suddenly she knew where he was going with this.

"Yes," she admitted.

"If they had binoculars, I could do a performance of Alfred Hitchcock's *Rear Window* once a night." He quirked a corner of his mouth.

She knew that movie was about neighbors spying on neighbors, and she recalled the little black bar photoshopped over J. T.'s penis. Some determinedly, greedily hateful photographer had worked hard for that shot. In a house comprised of glass windows, John Tennessee McCord would be pretty exposed.

Right now the only scene she could distinctly remember from that movie was the famous one: Grace Kelly swooping in to plant a long, slow kiss on Jimmy Stewart.

He pivoted abruptly then.

She couldn't be sure what expression he'd caught her in

the middle of, but it was probably the basic lustful sort. Nothing he hadn't seen before, doubtless.

It didn't save her from feeling mortified.

"Or you could push the couch over and enact puppet shows from behind it," she said hurriedly. "My nephew would like that."

Wow, Britt, she thought sadly. *You are a dork.*

His eyebrows dove in surprise.

But then he grinned. "I was a guest on *Sesame Street* once," he said. "I sang a song with Kermit. "Ev-ery-ONE needs a friend, it's just so FUN to BE a friend . . ."

He sang with complete and barely tuneful unselfconsciousness. She laughed, utterly disarmed.

"I put it on my acting resume," he said. "The singing. Even though I did it exactly once."

"Yeah, once was probably enough," she teased.

This just made him grin.

And now he was watching her in the same way he'd perused the view of the canyon a minute ago, only with significantly more pleasure and a degree of purposefulness that shortened her breath.

The backs of her arms heated to match the temperature of her face.

He took a little step forward.

"So, Britt . . ." he mused. "You ever watch any cop shows?"

She took a step backward.

"Nope."

"Watch any other TV shows?"

"Not really."

"Got any . . . favorite actors?" he said softly, teasingly.

"Are you still tight with Kermit? I would do just about anything to meet him."

It was an attempt to shut down this line of questioning and get the house tour on track.

She realized belatedly how very much like an innuendo it had sounded, when he went stock-still.

He tipped his head and considered her.

"Oh, sure. I'd introduce you. But Miss Piggy is the jealous type. One look at you . . ." The look he settled upon her here was somehow both soft and molten enough to dissolve steel. ". . . one look at you and she might . . ."

And with that silence he was like a sentry waiting for her to deliver the password into flirtation land.

She knew that password. Once upon a time she could have given J. T. a run for his money when it came to flirtation. But she wasn't going to say it. She wasn't going to say it.

"Flail?" she heard herself say faintly, anyway. "Would she flail when she saw me?"

His eyes gleamed a sort of wicked mischief.

"She might just angrily flail," he confirmed solemnly, with feigned regret.

It might be the first time in history anyone had flirted using the Muppets, but she wouldn't put anything past the human race.

They stared at each other in absurd, mute delight.

It occurred to her that she could probably toss any awkward, clunky observation to this man, and like Rumpelstiltskin, he'd spin it into flirtation gold.

"Well, then, I guess I'll have to settle for your autograph," she said finally, into the crackling silence. "On the lease to this lovely house!"

He dismissed this with a single sardonic flick of one eyebrow. "How about you, Britt? Do you sing?"

"Do I sing?" she was astonished. "Let's put it this way. The first time I met my next-door neighbor, it was because she'd called the police to tell them someone was being murdered in my house. Turns out I was just singing in my shower."

There was a beat of silence.

"Seriously?" He actually sounded hopeful.

"Seriously."

"Wow." He was thoroughly pleased. "What were you singing?"

"'Whole Lotta Love.' Led Zeppelin."

He mulled. "There is kind of a lot of wailing in that one," he conceded.

"Yeah."

"Great song, though."

"Heck, yeah."

"We should do duet at the Misty Cat on Open Mic Night. You, me, 'Whole Lotta Love.' We'd kill it. Or kill the audience," he said.

Her heart stopped. Was he . . . was he asking her out?

She stared at him blankly.

He stared at her expectantly.

Her phone dinged a reminder of her next appointment—a maintenance inspection of a cabin rented by a sweet elderly couple.

She lunged for it like a thrown life preserver, pivoted abruptly and headed for the kitchen and put the counter between the two of them, her heart thumping like John Bonham's kick drum.

She looked up to see him watching her with a puzzled furrow between his brows.

"Um . . . J. T., as you can see, you have more drawers than you can possibly use for your various cooking implements and . . . Scotch tape and cat toys and . . . er . . . batteries."

She had just inadvertently revealed what she kept in her own kitchen drawers.

"It's amazing what you can keep in drawers these days." He humored her. He was frowning ever so faintly.

And then he turned and wandered out of the room to

inspect one of the bedrooms. "Want to guess what's in here?" he called. "More carpet, that's what."

Britt didn't follow him in there. Because even though there wasn't a bed in it currently, which really made it more of just a room than a bedroom, the implication was still there.

He popped out of the room. "So how old is your nephew?"

She was startled. "Er . . . nine. Nine and three-quarters, he'd tell you immediately."

"He likes the Muppets, eh?"

"The Muppets, Minecraft, computers, and anything butt-related."

His smile grew bigger as she recited this. "Yeah, most guys never really outgrow any of that."

"I guess I kind of understand it," she said, hesitantly. "I mean, the first time you discover your own body and everyone else's can make a sound like a vuvuzela it's kind of a cause for celebration."

The smile dropped off his face.

He froze as if she'd pulled a gun on him.

He stared at her. This time, absolutely thunderstruck.

Silence ensued, during which Britt marinated in horror and wished she could vacuum the words from the air right back into her mouth.

She could hear her sister's voice in her head: What did I tell you about needing to socialize with adults? Now you've gone and made a fart joke to John Tennessee McCord.

She was never, ever going to tell her sister she was right, though.

"Vuvuzela?" he finally choked out.

"Yeah. Um . . . stadium horns?" The shame had scorched her voice right down to a thread. She mimed holding one up and blowing into it.

She was nearly floating up out of her body watching herself mime blowing a freaking stadium horn to John Tennessee McCord.

This wasn't just a fart joke. It was a never-ending fart joke.

"I know," he said dazedly. "It's just . . . that . . . that . . . that might literally be the funniest thing I've ever heard."

He looked awestruck. Almost beyond laughter.

His face was lit up like a sun.

He was staring at her as if she were better than Cirque du Soleil.

Her face, on the other hand, felt hotter than the sun and there was no way she wasn't tomato red.

"I guess . . . I guess if they sounded like wind chimes he wouldn't find them as funny," she expounded desperately.

He threw back his head and shouted with laughter. It echoed all around the place and the hideous knot in her stomach unwound and she felt light as a helium balloon.

Damn. Oh, man. She loved his laugh. It was the freest sound she'd ever heard.

And then he sighed happily, finally, and shook his head.

"I bet women might be more tolerant of them if they did. Though I swear a wind chime on the porch of the Angel's Nest tried to kill me."

She smiled at him, basking in his delight as if it were the first day of spring. "Yeah, it's a minefield of wind chimes over there. You have to watch your step, especially if you're tall. I mean, I can understand why you'd want to move out of there immediately . . . into this place."

He just gave her a "nice try" eye roll. "It's not just the wind chimes. It's all the purple, and the frills, and dear God, the potpourri, and did you know the soap is shaped like angels there, too? I can't bring myself to rub an angel in my armpits. And it's noisy. I'm next to the honeymoon suite. I didn't get a wink of sleep last night thanks to Cherisse and Kevin."

"Oh, you met your neighbors?"

"Not formally. They kept name checking each other. 'Oh, Cherisse. Oh, Kevin.' And their headboard. BAM. BAM. BAM. All. Night. Long."

"Their head . . ."

She trailed off when she realized what he meant.

She froze.

"Can't remember the last time I did that to a headboard," he said thoughtfully. Pinning her with his blue gaze.

And her every cell briefly surged with electricity.

And boom, or rather, BAM, like that, her breath was gone again.

She didn't know if she was wildly aroused or panicked. Both, probably.

They stared at each other.

She did know that was her cue to say, "Neither can I." Or, "I can offer up a refresher." Or "I bet this carpet is pretty comfortable. Didn't they have a lot of orgies in the seventies?" "Or surely you have a lot of opportunities to do it."

Because she used to have "game," as Kayla called it. She knew this particular dance from way back in the day, before she'd married Jeff. This exchange was the sort of coded language that men and women laid down to test sexual interest and intent. No one just flung off their clothes and leaped upon another. Well, hardly anyone just leaped upon another.

But she stood there like a deer in the headlights of his fixed gaze.

"Me, neither," she said finally. It was practically a whisper.

And instead of sexy or clever, it sounded pathetic.

And scared.

His expression subtly shifted. "I always wondered why angels wore dresses," he mused. "Those long robes? Seems they'd get their feet tangled up in them when they flew. Wouldn't it be more convenient to fly in a unitard?"

She was both grateful and a little alarmed at how skillfully he'd given her a way out of that flirtation corner.

She exhaled. "Like . . . Superman?"

That made him laugh. "But do angels actually fly?" he wondered. "I mean, do they need to, to get wherever they're going?"

"Good point. I think they can materialize wherever they please."

"Then why do they even need wings?"

She considered this. "Because wings are pretty?"

He smiled slowly. "That must be it, Britt Langley. It's important for things to be pretty."

He was teasing her. She wondered if she'd ever be able to talk to him without blushing.

She exhaled. "If it helps any . . . Rosemary?—you know, the lady who runs the Angel's Nest with her husband?—well, she was raised in Coyote Creek and that is one scary place—it's a settlement, kind of an annex of Hellcat Canyon, up there deep in the hills." Britt waved an arm up toward where the trees were thickest. "They say most people usually leave there in a cop car or a casket. Her life was pretty austere when she was growing up, and she and her husband really wanted a family but it didn't happen for them. And then they tried to adopt, but I guess it hasn't worked out, maybe because they're getting up in years now and they don't have a big income. Anyway, I always thought that maybe she went overboard with the fluff and the angels and the pillows and whatnot because of all of that. Wanted it to be soft and pretty so people would feel loved and protected in there in a way she never felt."

She began to feel like she was babbling.

Because gradually a shadow, almost a frown, appeared between his eyes.

"Funny. That's why my mama planted blue-eyed Mary's around our house when we were growing up. My dad used to call her his blue-eyed Mary." The corner of his mouth quirked. "Haven't thought about that in . . . oh, years, probably."

Her breath snagged. She realized she was frowning. A casual-enough sentence. Every word in that sentence had its own subtle character, from the faint bitterness of "dad" to the echo of an ache in "used to."

She could build a whole story around them and it wasn't a pretty one, and she realized her heart was aching as surely as if he'd told it all to her.

These were the kinds of things that lived between the lines of his Wikipedia entry.

He must have seen something in her expression because he added lightly. "This place makes the place I grew up in look like a palace."

"And I bet your current house makes this place look like a tool shed."

"Mmm. It might. Can't really recall."

"You can't recall your house?" She instantly regretted her astonishment. But still.

But he just shrugged. "I travel a lot. I rented a house in the Hollywood Hills and that's where my most of my clothes and stuff is right now. I travel pretty light these days."

"Do you miss Tennessee?"

"When I was eighteen it seemed pretty important to get out of there. Not sure it would still feel like home. I do . . ." He turned around to check out that view again, and his voice went kind of drifty. "Turns out I do miss trees and hills."

She took a deep breath. "You'll never have to stop looking at trees and hills when you rent this house."

Good God. The things she did for a paycheck.

He didn't turn around to look at her. J. T. just shook his head to and fro, slowly and a dimple appeared in his three-quarter profile. He clearly still found her entertaining.

A moment later he did turn around with an air of resolve.

"So how about it, Britt? I'd love to spend the evening in the company of a real-life angel instead of one staring at me from a frame. We'll go check out some live music, have a few drinks. You drink beer? I bet you drink beer."

Of all the things she'd thought he'd say, this had to be among the last. As shocked as if she'd fallen through a trapdoor.

She was afraid she was gaping.

"Did you . . . did you really just call me an angel?"

"I think I did." He was amused. "I don't know if you're incredulous or commenting on how cheesy that was."

"Kind of both, to tell you the truth," she said quite honestly. Still reeling.

She had to force herself not to take a step backward.

He just grinned again. The man was scrappy, she had to hand it to him. "Excellent news, as to the first. As to the second, I'll have to work on my patter. I might be a little rusty when it comes to asking women out."

Hoooolly. Crap.

CHAPTER 5

Her heart felt like a roulette wheel given a good brisk swipe.

"Oh." She drew in a long breath. "I . . . um. You were serious about that. Earlier."

That had emerged a lot more astonished and a lot less gracious than she'd hoped.

"Yeah. I was serious." It was his turn to be a bit incredulous.

She would probably remember this afternoon later in terms of its silences, each of them with their own character: tense, fraught, horrifying, painfully sexy, awkward.

"Um. I'm sorry. I can't."

"You . . . can't?" he repeated. As if she'd just taught him a new word in Turkish.

"I can't," she said firmly.

"But thank you," she added weakly a moment later, into the dead silence.

"Mmm," was all he said. A moment later.

He turned abruptly then wandered into the second bedroom. Where he was just going to find more of that green carpet.

She remained rooted to the spot.

And this time the silence was horrible because she had

no idea whether she'd offended him or hurt his feelings. But the room was practically spinning.

He'd asked her *out.*

He'd asked *her* out.

He'd asked her out.

Then again, she supposed he needed to do *something* to fill his downtime.

Or someone.

"So . . . is it *all* guys, Britt?" he called casually from the other room. "Asking for a friend."

"I beg your pardon?"

He emerged from the room. "Or maybe it's guys with tattoos? Or actors. It's actors, isn't it?"

"I'm lost. Why are we suddenly playing Password?"

"Just trying to get a bead on your current objection to me. You know, so I can refine my future approach."

Her jaw dropped. She gave a short, astounded laugh. The *nerve* of him.

"Is there another guy?" he pressed.

"J. T.—"

"Another girl?"

"Um—"

"Another guy *and* another girl? This is California, after all. People get adventurous here."

"J. T.!" And now she was laughing.

"You're into vampires, blindfolds, My Little Pony? I'm pretty open-minded."

"I'm just—wait. My Little Pony?"

"You live in Los Angeles long enough, you hear *everything.*"

She had the strangest urge to tell him about the mermaid and the fisherman.

"Huh." She was definitely going to Google My Little Pony.

He detected a softening. "Aw, c'mon, Britt," he cajoled.

"Just one night. Just a few hours. We'll sing badly, have a few drinks. See where the night takes us. I'm a person, same as you."

She almost snorted. The "same as you" part wasn't *remotely* true.

"J. T., it's just . . ."

She had no idea how to finish that sentence.

"Yeah?"

The moment was as taut as harp strings, suddenly.

"I'm busy."

His face all but blanked.

He was probably paralyzed by the crushing lameness of this excuse.

"Busy," he repeated, finally. As though he was tasting milk that had gone ever-so-slightly off.

He sounded more disappointed in her lack of originality than anything else.

She would have laughed if she didn't have a whomping case of vertigo caused from being asked out by a *movie star.*

One who had slept with Rebecca *freaking* Corday.

It was so wholly unexpected, she was as at a loss, and as breathless and panicky, as if her kayak had tipped over in the Pacific.

J. T. McCord made her feel way too many things all at once. Things she wasn't ready to feel again. She needed a wading pool before she entered the dating pool, and he was the whole damn ocean.

She wondered if he'd ever in his entire life heard the word *no* from a woman.

At least he'd remember her for that reason.

And as the silence stretched, his incredulity seemed to give way to a sort of curiosity. He was studying her as if he was determined to crack the code.

"Kayla Benoit is single," she volunteered desperately.

"And she's very pretty. *And* she owns a boutique. It's right there on the sign over her door. Kayla Benoit."

His face instantly became a flickering battlefield of emotions.

The one that settled in was pure hilarity.

"Are you seriously trying to distract me with another woman? Like throwing a steak at a rottweiler so you can make your getaway?" His voice was hoarse. "Are you attempting to *console* me in my disappointment with another woman?"

When he put it that way, it *was* pretty funny.

And pretty insulting.

"You sure came up with that rottweiler analogy pretty quickly," she hedged.

"I was on a cop show. That was in the script more than once."

That one tugged up one corner of her mouth, and then the other went up, and she was smiling, because that was pretty funny, too.

And that made him smile, too. It was an amused and wholly determined smile.

But a subtle little war was taking place. Something complex and dangerous and exhilarating was sparking between them. They were both pretty damn stubborn and accustomed to getting their own ways. Britt had forgotten just how stubborn she could be, in fact. And how much fun a well-matched sparring partner could be.

Her grin faded. "It's just . . . J. T., if you're just looking for, um, *company* during your downtime . . ."

His eyebrows shot up sardonically at how gingerly she delivered that euphemistic word.

". . . you must have infinite options."

He went silent again. She wondered if he'd been this astonished so many times in a single afternoon in his entire life.

Then his face got ever so slightly harder. "Spent a little time Googling me last night, eh Britt?"

More ironic than bitter, that statement. Though he had a right to both bitterness and irony, probably.

"Of course," she said instantly.

He seemed to like that. He smiled. If a little tautly. "Think you know everything about me now?"

"No," she said immediately, fervently. "Not for an instant do I think that. You can't know a person that way."

He blinked. And then she realized she sounded as though she was defending him.

"Okay," he said carefully, after a moment. "Then do you think that having, as you put it, 'infinite options' means discretion doesn't enter into it? That with me and women, it's like . . . I'm just reaching my hand into a bowl of peanuts and grabbing a handful and stuffing it into my mouth without inspecting each individual peanut?"

She was utterly arrested by this analogy.

"I'm sorry," she confessed on something close to a whisper after a moment. "But all that does is make me think of a bowl of lady peanuts."

His eyes flared in surprise, and then his face went abstracted. "Lady peanuts? Is it like a scene out of an Ethel Merman movie? Are they all wearing little swimsuits?"

"Yeah, they're all wearing little swimsuits. And performing a synchronized water ballet. All the lady peanuts."

He was staring at her not as though she was a lunatic, which might have been the logical response, but as though she was like a Russian nesting doll of delights and he kept uncovering new ones.

"Britt," he just said. Appreciatively. Almost yearningly. Sort of marveling. Apropos of nothing.

She could feel her face heating again.

She drew in a breath. "It's just, J. T., if the public record is any indication, my guess is you took your sweet time getting around to learning *discretion*, if you ever truly have, and had a lot of fun doing it."

That should have pissed him off.

Instead he whistled, long and low, impressed, as if she'd just deployed a tricky wrestling maneuver.

And then the devil actually *grinned*.

And planted his feet ever so slightly apart as if he was settling in for a good debate.

"When my career first took off, I could pretty much go out with any woman I wanted. I could flip through a magazine, call up my publicist, boom. It was practically like ordering something from Amazon. I might have gotten a little carried away."

"*Amazon?* Now you're only making my case for me."

This was actually kind of fun. She'd forgotten how thoroughly she loved to argue with someone who was good at it.

"Hold on. I was young then. Still figuring things out. What did I know? What would *you* do? And *everybody* is good-looking in Hollywood. What I learned is, when everybody's a four leaf clover, nobody is. Does that make sense?"

She hesitated. "In a Zenlike way, sure. I get it."

She did. And damn it, she liked it a lot.

J. T. McCord, she was learning, was not only hot. He was smart.

He might possibly even be soulful.

Something was asserting itself through her panic. The *Want* was still present and accounted for. But its gentler cousin, Yearning, had just shown up. Yearning was seductive. She hadn't felt anything like that in years.

Yearning was really only a few degrees different from pain.

"So I kind of had to learn about myself and women the hard way, Britt. And I did learn. Discretion, as you say."

She pictured the photographers hunting him through an airport and knew again a surge of outrage, as surely as if his happiness was critical to her own. It was hardly rational. It was just that she so hated injustice. And bullies.

"You ever learn anything the hard way, Britt?" he tried. Softer now.

She hesitated. She swallowed.

"Sure," she said faintly. Because she was fundamentally honest.

She could have said, *And how.*

She didn't have to. She was pretty sure that was the way he heard it.

He was studying her again.

He was a little too good at this persuasion thing and a little too intuitive.

"Okay. Ever think that maybe I'm hopelessly captivated by your command of the English language? 'Enigmatic.' 'Vuvuzela.' 'Lady peanuts.'"

She shrugged. "Who could blame you?"

He flashed a grin. "Well?"

". . . But that's not really why you're asking me out."

"Oh, for God's sake, of *course* it isn't," he said so exasperatedly and unapologetically she laughed. "I might be in Hellcat Canyon for just a few weeks, give or take, but I don't see a single reason why we can't kick off a beautiful friendship for the duration based on what you and I see when we look at each other. We were given five senses for a reason. It's how we connect as a species. It's part of the natural order. You have to start somewhere and I'm not gonna apologize for liking what I see when I look at you."

And just in case she missed his meaning, the way he looked at her now erased all thought except for what it might feel like to allow her five senses to run amok over this man like the starved little gluttons they were.

His faint little smile suggested he knew exactly which parts of her body were tingling right now.

"As much as I'm enjoying the nature lecture . . ." Her voice was a little frayed. ". . . and all your adroit rationalization, I'm not really looking for a"—she bobbed her fingers in air quotes—"'beautiful friendship.'"

Amazement flickered across his face.

"'Adroit . . . rationalization'?" He repeated slowly. His expression was frustration and amazement all shot through with delight.

They stood in a peculiar stalemate.

It was just that there was no way on God's green earth she was going to say to him, "My last relationship pretty much shattered me and I'm still collecting all the pieces and trying to figure out where they go, and most of those pieces are still jagged and raw. You are too much in every way and I have no business dipping my toe into those kinds of waters."

She didn't want to see the expression on his face if she said that.

"I don't believe for a moment that you don't like me, Britt Langley," he said suddenly.

Yikes.

His voice had gotten low . . . and . . . slow. It was absolutely knee-buckling. Erotic karate, she'd call it.

Her next words emerged a little low and hoarse. "Yeah? What makes you so sure of that?"

"Because I'm fully aware that I'm being a little obnoxious right now but you're still having fun. I think, in fact, we'd have a great time no matter what we did together. Because I'm more and more convinced, Britt, that you can give as good as you get. In any situation."

That last sentence was an innuendo par excellence.

They let that statement ring there, with all of its implications, and her silence was as good as a confirmation.

"Tell me I'm wrong," he demanded softly.

She, quite frankly, didn't know how any woman said no to him. Or why she would.

And she *was* really, really good in the sack.

The air was dense and crackling with suspense. This was a man who liked to win as much as she did.

"You're not wrong," she said faintly.

Triumph began to glimmer in his eyes. "And . . ." he prompted.

J. T. McCord might be kryptonite, but he was no match for Fear. Fear always won when it was part of the mix these days. It was just so much easier to say no than to say yes, and to keep her life small and safe. If she was a Russian nesting doll, she preferred to remain packed.

"And . . ." She inhaled deeply, exhaled. ". . . I'm sorry."

He went still again. Pressed his lips together thoughtfully.

He wouldn't quite free his gaze, however.

And she met it head on, because she might be damaged and squirrelly, but she wasn't stupid enough to forgo a single moment of staring into those blue eyes.

She took another long, deep breath, and it was a little shuddery.

"I have . . . I have another appointment right after this so I have to keep things moving. Want to see outside?" she offered finally, into the silence.

He hesitated a beat.

"Sure," he said shortly.

She wondered if she'd hurt his feelings. She was pretty sure J. T. McCord actually had feelings, rather than just an ego.

Then again, she suspected that whatever had gone on in his life between the lines on his Wikipedia page had toughened his hide.

She doubted he'd be nursing any wounds very long.

She managed to unlock the sliding doors, though once

again her hands were a little awkward, and it seemed to take an inordinate amount of time.

He waited in absolute silence, which didn't help her nerves in the least.

She slid the doors open onto fresh, already hot mountain air.

He beelined for the tarp-covered hot tub with a guy's instinct for gadgets, and she darted to the other side of the deck to collect her wits.

She'd just turned down a date with John Tennessee McCord.

She was certifiable.

Because she was both relieved and miserable.

The deck offered a panoramic view of the tops of the trees climbing the steep sides of the canyon. It was a flawlessly blue-skied California day. She'd seen the view of the canyon at this time of day dozens of times before. She'd never seen J. T. McCord in *this* light, though, so she peered at him out of the corner of her eye.

Her heartbeat hadn't quite slowed to pre-J. T. rhythms yet. Every part of her was lit up, from her brain to her nipples.

She heard a text chime into his phone. He lunged for it like a gunfighter being drawn upon.

He glanced hungrily at the text.

The tension went out of him.

He was clearly waiting for some kind of news.

And then she saw the ficus in the corner of the deck. Barely alive, left to crisp in the sun.

"Oh no!" She dove over to it and knelt next to it to investigate, lifting up one wilting leaf in her hand as if taking its pulse.

She was conscious of his feet thundering across the deck. When she looked up seconds later, it was straight into his blue eyes.

"Wow. Are you The Flash?" She was amused.

"I thought you were falling off the deck. You scared the shit out of me."

He did look scared.

"I'm so sorry," she said hurriedly, wildly flattered that he was going to try to rescue her. "It's just . . . the plant . . ."

"The *plant* was about to fall off the deck?"

"No! I'm sorry!" She wasn't sure how to explain. "It's just this poor plant was left out here and our landscape guy clearly forgot to water it . . . and that sort of thing makes me *furious*. I mean, it relies on us to stay alive, doesn't it? And we can't just let it down. It's a living thing."

He was watching her, apparently processing this in some inscrutable way.

"Sure," he said carefully.

If he thought she was a lunatic, so be it.

That might, in fact, be all for the best.

"I'm going to see if I can save it. Will you help me get it into my car, Mr. McCord? I have to get back to work. I'll give you a lift back to wherever you need to go."

Another brief hesitation, and then his eyes flashed a sort of wry resignation. "Sure."

Silently, like a pair of medics on a battlefield, they ferried the failing ficus down the stairs and installed it in her car. The plant got shotgun. J. T. buckled it in.

It reclined like a carefree tourist on holiday.

He was no stranger to manual labor, but honestly couldn't remember the last time he'd been conscripted into it. But then there wasn't much he wouldn't do for a beautiful woman who turned pleading green eyes on him.

Even if she had just resoundingly rejected him.

And *that* was still puzzling. He was puzzled less about the rejection, which was rare enough in his life to be at least a little interesting, but about the why of it. Some women found the whole actor/movie star/fame thing a little overwhelming, but he didn't think that was what was at play here. This woman was both smart and thoughtful and she could hold her own in any kind of debate. She would draw her own conclusions about a person. Lady peanuts or no lady peanuts.

Britt's car was a blue Ford Contour circa 1990 and one of the rear doors seemed to be tied shut with a rope. He chose the other door and squeezed himself into the backseat and buckled himself in. His knees were practically under his chin.

"Sorry you're a little squished back there," she said as she shoved it into reverse and backed away from the cabin. Not sounding terribly sorry.

"Don't worry about me. I always ride with my knees right under my ears."

She smiled at that, apparently utterly untroubled that she'd origami'd an Emmy winner into her car.

"Sorry the air-conditioning isn't the best," was the next thing she said, about three minutes later. Which was her way for apologizing for the rolled-down windows and the hot air blowing through the car. J. T. was pretty sure he saw a few insects, a dragonfly, and a skeeter hawk pass through the window on one side on their way out the other, like it was some sort of new and convenient insect bypass.

"These are *some* wheels," he said.

She grinned at him in the rearview mirror. "Thanks. So your truck is broken, eh?"

"Yep. They're diagnosing it right now."

"You're pretty attached to that truck, huh?"

"Yep."

"Don't you have one of those . . . what do you call it . . . fleets? A whole barn full of Bentleys and Porsches and

BMWs? Don't they issue you a fleet when you become a movie star?"

She was teasing him now. A little more comfortable, apparently, now that she had him strapped in and she was in control of the car. Perhaps throwing him a bone in the wake of the rejection.

"Oh, sure, *any* guy can have a fleet. But a genuine 1995 Dodge Ram with an odometer that's turned over twice? Just try and find one of *those* on Craigslist."

He couldn't quite see her whole face from his vantage point in the backseat, just a really lovely three-quarter view, but in the rearview mirror he could see that her eyes were scrunched in a smile. "I'll just bet they're rare."

"That truck was one of the first things I bought when it started to look like I could buy pretty much anything I wanted, which was kind of a strange adjustment. Like going from zero to a hundred, just like that. My life was kind of a kaleidoscope for a while—seems like it changed every day. And I just got kind of attached to having a constant. Something that needed *me* to take care of *it*. If that makes sense. Kept me sane."

"Sure," she said softly, almost reluctantly. "I get it. Like . . . finding a fixed point in a sandstorm. It's how you navigate through."

So she did get it. That was a damned poetic way to put it, too.

And she didn't *want* to like him, but she did.

She didn't *want* to want him, but she did. He *knew* she did.

Puzzling. But he could work with this.

"Great way to put it," he said shortly. "Know anything about sandstorms, Britt?"

She didn't answer for so long, he thought maybe she wasn't going to.

"Maybe," she said. A careful, neutral word. Issued after a hesitation.

In a way that didn't encourage further questioning.

He was determined, but he wasn't a brute. He was happy to let her be quiet if that was what she needed right now.

She handled the old car ably on the windy roads, because she'd likely driven them dozens of times.

He couldn't put his finger on it. It wasn't one thing about her. It was probably more a combination of externals and intangibles, like the beautiful eyes and a lacerating wit; a small curvy body and the way she moved; the sound of her voice; her soft, full mouth. All he knew was that she made him restless and almost ornery in a very fundamental way for a very fundamental reason from the moment he'd laid eyes on her. There was really only one way to scratch that itch.

She wasn't wearing a ring. But that didn't mean there wasn't a guy in the picture.

The notion bothered him a lot.

The notion that the notion bothered him a lot also bothered him.

And really, what was so hard about saying, *You know, there's a guy in the picture*?

He'd been pretty forthright with her because that was who he was. Rebecca had pretty much exhausted whatever lingering tolerance he'd had for games and strategy.

"So, Britt, what's your excuse for driving a beater like . . ."

"Margaret?" she completed.

It had definitely been a trap, if a whimsical one. "Now, how did I know you'd named your car, Britt Langley?"

Pink flooded into her cheeks, and he was completely charmed. "I usually do a sort of financial triage on my, um, priorities. So as long as the car door shuts at all, I wait until I can afford to fix her. But I make sure she gets her fluids and so forth."

"You ever think about what might happen if Margaret here quits on you in the deep dark woods?"

"Gosh, no, J. T., it *never* occurred to me to wonder about that," she said with such withering faux astonishment he blinked.

"*Wow.* Sorry."

"I'll be fine," she said easily, after a moment, somewhat conciliatory. "I can take care of myself."

Sure you can, sweetheart.

As much as he'd enjoyed arguing with her, saying that out loud would have been chucking a match into a gasoline puddle, he was pretty sure.

"I guess I just don't like to give up on things," she said after a moment. "Whether or not it always makes sense."

He wondered if she was talking about some other guy.

"Yeah," he said. "Neither do I."

He knew she'd see his smile in her rearview mirror.

She knew damn well he was talking about her.

He saw her dimple appear again. She cranked the wheel and steered the car into another sharp turn that sent his seat belt digging into his collarbone. Which he preferred to think of as a coincidence.

"So, Britt, will I see you under a car at the garage, too? Bagging groceries at the store? Running a vacuum in the hall at the Angel's Nest? Directing traffic at the stoplight?"

She smiled. "Nah, I just have the two jobs. Covers my mortgage and the basics. And my mortgage is barely anything, especially by California standards."

She pulled up in front of Ernie's Garage as she said that.

He managed to shoulder open the door, unfold his body with a modicum of grace and get out of her car.

He leaned into the driver's side window.

"Well, thanks for showing me that place. You gonna be able to get that plant out on your own?"

"Oh, yeah. I can just slide it onto a rolling chair and push it up to my front porch."

He stared at her, bemused. She said this as if she did it all the time.

"So I can tell my boss you'll move right into that house?" She gave him a bright, winsome smile.

He snorted. "You can tell him I'm a complete, hopeless diva. Or whatever the male equivalent of that is. You know how actors are, after all."

That was pure sarcasm, but this only made her grin, which only made him like her more, because he was perverse.

"I honestly can't blame you about the house," she sympathized.

He could tell it was true. Her sympathy was balm.

"So, Britt, you're clearly a compassionate woman. Have pity. Are you really going to consign me to the purgatory of the Angel's Nest? Those angels are *judging* me."

"If you behave yourself, you've got nothing to worry about."

"Darlin', I'm still hoping you'll give me a reason to misbehave."

She tilted her head. "Boy, it's like a faucet, isn't it, J. T.? The charm?"

"It's like a faucet, isn't it, Britt? The prickly rejoinders?"

She paused.

"'Prickly . . . rejoinders'?" she quoted.

With great, slow, wondering, savoring pleasure.

Amusement lit up her whole face.

Damn, but he liked this woman. She was *maddening*.

"I know a lot of other words you might be interested in, Britt Langley. I'd be happy to whisper them to you right now."

"I know a two-letter word you ought to look up, J. T."

She didn't sound or even look angry. She was smiling,

and she'd swatted that back to him like a tennis pro. There was an accomplished flirt in there somewhere underneath all the thorns.

She did, however, sound firm.

He'd never had so much fun being thoroughly blown off.

"I have to get going," she said. "Gary will get in touch with you if something opens up."

J. T. sighed deeply and with great resignation.

She laughed at his suffering and drove away with a wave.

CHAPTER 6

He walked into the garage, smiling in a way no man who'd just been resoundingly rejected ought to smile, and inhaled with pleasure the good, masculine motor-oil-and-gasoline perfume of the garage.

A big gray-haired guy sporting a really high quality mustache and a significant belly was waiting for his own truck, which was getting its oil changed. The two of them gazed up at their vehicles on the rack as if in moral support.

He turned and saw J. T. "You must be that Hollywood fella."

"So I am. You're that Misty Cat fella."

"So I am. Glenn Harwood. Me and my wife, Sherrie, we own the place."

"J. T. McCord." J. T. shook Glenn's outthrust hand.

"This your truck?" Glenn gestured upward at J. T.'s old Dodge Ram.

"Yep."

"Had her for some time, eh?" Glenn diagnosed.

"Since she was born, you might say. She breaks, I fix her."

Glenn chuckled. "A truck's a commitment. Not just a commodity."

"Agreed."

They stood in silence a moment longer.

"Was that our Britt dropped you off?" Glenn said, almost idly.

"Our?" Interesting choice of words.

"Oh, we kind of think of our employees that way, me and Sherrie. A bit like family."

"Family, huh? Even that glowering guy behind the grill?"

"Oh, sure. Nice kid, Giorgio, underneath it all. Talented cook."

Sure he is, J. T. thought. *Nice like a snakebite is nice.*

"Yeah, thought I recognized that car of hers," Glenn said. "Damn thing is held together with chewing gum and paper clips and string, practically. Wonder when the last time she changed her oil was? Women and their cars." Glenn gave his head a long-suffering shake. "I have two daughters. Two boys, too. One's a surgeon at the hospital in Black Oak. But that Britt has some smarts, though, I'll hand that to her."

J. T. thought about Britt and that poor, sad ficus. "Something tells me she's good about stuff like oil. I had in mind renting a house in Hellcat Canyon for a time, since I'll be filming near town. The house I saw today wasn't quite right, however. Britt was kind enough to drop me off here."

Glenn grunted an assent. "House has to fit a man. Like a truck."

This might in fact be true. J. T. didn't know. He hadn't lived in any single place that felt like home since he'd left Tennessee, and he hadn't thought it mattered. Thanks to what Britt had said today about Rosemary, he now knew his notion of home was lodged in him like an old bullet: it was blue-eyed Mary's, shirts drying on a line, green everywhere your eye fell, living things rustling about in the trees and brush. An old pain that couldn't be reached or removed.

He felt a sudden irrational surge of envy for the guy standing next to him. Glenn Harwood knew what home was.

"Yep," was all he said.

They were quiet again as someone in the garage clanged some metal part good and hard.

J. T. had the distinct sense that Glenn was working up to something.

"She's a good girl, Britt. A real sweetheart with a wit on her. Everyone here likes her. She keeps a bit to herself, though. Like something spooked her once."

It was admirably subtle.

But J. T. was pretty sure this was Glenn's way of warning this Hollywood Casanova to not be cavalier with Britt.

If not to stay away completely.

He instantly seesawed between being amused at the guy's nerve and sizzlingly angry at the insinuation.

Glenn didn't know him at all.

But then, only a few people really did. But there was a trail of photos and articles implying things about him, not all of which were wrong, and J. T. had to admit he would draw the very same conclusions about himself if he saw the photos.

He went absolutely silent and rigid for a moment. But one of the advantages of being just a little older was that he thought now before he spoke and good sense more often than not elbowed aside his ego.

He was the interloper here in Hellcat Canyon, after all. He'd had to prove things to people his entire life. *Why stop now?* he thought ironically.

He guessed, in the end, he was glad someone cared enough about Britt to issue a warning.

"I kind of got that sense, too," he said carefully.

It wasn't really reassurance, but something told him that Glenn was no dummy.

They didn't look at each other.

Glenn just gave a short nod.

Spooked. An interesting choice of word. But the more J. T. thought about it, the more it kind of fit. Because . . . how had she put it? Why would she only "want the basics"? In his experience, people like that were made—through some kind of experience—not born.

When he'd asked her whether she'd learned anything the hard way . . .

Well, no person with a heart would have asked her a single other question after seeing her expression.

Britt Langley might be hiding something. But hiding didn't come naturally to her.

Her eyes gave her away.

They watched their respective trucks for a little moment of silence.

"Film crew in the area will mean more customers at the Misty Cat," Glenn mused.

"Yep. I'll make sure they know about it, too."

They were guys, and they didn't really need to say any more than that. Glenn's satisfaction with this turn of events was palpable, and J. T. was a businessman, too.

"I believe I met one of your daughters and your granddaughter—outside the flower shop. Cute little girl. Smart. Annalise, I think her name was? A great speller."

Glenn glowed. "Oh, that'd be my second oldest, Edie—Eden, her name is—and her daughter. Smart doesn't cover it with the little one. She can spell like a sonofagun. And *stuuuuborn*. Like her mama. My wife is a softie. So Edie must have got her hard head from me." He said this with a sort of regretful, abstracted pride.

J. T. smiled at that. "Stubborn women," he repeated. Vaguely but approvingly.

"McCORD!" A guy with a clipboard appeared, like a doctor. "Got a sec to talk about your truck?"

"Well, I'm up. I'll be back for another Glennburger soon. Best burger I've ever had."

Glenn beamed at him. "Tell me something I don't know, son."

A bent rocker arm was no small thing, but they'd actually called around and were able to find the part and they could have it messengered over, courtesy of some internet magic. J. T. could have the truck back tomorrow.

He sighed with the same relief he experienced every time he managed to patch his truck back together again and signed the estimate.

Then he stopped in at the little service station mart attached to the garage to grab a couple of bottles of water and peruse the selection of snacks, most of which were packaged in lurid cellophane and comprised of preservatives.

He paused suddenly before a collection of black plastic cone-shaped bins that usually held bunches of flowers. Only one bouquet was left, a haphazard cluster of daisies and carnations and marigolds and some kind of purple flower embellished with frayed greenery, all of it just hours away from going limp, if he had to guess from the looks of things. Yesterday, he wouldn't even have noticed it.

And he thought of Britt kneeling next to that poor dying ficus, and about people who went nuts flailing for ways to make their lives something safe and comfortable and bearable, him included, his mama, maybe even his pa with his bottle, and he thought about the oppressive clutter at the Angel's Nest. It seemed to J. T. his life had comprised torrents of things he was either trying to dodge—like his dad's fists, matrimony, or bad publicity—or things he ought to grab, like women, opportunities, and good publicity. He was good at shooting those kinds of rapids.

It was the damnedest thing, but helping a beautiful, prickly woman carry a half-dead ficus felt like a grace note amid all of that. Maybe because, while his entire life had been pretty eventful and glamorous and enviable, none of it had been . . .

It occurred to him that the word he might be looking for was *gentle*.

He snorted at himself. But he added the bouquet to his things on the counter, anyway.

He walked back to the Angel's Nest and paused a moment outside to watch the guys clambering over the billboard with big roller brushes.

The words . . . *wish they were you* were now readable.

"Damn straight," he told the sign.

Most days, being him was a pretty good thing to be. Even days when thorny little blondes blew him off.

And then he held his breath like a deep-sea diver against the wave of potpourri and pushed open the door.

Rosemary was still working on the ledger, fingers deftly tap tap tapping at the keys. She glanced up briefly and her fingers didn't stop.

"There are cookies in the lounge, hon, if you want some, fresh out of the oven."

He could *almost* smell them through the potpourri. Chocolate chip, if he had to guess.

"Thanks. I could use a cookie."

She paused and looked up when she sensed he hadn't moved on.

He thrust the gas-station bouquet out at her. "These looked kind of lonely at the gas station. Thought they might look nice right up here on the counter."

Her eyes widened. She nervously pushed her glasses up onto the bridge of her nose.

And then she slowly flushed a pleased shade of red

that complemented the one on her head and took it from him.

"Oh, my goodness, aren't you a *sweetheart*."

He'd managed to fluster her again.

He'd actually managed to fluster himself a little. Somehow he'd forgotten the sort of pleasure that could be had in making someone happy for no reason at all.

He frankly couldn't think of the last time anyone else had tried to make him happy for no reason at all.

She took the bouquet and buried her nose in them. "It was *just* what the room was missing."

It was the *only* thing the room was missing, more specifically.

"My thoughts exactly," he said.

She naturally located a vase shaped like an angel. It was sporting wings.

He begrudgingly allowed that they *were*, as Britt suggested, kind of pretty.

He was two steps toward the stairs, on his way to hunt down a cookie, when Rosemary said, "You just missed meeting Cherisse and Kevin, your neighbors. They came in from a hike and went back up to their room."

He froze mid-step. Closed his eyes. Swore silently.

He couldn't do it. He couldn't stay trapped in that purple room with Kevin and Cherisse boffing noisily away all afternoon.

He pivoted smoothly.

"You got some trail maps down here, Rosemary? I'm in the mood for a hike."

She licked the tip of her finger and swiped a turquoise flyer from a stack next to the pink ones. "I sure do, hon, and this has all the best routes and landmarks marked. The Eternity Oak, now that's worth seeing." She laid it on the counter and pointed to an illustration. "Big beautiful old live oak they say was just a baby when the Maidu

Indians lived in these hills. Legend has it that if you carve your initials and your sweetie's initials into it, *nothing* can ever sunder your union—you'll be bound to that person for life, for better or for worse. So you better be damned sure about that person before you do it. People around here take that oak seriously. You won't find too many initials on it."

"Hell. Do you use that story to scare the kiddies on Halloween?"

Being bound to the wrong person for life sounded like the worst kind of purgatory. Given how long it might take to find out that person was *really* wrong. Say, something like five years.

"I take it you're not a romantic, Mr. McCord?"

"Let's just say I have a healthy sense of self-preservation," he said dryly.

"Well, we all need that, too, don't we? Oh, hon, there are a few awful stories around here about what happens if you don't get the right name up there. And they say the oak grows over your initials if your love is destined to die."

"Damn." He was impressed. "That is one brutal tree."

"I don't make the legends up, I just repeat 'em. Now, you got yourself a black belt, hon. I know because I read it on Wikipedia. Won't work against a bear but any random crazy hill folk might be startled if you start in on them that way, so you stay on the trail."

"I'll be ready for random crazy hill folk. I *come* from random crazy hill folk."

"I believe you, hon, but you also don't want to go too far and make a wrong turn up at Coyote Creek settlement, because some folks have been known to grow"—she lowered her voice to a whisper and held her hand against the side of her mouth—"*marijuana* . . . way, way up in those hills and, well, let's just say they're enthusiastic about their privacy."

"Gotcha."

"But you're pretty safe with any number of these options. If you keep to the Grubstake Trail, you can follow that on up to Whiskey Creek or Whiplash Ridge. You take the South Route, there's a good trail about a mile from Rustler's Ridge along Sassy Hooker Crossing, right on up to Full Moon Falls, and you'll pass the Eternity Oak on the way there."

"Those miners sure were colorful fellas." Sassy Hooker Crossing, for some reason, made him think of lady peanuts. Just as colorful.

"They were at that."

"I like falls."

"Well, that's your route, then. And you'll like these falls. They are the *prettiest* thing ever. Now, if you're a country boy, I don't need to tell you what to do if you encounter a snake that rattles, or a bear or a mountain lion or coyote."

"Don't try to pet it."

"Want me to tell you what else to touch and what not to touch?"

Rosemary had just lobbed him a good one.

"I wish you would have told me that years ago, Rosemary. Could have saved me some trouble and made me even *more* popular than I am."

She grinned at him. "Leaves of three, let it be, sweetie. Don't pick me any wildflowers if you don't know the names of them. And don't you slip up and carve the wrong initials in that tree."

"Yeah, I don't think you have anything to worry about there."

Pines, manzanita, Indian paintbrush, oaks, firs, redwoods and all manner of greenery kept the trails shaded for the most part, but the sun was ruthless where it made it through the tree cover, and it helped incinerate a little of J. T.'s restlessness.

He was halfway up the trail when his phone chimed in with a text.

He scrambled for it. He exhaled.

Still not his agent.

It was from Linda Goldstein.

> John Tennessee, I have a stash of signed photos from Blood Brothers days. The ones with floppy hair. Do you still want to use them? If not, what would you like me to do with them?

Linda was the president of his fan club. He was bemused he still *had* an official fan club, let alone one with an elected officer; it was really more of a skeleton crew of women who never abandoned anything they started, bless them, whether it was a knitted afghan or organized adulation for star of a program that was popular before most of them were moms.

J. T. texted back:

> Laminate them and use them as placemats for your cat's dinner? Offer them to your boys for target practice?

A moment later a message trilled in:

> HA HA HA! You're the BEST. I know The Rush is going to be GREAT!

Accompanied by a flurry of emojis: various smiles and clapping hands and one inexplicable cat.

Linda had evolved from a gushy, giddy, alarmingly

well-organized Tennessee McCord worshipper into a happily married, cheerfully harried, alarmingly well-organized mother of two teenage boys. And now she treated J. T. more or less like one of them: with a blend of affectionate "Go get 'em, Tiger!" and concerned clucking. She'd always been unequivocally on his side, which he obviously didn't always deserve.

He texted back:

> You can recycle them if you want. I'll get you some new ones. We'll have some great stills from The Rush.

Emojis in principle got on his nerves the way cherubs did.

But he hesitated.

And then added a smiling emoji before he sent it. Just a basic one. Because he knew she would enjoy it.

He wondered what Britt Langley's policy on emojis was.

He smiled to himself, and then the smile evolved into a frown.

He was positive she hadn't believed him, but he *hadn't* asked a woman out in a long time. Not in so many words, anyway. For the past fifteen years, before Rebecca, it was more often than not his people calling some actress's people and arranging a date. Or him saying yes to some hot woman who had flung herself into his path. Not that he was complaining, necessarily.

And he hadn't gotten laid in . . . well, it wasn't like he'd made marks on his wall like a prisoner in a cell. Months had gone by, though. Long enough for him to start feeling twitchy.

It was hardly for lack of opportunity.

It was just that the whole thing with Rebecca had left him feeling scorched and sobered. Together they'd been any publicist's wet dream. They really should have worked. They were probably too dazzled by each other and their own publicity and mostly too busy to realize they excelled at making each other miserable, and it started to become really clear when her career took off and his foundered. He felt like he'd given the relationship his best shot. But there was no getting around the fact that they'd been hurtling toward the inevitable messy end for some time.

In inimitable Rebecca Corday fashion, she'd picked her moment to maximize drama and publicity. She'd needed to punish him, and boy had she.

Five years ought to be long enough for another person to make a mark on you, to reshape you a little, he thought. Apart from feeling disoriented for a while—every relationship was like a culture of two, with its own language and customs—mostly he felt like he'd been evicted from a small, hot, noisy party.

And maybe that said more about him than it did about her. Maybe he was indeed the problem.

He didn't pass a single other soul on the trail, unless you counted deer and squirrels, the former of which galloped off, the latter of which scolded him from high branches. A blue jay followed him for a time, from tree branch to tree branch, squawking. A hummingbird strafed him, then moved on, satisfied it had shown him who was boss. He didn't encounter any mammals of the kind with fangs or claws, but that didn't mean they weren't in there, watching him.

He hiked past sheer drops—thoughtfully labeled by the Forest Service—and staggeringly beautiful vistas of the canyon, carved out by a relentless river.

He heard Full Moon Falls before she saw them. The low roar was like a lover's breath in your ear when things were just starting to get hot.

He forgave his mind for still being a little one-track. Nature was all about sex and death, anyway.

The roar was growing louder when he stopped at a respectful distance by a tree that could only be the Eternity Oak. The thing was immense.

A little bronze plaque at its base verified his supposition.

He moved closer to it and discovered the Forest Service hadn't splurged on any engraving to describe the legend.

But someone *had* affixed a little note to the plaque. Folded like a note card, attached with tape.

He lifted it to read.

Think twice, man, it said.

He laughed. His laugh echoed eerily.

The tree's arms—branches, he corrected himself, but their graceful, twisting reach really did seem more like arms—spread way up and out, and the whole thing was as vast and intricate as an apartment complex or a little city, which it likely was for various forest fauna. Sun could hardly get through the branches, and when it did, it dappled the ground like a scattering of gold coins.

The place was arrestingly beautiful and as calm as a temple. And yet it made him a little nervous, as if there were something he needed to do in order to earn the right to even stand there. Like this was the Temple of True Love, or something, and he hadn't paid the price of admission yet.

"Paid the price." Now, there was a phrase calculated to chill a man's blood.

He stepped closer to the tree.

On first inspection he saw only one set of initials.

ELB + GHG

But then he squinted, and an errant ray of late-afternoon sunlight picked out a few other sets of initials, scattered over it. He couldn't read all of them clearly.

But one set was spotlit, set on a high branch, old and scarred now:

GEH + SLO

Who were they? He wondered what it felt like to be that *certain.* Or did their hands shake when they dug those initials into the tree?

He was pretty sure Felix Nicasio and Michelle Solomon would have no compunctions about carving their initials in that tree.

J. T. recalled an infamous article in the wake of his breakup: "Top Ten Reasons Rebecca Corday is better off without John Tennessee McCord." The list read like some unholy brainchild of Rebecca's publicist and her mother. Number Eight was, "He's allergic to the 'L' word."

Now, that was low. It wasn't an *allergy.* He was more like . . . a self-proclaimed agnostic who refused to use the Lord's name in vain, just in case he might be wrong. An awful lot of misery was perpetrated and endured in the name of love. Just look at what it had done to his mama, for instance. As far as he was concerned, the word deserved the type of fear and awe reserved for the Old Testament God.

He would have said it if he'd felt it.

Maybe he *couldn't* feel it.

J. T. restlessly turned his back on those initials and the poor fools who'd carved them. He wanted to see the falls and get back before it got dark.

The roaring grew louder, and a few dozen yards later

there they were: a lacy, foaming spill that cascaded over a terraced series of jagged stones and terminated in a pool, that turned into a stream, that likely ran off and joined the river. He looked up: the trees, as if in deference to the falls, stood way back from it, and he could imagine that a full moon would pour down through and light them up.

He did enjoy a good spotlight.

He stood and breathed in silence. He was beginning to recall one of the problems he always had with big swaths of unstructured time: a restless feeling set in, a niggling sensation that might be missing out on something. It could explain why he'd just kept moving in recent years.

So he turned around and headed back.

But he stopped at the Eternity Oak and listened.

One long, low branch reached down the road toward the falls.

Not that I would, but if I ever carve initials here, he thought, *that's where I'd put them*. Closest to the falls. So it's like you're hearing the breath of a lover in your ear while you're sleeping.

"Britt, honey, are you all right in there? I heard screaming."

Britt popped her head out of her screen door and looked across at Mrs. Morrison, who, leaning over her porch rail, was limned in the last bit of the day's sun. Her hair looked like a silver crown.

"Sorry to worry you, Mrs. Morrison. I'm just watching a movie. Someone just got murdered."

"How exciting! Well, all right then. We won't be needing this." Mrs. Morrison lowered the Remington shotgun she was holding and leaned it next to her front door. She retrieved her Dr Pepper and rum on the rocks from the railing she'd placed it on and toasted Britt with it.

"Thank you for picking up my prescriptions," she called.

"Oh, you're welcome. It's never a problem, Mrs. Morrison."

"Well, good night, dear. Enjoy your film."

"Sweet dreams, Mrs. Morrison."

"They always are. Tonight I think I'll dream of the day my Elwyn and I carved our names in the Eternity Oak."

"Well, you tell Elwyn I said hi when you see him tonight."

Mrs. Morrison chuckled. "I will, dear."

Britt ducked back into the house and collapsed back onto her sofa, snatched up one of the pillows she'd recovered with thrift store silk and clutched it to her, then held her breath as if going back under water and took the movie off pause.

She'd spent the last five minutes in a shabby, 1970s-era kitchen in Boston, immersed in the life of a cop, a simple guy who was kind of awkward, but good and solid and ferociously loyal. He'd been in love with the same woman his entire life . . . but she'd married his best friend. And just when he'd won a declaration of love from her—in bed no less—his best friend stabbed him.

And his friend hadn't meant to stab him, they'd been fighting and it was all in the heat of the moment and quite an accident, and dear God in heaven it was quite a mess and very upsetting.

John Tennessee McCord was really, really good at dying.

He was also really, *really* convincing in the love scenes.

There were two of those.

They were real and raw and mostly naked and of the many powerful impulses that assailed her as she watched them, all were surprising, but two of them seemed strongest: she'd wanted to crawl in there and pull that woman off him. The word that had throbbed in her head throughout that scene was *MINE.*

The other impulse was to nibble on one of his smooth, hard brown shoulders.

But it was particularly fascinating to witness his transformation into that character: His posture, his diction, his mannerisms, his accent—he was seamlessly, one hundred percent a different person in his role in *Agapé.* It was a bravura performance.

Except his eyes. His eyes were the same. His eyes were so eloquent they were an entire movie unto themselves.

How did he know how to do that? Embody heartbreak and passion and fury and mute longing?

You either channeled that from some divine source, she figured. Or . . . you had to know how those things felt.

Good grief, that was hot.

God. She dabbed at her eyes as the credits rolled. Phillip laid a sympathetic paw on her knee.

She really had a problem.

Or maybe it was a solution.

A little Googling would help her decide which it was.

The problem was that she'd gone about the business of Gold Nugget Property Management all day, marking up big "For Sale" and "For Rent" signs with a big Sharpie, talking to tenants about trimming trees and fixing sprinklers and the like, and all the while she'd fully expected the John Tennessee McCord effect to fade from her body and mind, the way you eventually got your hearing back after a loud and fabulous rock concert.

But instead the rest of her day had been like that scene in *The Wizard of Oz* where Dorothy opens the door and suddenly everything changes from black-and-white into blazing color.

Only in reverse.

Everything was now dimmer. She was a little afraid he'd permanently altered her body chemistry by his mere proximity.

Just two days ago she'd been content with the rhythm of her days. Now she knew "content" was a synonym for "safe little box."

She took a deep breath and typed some search terms in the browser window.

She'd promised herself she wasn't going to Google him again. But this wasn't frivolous, voyeuristic Googling, she told herself. It was a fact-finding mission inspired by a sentence he'd uttered today. Which was:

"Can't remember the last time I did that."

Slammed a headboard, that was. With a noisy and willing partner.

What she discovered was that while Rebecca Corday was linked with Anthony Underhill and was seen in photos grinning her eight-mile-wide grin alongside him in various venues, from restaurants to red carpets, as far as she could tell, J. T. hadn't been photographed with a woman anywhere.

She couldn't find a single photo of him with a woman on the internet for at least the last six months.

Though there were photos of him out with what looked like his buddies at lunch, and one of him leaving a karate dojo in Los Angeles. But if any women had been in the picture, J. T. had definitely kept it on the down low.

He was only going to be in Hellcat Canyon for a little while. He'd be out of here in time for Felix Nicasio's wedding for sure, which was in about a month.

Some women might put that in the "con" column.

For her purposes, she decided it belonged in the "pro" column.

In the sidebar of one of the pages with the photos was a link to an article intriguingly entitled, "Top Ten Reasons Rebecca Corday is better off without John Tennessee McCord."

Yikes.

It was quite a list. Snarky and juvenile and absolute clickbait for lovers of Hollywood gossip. But it was Number Eight that caught her eye.

8. Because he's allergic to the "L" word.

Britt exhaled.

Ironically, she'd put that in the "pro" column, too.

Her plan was taking shape.

She liked that her solution was still technically a box, in that it had parameters and a finite volume. So there was comfort in that. The parameters were defined by a guy who in all likelihood wouldn't want anything more from her than a good time, who had known commitment issues (he'd never moved in with Rebecca Corday, after all), and would be gone in a couple of months.

Inside that box could be lot of hot sex.

Provided, that was, she saw him again. He didn't seem like a guy who gave up, however.

She sat in thoughtful silence for quite some time. She pulled her sketch pad into her lap, and stared down at that empty white page.

And then her pencil began to fly.

She reveled in creating in the arch of a neck, expressive angled ears, the curve of a haunch, the length of the spine, the flow of a mane and a tail.

And because it was standing on its hind legs, she dressed the horse in jeans.

And cowboy boots.

And then, as a coup de grâce, she drew a black T-shirt on him. It was snug at the top and a little loose at the waist.

She laughed at herself.

But with that one final touch, John Tennessee McCord was officially a horse.

The one she intended to get back up on.

CHAPTER 7

J. T. had his truck back at around three o'clock the next day. He immediately took it for an almost giddy drive around town, as if he'd just been sprung from the pokey. He stopped in at the grocery store for some real food, including sandwiches and a few packaged salads, startling all the clerks into wide-eyed speechlessness. He drove past the fountain in the town square, past the town hall, past a few Victorians that straight-up qualified as mansions, and through, on a whim, a pretty little trailer park called Heavenly Shores even though no body of water was in sight. It was apparently a retirement community. He waved at two senior ladies hanging out on their porches, chatting and knitting. They waved gaily back.

All roads, alas, eventually of course led right back to the Angel's Nest.

J. T. took a long hot shower and rubbed his own sandalwood soap in his armpits lest he besmirch the angel soap. He ate his grocery store sandwich and salad and tried to write his damn wedding toast for Felix, but he couldn't hear his own thoughts over Kevin and Cherisse. The headboard bamming next door had yielded to loud arguing.

"You never listen to anything I say!" poor Cherisse was sobbing.

"You never stop talking! How am I supposed to listen to *all* of it?"

Kevin, the poor schmuck, sounded genuinely tormented.

J. T. sighed, made a fist and gave the wall a couple of good hard thumps.

They clammed up.

"Don't go carving your initials in the Eternity Oak, now, ya hear?" he muttered dryly.

He was just reaching for his Kindle again when another text chimed in. He glanced at his phone.

It was Missy Van Cleve.

Tensnesseee I'm drunk and homey.

He frowned. "Homey" was the last thing Missy Van Cleve was. He'd heard the word "flawless" used to describe her, but an allegedly perfect waist-to-hip-to-bust ratio (which she'd once pointed out in an interview) did not, in his book, add up to flawless. She was famous for being famous, and she was most guys' definition of hot, but she was also so vapid it entered the realm of surreal and was *almost* funny. He'd gone out with her once, and decided life was too short, which is how he knew he was getting older.

But apparently he'd made quite an impression on her. Because she kept in touch. Usually when she was drunk.

A few seconds later:

I mean drunk homey.

A few seconds later.

Homey! I'm drunk and homey!

Where are you Tesnnsesse I'm drunk and homey!

I'm coming right over

He could ignore her and hope she got tired of sending drunk texts and eventually passed out.

Or . . . he could have a little fun.

He texted:

> Do you mean by any chance drunk and horny, Missy?

She texted back:

> That's what I said!

He texted:

> Get a cab from wherever you are to 11493 Excelsior. Tell the driver the guy who answers the door will pay your fare.

In about a half hour, Franco Francone would have his hands full of a drunk, homey, unruly, incensed Missy Van Cleve.

J. T. grinned.

His smile vanished when "Taking Care of Business" erupted from his phone. His agent was calling instead of texting. Which could pretty much only mean one thing.

J. T.'s heart went from about zero to ninety just like that.

He took a couple of deep breaths before he answered.

"Hey Al."

"It's a no on *Last Call in Purgatory*, J. T. It's a no they delivered with convincing anguish, but it's a no."

Al was a big believer in ripping the Band-Aid off quickly.

J. T.'s breath whooshed out of him.

"They thought you were amazing," Al went on. "They

never dreamed anyone could be so perfect for a part. They made it sound like it was a reenactment of *Twelve Angry Men* in there, deliberating every point of your performance for days. They really wanted you. They pleaded for you. The director says you're everything he ever envisioned. But the producers are worried you can't open the film big enough, and your sketchy track record . . ."

". . . is ten years old," J. T. said tersely. "If that's what they're worried about. I mostly haven't been an asshat in public or on a movie set for ten years, anyway. Look at my work on *Agapé* . . ."

Even as he said it, J. T. knew that the producers knew all of this, and knew all about *Agapé*, too.

"Yeah. Well. I think they know that and the producers just wanted to whip out an excuse. You know how jumpy they get when money's at stake. I guess they want the pope or someone infallible for the part. But it's really about the money and the numbers, J. T. It's what it always boils down to."

J. T. was numb. The word *no* hadn't quite sunk all the way through him yet.

"Do they want me cheaper?"

"They won't get you cheaper. We both know what you're worth."

J. T. was in agreement with that.

He was silent.

Al let him be silent.

"They have anybody else yet?" J. T. finally said.

"Nope. They're still looking for the female lead, though. Threw out a few names you might know."

Al did irony *very* well. J. T. could just imagine what one of those names was.

He closed his eyes, mouthed an expletive.

"Would you rather I'd waited until morning to tell

you?" Al was sympathetic but there was a hint of laughter in his voice, as if he'd once again heard loud and clear the word "Fuck."

"No, because I needed an incentive to go out and get drunk tonight and you provided it."

"That's my boy," his agent said complacently. "Just don't do it in front of any cameras, if you can help it."

J. T. gave a short, humorless laugh.

"I *am* sorry, J. T."

"Yeah, don't be. We both know how it is."

"And you never know," his agent said.

"You never know," J. T. said.

The Hollywood motto. You never know.

They signed off.

He sat motionless on the edge of the bed for a moment. He took a long breath. His lungs burned strangely. No matter how hard you tried, hope took up residence almost like a pumping organ and when it was gone you sure noticed.

When it was gone was when you truly knew the measure of how badly you wanted something.

He'd *badly* wanted this part.

"FUCK," he said, with great, resonant sincerity.

Either Kevin or Cherisse thumped the wall.

J. T. thumped it back twice, harder. "Take it as a suggestion!" he yelled. Even though they'd probably miss the irony.

There was no return thump.

There might, however, be a return noisy revenge hump.

He had to get out of this room.

He looked up at the wall. A cherub was gazing at him with limpid sympathy.

J. T. *almost* appreciated it in that moment.

His eyes flew around the room like a prisoner in a cell looking for an escape. And his eyes lit upon the little bright pink flyer featuring Hellcat Canyon's Calendar of Events.

Tonight was Open Mic Night at the Misty Cat.

He plucked it off the desk and stared at it.

And then something occurred to him.

There was a silver lining here, and she had green eyes and a sweet body and a sharp wit on her.

He'd never gotten more than three no's in a row in his entire life.

That could only mean one thing: he sure as hell wasn't going to get another one tonight.

The tables at the Misty Cat were about a quarter full when he arrived a little before seven in the evening. Plenty of parking on the street. Not a really hopping night, apparently. Possibly because it was a weeknight. Possibly it never was.

A few tables were occupied by guys who were already loud thanks to beer.

A big chalkboard had been propped up on an easel and it read:

TUESDAY IS OPEN MIC NIGHT!
Open Mic Night Sign-up

Glory Hallelujah Greenleaf was written on the board in pink chalk. It was the only name so far.

He looked about, but he didn't see Britt right off.

But a girl who must be Glory Hallelujah Greenleaf was up on the stage, an acoustic guitar on her lap. She was tuning it.

An old bearded guy, wiry and small but surprisingly lissome, was on the floor in front of the stage, swaying and waving his arms around.

"You sit down, Marvin Wade, I don't care how many

drugs you did in the seventies, this ain't no Grateful Dead show and I will not have you doing a swirly dance while I'm playing. This is a listening song. Or maybe . . . a make-out song."

She flipped a sheet of long black hair over her shoulder, to a chorus of whistles and lascivious hoots. She was wearing a lacy sort of bustier-esque top that owed something to Stevie Nicks, and she had a very appealing rack.

"Take it off!" some doofus inevitably shouted.

"Yeah, Glory, show us your ti—"

"LANGUAGE!" Glenn bellowed as he strolled across the floor scooping up empty beer bottles, probably the world's most futile admonishment. "This ain't the Plugged Nickel!"

J. T. made a mental note to find out what the Plugged Nickel might be and where it was. If he had to guess, it was in the scary, in other words, interesting, part of Hellcat Canyon that Rosemary had warned him about and Britt had described pretty colorfully.

"There ain't enough money in the world to get me to show them . . ." Glory Greenleaf paused. ". . . to you, Truck."

"Hooooooeeee!" A gleeful chorus and a few high-fives were exchanged.

The inevitable heckling lunkheads aside, this was a girl, J. T. was certain, who knew how to incite a riot, and might just do it in order to observe it, the way a pyromaniac stands back and admires the fires he sets.

She settled onto the chair and pulled the microphone up to her face, squinting in the overhead stage light. She had cheekbones cut like diamonds.

He suspected she was a dangerous little thing.

He'd been completely inoculated against dangerous little things ever since 1995, when one had keyed his car and set fire to the ficus on his front porch after he'd been photographed with his arm around another woman.

Lighting something on fire was a surefire way to get a lesson to stick, as far as he was concerned.

A brief shot of warm air against his cheek made him turn toward the door. A guy with a badge, who must be the sheriff, had quietly slipped into the Misty Cat and was leaning against the wall behind him, mostly in shadow, unobserved, as all faces were turned toward the stage.

He looked like a former halfback who'd parlayed a knack for busting heads into a career in law enforcement.

He intercepted J. T.'s glance and nodded politely. He had a cop face. Pleasant and unreadable.

Maybe the sheriff knew that drunk men and the girl with the guitar were a combustible combination and had stopped in to throw a nice wet blanket over that.

There were three names on the chalkboard now.

And then he saw her. She slipped out of the poolroom, carrying a tray.

His heart rate actually ratcheted up in speed.

He watched her move from table to table, taking orders, giving smiles, and it was ridiculous.

And then she was next to him.

"Hi," she said.

The pleasure of being next to her washed through him with such surprising force that he felt his stomach muscles contract. And for a second he didn't say anything. He nearly stood up, a reflex born of Southern manners. He stopped himself just in time.

Her hair was swept up off her face with a clip and waved on down to her shoulders. Which was how he noticed, suddenly, that it was shaped a bit like a heart, thanks to some magic collaboration between her cheekbones and chin. She was wearing a sort of floaty floral shirt tied at the waist over a low-scooped pink camisole, and a short denim skirt that inspired an ungentlemanly impulse to invite her to sit down so he could see just how far up her tanned thighs it rode. Just enough to leave a little mystery, he was pretty certain.

"Hi," he said, belatedly. "I nearly jumped up like an eager golden retriever when I saw you coming, Britt Langley."

She tipped her head and studied him. "A golden retriever? Funny, but you don't strike me as the obedient type, J. T."

He leaned back in his chair. "Oh, I can take instruction on occasion. Like Kevin."

"Kevin?"

"Of Kevin and Cherisse, in the room next to mine? He takes instruction from Cherisse. All. Night. Long."

Britt froze.

From her expression, she was clearly imagining him listening to "Faster!" "Harder!" "A little to the left!" all night long.

"Just imagine what Cherisse is taking," she said, finally.

And he gave his head a slow shake to and fro and smiled, as if her answer was better than anything he could have anticipated. As if he'd known she'd had it in her.

She smiled, too. And then she surprised him again: she put a Sierra Nevada Stout down in front of him.

He looked at it, then up at her. "I'm touched you remembered." He was, in fact, as absurdly pleased as if he'd won a prize. She must have seen him come in before he saw her.

"I'd memorize pi out to twenty digits if I thought you'd tip me well for it."

She was teasing. Probably even officially flirting.

If anyone with bionic vision had looked their way surely they would have seen tiny sparks flying from both of them.

"Actually . . ." She took in a deep breath. "This one is on me."

Well.

Surprise number three.

There were an awful lot of things he could have glibly said aloud in response to what she'd just said: ". . . which is exactly where I want to be," chief among them.

He let his expression do the talking for him.

From her expression, she heard him clearly.

He was pretty sure she was blushing, though it was hard to tell in the dark.

But neither of them blinked.

Britt Langley seemed to have done a little thinking since he'd seen her last. He could work with this.

He fished out a five dollar bill. "Will this do for a tip?"

"Nicely." She whisked it away.

"Funny," he mused, "but now I want pie."

She laughed.

It was impossible not to notice when the big red-faced guy turned to the sound of her laughter. It was like someone had set a building on a turntable and rotated it.

He flicked his eyes from Britt to J. T., where they remained.

J. T. leveled his head up and locked eyes with him.

If they'd been dogs, he'd have been over in an instant, fur on end, for a bout of mutual, stiff-legged butt-sniffing.

Before they attempted to tear each other to pieces.

"Anything between you and Jughead?" he asked Britt idly, returning his eyes to her, where they infinitely preferred to be. It was absolutely none of his business, but that had seldom stopped him asking anything. And he was more than prepared to vanquish Jughead, if necessary.

"Oh, Truck Donegal?" she said, casually enough. She'd glanced briefly at him, offered a polite smile. Truck was clearly torn between watching the girl onstage, who was still tuning her guitar, and his new fascination with J. T. and Britt. "He seems to have given up asking me out after the third 'no thank you.'"

There was absolutely no need to ask why the guy was called "Truck."

"Three times, huh? Polite of you to add the thank-you."

"Oh, yeah. Etiquette is the glue that holds society together," she said dryly.

"Can't say"—he leaned back in the chair, as if relaxing into the sheer luxury of looking at her—"I fault him for trying so hard. Because if I got three no's from you it might just about end me."

She appraised him with a slow crooked smile that he felt like warm honey poured down his back.

The implication was that he'd give her another chance to issue one.

But he was going to leave her in suspense until then.

"I told you to sit down, Marvin!" came over the P.A.

"She any good?" He gestured with his chin toward the girl on the stage, whose dark head was down as she tuned her guitar. Which seemed to be taking forever.

"Yeah. I don't think she realizes how good."

He arched a brow skeptically. "I'd be willing to bet that girl is fully aware of and uses every one of her assets."

Britt laughed. Which he loved, given that after that sentence a lot of women would bristle or immediately begin mentally inventorying their own assets.

"BRITT!" Truck had a big arm up in the air and was waving it at her. "Gettin' thirsty over here."

"Look at her hands," she said, leaning toward him, as she slipped off toward the beckoning behemoth. She arrived and gave Truck one of her smiles. Mollified, Truck basked in it.

J. T. couldn't very well tug her back. But she'd come around again. He knew that for certain.

And he somehow knew for certain he wouldn't be leaving without her.

So he closed his hand around his beer and looked at Glory Greenleaf's hands.

Sure enough, she fumbled a little as she turned the pegs.

He could have, in fact, sworn that they were shaking.

Huh. So the wild, cocky thing was nervous.

He wondered if anyone here besides Britt noticed.

Or would bother to notice.

Glory Greenleaf sure threw out the kind of sparks that would camouflage it.

The advantages of getting the ficus burners—hot women who were easy to get but hard to handle at best and got your insurance rates raised at worst—out of his system early in his career were that now, in contrast, he could appreciate a ficus whisperer.

Not that this particular ficus whisperer didn't have thorns. And she was also insanely hot. But it was just that she bothered to notice when someone's hands were shaking and for some reason this made all the difference in the world.

Rebecca hadn't been a burner or a whisperer. She in fact occupied her own category on the planet, which was the way she'd always wanted it.

He glanced over at Britt again. Just in time to see Truck accidentally-on-purpose brush his hand across her ass.

She jerked and stepped backward, her smile frozen.

J. T.'s hand gripped his beer so hard it was a wonder it didn't shatter.

Hazards of the trade when you were a waitress. Probably wasn't her first ass grab. She could probably cope. She'd probably be the first person to tell him she could cope.

Didn't stop him from kind of wanting to break the arm of an ass grabber, however.

Neither his agent nor his publicist would thank him for that.

Truck chose that moment to look at him.

For whatever reason, meathead was declaring territory. J. T. didn't know if it was about Britt or the Misty Cat or the whole of Hellcat Canyon or because he was miserable about life and wanted to take it out on someone in any way he could, but it was both tiresome and timely.

Because J. T. was really in the mood to take someone on.

And then the girl on the stage, without preamble, began plucking out a song.

Her guitar was an old Martin acoustic, and each note rang with depth and richness you could feel right in your rib cage. Beautiful instrument. Expensive, too. The Misty Cat really did have amazing acoustics. The whole room seemed to soak up and amplify that song until you felt surrounded by it.

And a few chords in, J. T. was shocked to realize he recognized it.

It was an old Linda Ronstadt song. "Long Long Time." A song that was popular long before that girl on stage or Britt had been born. Before even he was born.

He hadn't heard it in . . . God, must be at least a decade. It was a straight-ahead, brutally poignant, unpretentious ode to unrequited love. Just beautiful.

And Glory Greenleaf was good.

Possibly even amazing.

She sang most of the song through her hair, and when she looked up, her eyes were closed.

Every guy in the place—maybe ten of them—was frozen, listening. And even on this Tuesday night in the middle of nowhere, with all these disparate people, misfits, travelers, drunks, lunkheads, famous and anonymous, it was the kind of song that could burrow into a person and find that sore place of heartbreak, recent or remembered, and really make it hurt bad all over again.

J. T. was not unaffected.

He reflexively did what every person who'd had an ache stirred would do: searched out comfort.

Which is how his gaze collided with Britt's at that precise moment.

He knew a surge of triumph. She looked away again, swiftly, self-consciously.

But she had to keep moving, because that was her job.

The room was held in such thrall that a minute, restless motion in his peripheral vision made J. T. turn around.

It was the sheriff.

Whose eyes were fixed on the stage. But something raw and fierce, very like pain, so vivid that J. T. actually held his breath, flashed across the guy's face.

A moment later he slipped out the door and was gone.

A few seconds after that, Glory Greenleaf abruptly stopped singing. Almost as though she'd forgotten the words.

She held perfectly still a moment.

Then she stood up, stuffed her guitar into her case, snapped the latches down, walked across the silent, startled room and right out the door of the Misty Cat.

They all watched her silently go.

There was a stuttered scattering of confused applause.

"Women," he heard Truck Donegal sniff.

Glenn, clearly accustomed to rolling with whatever happened in his establishment and completely unaffected, stepped up to the microphone.

"You're up, Mikey McShane!"

A skinny young guy with dyed black hair clutching a battered acoustic guitar in one fist moved toward the stage. He gave a head toss to get his long bangs out of his eyes. He had a single stud in his nose, and the piercing looked fresh. And possibly infected.

He cleared his throat and leaned toward the microphone. "This one's called 'Fuck Small Towns,'" he said shyly.

"Go Mikey!" Truck called. Not entirely ironically.

If the kid was born here, he'd probably be known as Mikey his whole life, J. T. thought. Which was reason enough to write angsty songs about small towns.

And with no one to tell him not to, Marvin Wade got up to dance.

Britt brought her beer orders to the counter and Sherrie sorted through them with practiced speed. Casey Carson was waiting there. She'd sneaked one last take-out order in for the day to bring home for her dinner. She had an early morning and she couldn't stay for Open Mic Night.

"Mr. McCord likes you," Sherrie said as close to Britt's ear as she could get, over the sound system as she plopped beers on her tray.

Britt's heart gave a lurch. "Of course he likes me. I'm nice to everyone. Isn't that why you pay me the big bucks?"

Sherrie snorted. "Don't be ridiculous. *Likes* you, likes you."

Britt stopped herself just in time from saying, *Really? You think so?*

Because, frankly, she knew so.

It was an interesting blend of terrifying and enthralling to hear it from other people.

Casey took the take-out bag Sherrie extended and leaned toward her so she could say it quietly. "Greta was in here a minute ago and saw you talking to him, and she said your *auras* were *merging*."

Greta worked at the New Age shop and read palms and futures in the back room behind a red curtain, between selling books and crystals and other accessories.

Casey looked genuinely excited about the prospect of this. As if her team had made the playoffs.

Britt was touched to realize that both Sherrie and Casey were rooting for her. And Britt wasn't an unbeliever in auras and that sort of thing, not really. But now felt like flinging her hands up over her head. How did one disguise an aura? Could you wave it away, like a gas?

And was this what life felt like to J. T.? Her life viewed through a telescopic lens, wide open to the interpretation of any casual observer?

The real danger in Mr. John Tennessee McCord wasn't his considerable sexual appeal.

It was in his subtlety. In the way he calibrated what he said to her. That little silence when he saw her, as if some sort of internal adjustment was taking place to absorb the pleasure of her impact.

All of this suggested that he likely not only wanted to *do* her . . . which she could get on board with . . . he wanted to know her.

She wasn't certain this was what she wanted.

"Don't worry," Casey said, maybe correctly reading her expression. "I'm not convinced she actually sees auras. I think she brought some peyote back from Burning Man and it's giving her notions."

Britt laughed.

"Gotta go." Casey waved good-bye and marched out the door with a mighty flick of her blonde hair in the direction of Truck, who was forced to look, and then watch her leave, because Casey was, in a word, fierce.

The inevitable occurred about ten minutes into Mike McShane's angsty, sensitive-boy acoustic set.

The big guy stood up from his table and made his way over to J. T., seized an empty chair, turned it around backward and straddled it.

Two of his friends followed him: smaller, wiry guys, the sort grown in the hills everywhere, it seemed, because J. T. had seen that kind before. Underfed.

"Truck Donegal." He thrust out a hand.

"John Tennessee McCord." He didn't want to touch that guy. He was certain he would attempt to demonstrate his virility by crushing his knuckles.

Then again, he'd touched worse things in his life.

He extended his hand, did some alpha staring, got it briefly crushed and did some return crushing, and took it back and counted the moments when he would be free to wipe it on his jeans.

"You're that guy from *Blood Brothers*, ain't ya?"

"Yep." He didn't blink. He also didn't smile.

"Can you say that thing?"

"Nope. Sorry. Contractually forbidden." He was all unblinking politeness. He was pretty certain a grown-up word like *contractually* would frighten off a guy like Truck.

"*I'll* say it. *Daaaaaaamn*, Truck!" one of his friends snickered.

"Shut up, Moses," Truck said tersely, without turning around.

Moses shut up.

"Saw that movie you were in. Sorry, but I didn't like it."

"That breaks my heart." J. T. didn't ask which movie.

He saw Britt move into their orbit with the beers on a tray.

"Thought it was kind of . . . gay," Truck expounded.

Her eyes went wide. They darted from J. T. to Truck.

J. T. actually sighed. It was such a grade-school attempt at an insult. It didn't register remotely as one. Truck would have to do a helluva lot worse to top some of the things J. T. had heard about himself over the years.

J. T. took a sip of beer, and leaned back, as if preparing

for a nice long chat. "Are you doing your master's thesis on homoerotic subtexts in big-budget action films, too, Truck? Because I was interviewed by a film student on that very subject."

He managed to say this evenly, and with every evidence of faint interest.

Truck froze.

And then his spine slowly straightened as if he suspected those were fighting words, but he didn't know whether to be insulted or flattered that J. T. might think he was doing a master's thesis.

He was absolutely the picture of tortured indecision.

He defaulted to staring J. T. down.

J. T. gave him back polite, unblinking boredom.

He had, in fact, been interviewed by a film student on that very topic. He supposed there were only a certain number of thesis topics for students in the world.

"You gonna give me that beer I ordered, Britt?" Truck said, finally.

She handed it to him. "Here you go, Truck."

Truck took it from her. His hand briefly covered Britt's hand when she reached for his money.

Her smile froze again and J. T. could see that she was struggling not to snatch her hand away.

A surge of black temper made every single one of his muscles go rigid.

He didn't have a claim on Britt. But if Truck pulled that crap again J. T. would be in the headlines for the wrong reason again.

Truck knew exactly the effect he was having on him, too.

Because he gave J. T. a little smile.

"You play pool, McCord?"

"Oh, sure. Some." J. T.'s voice had gotten soft. Abstracted.

Anyone who knew him well would have worried about it. It meant he was furious.

In that significant divot of time between when his last rom-com had tanked and the relative triumph that was *Agapé*—during which his phone got almost eerily quiet and the scripts dwindled—the first thing J.T. could think to do was play pool against himself. It had helped channel the mounting panic.

To this day that *pock* of a cue striking a ball felt like his personal soundtrack to failure.

Which was ironic, given that he'd become a *great* pool player.

"You should come on back and play some pool later." Truck made that friendly invitation sound somewhat sinister. "I'm going back there now."

"Just might." And J. T. made that sound just a little bit like a threat.

Truck nodded, satisfied that the two of them understood each other, hoisted himself out of his chair and turned it around again. They returned to where they were sitting originally.

"Homerotic *subtext?*" Britt murmured as she handed him the beer. "That was inspired."

He would have ridden into battle on a charger for the chance to see her smile the way she did now: slow, soft, thoroughly amused and impressed.

"I've heard Truck can really stomp a guy," she added.

"You worried about me, sweetheart?"

She grinned. "Not in the *least*."

She slipped away again.

He had just about finished half of his second beer when Mike McShane ceded the stage to a skinny guy with a big drooping red mustache.

"Let's hear it for Mikey McShane! Next up: Dan Ludlow, ladies and gentlemen!" Glenn announced.

Mickey McShane left the stage to a scattering of indifferent applause and one loud belch.

Dan Ludlow was carrying a square case. He carefully lowered it to the stage, flipped up the latches, and to J. T.'s horror, lifted out an accordion.

J. T.'s policy had always been to head in the opposite direction of any given accordion. It occupied the same musical strata as kazoos, as far as he was concerned, and he would almost rather listen to fingernails dragged down a chalkboard.

He got up casually, aware of eyes on him and strolled to the bathroom, where he had an interesting view of the stage through the high little window.

That guy was really jamming on accordion.

And then he finished up and slipped out of the bathroom into the poolroom.

It was to make a point.

CHAPTER 8

That was it for the open mic, and some stragglers—the people who didn't have to go to work the next day, or had no place else to go that was particularly appealing at the moment—migrated into the poolroom to join the people already there. All those faces were cast into strange shadows by the lurid light of a dozen or so vintage beer signs. A chalkboard on the wall was apparently for sign-ups and keeping score. Right now it said *Moses and Truck.*

"Thought I'd take you up on that offer of a pool game, Truck."

The murmured conversation stopped and the people in the room—about seven of them, two couples, the guys J. T. had come to think of as Truck's henchmen—stared at him in awe.

A beat of silence later, Truck said, "Moses."

Moses abandoned the game in progress and Truck racked the balls.

J. T. took the pool cue Moses proffered as if he was being handed a dueling pistol.

"You go ahead and break," Truck said magnanimously. And somewhat sinisterly. He apparently had a lot of faith in his skill at pool.

It was pretty clear that those in the room saw Truck as some sort of authority.

But J. T. was John Tennessee McCord; charisma was in his DNA, and all eyes were on him, and everyone could nearly feel the molecules in the room re-aligning behind J. T.

Truck was going to need to fight for supremacy.

"You got a new show coming up I hear, Mr. McCord?" A blonde girl asked this shyly.

"Yep. Called *The Rush*. Set right here in Gold Country. It's going to be *fantastic*. Best script I ever read. Thrilling and hot and funny. On AMC."

Part of his job as an actor was to never, never stop selling.

And everything he'd just said was true, as far as he was concerned. *The Rush* was going to be a freaking triumph, or his name wasn't John Tennessee McCord.

"Don't about ten people watch that channel?" Truck asked.

This got a couple of snickers.

J. T. took his shot. The green 6 rocketed into the side pocket.

"Twelve. Thirteen if you count that guy in Omaha who lost his remote and is too lazy to get up to change the channel."

Everyone laughed.

The answer would likely be more like 2 million at least, when you factored in DVR viewing and the like. A drop in the network bucket. It could, of course, explode into much bigger numbers, the way *The Walking Dead* had. It didn't pay to wonder and it didn't pay to project.

Anything could happen. In fact, J. T. often thought there should be a giant asterisk next to the Hollywood sign, and at its foot the words *Anything Can Happen* should be erected.

J. T. pointed to the corner pocket and shot the three ball in.

Truck was looking pretty tense now. He was holding his cue the way a Beefeater at Buckingham Palace holds his rifle.

"Mr. McCord . . ." A shy girl presented a napkin and what appeared to be a purple eyeshadow pencil. "I loved *Blood Brothers*. I'm sorry to interrupt, this is all I have to sign, but would you . . ."

Her boyfriend was wearing a strained smile, and he kept a loose grip on her, as if McCord were a magnet and she were an iron filing in danger of being sucked into him.

"You'll love *The Rush*, too, darlin'." She would never forget the "darlin'."

He scrawled *John Tennessee McCord*. The pencil proved no challenge. He'd written his name with any number of implements, from lipstick to erotic lubricant, and across any number of things over the years, from Maserati dashboards to cleavage.

He handed it back to her. She clutched it happily, beaming up at her boyfriend.

J. T. turned and eyed the four ball, pointed casually to a side pocket, lined up the shot, and slapped the sucker in.

He saw Truck's nostrils flare. Though the rest of his face remained admirably stony.

"You'll be filming here, in Hellcat Canyon?" someone else ventured.

"Yep. Quite a bit of the series will be filmed in the mountains around here, along the river and such. Ya'll will get tired of seeing me and the rest of the cast around town come next fall."

More laughter, and someone fervently muttered, "Never!"

He chalked the cue again. Pointed at the left side pocket.

Eyed it a moment, for the sake of drama. And then shot the sucker in.

"Hey, McCord," Truck said suddenly. "You know the Misty Cat is haunted?"

"You don't say," J. T. said idly.

"You like ghosts, McCord?"

"Not sure anyone *likes* ghosts. Seems to me, you either have 'em or you don't."

Scattered laughter greeted this.

"It's just," Truck drawled, "I figured you might know a bit about dead things. Seeing as how your career is pretty much one."

J. T. straightened and examined Truck thoughtfully.

"Not bad, Truck. A bit labored as insults go, but nonetheless fairly well constructed. I give it an eight. Always good to know someone is following my career."

Nervous laughter greeted this.

He bent over the table again, picked out the red 3, lined up his shot, and slammed it into the pocket.

"Daaamn!" someone murmured.

"Who says *nonetheless* when they're playing pool?" Truck addressed this to the crowd at large.

Only one person laughed. Nervously.

J. T. did, that's who said *nonetheless* while he was playing pool. Especially when he knew it would piss Truck off. Which was his whole objective.

"Naughty Nellie, they call her," Truck continued. "The ghost. She was a prostitute."

"How'd Nellie die? She see you coming, Truck, throw herself out the window?"

The room erupted in laughter.

He lined up a shot; the seven was about a 60 degree angle to the left side pocket. A tricky one. He took a moment to commune with the shot.

He aimed. And he got it crisply in, to a rustle of oohs and aahs.

Truck was tenser than a drum skin now.

The air felt hot and close, and waves of something hostile and dangerous were coming off him.

J. T. lined up the blue ball and tapped her delicately in, just as Britt wove into the room, tray balanced on her arm, handing out smiles, beers, and change.

She pushed past Truck to get to Moses. And Truck didn't even look at her, but somehow, magically, he managed to brush her ass with his hand.

J. T. saw her scoot out of the way and every muscle in his body went rigid.

"Nobody sees *me* coming, McCord," Truck claimed.

"Aww, now that is a shame. Just you and your right hand these days, Truck?"

More raucous laughter greeted this.

"*Right hand!*" half the crowd crowed, like a Greek chorus.

Truck's complexion went a full shade redder. He was now fully as radiant as the beer signs.

"Means if I want to take you out, McCord," he said thoughtfully, "you'll be on the ground before you even see me coming."

Britt tried to maneuver by him again with a tray and Truck's hand slipped down and swiped at her ass again.

She dodged and handed beers to the girl with the eyebrow pencil and her boyfriend.

"That so?" J. T. said softly. "You're a ninja, eh, Truck?"

"Bam," Truck said softly. "On the ground. Before you even see me."

J. T. nodded thoughtfully, as if taking this in. "See, the problem is that I've *seen* you grab at our waitress's ass three times tonight. And every single time I saw that move coming a mile away." His Tennessee drawl had gone as slow and taut as a stalking predator. "I'm going to recommend that you stop doing that. Right now."

Conversation dwindled uncertainly and then came to a decided, uneasy, fascinated halt.

There was a fraught silence.

"Aw, she don't mind, right Britt?" Truck didn't address that to Britt, who was getting ready to dart by him with an empty tray. Truck curled a hand around her arm to stop her.

J. T. saw raw terror flash into her eyes.

It was there and gone, so quickly he might have even imagined it. But it nearly stopped J. T.'s heart.

And this time she didn't dodge or object or demur. She was frozen.

"Yeah. I'm going to need you to take your hand off her, Truck. Now."

He knew that was all that was necessary to get that big dumb bomb to go off.

He touched Truck gently on the back.

It was like touching a bank of file cabinets.

Truck whirled on him and brought his pool cue whipping down toward him like a club.

In a series of smooth blink-and-you'll-miss motions, J. T. blocked it with one hand, snatched it from Truck's fist with the other, and then snapped it over his knee.

The ensuing silence was so instant and total it was like something had vacuumed sound out of the world. He would have sworn even the neon signs had stopped humming out of shock.

He hung on to the cue. The top half dangled from a single shred of wood, like a man hanging from the gallows.

The silence rang.

And then J. T. became aware of a tiny sound. Like a hungry mosquito had zipped into the silent room.

The sound swelled until it became a gleeful "*oooOOOoooo . . .*"

The universal sound of glee that accompanied the anticipation of a fight.

He shot a censoring black look at the culprit.

The sound stopped.

"That's my lucky pool cue, you son of a bitch!" Truck, when he found his voice, sounded perhaps a bit more surprised than furious.

But it was fair to say he was a *lot* of both.

"Damn straight it's your lucky cue. You're lucky I didn't skewer you like chicken satay with it."

Truck was scarlet. "What the fuck is satay! Quit saying things like satay!"

"You're lucky I didn't puncture you like a toothpick in *fondi de carciofi*."

He'd never before used hors d'oeuvres as weapons. But he was resourceful, and Truck had just handed him a weapon, and as he'd told Britt, he didn't see the need to fight fair.

He decided to put Truck out of his misery.

"What I mean to say, Truck, is, you're lucky . . ." J. T. leaned, perhaps inadvisably, forward and said, very, very slowly, with tenderly menacing patience ". . . I didn't ram it up your *ass*, Truck."

"It's broken now. One of those pieces ought to fit on up there," suggested some wit.

Truck whipped around on him. "You shut your hole!"

"You don't want to fight me, Truck. You ever been in actual prison? It ain't the cozy hometown drunk tank I bet you have here. And what I did to that cue? I can do to your neck. And just as fast."

Ain't? Where the hell had that come from?

When in Rome, he supposed. He didn't like discovering his veneer of civility was tissue thin.

J. T. didn't like knowing it was a veneer.

Britt had sidled up next to him and gently laid his beer tab down on the table in front of him. Deliberately.

He glanced at it. It read: *Mention his mama.*

"You think your mama would be proud, Truck?" he said seamlessly.

Bingo.

Truck froze.

Doubt rippled across his expression. He made a visible effort to collect his temper.

Satay was one thing. His mama was apparently a whole other level of combat.

J. T. sighed a great gusty sigh of exasperation. "The trouble with you, Truck, is you're boring. I'm willing to bet everything that you circle around and around, doing the same damn things, in the same damn way, blaming the same damn people, throwing the same damn tantrums. Like a damned baby with a dirty diaper. Am I right? Ain't you *bored* with yourself?"

J. T. seized the chalk used to keep score on the board and dashed out, in huge, sweeping letters:

GOOGLE
SATAY

He slapped the chalk down on the pool table.

"The internet," he said. "Not just for porn anymore."

Truck was speechless.

"You follow me now or if you ever again touch Britt here when she doesn't want to be touched, or say anything untoward to her or anything that so much as raises a blush, I *will* kick your ass in ways so surprising and painful you'll have to Google your own name to remember who you are."

He knew an exit line when he uttered it.

He threw the destroyed cue down, snatched his cue up, shot the eight ball in the corner pocket, and flung the cue down again.

And then he headed out the door.

"*Untoward?*" Truck's voice was frayed with shock. "Who *says* shit like that?"

"*Aren't*," Britt heard J. T. say viciously to himself, once he stood outside. As though he were pressing a reset button.

She'd started after him and paused to give Sherrie an imploring look. Sherrie gave her the "go on, go after him" nudge with her chin.

The street was so peaceful compared to the inside of the Misty Cat, it was like entering another dimension. The hills were purpling now and it would be full dark in minutes, but it was never really dark on a clear night, thanks to all the stars.

He glanced over at her. "You okay?"

"I'm fine. A little shaken. Impressed. But fine."

He was quiet a moment.

"Wasn't all that long ago *I* didn't know what satay was. That was playing even dirtier than I'm normally willing to do."

"I'm sorry you had to do that."

"It's not me I'm concerned about. I have plenty of experience with the Trucks of the world. If I had to guess, he's a big fish in a small pond that doesn't have the guts to ever leave. Guys like Truck, when they see something different or new, they either want to own it, be it, or kill it. Metaphorically speaking. Or, if you'll excuse the vernacular, fuck it. Anything to make him feel like he has some control over it."

Only someone who was used to feeling like an outsider would know these things.

Her first impression of him had been right: John Tennessee McCord was probably fundamentally lonely.

"You nailed him pretty perfectly," she told him softly. "Add to all that the fact that he hasn't worked in over a year. Got laid off. His mama's on disability."

J. T. gave a short laugh that tapered into a sigh, and he swept his hair back with his hands. "Now I feel like even more of a jerk."

"No, Truck had every bit of that coming. He wasn't going to hurt me, though."

"Oh, how the hell do you know that?" He sounded more wearily exasperated than anything else and she almost laughed.

"I just do. He's an equal opportunity asshole. He mostly just blunders about and people put up with it because they know him. Everyone in town seems to have their own role. Seemed like he had something to prove tonight, though."

He turned and even in the dark his eyes seemed brilliant.

Normally she would have enjoyed an uninterrupted opportunity to stare into his blue eyes.

At the moment they felt like lasers.

"But you didn't like him touching you, Britt."

She hesitated. "No."

"Has he touched you before? Like that? Grabbed you?"

Suddenly she was wary.

This was a man who noticed things.

"Not quite like that. No." Her voice was fainter now.

"And you're certainly not scared of *Truck*, necessarily."

She hesitated again. "No."

Her voice sounded small over the pounding of her heart in her ears.

He was just a few questions away from cornering the truth about her, the one that no one in Hellcat Canyon knew.

"Because here's the thing, Britt. You weren't pissed off when he grabbed your wrist." He pointed this out, gently but relentlessly. As if he somehow knew she didn't want to hear it. "Or just annoyed. Or amused. You were terrified. I saw it in your eyes. You were scared to death."

She was speechless. Her mind blanked.

He held her gaze with a sort of sympathetic remorselessness. He would have made a good actual cop, she thought, because she doubted he'd miss an eyelash twitch.

And she simply couldn't deny it, because it was true.

She suspected she'd told him quite a bit with her silence.

And he seemed to take it as confirmation.

"I just couldn't let that stand," he said gently. "Is that all right?"

Her throat was so tight the words couldn't emerge. Her mind couldn't seem to line them up in any proper order anyway.

"I'm sorry you had to . . . but . . . thank you. Yes. That's all right."

He exhaled, as if he'd been waiting for just those words.

"Good," he said softly.

And suddenly they were quiet. J. T. sought out the moon, a sliver of light over the mountains.

The silence thrummed with intensity. She was grateful he didn't ask any more questions. Though she had a hunch his thoughts were full of them.

"Just so you know, J. T., I *can* actually take care of myself."

He turned very, very slowly toward her. He stared at her with unflattering incredulity. "Do you really *believe* that?"

She was shocked. "I'm—"

"Or is it just something you say, a formality, like offering to pick up a check when you know someone else is going to pay for it anyway?" he demanded.

She was speechless. "Maybe," she admitted faintly, after a moment. "But you sure use a lot of food analogies when you want to make a point."

He blinked.

And then the tension visibly went out of him. He smiled faintly. "Something new I'm trying."

"I'm not saying you're helpless, Britt. I don't think *that* for a minute. It's just that *no one* can completely take care of themselves. Not even me, and I have a freaking black belt in karate. It's not a man versus woman thing. It's a 'let somebody care about you thing.' And sometimes *that* takes more guts and sense than taking on the whole damn world by yourself."

She was awfully tempted to argue just for the sake of arguing, but it would get her nowhere. He was every bit as stubborn as she was.

And the thing was, he was exactly right. With this little lecture he'd just chipped off another layer of her crusty old defenses. Trust and vulnerability had once led her into danger. Add that to her own native stubbornness, and you had a recipe for a wall.

"Got it," she said finally, tersely. A concession on her part.

And the perverse man smiled slowly at her. He seemed to actually relish her stubbornness.

She sighed. "It's funny," she mused. "You'd be surprised, but plenty of women are into Truck. Kayla Benoit and Casey Carson once got into a fight right there outside the Truth and Beauty over him. It started when Kayla told Truck she could tie a knot in a cherry stem with her tongue, and I'm not quite sure what happened after that, but everyone was torn between selling tickets or getting the fire hose. Even the sheriff hesitated to wade on in there. They both had fresh manicures and those nails can do some damage."

Bemusement bloomed into unadulterated wicked delight on J. T.'s face. "Who won?"

"Casey pulled out Kayla's new hair extensions, which upset both of them, since Casey had just put them in and they looked great. That stopped it pretty quickly. They made up right there on the street. So I guess you can say it was a draw. Kayla offered Casey a twenty-percent discount on anything in her store, but she told her she had to come into the store to use it, and she hasn't yet. And they haven't really talked since. Which is kind of a shame, since they've been friends since grade school."

He was smiling in earnest now. "Well, I'm a little sorry I missed that."

"Casey's pretty talented with hair."

"All artists are temperamental." Said the man who ought to know.

She smiled back at him.

His grin faded. "You get a little older, you get to know what or who is worth fighting over."

The implication, if she wanted to read it that way, was that he considered her worth it. Worth the risk to his reputation, worth the risk to his person, worth lecturing her about unclenching.

And her heart lurched.

The low hum of want that thrummed between them was textured now with the things they weren't saying, the questions he wasn't asking, the admission she'd just made that wasn't really an admission. The admission he'd just made.

"I'll see you home if you want," he said finally, easily. "My truck's right's over there."

The silence between his question and her answer nearly rang like a note.

This is it, she thought. It was her chance. It wasn't quite the way she'd expected, but she'd better take it.

"All right," she said finally, softly. "Thank you."

He released a breath he seemed to be holding and immediately aimed his keys at his truck and beeped the locks open, and he pulled open the door for her. She climbed about two stories, or so it felt like, and slid into cushioned comfort.

He shut the door behind her. "Seat belt," he murmured.

She smiled and clicked into it as he started the truck up and pulled away from the curb.

J. T. was silent. He was still waiting for the last of the adrenaline to ebb. Running like a deep seam through the pure carnal triumph of finally spiriting away a woman with whom he badly wanted to have sex was the satisfying knowledge that he'd protected her.

It had been a reflex. And he'd known he would do it again, in a heartbeat, career be damned.

In this moment, next to him, Britt Langley was safe. This, for whatever reason, seemed to be the only thing that mattered in the moment.

"I like this," she said, pointing at the stereo.

"It's Wilco." He turned it up a little.

It was loping and jangly and acoustic, lovely and wistful, not country but not *not* country. A song about resting your head on a bed of stars, one he'd heard dozens of times, one of his favorites. It seemed sort of prescient given how he'd ended up here in Hellcat Canyon.

"This is how I felt when I first saw night in Hellcat Canyon," she said.

He could have guessed that. He and Britt Langley, he had a hunch, saw much of the world in much the same way.

There was a whole lot of strategy and very little delicacy in most Hollywood relationships. When people were so easily had, it was easy to forget the serrated thrill of uncertainty. The pleasures of *wooing*. Of actually earning someone's regard.

He began to think that inner peace just meant knowing someone needed you. The essential you, whoever you might be when all the other nonsense was stripped away.

"Maybe you should get a dog," he said, finally, to her. "Or do you have one?"

"I have a cat."

"I hope by *cat* you mean 'puma.'"

She smiled. "The dog a few houses down from me barks when a squirrel so much as sighs."

He jerked his head toward her, feigning astonishment. "What do squirrels have to sigh about? You got world-weary squirrels here in Hellcat Canyon?"

She laughed. "I do have a blue jay who's a bit of a dick."

"Oh, blue jays don't take any guff," he said in all seriousness.

She laughed again. He loved the sound of her laugh.

He took the nearly U-shaped bend she silently pointed to and aimed the truck up the hill.

"I'm . . . riiiight . . . there. On the right. That yellow cottage with the red mailbox."

He maneuvered the truck over and cut the engine and the party of deer arranged in front of her house like ornaments scrambled to their feet and trotted at a swift but hardly urgent pace up the path and out of her gate. They seemed less frightened of than guilty about being caught holding a lawn party.

Their hooves echoed on the hard earth as they all vanished.

"That's one of my favorite sounds," she said absently.

"What, deer hooves?" Somehow he just knew.

"Yep."

"It's a good one. Flapping's good, too."

"Flapping?"

"Wings, flags, sails, the ears of dogs and cats when they shake their heads."

She turned to stare at him.

"All good sounds," she said softly. As if it was the most perfect thing she'd ever heard.

He realized his hands were still gripping the wheel. Albeit loosely. He still hadn't quite turned all the way to look at her head on.

He knew it was because the minute he met her eyes he would need to make a decision.

The atmosphere in the cab of the truck was a bit like the air just before a lightning storm.

His head turned, his hand left the wheel.

And it rose slowly, to slide along her cheek, and she tipped her head into it with a sigh. And then her eyes closed, and magically, as if they both knew this was the next step in the dance, they were leaning into each other, and his lips leisurely, softly, brushed across hers. It was the kind of caress, he knew from cxperience, that let all your other nerve endings know that mind-blowing pleasure was on its way.

It was very nearly a chaste kiss.

If, say, a burning match touched to a fuse could be considered chaste.

And the little carnal catch in her throat . . . well, he'd remember that sound forever.

He unleashed himself just a little. He let his mouth sink against the softness of hers.

He could all but taste desire in the back of his throat, electric and nearly desperate. It was as if every muscle in his body was pulled taut as a bowstring.

Her lips, her skin, her hair. So soft. Christ almighty.

His lungs moved shallowly. He could feel the answering tension in her. Her mouth parted softly against his; he pulled her lower lip gently, gently between his. Her breath was hot and shuddery and he wanted to slide his hand up under her skirt and between her thighs, watch as her eyes went hot and dazed and her head thrashed back as his fingers worked their magic.

And to get from here to there, all he had to do was take that kiss deeper.

In minutes have her in his lap, riding both of them to climax. This was hardly his first rodeo.

He knew exactly what to do to get what he wanted.

He ended the kiss.

It about killed him, though.

Their mouths hovered a hairsbreadth away from each other for a second.

He sat back slowly, as if he didn't want to jar his body. He felt like a naked wire. Almost dangerous to touch.

He closed his eyes briefly and sucked in a long steadying breath. Released it at length.

His body, particularly his hard cock, thought he was nuts.

There was no sound in the cab of the truck apart from the two of them breathing, and that sound, in its intimacy, was purely erotic. And he remembered the Eternity Oak, and the sound of the falls near it.

"I'll watch you get in your door." His voice was a husk.

If she was surprised, she didn't betray it.

She hesitated.

"Okay," she said softly. "Thanks."

She got out and the door shut with a thunk behind her.

She flapped a hand behind her in farewell, tossing a little smile over her shoulder.

He watched her go up the little flagstone walk to the raised wooden porch, surrounded by a railing that he doubted would survive a good lean by a person any heavier than she was.

And the porch itself had a definite curve. Like a slight smile.

Or her butt in that skirt.

When she leaped that top step like a pro he winced. One wrong move and she might just drop through that thing like it was a trapdoor. He remembered her "triage" on priorities, and the muscles of his stomach tensed again. He could so easily fix that porch.

Now she was in the warm, yellow pool of light on her porch.

It briefly turned all of her a shade of gold.

Funny, he felt a little like that inside. Gold and lit.

She tucked her hair behind her ear, away from her face, to jam her key in the lock. She turned around, paused, and flashed him a smile, and disappeared inside.

He watched a moment longer. Unwilling to move just yet.

He'd have to go back a long, long way to the last time he'd felt quite like this.

Back at least before he'd learned that he could be cavalier about sex and still live with himself.

Whatever had happened to Britt Langley made him want to protect her, and if that meant from him, too, so be it. If she wanted him—if she really wanted him—she would let him know. In the same way she'd dropped off that beer this evening.

They'd both be lying awake burning tonight, he was pretty sure.

It wasn't really strategy on his part. But it might work out that way, anyway.

Then he swiped his hands down his face and turned up the music again, and started the truck.

CHAPTER 9

During the last bad winter storm in Hellcat Canyon, a power line had snapped and lay arcing and sparking on the ground in front of Britt's house until Pacific Gas and Electric came to take care of it.

Britt's body felt like that all night long.

She could feel the tension in J. T. when he'd touched her. She could all but *taste* how badly he wanted her.

But now she suspected the man who had once blithely partaken of women as if they were a bowl of peanuts and probably would have blithely partaken of her, too, before last night . . . was being careful with her.

She was frustrated. Maybe a little amused.

And also, when she thought about it, unaccountably moved in a way she didn't necessarily want to feel. Because it made her feel a little exposed. Like that snapped power line.

He'd ferociously protected her last night. The funny thing was, however . . . she'd felt oddly protective of him, too, from the moment he'd walked into that diner.

J. T. was missing something, she was pretty certain. She wasn't certain it was only sex.

She did know that she needed to make it clear to John Tennessee McCord that part of taking care of herself meant partaking of *his* body with wild abandon.

The sooner the better. Or the two of them might never sleep restfully again.

She must have eventually slept.

Because she opened her eyes to a soft early-morning light. She didn't have to work until this afternoon.

But an inspiration had brewed while she was sleeping.

And now she was quite breathlessly eager to call Gary, which was a first.

She had the pleasure of hearing *his* morning voice, which was gravelly and very, very irritable.

"This better be good, Britt. I got an early tee off time and I need all my beauty sleep."

"Have you lost your mind?" was his response when she told him why she'd called.

"Maybe. I just have a hunch."

Gary sighed noisily and cleared his throat in a phlegmy way that made her wince. "Okay. I'll set it up. If you can rent that place to him I'll know for sure they're weirder in Hollywood than we ever imagined."

She'd scrambled to get ready, but J. T. had beat her to the Greenleaf place.

She saw him through the trees as she approached in her car. He was standing in front of the house, his head tipped back, hands in his pockets. He appeared to be studying the roof. Probably critically eyeing the gutters. A very guylike pose.

He turned around when he heard her car. And went still.

She turned off the engine and shouldered the door open.

J. T. tracked her with his eyes when she got out of her car.

Today's tank top was white and her shorts were denim and the buttons came undone pretty easily.

He remained absolutely, almost unnervingly, silent.

And then he smiled. Slowly, crookedly, purely wickedly.

It was almost knee-bucklingly sexy.

He knew why she'd called him.

That smile was his way of telling her that he would be calling the shots.

And he would leave her in suspense as to when the shot calling would commence.

She stood next to him.

The Greenleaf house was a tiny two-bedroom Craftsman-esque residence built circa 1920-something. Geographically, it occupied a fairly indeterminate place in the hierarchy of Hellcat Canyon territory. Sort of in between all those vacation palaces and the deep dark of the hills. She doubted Jonah Greenleaf was trying to make a statement with the location, but you never knew with the Greenleafs.

And it was kind of falling apart. The porch was caving in; there was a hole in the roof; the back deck was hazardous.

He was still quiet.

"There's only a little hole in the roof over *one* of the bedrooms," she said. "I don't think it needs a whole new roof. You might need to shoo the squirrels out. I don't think a raccoon has gotten in yet. Plumbing's good. Wiring's good. The porch is bad, as you can see. The back deck needs help. Gotta watch your step out there. Nice woodwork inside. Your basic Craftsman."

Her words were clipped and nervous because he looked utterly absorbed by what she was saying, while he was clearly thinking something else.

"Love Craftsman homes." He said this after a funny pause. As if his thoughts were on a time delay.

"You're tucked in off the road here among the trees, but there's a really wonderful view of the canyon nearby. One of my favorites. I go there a lot. It's a sort of vista point not far from my place. Kind of set back a bit off the road."

"Mmm," was all he said.

He patrolled the front of the house, looking a bit like a stalking panther.

She decided to take his lack of glib commentary as a good sign.

"If you stand here, you can hear the river. A little creek runs around back of the property. No one can see in through the trees, but you get plenty of sun in the afternoon in the back of the house, especially in the kitchen."

They stood together and listened to the creek.

"Another good sound," he said.

It was a reference to last night, and that kiss they weren't talking but in a way was all they were talking about. It thrummed through every word and every silence.

He turned to smile faintly at her again. And then strode off suddenly, heading toward the corner of the house. It looked as though he intended to go around the back of it.

He went stock-still just as he turned the corner.

Her heart lurched.

He must have seen the blue-eyed Mary's.

This was the thing that decided her. She knew they grew in a sort of unchecked abundance up against the back of this house.

She didn't know if it would be a painful memory for him, or a sweet one. But she wasn't sure it mattered. She had a hunch they meant home to him, regardless, and she knew deep down that John Tennessee McCord needed a place that felt like home, even if he didn't know it.

He didn't turn around for so long she started to worry.

But she half suspected it was because he didn't want her to see his expression.

She cleared her throat. "It's just . . . I saw them and thought of you, and I just thought . . . I thought the house might give you . . . something to take care of. A fixed point in the sandstorm."

He turned back around slowly then and looked at her full on.

His expression was carefully inscrutable.

And then his face lit, and his slow smile about yanked her heart out of her chest like a lariat.

"I don't mind." His voice was low, and smoky. It was like being stripped nude and laid down on velvet in a dark room.

She lost her breath.

"Can I see inside?" he said mildly.

She couldn't speak. She could hear her own breath, swiftly now over the beating of her heart.

She just turned and climbed up the steps, and he followed.

She fumbled with the key yet again. She could feel the heat of his body against her skin.

Behind me. Over me. On me. In me.

Her dirty little prepositional phrases started up like a chant again.

She turned the key and pushed open the door.

He stalked through this room, taking it in thoughtfully. The entire house was *maybe* a thousand square feet. The living room looked out onto the porch and the woods; the little bedrooms flanked it. It wasn't as moldy as it might have been, mainly because the hole in the roof was recent and the intense Gold Country summer heat tended to dry things out. The prevailing smell was good, aging wood.

He stepped into the tiny bathroom, his hand lingering with bemused pleasure over the original porcelain knob. All the fixtures in the house—knobs, latches, hinges, lights—were pretty much original. There was a shower over an old claw-foot tub, and a vintage porcelain sink, a little rusty now, with a separate knob for hot and cold. He tried both, casually. Water spurted from each.

And still he didn't say a word.

She felt like he was mulling over a decision, and it had more to do with her than with this house.

She found her voice, but it emerged pitched a little high. "Want to see the kitchen?"

She led him in there.

He followed in almost dreamlike silence.

The floors were wood, and a huge old farm sink sat below a little window letting in leaf-filtered sunlight. A bird flew up to it and split when it saw them.

A huge, sturdy slab oak table sat in the middle of the kitchen. It was the only piece of furniture in the house.

Britt touched it. "Jonah Greenleaf owned this house. He made this table. Apparently he was good at stuff like that before they hauled him off."

"'Hauled him off'?" J. T. was amused rather than alarmed. He was ready for another Hellcat Canyon story.

"Drugs. Sheriff Barlow arrested him for running drugs out of the Plugged Nickel. Scary bar up near the Coyote Creek settlement. He's doing time. Bank repossessed the house and Gary bought it a short time ago. Remember the woman from the open mic? Glory Greenleaf? Her brother."

"Mmm," was all he said.

The stove was an ancient gas model, gorgeously made. She touched it, too.

"It works," she told him. "But you'll need to get a fridge in there. A wood stove heats the place, and I don't know if the heat reaches the bedrooms very well. There are fans in the bedrooms, though. Want to check out the back deck? It's a little on the rickety side."

Her voice was still rushed and breathy, as if he'd been chasing her through the house. It was pure anticipation.

She opened the kitchen door, which creaked on its hinges. She took two steps out onto the deck. J. T. wrapped his hand around Britt's arm and drew her swiftly backward.

And then he pointed upward silently.

Her eyes followed the direction of his finger.

A huge black widow spider was hovering up high in the web in the eaves of the house over the kitchen door. Clearly hoping not to be noticed.

"Holy. . . ." she breathed.

The spider backed swiftly up like a square dancer getting ready to do-si-do with a partner, scrambling to get away from them.

"You know what they say. It's more afraid of us than we are of it," he said dryly.

"Then we'd better get out of the way in case it faints and falls out of that web."

Simultaneously, it seemed, they both realized his hand was still on her bare skin.

She looked down at it, curled around her, and suddenly her skin felt feverish.

"Britt?" he said softly.

She raised her head slowly and looked up into his eyes. Which had gone so black she could see herself in his pupils. She couldn't speak.

And then his hand slowly, deliberately, slid the length of her arm, down to her wrist.

A bold, unabashed, caress. And if she had to guess, a statement of intent.

And he released her.

Her heart drummed so hard her blood whooshed in her ears. Her every cell was lit up with hunger.

"Let's go back inside," he suggested in something close to a whisper. Oh, so casually. Like the sexual hypnotist he was.

He turned, apparently confident she would follow.

Of course she did.

He held the door for her. It clanked shut behind them. The sound seemed to echo, but then all of her senses were wildly sensitized.

J. T. stood in silence near the sink, studying her.

She stood a few feet away from him.

The quiet in the kitchen almost had a roar, like a river.

And then J. T. reached out, curled his fingers into the hem of her tank top, and furled it up as smoothly as a window blind.

Her arms came up to help him, probably more out of sheer surprise than anything else.

Now she was nude from the waist up.

And then, absurdly, he handed the tank top to her.

As if to say: "There. Problem solved."

She took it, with a short stunned laugh.

The sight of her went straight to J. T.'s blood like Everclear.

She was smooth and tanned gold except for her breasts, which were white, small, tipped in little pink ruched teepees and curving up at him. Her little waist flared into round hips. Her low rise denim shorts showed him her belly button. He was going to make short work of those shorts.

Lust sank its talons fully in.

He made a little sound, almost of pain. The breath went out of him as if he'd been dropped suddenly from a height.

She dropped the tank top.

Later he couldn't remember what happened between that moment and the next.

Only that one moment she was standing half nude, illuminated in filtered sunlight.

And the next their bodies and mouths were colliding with greedy near-violence.

They all but climbed each other. Her arms went around his neck and he pulled her up roughly against him, his hands slid over the satiny heat of her skin, over the delicate blades of her shoulders, the nip of her waist, sliding down into her shorts to cup her cool, smooth butt. He groaned with a shocking surfeit of pleasure.

He was awkward and greedy and practically shaking with the effort of asserting some sort of control on all that unleashed lust.

She was shaking, too. "Oh, God, yes, J. T. . . ." She whispered this against his mouth.

And she tasted amazing, dark and sweet and hot and set. She kissed with carnal strategy and so did he, each curl of the tongue, each brush of their lips designed to make each other crazy hot. They both knew what they were doing and they were good at it, and if they weren't wild before they started, they were beasts now.

In her ferocity she was hurting him a little. But he liked it. He was likely hurting her a little. It only seemed to spur them on. They were both so hungry they'd forgotten how to calibrate and it was all urgency and take take take. She came at him so hard he nearly staggered backward.

He slid his hands beneath her butt, lifted her up against his swelling cock, and they ground together gracelessly groin to groin, and her head went back on the most erotic gasp he'd ever heard. He buried his mouth in her throat beneath her ear, where the skin was tender and satiny and her heart was beating hard as a kick drum, and he licked, then laid his lips there and her head fell back.

And he carried her like that three feet to the old slab table and laid her down.

He hovered over her for a moment of near quiet, and he propped himself above her on his arms and kissed her, more softly now. He was like a drunk man. Her fingers wound through his hair, traced his ears, dragged lightly down his throat and it was like her fingers were magic wands lighting fires everywhere in him.

He touched his tongue to her nipple, then drew it into his mouth and did fancy twirls with his tongue and then sucked until she was writhing from the pleasure. His other hand savored the silky give of her other breast, his thumb chafing the hard peak. Never let it be said he couldn't multitask.

He knew how to get the job done fast. And the job was to make her wet and begging.

She arched upward, groaned and slid one bare foot up between his legs, and dragged it hard and surprisingly dexterously up over his bulge, and stroked by way of encouragement.

"God," he swore.

He was going to lose his mind.

"Take them off." Her voice was ragged.

He didn't know whether she meant his or hers, but he started with hers. He dragged her shorts down over her legs, and with them came a practical pair of underwear. Two birds with one stone! She gave a little kick and they were on the floor. He kicked them aside.

She was completely nude and lying on that table like a feast and he leaned over to kiss her and murmur, "This is going to be fast." Part apology, part promise.

"It had better be," she rasped.

He got his own jeans unfastened and open and his cock sprang free, and then he dangled his fingers in the dark blonde, neatly trimmed fluff between her legs and then slipped one finger into the slick heat of her, dragged it over her hard again.

She moaned low, and it tapered into something like a despairing laugh. "J. T. . . . I swear . . . I'm so close . . . *please* . . ."

And then he tucked her calves against his rib cage and

she locked them around his waist, and he was inside her in a swift thrust. His head fell back and he swore hoarsely at the staggering pleasure. He was sure nothing in this world could ever feel as good as his cock sheathed inside the tight heat of her, right now, in a falling-down house in the middle of the woods.

There was no finesse attempt. He was dying for it and she was begging and it was, as he'd promised, fast. He drew back, dove in again, and she hissed at the pleasure of it. And then plunged and thrust with a speed his eighteeen-year-old self would have been proud of, and he was going to come with almost embarrassing speed, he could *feel* it, hovering like a presence about to yank him from his body right into the stratosphere. He kept his fingers on her in a steady rhythm, too, and judging from the moans torn from her this pleasure was nearly impossible to bear, which was reasonably true for him, too.

And then her body whipped upward and her head fell back and he could hear the raw soundless scream of his name and her fingers clutching the edge of the table as if to brace for an earthquake, as she pulsed around him, absolutely coming apart as she came.

And then he was right there with her, his head thrown back, and he roared like an animal, racked with wave after wave of white-hot pleasure.

When it was over, it was, in fact, like the aftermath of a real earthquake.

The part where everyone looks around and says, "What the hell was that? And how did we survive?"

Sounds sifted into his awareness again. Singing birds outside. Her breath. His.

He leaned forward to kiss her mouth lightly. Her hot, swift breath mingled with his. He rested his head lightly on her sternum. She was damp with sweat. He could feel her heart hammering beneath his cheek.

"You okay?" he murmured.

"I'm good. But you're breathing pretty hard there, J. T."

He laughed. "That was a sprint. You got to do most of it lying down."

Her rib cage leaped in a short laugh.

Slowly, reluctantly he stood up. And looked down on his conquest.

She sat up and leaned back on her elbows, still disheveled and nude, looking pleased with herself and with him and the entire world. Her mouth was rosy and swollen and her face was flushed and her eyes were heavy. She was really astoundingly luscious. He felt a fresh wave of hot weakness.

He retrieved her tank top from the floor and tossed it to her.

She caught it one hand and shook it out and pulled it down over her head, then gave her hair a cursory rake with her fingers.

He watched all of it with great satisfaction.

She was just as sexy in that tank top as out of it. More, maybe. Because now her hair was a shambles and her skin glowed with a slight sheen of sweat. All caused by him.

"Foreplay. It's overrated," she teased.

"Everything from the moment we met up until now was foreplay."

She went still for a moment.

Their eyes locked again.

She didn't disagree. She smiled slowly and stretched.

"Shorts," she demanded lazily, as if he were a peasant.

He fetched her shorts and tossed them to her. She wriggled into them and buttoned them up, graceful, swift, natural.

Then she slid from the table.

They were quiet a moment, studying each other almost

shyly. As if hot sex on a wooden table was a long overdue conversation they'd been meaning to have and now there was nothing left to say.

"Hey."

He curved his arm loosely around her and spooled her back against his body. Her arms went around his waist.

He wrapped his around her, and when her body was against his, lust surged up again in her like a wave.

There appeared to be a whole ocean of it.

She closed her eyes.

She could feel his heart beating hard against her cheek. She savored the triumph and pleasure of making his heart beat that hard.

He didn't say anything else.

She held him close, because it seemed as though he needed it.

Or maybe it was because she needed it.

He kissed her lightly on the temple.

"Thanks," he murmured.

She eased from his arms with great reluctance.

"Thank *you.*"

For God's sake. Next thing you knew they would high-five each other.

But they both knew this casual stuff was a way to diffuse the shocking intensity of what had just happened.

"I . . . I . . . have to go," she said. She was already backing away. "My other job . . . the Misty Cat . . . afternoon shift . . . have to get to it . . ."

"Sure," he said lightly. "You want to leave the key? I'll lock up."

She fished it out of her pocket and handed it over to him, and even though they'd been naked savage lovers a moment ago, the feel of his big hot hand against hers as she handed him the key made her blush all over again. And their hands lingered.

"I'll see you, Britt," he said softly.

And she left.

Quickly.

She did have somewhere to be. Though in truth she was kind of running away.

At least she left backward.

And she walked backward for as long as she could, so she could see his smile until she got into her car.

CHAPTER 10

Oh my God oh my God oh my God oh my God.

A hosanna, a prayer, three useful little words that could be used to express anything huge and inexpressible. They were a song in her head as she drove down the hill again.

Then she turned the radio up, because the universe knew the perfect Led Zeppelin song for this moment and here it was, all about levees breaking, replete with thundering drums and squealing harmonicas.

It was safe to say the levee had broken. And how.

She supposed there was a chance her incredible glow of self-satisfaction and well-being that might fade into shame and self-recrimination when she pictured herself spread-eagled on a big wooden table with J. T.'s face over her, intent, shining with sweat . . .

Nope. Nope. Nope. That wasn't shame she felt.

Shame might kick in later.

But for now it was a fresh, new, great unfettered wave of undammed lust and she needed to get a grip or she'd drive her car off the road.

She had just turned onto the road that led to town when her phone rang. Mozart.

She fumbled with her Bluetooth and shouted over her noisy air conditioner.

"Hi Gary!"

"Mr. McCord just called. He's not going to rent that place."

Huh.

But Gary's voice was vibrating with glee, so she waited for the rest.

"No. He's going to buy it. He's going to have his accountant wire the money to us this afternoon. His accountant! Wire it! Has anyone with an accountant ever wired anything to me? No. No, they have not. He wants to take possession of that place today! You're a genius, Britt. I always said that house had great bones."

She was stunned silent.

"I'll shoot you over a little bonus, Britt. Maybe I'll even wire it. Enough so that you can buy a shiny new rope to hold your car door shut."

"Ha ha."

"Whatever you did to sell him on it, keep doing it."

She smiled hugely and privately at that suggestion.

"Oh, I plan to," she said.

J. T. put his phone away. Smiling.

Early in his career, he'd been bewildered by the sheer endless volume of money he'd been showered with. How in God's name did people spend it? It seemed to him that you either bought more things or bigger things, which was how he'd learned there really wasn't much he wanted or needed beyond a few basics. For a confusing time, he'd bought things in multiples simply because he could.

And now he could outright buy a shabby little house that was somehow perfection by just pressing a few buttons on his phone.

Not for the first time did he realize that it was good to be a movie star with a fat bank account.

Dust kicked up by the departure of Britt's car was still dancing in motes. It would settle soon enough. He watched it the way he always waited out that last endless note in the Beatles' "A Day in the Life." Something that magnificent deserved every bit of his attention.

He touched his face, realizing he'd pretty much been grinning since she'd left. *Bolted*, was more accurately what she'd done. He thought he might understand why. They'd have to come up with a new name for what they'd just done on that table. Because it had been so much better than all the sex he'd ever had, it hardly seemed to be the same activity. Maybe he'd forever call it the Britt Langley Memorial Superlative Explosion Experience.

He washed up a little in the dusty bathroom. And he took his smile out on that porch. And wandered around back again to look at those blue flowers.

His smile faded.

Damn. That girl had just given him two things he'd wanted.

And he hadn't even known he'd wanted the second one.

That, frankly, was a little unnerving.

And while he felt replete, which was always excellent, he also felt a little uncertain, as though his internal equilibrium was off. Uncertain and a little raw, though not in the physically abraded way. More like some brand-new part of him was suddenly exposed to the light of day. Like any new thing, it might get burned or snatched by a metaphorical coyote.

He didn't have to think about it. Because they would be doing *that* again, and *that* only required feeling.

He smiled to himself. He rotated slowly again, like a divining rod, and through the surround of enormous ancient pines and redwoods he spotted what he thought was likely a narrow dirt track heading steeply down toward the river.

And on impulse he headed out that way,

He followed the sound of the creek for about ten minutes, picking his way through instinct down the faint, slightly overgrown path, knowing it had been created because it led some place in particular, and he had a hunch about what it might be.

A hundred or so yards later, the trail opened up and there it was. Just as he'd guessed on the day he drove into Hellcat Canyon.

His own, beautiful, private swimming hole.

Well, more or less secret. He knew the mountains were full of places like this, And because he was a country boy, there was no way the natives, the people who had grown up here, and whose parents had grown up here, didn't know about this hole. But if Jonah Greenleaf had indeed been "hauled away," as Britt put it, odds were pretty good it didn't get as much use these days. There were no other homes nearby. And it didn't sound as though Jonah would have been thrilled about trespassers, given his line of work.

He stood and just listened and thought about what it might be like to bring Britt here. He was reminded of her—something beautiful and naturally wild, but a little guarded.

He'd noticed something a little troubling about her tattoo. Something that might hold the secret to why she was so squirrelly. Everyone had secrets, he knew. The trouble with sharing them with someone else was that they tended to bind people together. And any woman who had ever known him could have spoken to his own utter slipperiness when it came to being bound to someone.

Trouble was, he already felt kind of responsible for her. And had ever since he'd laid eyes on her.

He hiked back up, hopped into his truck, did a search for the nearest Home Depot on his phone (fifteen miles away), and started the engine.

He rolled the window all the way down, and essentially coasted down the road so his senses could bask a bit. Even over his engine he could hear birds and the chattering of squirrels and the low rush of a river. And the trees somewhat broke the brutal aim of the sun, but it was near blistering on his forearm hanging out the truck window where it pushed its way through.

These sounds and sights were like an essential soul nutrient he'd been missing probably since he'd left Tennessee. Something in him that he hadn't even known was knotted loosened.

A mile or so down the road he slowed. There was indeed a sort of dimple off the shoulder, a clearing that promised an extraordinary view of the canyon and sunsets. He suspected this was the view Britt mentioned. That girl knew how to sell him on something. He smiled again.

And then he finally gunned it and drove through town. Happier, lighter, than he could remember being in a long time. But then, sex endorphins did do that to a guy. He opened it up out on the highway . . .

And unconsciously slowed down as he approached that billboard. They had finished slapping it up.

He pulled over.

He gave a short, incredulous laugh. "You have *got* to be *kidding* me."

The left side was almost entirely white, which made the rest of the visual quite striking. A twenty-foot high profile of a woman. Her gigantic, sparkly, neon raspberry-colored lips were aimed in a coy exaggerated pucker toward the highway as she blew a dandelion, her hair streaming out behind her like a flag.

They'll all wish they were you, said the words across the top.

Below that it said, *Goddess Cosmetics*.

"You have *got* to be fucking kidding me," he said blackly.

The woman, naturally, was Rebecca Corday.

He banged his head twice theatrically on his steering wheel. And then he sat back and sighed, which tapered into an ironic laugh. "Well, good for *you*, Becks."

His ex-girlfriend might be taking over the world one billboard at a time. That had always been her goal, anyway.

He'd just taken a beautiful blonde on an oak table, and frankly, he considered himself the winner.

"Well, hello there, McCord."

J. T. turned abruptly to see Glenn Harwood of the Misty Cat.

"Hey, Harwood. Doing a little Home Depot shopping, eh? Yeah, that one, thanks," he said to a sales associate rolling a green wool carpet onto a huge cart loaded with other things he'd just requested.

Glenn was holding a big mag light and a lantern. "Had a few repairs to do at the Misty Cat, but these were on sale this week. Can never be too prepared for winter blackouts. Storms up here can get nasty."

"Always smart to plan ahead." J. T. made a mental note to add a mag light and a lantern to his list.

"Ran into one of my sons over in the bathroom fixtures and he said some guy said someone was buying everything in the store by just pointing at it," Glenn added. "Figured it was you."

J. T. laughed. "Yeah, I need a lot of stuff. I just bought the old Greenleaf place. I'll have some place to stay while I'm filming here."

Glenn whistled. "Congratulations. Good bones, that place. Smart little house."

J. T. was charmed by the use of the word *smart*. "I thought so. I need a few basics. Refrigerator. A couple of lamps. A sofa. And chairs. A rug. A bed. A new deck. Possibly a new roof."

"Yeah, I'd say that about covers the basics," Glenn said dryly. "You have some work cut out for you, though."

"I like work," J. T. said easily. "And I still have a little downtime."

J. T. needed to get his basics picked out quickly, before a crowd gathered or anyone looked set to rebel against the blast of charm he'd used to cajole them into keeping their phones sheathed. When it was choice between photos and selling a lot of stuff to a rich guy, the staff had shown their practical side.

"I can probably knock off most of what the porch needs in an afternoon. I'll have some time to do the work in a few days. I'm pretty determined to sleep there tonight whether or not I get a bed in there. A guy can only stay so long in Angel's Nest."

Glenn nodded sympathetic agreement with this. "You got any carpentry skills, McCord?"

"Oh, yeah. Some. Did some carpentry work as a kid. Worked a little construction in L.A. when I got out of the army. Before I got my first TV gig. Pretty sure I can handle what needs to be done on that house. Yeah, that's the one," said J. T., when a couple of guys gestured with wide questioning eyes at a big stainless-steel refrigerator.

The guys in Home Depot were all wearing dazed grins.

"Remember, *huge* tip for all of you if you get this delivered up to Hellcat Canyon tonight," J. T. added.

A little silence went by as Glenn watched all of this with every evidence of absorption.

Some men dreamed of dating any woman in Hollywood they chose. Some guys dreamed of walking into a Home Depot and just pointing at anything they wanted and being able to take it home.

"Our Britt show the Greenleaf place to you?" Glenn asked.

"Yep."

Here we go, thought J. T. Though he thought he understood it better now, and he was mostly fine with it.

Another little silence ensued. Just a trifle tenser than the silence before.

"Her porch could use a little work, too," J. T. said offhandedly, just as a couple of guys rolled a huge cart covered in two-by-fours, a saw, hammer and nails up to him for his inspection. Which, as the two of them knew, were exactly what he'd need to fix Britt's porch.

The Home Depot manager came over with a receipt for J. T. to sign.

Glenn shot a wondering look at J. T.

J. T. missed it. His head was bent as he applied his signature with a flourish.

"Say, Glenn?" J. T. said, when he'd finished spending thousands of dollars with the stroke of a pen.

"Yeah?"

J. T. almost said, "Never mind." It was the damnedest thing. He was a little nervous about asking.

"I think the Misty Cat food is great. But I'm looking for a recommendation for a different kind of place. You know, the kind with white tablecloths. Candles. Wine. Romantic."

Glenn mulled. "Can't go wrong with Maison Vert up in Black Oak. About fifteen miles up the highway. French, has a maître d' and everything. Great food. Atmosphere just like you want. Place has been there fifty years. Took Sherrie there on our first date."

Glenn didn't look at him as he said this. But his inflection on those last three words had been on the word *our*.

Kind of like the way he'd said "our Britt" that day in the garage.

"Thanks," said J. T. abstractedly. Without looking at Glenn.

But Glenn could see J. T.'s reflection in the broad, shiny

stainless-steel surface of that refrigerator. And he took special note of his expression, which was just a little different than it had been earlier.

"Well, I got to get back to the Misty Cat, McCord. Welcome to the neighborhood."

J. T. flashed a grin. "See you around, Glenn."

"I was a little worried when I first saw him standing there," Glenn told Sherrie later that night, as they sat on their porch swing. "Because he was pointing at stuff and he had that look, Sherrie—know the one I'm talking about? Grin ear to ear, like he was king of the world, kind of dreamy?"

"Oh, the 'I just had great sex smile,'" Sherrie said knowingly.

Glenn was glad he had his wife to finish his sentences, because that kind of sentence was never not going to embarrass him.

"Britt was walking around like that all day, too," she added. "Bumping into the things at the Misty Cat. Smiling so wide it was like she had a coat hanger in her mouth. Worried me a little, too."

"But *then*," Glenn added triumphantly, "he asked about a restaurant with white tablecloths. And when I left he was smiling a completely different smile. Know what I mean?"

Sherrie thought about this. "I think I know the one," Sherrie said. "See it on you every day."

Glenn gave her that smile now. He was a lucky, lucky man.

Sherrie gave that smile right back to him.

He slung an arm around Sherrie and she leaned her head on his shoulder and sighed.

"Sherrie Lynn, I'll be surprised if Britt doesn't come in some time this week and tell us he fixed her *porch*."

They were both old enough to know that hot sex was one thing, and it was all well and good. Fixing a porch was something else altogether.

If Britt had a shift at the Misty Cat, J. T. figured he had just enough time to do the work before she got home.

Problem was, he knew that Britt's house was yellow and had a red mailbox, but that was about it.

After a wrong turn or two, he was finally confident he'd found the place.

Mostly because it was the place that looked the most like *her.*

He pulled up outside it, and got out to take a look in the full sunlight.

It was a dollhouse of a cottage: tiny, wood-framed, painted pale yellow, set back from the road in a sheltering horseshoe of pines. A fruitless little white picket fence circled a little yard—fruitless, since a determined deer could yawn and stretch and just step over it to eat flowers and crap on the small green lawn if it so chose. But the fence seemed *right*; the house would seem incomplete without it. Poppies and wild lavender and irises and other cheerful, colorful wildflowers on long stalks peeked in and out of the slats in disarray. A neatly trimmed little flagstone path led to the porch, which wrapped around the front of the house.

That big French-paned window would let in sunlight during the late afternoon, if he had to guess. And it would be shady and cool the rest of the time.

The raised porch was railed in white and the center step was the one that sagged. He could replace the boards in a couple of hours, and he could do the same with the railing, too, provided there wasn't any dry rot.

And then he was positive it was Britt's place, because,

flanking the window on the deck, pressed up against the wall, was that rescued ficus, already looking happier. It cheered him. Oddly, he felt somewhat personally responsible for its health. Alongside it, on a tall metal baker's rack, were what looked like other little plant patients: a tomato, he was pretty sure. Some basil. A poinsettia, probably a Christmas orphan. An African violet. A coleus, at least that's what he thought it was called. Some others he couldn't identify.

He smelled varnish, too, and located the source: an old chair that had clearly been stripped and repainted and antiqued in shades of cream and white. A skillful, elegant job. Another chair was lined up next to it, battered wood, with a shredded cane back, but it had good lines, simple, elegant, well made.

Rehabilitation seemed to be a theme up here on Britt's porch.

He smiled. This was kinda funny, given that the porch itself needed a little rehab.

Her neighbor's house was similar: a little bigger, minus the picket fence, painted a sweet pale blue. They must have kids, or maybe they hadn't put their Halloween decorations away yet: a big old rag doll with little stick legs was slumped in the wicker chair on the porch.

J. T. whistled as he pulled his toolbox out of his truck, then lifted the latch on the little gate and headed up the flagstone path to Britt's house.

Cha-chunk.

He froze.

Because that's what anyone with any sense would do at the sound of a shotgun being cocked.

A Remington, if he had to guess. Like his first gun. *Absolutely* unmistakable sound.

He turned his head very, very slowly.

I'll be damned.

The rag doll on the porch next door and had come to life and was aiming the shotgun right at him.

"Jesus," he said.

He dropped his toolbox and slowly raised his hands.

"You a praying man, mister?" she asked.

"Isn't everyone when they're staring down the business end of a shotgun?"

To his surprise, she chuckled.

They spent a moment in a silent stalemate while she studied him. Her white hair was scraped back into a neat chignon. Her eyes were brilliant blue, even if her face was like a pale crumpled tissue. Her arms were as wiry as her legs, and her dress, floral and cheerful, hung from her spare frame.

Finally she spoke. "You're a little too handsome . . ."

"Thank you?"

". . . for a housebreaker."

"I'm not a housebreaker," he said soothingly. "Just here to fix Britt's porch."

She took this in, apparently deciding whether or not she thought it was true.

"You're a bit hairier than I prefer, though," she assessed.

"Now, that's a shame," he said.

Apparently he intended to go down flirting. Interesting what one learned about oneself in moments of desperation.

She chuckled again, but the gun stayed pointed at him. "You're quick. Like my Elwyn."

"Elwyn your husband?"

"Was. Dead ten years."

"Sorry to hear that, too. I'm not a housebreaker. Did I mention that?"

She still didn't lower the gun. "I'm ninety-two," she volunteered.

"See, I would have guessed sixty at the most. Because that there Remington isn't a lightweight gun, and you're holding it as straight and true as someone a lot younger would. I know how to hold a shotgun. I can even identify what kind of gun it is from the sound it makes when you cock it. I'm from Tennessee."

Maybe he could bond with her over guns, was his thinking. He'd learned from his cop show that hostage negotiators try to find common ground with criminals that way.

"It's a Remington, all right. This was my daddy's gun. And you sure say all the right things, son. But Britt didn't mention anyone coming to fix her porch, and she would have, because we look out for each other. She's got nothing in there worth stealing, so you can just take your pretty self off."

"Well, you see, I wanted to surprise her by doing something nice. If you take a look in my truck"—he wasn't going to make any sudden moves, so he didn't turn his head—"you can see the boards I plan to use. Britt is a . . . friend of mine. I helped her carry that there ficus plant down from that old cabin up the hill."

The woman turned toward the plants thoughtfully. She kept that gun aimed right at him, though.

"And something tells me Britt would never ask anyone for help," he added. "So I wanted to do this for him before she fell or tripped on it and got hurt."

As it turned out, this was the right thing to say. At least it was the thing that got her to lower the gun.

A little.

"Well, that does sound like Britt. And that porch of hers is a hazard. She's got a good heart, that girl. She loves those plants up until they're thriving and gives them away again. But she needs someone to look after her. And she needs something to look *after* that isn't a plant or a cat."

"I kinda got that sense, too."

The gun lowered a little bit more.

"You must be the neighbor who called the police when Britt was singing in the shower," he tried.

He hoped Mrs. Morrison's memory was still sharp.

"I might be at that," she hedged.

They continued eyeing each other, though she was a bit more thoughtful now.

"You like her quite a bit, don't you, young man?" Mrs. Morrison shrewdly guessed.

He hesitated. "I might just."

"I might be a might twitchy because you're her first male visitor since she's moved here."

He smiled at that. "You don't know how happy that makes me."

She chuckled again.

Finally she sighed, locked the gun and set it aside, leaning it up against the house as casually as if it were a cane. She brushed her hands off on her apron.

"I'm Althea Morrison."

J. T. exhaled and wiped his own hands, admittedly a trifle damp, on his jeans. "Pleased to meet you Mrs. Morrison. I'm John Tennessee McCord."

"Huh. A man with three names is usually an assassin or a president."

"Believe it or not, I'm an actor."

"Well, that makes sense, too. That's why I can see your teeth from here. You ought to be careful. You can blind someone with those things."

"It's a job requirement, the white teeth. It's like a uniform."

She chuckled again. "All right, no monkey business, Mr. John Tennessee McCord. You just fix her porch."

"I'll be in and out of here right quick. I'll try not to make too much noise. You need anything done around your house while I'm at it?"

"I got some lightbulbs need changing. A few holes in the wall need patching. Sometimes this gun just goes off all by itself."

"I'll just bet it does," he said soothingly.

"You want a Dr Pepper with a little rum on the rocks?" she called. "I'm about to fix myself one."

"Dr Pepper and rum, huh? That's a new one on me. That drink have a name? You should call it a Visit to the Doctor."

She laughed merrily. "We might just get on, John Tennessee McCord."

"Make mine with whisky," he suggested. "We'll call it the House Call."

"House call!" she hooted, then disappeared into her house.

J. T. watched her go with a smile on his face.

And then he sighed and picked up his toolbox.

A sane person who'd just been drawn upon by shotgun-toting nonagenarian might feel a little put out, but perversely, he felt there was something right about neighbors caring about neighbors enough to pull a shotgun on a stranger. That of course could be the result of growing up in a place where shotguns got pulled for nearly every occasion, from weddings to poker games. But there was something unassailably right about this pocket-sized house set among the trees and the youngish woman and the old woman who looked out for each other.

He didn't even know who lived on the opposite side of him in Los Angeles. He didn't even fully understand his compulsion to fix the porch.

But she'd known he'd needed a beat-up old house.

And he thought he might know what Britt needed, too.

CHAPTER 11

Britt gave Phillip his dinner, showered off the restaurant smells, threw on clean shorts and an old halter top, and then bolted out of the house. She halted in the doorway, then stepped deliberately, wonderingly on that brand-new fixed step. Like Queen Elizabeth stepping on Walter Raleigh's cloak spread out over a puddle. She and her sister used to take turns acting out that scene when they were little.

She walked. She needed to move.

Faster and faster, until she was almost running.

She realized she was heading for her vista point, where she could look out at the huge wide open sky and the vast canyon. It seemed the only place that could accommodate the multitude of things she felt, from anger to panic to something too bright and too big to contain, the thing that had all but launched her from her house likc a firework.

When she was in a leisurely mood, she could get to that vista point in about fifteen minutes. Today she took it at a near run, gulping great drafts of dusty, pine-scented air.

And she was almost there when she stopped abruptly.

Her heart leaped like a kite jerked into an updraft.

An unmistakable red truck was parked there.

And J. T. was leaning against the hood, watching the

canyon as avidly as if it were the Superbowl. She had told him about the view.

She hung back. Breath lost.

He was wearing faded jeans and apparently nothing else, unless it was boots. That smooth burnished gold of his shoulder and the eloquent wedge of his torso vanishing into the waistband of his jeans made her knees watery.

He looked like every fantasy of every bad boy she'd ever had. Times a million.

She gawked.

"Out walking your mountain lion?" he called.

She was pretty sure he hadn't even looked up. But then maybe he had, and she'd been too busy feasting her eyes on his torso to notice.

His torso disappeared a moment. She heard some rummaging and clinking and then the pop and hiss of a bottle being opened.

His head popped back up and reappeared and held a beer out to her.

She closed the distance between them, took the beer and tapped it lightly against his, and took a sip. Because he'd been right before. She did like a good beer.

"So how did your day go, Britt Langley?"

"Well, J. T., my day was pretty great. I got home from work at the Misty Cat today, and discovered that someone had fixed my porch. I couldn't finagle who it was out of Mrs. Morrison. All she would tell me is that it was someone with three names. And that he took off his shirt to do it. And that he patched some holes and changed some high-up lightbulbs for her and invented a new drink."

His eyes lit as he listened to this recitation.

His mouth still sort of somber.

"You mind?" he said, after a moment.

The same thing she'd said to him when he'd turned the

corner of his house and was stopped in his tracks by those blue-eyed Mary's.

"That I missed the shirtless part? Heck yeah, I mind."

He didn't reply. Just wrapped her in a slow smile.

She could have said a million other things. That he had a lot of nerve. Because she could in fact take care of herself, and she would have gotten around to fixing that porch.

And that it was the nicest thing she could remember anyone doing for her, let alone a man, because it wasn't just about a porch, it was about her safety and the integrity of a little house she loved, and she knew damn well he knew it, too. But she struggled with surrender, because surrender felt like vulnerability and still carried with it a whiff of danger, just like the old sagging top step of her porch, for example. It could be a trap she fell right through.

She supposed she knew in her heart that his little lecture of the night before was exactly right: sometimes it was okay to just let go and let someone fix your porch. Maybe it didn't have to be anything more than that.

But she kind of had the sense that allowing him to give to her was her way of giving to him too. And frankly, when she was standing next to him, she wanted him to have whatever he wanted, particularly if he wanted her body.

"Thank you," she said shyly. And somewhat stiffly.

He just smiled at her. Like he knew everything she wasn't saying.

"I'll paint it, if you want. Still got some downtime."

"If you want to."

"I want to," he said easily.

"Okay," she said. It was getting easier to agree to stuff.

He flashed her a smile. "Saw some of the old furniture you refinished up there, too. Nice job on those. You got yourself a little plant hospital, too. You like rescuing things, Britt Langley?"

It sounded a little innuendo-y, that question.

"Mmm . . . maybe I just think that everything should get a shot at being beautiful. Or . . . maybe I think something that's a little battered and scarred can still be beautiful?"

They locked eyes.

Something in his expression, some light in his eyes, made her feel shy and restless. She found herself turning to walk to the edge of the canyon.

Neither of them spoke for a moment.

"You were right about this spot. The view *is* pretty spectacular," he said.

Given that he was currently watching the back of her, she was pretty sure this was a double entendre.

She aimed a quick little smile over her shoulder at him then turned back around.

"It's different at every time of day. In different lights," she told him. "With different clouds. In different seasons."

"I got good at guessing the quality of views and vistas back in Sorry, Tennessee. We didn't have a TV, so that's what we watched instead. 'What color is the sunset tonight, Jeb? It's purple and orange over at the ridge.' 'Yeah, but did you see that big cloud from McCarthy Peak? Looked like an angel.'"

She laughed. "I can't tell if you're joking. I kind of want it to be true. And I kind of hate that it might be."

"Well," he said easily enough, "we did have a TV once, then my dad sold it to get more money for booze, and then we got another one, and then he sold it to get more money for booze, and then we got another one, and we sold it to bail him out of jail . . ."

"Jesus, J. T."

"The circle of life, right?" He flashed an ironic grin.

"Yeah, Dad was worse after Mama left when I was eight. She died when I was ten."

She was speechless.

"God, J. T., I'm sorry," she finally said. Softly. *Sorry* sure didn't cover it. He'd been about her nephew Will's age then. He'd had his life kicked out from under him, and look what he'd become.

She knew everyone was shaped by their past. Still, she wished she could go back and fix his for him. Take away the fear from that little boy and tell him he was going to be magnificent one day.

"We've all got a story," he said. "So what's yours, sweetheart?"

Damn.

She knew that wasn't an innocent question, and he'd walked her on up to it, too, without her even noticing. He was really pretty damn clever, J. T. McCord was.

There was a tense, almost waiting quality to him now.

She looked out over the canyon, thick with trees, going shadowy in places and gilded in others.

"I came to Hellcat Canyon from Southern California," she said finally.

She didn't turn around as she said it because she knew exactly how he would hear it.

Ironically, given the slant of the light and the shape of the clouds, she was pretty certain tonight's sunset was gong to be purple and orange. There might even be a cloud shaped like an angel.

She heard him take a sip of beer. Mulling this bit of non-information.

"California's a big state. I know, because I drove ten hours from down in Los Angeles all the way up here and there's still a lot of state left over."

"Mmm."

"Looooot of people live in Southern California."

She gave a short, humorless laugh. "Which is your way of saying I've told you nothing at all."

"Your words," he said shortly.

She glanced over her shoulder at him. And then her heart about did a back flip. She was tempted to just do that over and over: Turn away. Turn back. Turn away. Turn back. Just to get that fresh, shocking impact of him over and over.

"We all have life stories, Britt. I sure as hell don't tell mine in all its glorious detail. You can't even Google for it," he added dryly.

"Not even that warm, fuzzy story about the TV?"

"Not even that one. I'm lucky half my relatives can hardly read or write, let alone get on a computer, or my Wikipedia page would be a real eye-opener."

She laughed.

"So where'd you go to college?" he asked.

She was startled. "How do you know I went at all?"

That was equal parts dodge and curiosity. She was beginning to savor how his mind worked. She genuinely wanted to hear how he'd drawn that conclusion.

"You have a different kind of confidence. Small town girls usually have . . . oh, sass, I guess you'd call it. Like that handful with the guitar at the Misty Cat?"

"Glory Greenleaf?"

"Yeah, that's the one. Sass is sometimes kind of a defense. Sometimes it's even combative—I'll get you before you get me, that sort of thing. But you," he mused, "you're intelligent and you know it. You don't have anything to prove. It's the thing that Truck senses in you, though he'd never be able to put it in so many words. I think he sees it as a judgment of him."

She was astonished.

And then speechless with admiration.

She met his eyes. His gaze, mild but fearless and amused, dared her to contradict him.

"I watched *Agapé*. You're a very good actor," she said finally. Faintly. "You're really gifted."

It might have seemed like a whomping non sequitur. But she understood at once what made him not just a good actor, but a truly special, powerful one—this power of quiet observation—and she wanted him to know she understood it.

He just gave a courtly nod.

They both knew being good at something was no guarantee of anything.

"I take it you didn't go to college?" She strolled over and came to lean next to him, and the speed of her heartbeat ratcheted up. The truck's hood was pleasantly, almost lullingly warm against her bare skin. His warm bare skin was pleasantly close to her arm. She could lean into him. But she didn't, not yet, simply for the luxury of ramping up the anticipation.

"Nope. I went from Tennessee to the army to Los Angeles into stardom into whatever this is now. Not sure I had a plan. Just sort of reached for what looked like the next rung further up out of the hellhole that was Sorry. I never could have predicted exactly what happened. But my plan was always spectacular success, no matter what."

"That took a lot of guts."

"Or pigheadedness. Or desperation. Or imagination. Choose your word. I didn't know enough to consider it might be well-nigh impossible."

She completely understood. "I know what you mean. Life seems so much roomier before you learn that word."

He smiled at that. "'Roomier.' Great way to put it. I guess during all those years I always noticed how people who went to college behaved. They held themselves differently. Spoke differently. It was as though knowing just the right word for something, or the history of or the *why* of things . . . every thing you knew was like you had one more piece of a treasure map. It was like you felt you had more a right to even be in the world, if you went to college. I wanted to be like that. Anyway, I never did go. Read a lot, though."

"In your downtime," she teased softly, in return.

"In my downtime," he confirmed. Amused.

She was willing to bet he'd read a lot more than she ever had, and she'd read a *lot*.

It was impossible to imagine this elemental man, who somehow seemed at home everywhere, not feeling at home in the world. Or ever feeling small.

Or being made to feel small.

"I went to UCLA," she said suddenly. "I studied art and writing. I was working on my master's for a while. And I read a lot, too. Everything." She hadn't said this to anyone in Hellcat Canyon.

She didn't expound and he didn't ask her to. She wanted him to know just how right, just how intuitive he was.

He smiled. "Makes sense," he said finally, draining his beer and adding the empty back to his cooler. "The writing thing. And the art thing. You see things from a slightly different angle. Original minds generally do."

He sighed then, a sound of pure contentment, hooked an arm about her and then drew her against his body and wrapped her loosely, so that he could rest his chin on top of her head. Her butt was nestled against his groin. She rested her hands on his corded brown forearms. It was both unutterably peaceful and yet so very much the opposite of peaceful, because want hummed between them like a plugged-in appliance. They each settled into the luxury of that sensation. Knowing they could afford to savor. And that savoring was really only honing the edge of something spectacular.

"You still write? Or paint or . . . ?" His voice was a murmur above her head.

"I draw. I stopped for a while, but I started up again."

They admired the view, changing ever so slightly every second thanks to the shifting light.

"You ever been married?" His voice had gone a little husky.

There they were, at the crux of it.

And yet she sensed he was only looking for confirmation of something he already suspected.

"Yep."

"Mm."

He didn't say anything else. Then again, it was amazing what could be conveyed in one syllable.

He tucked his chin into the sensitive spot between her ear and shoulder, the one near the small, small, ugly scar that now formed the heart of her flower tattoo.

She was positive he knew how erotic his little bit of stubble felt against the tender skin there. And how his breath sent her nipples erect.

Speaking of erect things, she was beginning to feel one against her backside.

But they just lingered and watched the sun paint the canyon gold, quietly.

She was conscious of the movement of his chest swaying ever more swiftly against her back.

"Red-tailed hawk, right there," he murmured as the wedge of the bird cut across the sky.

"Looking for dinner," she mused.

"Sometimes they hunt in pairs. Maybe we'll see another one."

As he spoke, he was casually working loose the tie at the waist of her halter top as if it were the most natural thing in the world, an extension of the conversation. Just like they were two animals out here doing what came naturally.

When it was undone it fell open. The breeze slipped in. A glorious sensation against her hot skin.

He slid his hands up over her ribs. His thumbs fanned beneath her breasts, casually, oh, so leisurely, without preamble, cupped them, and then stroked, and traced them with his fingertips, took his sweet time with her nipples. Dear God, the layer upon layer of bliss.

She moaned shamelessly.

She arched beneath his hands, reached back to latch her hands behind his head, her head fell backward and she found his mouth waiting for hers. They met in a take-no-prisoners kind of kiss, hot, deep, thoroughly carnal, and just like that her blood was lava.

He slid his hand slowly, steadily down over her rib cage, her belly, straight into the gap of her shorts' waistband, right between her legs, where she was already slick and wet and getting wetter. She groaned when his fingers slid over her and lingered to rub, and she arched up against his hand to help him reach exactly where she wanted to be touched.

The man was no frills and knew exactly what she wanted.

Which was exactly the same thing he wanted.

"Take them off," he murmured, making it sound more like a suggestion than an order.

He tugged at her top button until it came loose to get her started, and she gave a yank and all the butter-soft worn buttonholes gave and the buttons on her shorts rippled open in a cooperative little row. He pushed them down her hips; she shimmied them down to her ankles.

He turned her swiftly, and thrill roared through her as she lay with her cheek down and her arms flat against the still warm hood of his truck.

His hands slid over her back and he sighed with a surfeit of pleasure and satisfaction.

He guided himself into her with a single deep thrust.

He swore softly, a sound that tapered into a groan. She

heard the roar of his breath. He palmed her bare cheeks and pulled himself back, then drove himself in again, slowly this time.

She whimpered and it trailed into very nearly a keen of pleasure, which seemed to spur him on. Fast now.

Her breath came in gusts, and half begged, half threatened him with tattered words and threats. "J. T. . . . I swear to God . . . *so good* . . . if you don't hurry . . ."

She could hear the roar of his breath. And then he was plunging into her, swift and hard, pulling her back against him to take it as deeply as he could, their bodies colliding hard again and again. Her nails skidded along the hood of his truck, and she was already near exploding when his hand sneaked around front between her legs and stroked hard.

Her mouth opened on a ragged, near-silent scream of his name, and she writhed, her body bucking upward, racked again and again by an onslaught of bliss. She could have sworn she saw the whole Milky Way behind her eyes.

"Britt . . . *sweet Jesus* . . ." His voice was a raw scrape. "I'm going to . . ."

The missing word was either *come* or *explode*, but he gave a hybrid groan-battle cry instead and then went still like he'd been shot.

But she could feel his body shaking, too, and even replete, she knew a purely primal satisfaction, that she could have rendered this hot-as-Hades man limp as a rag.

She heaved an enormous sigh. Dear God, she was disheveled and bent over the hood of a truck in the woods. It was as trashily sexy as it got. It was practically porn.

She was too pleased with herself to think too hard about this.

For a moment they were apparently both trying to remember how to breathe normally.

He gave a short, dazed laugh. "You alive?"

"Give me a minute, and then I'll tell you," she murmured.

He slipped back away from her, his hands sliding along the length of her back, claiming her, a sort of possession.

She peeled herself away from the truck and dragged her shorts up, buttoning them swiftly.

He watched. His eyes were still dazed and dark. She wanted to lick that little bead of sweat that was traveling from his clavicle down the seam that divided those gorgeous sections of muscle on his torso.

So she moved up against him and did just that.

And his hand came up to cup her head. He stroked her hair, threading his fingers through it. She turned her face up to him, and he kissed her. Gently. Her mouth felt a little bruised, which she didn't mind. It felt amazing in a cathartic way. She suspected he felt that way, too. They'd gone at each other ferociously.

"I *can* do it when I'm lying down, too," he murmured against her mouth, "and at a leisurely pace."

She laughed. "Your thighs are probably sore, J. T., but I think you need to hold me up for a moment. I am replete."

He obliged and wrapped his arms around her tightly. "My *thighs* are probably sore? You think I'm that out of shape?"

"Not really. I just don't think any gym has a thigh workout quite like that."

"If it did, no membership would lapse ever again."

She laughed. He kissed the damp little hollow beneath her ear. She could feel his heart thumping against her cheek.

And then he loosened his arms and retied her halter top as if he were buckling her in for safety.

She pulled away from him and then turned around again and leaned back against the lovely hot, damp wall of his chest, blankly, blissfully replete. He smelled amazing—

sweaty and musky and male, with a hint of soap. The air was cooling and releasing the whole bouquet of mountain smells.

"I think we could bottle how tonight smells, and call it Sex on a Truck," she said dreamily.

He gave a short laugh. He said nothing for a time.

He was either still recovering, or lost in thoughts of his own.

"Can I have your phone number?" he said, suddenly. Almost diffidently.

She gave a short laugh. "We're doing things all out of order, you and I."

"Maybe we're a little rusty at . . . whatever this is."

"Yeah," she said.

They were quiet a moment, both of them feeling a little awkward. Because it was true, neither of them really knew what this was, only that they liked it. And maybe they even feared it a little.

And then he fished out his phone and wordlessly handed it to her.

And like a shy girl who had just met a cute guy in a party, she wordlessly took it and typed her number into it.

"Thanks," he said.

She handed him her phone and he did the same thing.

And then she stood back. And that need overtook her: to get some space, to process what this was.

Then she stood on her toes and gave him a swift kiss on the cheek and had already taken about five steps away from him before he could say another word.

"I think I'm going to walk home now," she told him, in case that wasn't clear.

"Got what you came for, eh?" He was teasing.

"You know it." Who was this saucy person who had a quick answer for everything? It was the real her, that was who.

"You sure you don't want a ride?"

"Just had one, thanks."

He smiled crookedly. "If you can still walk, then I didn't do my job right."

She turned around and walked backward. "Well, that gives you something to aspire to, doesn't it? Wouldn't want you to get *complacent*."

"*Dammmmmn*," he murmured, with great admiration.

The first time he'd willingly said that word in that way in years.

She tossed him a saucy smile over her shoulder.

J. T. smiled to himself. He'd rather see her home, make sure she was tucked safely behind her own locked door. But he suspected she needed a little time and space.

And he could give that to her.

He was aware as he watched her go of a shortness of breath that was less about the rigors of Sex on a Truck. Funny. It was more like one of those damn cupids at the Angel's Nest shooting him straight in the heart with an arrow.

CHAPTER 12

Britt got the text around the middle of the lunch rush at the Misty Cat, which meant a half dozen people, including Casey Carson, heard her squeak, then saw her clap a hand over her mouth.

> I was wondering if you were free for dinner at Maison Vert this week? Any night is good for me.
> J. T. M.

"I have to sit down," she said faintly.

To Giorgio's great, glowering disapproval, she took a precious empty stool in front of the grill at the counter and sat down, just like a paying customer.

"Oh my goodness, honey, are you all right?" Sherrie noticed her immediately. A motionless Britt during the lunch rush was like the earth ceasing its rotation.

She held out her phone mutely.

Sherrie and Casey craned their heads to read the text.

They both promptly made similar squeaking sounds.

"Oh my goodness gracious God in heaven." Sherrie clapped a dramatic hand over her heart. "Is that text really from John Tennessee McCord?"

Britt nodded.

She was vaguely aware she was wearing a huge stupid smile.

Which faded.

Doing it on a table and against a truck was one thing. Dinner at a white-tablecloth restaurant seemed to be another thing altogether.

She considered that she might have stepped into a riptide.

Though maybe he just wanted to sample cuisine outside of the Misty Cat. As excellent as Glennburgers were, one could hardly blame the man.

Her heart was hammering painfully.

"*And* he fixed my porch," she said. As if they were all following her own internal conversation.

"GET. OUT." Casey was agog.

Glenn exchanged an "I told you so" glance with his wife that Britt didn't quite understand.

"He just showed up and fixed your porch? When you weren't there? For no reason at all?" Casey said this as though she were collecting clues to a mystery.

"It needed fixing, was the reason," Britt said shortly.

Casey studied her with a tipped head, and her knowing, wicked little expression told Britt that she knew exactly what the reason was.

Britt couldn't help but grin that same grin right back at her.

"Okay." Casey took charge. "You have to pick a night where you don't have to work the next day. Because, you know."

Britt did know. Warmth swept through her whole body at the merest suggestion of what she and John Tennessee McCord could do with a whole night together.

"I'll do your hair and makeup. For free," Casey said briskly.

Britt was astounded. "Casey, that's just . . . what a sweet

offer! Are you sure? I've practically forgotten how to do makeup."

"I can tell, sweetie."

Britt laughed.

"And do you have anything to wear?" Casey was on the case.

"Not really, no. Maybe I'll stop in at . . ."

She thought yearningly of that white halter dress in the window of Kayla Benoit's boutique. Maybe she could bring in her coupon and make puppy dog eyes at Kayla. Things were going her way lately. Why shouldn't she get the dress, too?

"Not really, but I'll figure it out," she told Casey.

She didn't work tomorrow morning. She *did* work the rest of the week in the morning.

And, really she had no shame. She wanted what she wanted.

She texted J. T. back:

Is tonight too soon?

His reply chimed in:

Ten minutes from now wouldn't be too soon.

The man really *was* an Olympic-caliber flirt. And he knew what he wanted. She had to hand it to him. He was confident enough, or mature enough, to be completely direct. There was a surprising amount of comfort in that.

She texted back:

I'm off at two.

Her phone chimed in:

I'll pick you up six thirty.

And then she moved her butt off the stool in case Giorgio's glower burned a hole in the back of her head before her date.

At ten minutes after two Britt hovered on the sidewalk outside of Kayla Benoit's boutique, still shiny with lunch-hour sweat and redolent of the diner smells that made her cat sniff her so happily when she came in the door for the day. The halter-necked sheath was still in the window worn by a nearly flat chested, featureless mannequin. Lucky mannequin. White eyelet over silk acetate. Simple, gorgeous, expensive, taunting. It had been there for so long it ought to be sporting cobwebs. Kayla was pretty meticulous about that sort of thing, though. The dress was spotless.

Britt took a deep breath and pushed open the door and stepped inside Kayla's fragrant, elegant boutique. There wasn't another soul in there currently.

Kayla was rearranging one of the racks by color. She whirled about and her face lit up.

"Britt! What brings you by?" Kayla Benoit sounded pleased but faintly concerned. As if Britt might have taken a blow to the head and staggered into her boutique by mistake. She was fully aware that Britt's budget didn't extend to most of her merchandise.

"Hi Kayla. How's it going? I find that I . . . need a dress."

Kayla paused, her pretty brow furrowed faintly. "Are you getting married?" she wondered.

"No."

"You pregnant?" was her second guess.

Britt looked down at herself, then back up at Kayla.

"Well, *no*, you don't look it, but you strike me as the sort who likes to plan ahead," Kayla said, answering that unspoken question.

"I am that type," Britt admitted. Surprised and a little flattered that Kayla had been deciding what she might be like. She was realizing lately that people all over town were probably drawing all kinds of conclusions about her. Funny, she'd thought she was so inscrutable. And funnier still, she didn't really mind. It made her feel more as though she belonged.

"Okay, I give up, Britt," Kayla said brightly. "What kind of fabulous dress can we find for you?"

"Truthfully . . . well, I'm going on a date."

Kayla's brow furrowed a little. As if she were rifling through all the men in town that Britt might actually consent to date. Men who would warrant a special dress, no less.

And then her face went all but neon with realization.

"With John Tennessee McCord?" Her voice was a hush.

"He asked me out to *dinner.*" Britt whispered this, too. As if they spoke at the volumes the news warranted they'd violate the neighborhood noise ordinances.

"Oh my God oh my God *oh my God.*" Kayla was practically bouncing on the toes of her peep-toed pumps. She was touchingly thrilled, just like Sherrie and Casey, and it warmed Britt's heart clean through.

"At Maison Vert." Britt pronounced this with the gravity it deserved.

Kayla froze.

"Britt . . ." she said portentously. "That place has *white tablecloths.* And candles. Holy crap."

"I know. It's a real date."

"I mean, we all thought you and he were probably doing it, but if he's taking you *there . . .*"

We all? Was there some kind of Hellcat Canyon phone tree Britt didn't know about during which her sex life was discussed?

She decided to neither confirm nor deny this. People

weren't stupid, and Britt wasn't coy, and she supposed she and J. T. had been shooting off sparks.

"I've got a black dress. But it's old and the fabric is starting to pill. And it would take me some time just to blow the dust and cat hair off it."

"So yeah, you can't wear that," Kayla agreed. "That would just be sad. And you can't wear one of your umpteen camisole-and-shorts ensembles."

Britt gave a startled laugh.

"Sorry, it's my curse." Kayla sighed. "I can't help it. You don't *know* how I suffer, Britt. I notice what *everyone* is wearing and my mind is constantly giving them all makeovers, and in this town it's exhausting. Practically everyone needs one. You *do* have a good sense of color."

"Thanks." She'd take a compliment where she could get it. "You know . . . I think I'd look good in white," she tried, tentatively. And she shot a sidelong speaking glance at that dress in the window.

Kayla became a lot more cagey and a little sad.

"I know where you're going with this, sweetie, and oh, I wish I could, I really do, but that dress costs a lot. And I have margins to meet."

"I *do* have a coupon . . . that one you sent out in the mail . . ."

"That will take it down to the high two figures," Kayla said succinctly.

Aargh. Still too high. At least for her budget.

So *this* was how Kayla managed to stay in business. She wasn't a patsy. Britt both admired it and rued it greatly in the moment.

She was pretty sure Kayla would be immune to her puppy-dog eyes.

"Let's take a look at the sale rack," Kayla said briskly, "and see if we can't make something work. We'll make you look *gorgeous*, I promise."

The sale rack usually comprised rejected bridesmaid gowns.

They both pivoted sharply when the bell on the door jingled. A gust of air fluttered up the white dress on its stand portentously.

Casey Carson was standing there.

She closed the door behind her, and stood motionless in the doorway.

All was shocked silence.

"Casey," Kayla said coolly.

"Kayla," Casey said primly.

And that was the last word anyone said for about half a minute.

Britt half expected the soundtrack from *The Good, the Bad and the Ugly* to play over the sound system, but no.

It was Lady Gaga. "Bad Romance," which she thought was rather ill timed.

"You said if I wanted to use my discount, Kayla, I needed to come into the store." Casey sounded ever-so-slightly defiant.

"I did say that." Kayla was trying to look hard and cool but a very poignant bit of hope was creeping into her expression.

These two missed each other a lot, Britt realized.

And then Kayla's face paled when something ghastly apparently occurred to her.

"Are you . . . are you getting married?" Her voice was faint.

"No. And I'm not pregnant, either," Casey said hurriedly.

Apparently Casey knew the drill.

Some of the color rushed back into Kayla's cheeks.

It occurred to Britt then that the whole kerfuffle regarding Truck Donegal *might* not be completely resolved. Which meant things could get potentially a little sticky. If not today, then at some point.

"No, I was wondering . . . can I use my twenty-percent-off discount for Britt?"

Britt's jaw dropped. That twenty-percent discount was part of Kayla's peace offering after their fight in the street.

She swiveled toward Casey. "*Casey* . . . that's so . . . I just . . ."

"We can't send you off on a date with John Tennessee McCord in any of the stuff you usually wear, Britt," Casey explained practically. "You're like an ambassador to Hollywood for Hellcat Canyon."

"That's what *I* just told her!" Kayla was delighted. "The first part."

"I don't know if Maison Vert is in *my* near future. I make pretty good money at the Truth and Beauty," she said, rather defiantly. "And besides . . ." Casey faltered. "I just wanted to see . . ."

And then she smiled a watery sort of smile and shrugged with one shoulder.

Kayla very, very carefully removed a tear from the corner of her own eye with her pinky nail, lest it mess up her mascara.

"I missed you, too, Casey," she said.

And then they practically leaped into each other's well-dressed, flawlessly made up arms. And now the atmosphere was zinging with delighted relief and rejoicing.

"Casey, Britt wants that white halter dress in the window. With your discount, that brings it down to about thirty-five dollars."

"I bet she can *totally* do that!"

Britt totally could.

"That dress is perfect for her!"

"I'm going to do an updo for her. And I'll do her makeup, too. She will look *amazing*."

For a moment, it was like Britt wasn't even there. Britt didn't mind, not really. It was hard to begrudge being forgotten for a moment, because she'd reunited a pair of friends, she'd *gained* a pair of friends, and she'd be getting the man *and* the dress. Not bad for a day's work.

Her heart felt like a big sun shining in the middle of her chest.

Kayla leaped back from Casey when her phone chimed as a text came in.

She scanned it swiftly. "It's Edie from the flower shop. She says John Tennessee McCord just came in!"

The whole town was apparently tracking her date like NORAD tracked Santa.

"Flowers are hard core, Britt," Kayla said with a sort of grave awe.

This was unassailably true. A date was one thing. A date who brought flowers to her was something else. Maybe he brought flowers to all of his dates. He was Southern, after all. He was a sex machine but his manners were lovely.

She didn't have to think about that right now. Right now, all she had to do was try on that dress and then count the minutes until six thirty.

"Well," J. T. said on an exhale. "Lucky me."

He'd arrived on the dot, and he'd spent nearly half a minute speechless, admiring her in the lowering evening sun when she stepped out on her porch. And stood, like a diva on a stage, on her brand-new step.

"I'll say," she teased, gently. But her voice was a little threadbare.

Because her heart was pounding. And his expression *was* genuinely awestruck.

"You look very handsome," she said almost timidly.

Dear God, that was an understatement.

"Yeah?" he said distractedly.

He was wearing a jacket that fit him like a freaking poem over a crisp button-down shirt and, naturally, a pair of jeans and his favorite boots, which seemed to have been polished for the occasion.

She noticed then that he was holding something behind his back.

He followed her curious gaze. Those must be the flowers.

"Well, I was going to bring roses," he explained, as if she'd asked that question aloud. "Who doesn't like roses? All women do, right? But then I thought, maybe roses are a cliché. And I've brought them to so many women over the years . . ."

And he stopped.

"Sure," she prompted carefully. "Roses are nice." She wasn't necessarily enjoying the reference to "so many women," but it wasn't as though she didn't know this part about him, and he clearly was heading someplace with this little story.

"But then I saw something and it made me think of you, and I thought it might be better."

He brought it slowly out from behind his back.

It was a wilted, sad, anemic-looking azalea in a little pink-foil-covered pot.

She was speechless.

She could have sworn he was holding his breath.

"Oh!" And she scooped it into her arms as if it were an orphan being abandoned at the fire station.

"The poor little thing. I . . . it's . . . thank you! *Way* better than roses."

He laughed. "You are a funny woman, Britt Langley."

"Yeah," she agreed happily. "I know. I love it. It's perfect! Thank you for rescuing it. I will make it grow! I'll name it after you."

He laughed, clearly delighted.

She settled it next to her other convalescents on the shelf on her porch. And took a moment to admire it and bask in the luxury of being *known*.

Though he didn't know everything.

"Allow me." He strode over to his truck parked at the side of the road, and pulled open the passenger-side door for her. He held out his hand, and she gave hers to him, and he helped her up into it as if she were Cinderella boarding a gilded coach.

"I like your hair up that way," he said. "It's pretty."

She touched it. "Thank you. Casey did it. It's apparently a bit complicated. Seemed to take quite a bit of finesse."

She turned her head this way and that so he could admire it.

"How about that. She *is* an artist."

She smiled at him.

"By the way?" he said, hovering in the truck doorway a moment.

"Yeah?"

". . . I'm going to enjoy messing it up later."

And with that incendiary little statement, he shut her door.

She was lucky she was already in the truck, because the look he shot her would have buckled her knees.

CHAPTER 13

They drove there with the windows rolled down, and she kicked off her shoes and put her feet up on the dash and let the breeze free a few tendrils of her fancy updo.

"Love this song! Sing with me, Britt," he commanded, and cranked up the radio.

It was Neil Diamond's "Solitary Man," one of her favorites. She'd always loved Neil Diamond's huge, revival-meeting-style choruses. The two of them belted out the song, more concerned with volume and conviction than the key, and any dogs within earshot could not have been blamed for howling. And if this had been the sum total of their date, she would have been perfectly happy.

She went as silent as a canary in a coal mine when they drove past the billboard of Rebecca Corday.

"Boy, they really captured her likeness. Her head is really that big in real life," he said.

She gave a short laugh.

But it was oddly as sobering as a splash of water in the face.

Passing that billboard was like entering a portal into J. T.'s world.

He'd dated, and slept with, and was photographed with, a woman who was on a freaking *billboard*.

She'd forgotten how much more populated Black Oak was, in general, than Hellcat Canyon. Tourists with lots of money cruised the antiques stores and stopped in at the restaurants as they headed up to their Tahoe condos.

The street was aswarm with Lincoln Navigators and Cadillac Escalades.

And people. Lots and lots of people. Many of them leaving work for the day, but others pouring into restaurants for dinner.

Britt had grown up amid crowds in Southern California, and this hardly compared.

Still, it was a veritable stampede next to Hellcat Canyon.

And J. T. got even quieter.

She sensed he was even a little nonplussed.

She knew why.

One of these people, if not all of them, was bound to recognize him.

They'd spent a few days in the insular, wooded little bubble that was Hellcat Canyon. And she'd known all along he was famous.

She just hadn't had to *really* experience firsthand what that actually meant in real life. And she had a hunch he'd almost forgotten this, too.

That was what good sex could do to a person: make them lose their mind.

"I made the reservation under a fake name," he said absently. Almost to himself.

"Maybe we can whip up some kind of disguise."

He shot her a wry glance. "I used to keep a fake mustache in my glove box."

"Seriously?"

"No." He sounded a little tense and distracted.

She wondered, then, if he was concerned about being seen with her, in particular.

Which made her go quiet, too.

"Let's just have a good time," she said, because she gauged from his tension that he was worried.

"I can't imagine having any other kind of time with you, Britt."

There it was. The charm was back. And that was better.

They found parking practically outside the restaurant, and they were both smiling when he came around to help her out. His hand went possessively to the small of her back.

A genuine maître d' greeted them at the door of the restaurant.

"*Bon soir, monsieur, madame.* Welcome to . . ."

And then he did a near cartoon double take.

"*Mon dieu* . . ." he breathed. He clapped a hand over his heart. "*Vous êtes Monsieur John Tennessee McCord!*" he said with the awestruck gravity usually reserved for popes and presidents.

It occurred to Britt that nearly everybody said J. T.'s name in italics.

"Er . . ." J. T. began.

"*Je suis un grand fan de votre emission!* Daaaaamn!"

"*Oui.* Honored. *Excellent. Merci.*" And then J. T. smiled a smile Britt had never seen before. At least not in person. It was all-expansive, blinding charm—downright rakish. She recognized it instantly as the one he produced on red carpets, the one that showed up in all his photos. It transformed him as sure as if he'd put on a tuxedo.

"*J'ai regardé chacun de vos épisodes au moins trois fois. Je ne peux pas croire que vous êtes dans mon restaurant! Auriez-vous l'amabilité de bien vouloir signer ce menu et puis-je vous prendre en photo?*"

Britt's high-school French couldn't quite keep up with

that, but she did hear the word *photo* and knew exactly what that meant. And she hadn't considered *that*, either.

"I'll be just a moment," J. T. said to Britt crisply, apologetically. He put a chummy hand on the maître d's back, steered him aside, and murmured to him in rapid-fire French, "*Je suis en compagnie d'une belle femme . . . Nous souhaitons rester discrets, ni être dérangés, alors je crains de devoir refuser votre demande d'une photo.*"

Hearing J. T., he of the seductive Tennessee drawl, rattle off fluent French, was just one more surreal element to the night.

He returned to her swiftly with the smile she recognized. "Sorry about that. I told him I was having dinner with a beautiful woman and I'd like to be discreet because I'm going to mess her hair up later."

"You didn't!"

He grinned. "But I did slip him a fifty, the going rate for discretion from maître d's, told him we don't want to be bothered, and he couldn't take any photos. Though there are never any guarantees when it comes to privacy."

"Then again, everything's a little cheaper out here. Maybe you bought twice the discretion," she tried. She'd never had to buy anyone's discretion.

"Discretion," he said somewhat grimly. "Is priceless, and it's a bit of a gamble. That fifty may be wasted money if he figures out that a gossip site or TMZ might pay him more."

This was completely outside the realm of her life experience to date.

"If it helps any, I got all tingly hearing you speak French," she finally said.

He smiled for real again. "I got fluent between movies. In, you know, my downtime. It was useful in Cannes. I can do something French to you later, if you'd like," he suggested politely. With a wicked glint in his eye.

"I'll hold you to that."

They gave a start when the maître d' materialized next to them.

"Monsieur McCord," the maître d' stage-whispered. "Mademoiselle. This way, *s'il vous plaît*."

They were ushered swiftly by a phalanx of waitstaff through the dark, dreamily lit, white-tableclothed restaurant and installed at a table in the back of a room that was apparently deemed slightly more private. To get there they needed to sweep through the main room, and every single head whipped toward them, craning, both because of the hushed commotion and because one glance at J. T. was all it took to surmise that he was a VIP.

"I was the homecoming queen a thousand years ago, but that was nothing compared to this," Britt murmured.

"Damn. The homecoming queen? I've really come up in the world," he teased.

And then they were installed at their table, and J. T. ordered a bottle of wine, which was produced for them with lightning speed, and they sipped and were quiet.

J. T. fussed briefly with his napkin.

The easy rhythm of the day stuttered.

And Britt wondered if they would have been better off just keeping their little fling in the safe-ish confines of Hellcat Canyon.

"It's funny, but I feel a little out of practice. It's like switching gears. For a time in my life, paparazzi were everywhere. Like mosquitoes. You kind of just plowed through, maybe swatted a little bit."

He smiled a little tautly here.

"I read about your swatting."

"Ah, Wikipedia is so useful. *Really* not proud of that," he said shortly.

"My impulse would be to swat them away from you."

She said that before she could think it through.

He smiled. "I knew you were fierce, Britt Langley," he said approvingly. "I kind of feel obliged to show fans my best self, or a dazzling self, so they don't feel hurt or slighted. I'm sorry if it's weird."

It *was* a little weird.

"I get it. It's part of your job. It's not really the same thing, of course, but my dad was in sales. I watched him switch charm on and off. It wasn't so much a different persona as an amplified one."

"An amplified persona," he quoted slowly. "You are one smart cookie, Britt. I've never heard it put that way. What did your dad sell?"

"Insurance."

"In Southern California?"

"Irvine."

"What about the rest of your family?"

"Well, my sister's—"

"Mr. McCord . . ." The voice came from behind J. T. and both he and Britt gave a start. A skinny teenage busboy had crept up to the table. His voice was shaking. "I'm so very sorry to interrupt . . . it would mean everything if you would sign . . . I can't tell you what a huge fan my mother is of . . ."

J. T.'s smile switched on, and the charm enveloped the skinny kid in warmth and ease and he swiftly signed his name on the proffered notepad with the ballpoint.

"Thank you, thank you, thank you, Mr. McCord! Gosh . . . I hate to ask . . . if could just . . ." He held up his phone.

"Oh, I'm afraid I can't do photos when I'm dining. Contractually forbidden."

And he was all melting apology and steely unyielding denial and blue-eyed charm. The kid was helpless in the face of that and promptly took himself off.

There was another moment of taut silence between

them. The reality of sitting with someone half the world had seen every week for several years was sinking in.

And she was suddenly as speechless as that kid.

"I'm sorry about that, Britt. That maître d' pocketed my fifty and didn't say anything to his staff, or that kid has balls, and I'm betting on the former. It's just . . ."

"Please. Please don't apologize. We'll just roll with whatever happens."

This was the right thing to say, and that's why she said it. But she was out of practice, too: with rolling with things, with sudden interruptions, with changes, with hot men who comprised all of those things.

"So you were homecoming queen, huh? I bet you were a cheerleader, too, Britt Langley."

"*Head* cheerleader." Her old competitive streak kicked in. She'd fought for that top spot.

"Not surprised. I bet you liked it on top. Of the pyramid."

"Oh, yeah. The view is much better from up there."

He grinned slowly at that. "Still have the uniform?"

She laughed. "What *is* it with men and cheerleaders? It's cliché. Remind me to tell you about the mermaid and the fisherman some time."

"*What* the . . . you don't want to tell me about it *now*? You expect me to move on from a statement like that?"

"I don't know if you're ready for it. An innocent young movie star like yourself."

His head went back on a quick laugh. "Okay, you were about to tell me about your family."

"Ah . . . um . . . well, my sister's name is Laine. She's older than I am. She married her high-school sweetheart and they have a little boy, Will."

"The one who likes Muppets and flatulence."

"That's the one! We were a pretty ordinary family I guess. We had a nice little house identical to all the other houses on our street, except I had pink daisies on my wallpaper and my friend Dana down the street had yellow daisies. And she had a glow-in-the dark baton and I had a regular one, and man, I really wanted a glow-in-the-dark one. Oh, and my mom planted petunias and Dana's mom planted shrubs. Mom could make anything grow, really."

He visibly relaxed as he listened to this with pleasure and amusement.

"Is that where you got your love affair with plants? Your mama?"

"Yeah, probably. From Dad . . . I guess that's where I got my competitive streak. And my mom would say that's where I got my hard head. I got a scholarship, otherwise my parents would never have been able to afford college. They wouldn't have pushed me to go, though. They're pretty mellow people, my parents. They love us just because."

And he was smiling softly at all of this.

With a pang she wondered if anyone had ever loved J. T. just because.

"Your turn, J. T. Where you grew up, siblings . . ."

She said this swiftly so she could cut him off at the pass if he intended to ask about her husband.

His little silence, and that faint shadow between his eyes, told her he wasn't fooled a bit.

The muscles banding her stomach tensed.

But this was what people did on dates, right? They exchanged information about themselves.

"I have two brothers and a sister. We don't talk much these days. We kind of scattered like pool balls the minute we could get away from Sorry, Tennessee. You don't go revisit the site of a train wreck if you can avoid it, right? One brother is kind of a deadbeat, the other's all right. He's stubborn and proud and—"

"Mr. McCord." A waitress had slinked up to their table.

She was a beautiful girl, tall, pale, brunette and willowy, in a short black skirt and a white blouse open two buttons. She was clutching what appeared to be her own head shot, of all things. "I am *such* a fan," she gushed nervously, but she wasn't too nervous to lean down a bit in case he might want a little cleavage with his wine. She bent so low, even Britt got a look in there. Admittedly, a decent rack, but Britt thought her own measured up nicely. "Would you please—"

Britt had never seen someone smile another person into silence, but J. T. was doing it now.

His eyes were doing most of the work. They were like steel gates slamming down.

The sheer force of his personal authority and displeasure came off him like steam and his smile was practically a weapon.

The poor girl—Britt could think of her that way now—was frozen in place.

And if that girl was a little nervous before, she was a *lot* nervous now.

"I'm afraid we have an urgent situation," J. T. said pleasantly to her. "Would you be so kind as to ask your boss to come to our table immediately?"

She was off like a shot.

He turned back to Britt. His expression was thunderous.

She was frankly awestruck by what she'd just witnessed. J. T. McCord possessed the rare ability to be hot and charming and scary all at once, and he knew how to get what he wanted. She'd witnessed a variation on that theme with the snapped pool cue at the Misty Cat.

And he was clearly pissed off.

"Do you get used to it?" she tried.

"You just learn how to deal with it," he said. "I don't know that you get used to it. It's all part of it. Sometimes it's fun. Maybe a lot of times. Other times . . ."

"Maybe you have to ease back into it. Do sprints."

He grinned at that. Sprints reminded him of a certain oak table on a house he'd just bought, and that's exactly what she was intending.

"Don't worry, Britt. She was leaning pretty far over but I've seen breasts before."

He was a devil.

"Oh, I wasn't worried," she said idly. "I have a sense for where mine belong in the rack hierarchy."

"*Rack hierarchy?*" he repeated slowly. "Sweetheart, I'd put them right on top."

She laughed.

"You need to go back to work pretty soon, right? Get right back into the thick of all this kind of thing?"

"I have a few weeks before it all hits. I have a meeting with the location manager of *The Rush* and another with the director, and then I'm headed to Napa for Felix Nicasio's wedding. He was the producer of *Blood Brothers* and I'm supposed to give a toast. I don't have a single idea what I should say. And then after that I start back to work in earnest."

And that would be the end of his downtime. He'd be swept right back into the current of his old life, and Britt could remain on the island of Hellcat Canyon with her memories.

She unconsciously pulled her hand way.

"You were telling me about your family?"

"Oh yeah," he said, a little jarred that she'd taken her hand. "For the most part my family is pretty undistinguished, and that's putting it really mildly. Unless you count good bone structure and a way with the opposite sex. You like kids, Britt?"

Holy shit. *That* was so sudden it felt like an ambush.

She was so startled she couldn't speak.

"Love them," she said faintly.

"Me, too. I always wanted kids."

They could be interrupted any minute, so maybe this conversational gambit was more out of practical economy than anything else.

She doubted it.

She suspected it was more in the way of trying to startle her into deeper self-revelation. She was aware that it was patently unfair not to give anything of substance to him; then again, she hadn't signed up for substance.

"Yeah. Me, too," she said. Her voice was faint. She was unaccountably a little angry.

She'd both answered his question and hadn't really answered it. And her own deeply ingrained sense of justice niggled her, because she knew she was being unfair to him.

Her hand curled into the tablecloth as if to ward off any more questions in the same general vein. She made herself stop, because he noticed stuff.

And little blip of silence ensued.

She was actually glad to see the maître d' when he appeared.

"Yes, Monsieur McCord, please tell me how I may help."

J. T. crooked his finger so that the man would bend closer. "Two members of your staff have approached me for an autograph since we've been seated. I'll be filming in the Gold Country with a number of members of the Hollywood community in the near future and I would be pleased to highly recommend your restaurant to them if we are untroubled for the rest of the night."

That was some masterful diplomacy. The elegantly implied threat was that if one more person interrupted them, he might even say something decidedly uncomplimentary. Maybe even on television.

He was clearly a master tactician. The "punching his way out of frustration" days were clearly behind him.

Watching him like this was somehow both intimidating and erotic as hell.

"Thank you for apprising me, sir," the maître d' said faintly. "You will not be bothered again."

"Don't leave," J. T. ordered the man. "Britt, do you mind if I order for us?"

She shook her head.

She was hardly a complete rube. She could even speak a little French. But J. T.'s worldliness and authority, this earned sophistication, made her feel every bit of what she was, a middle-class California overachiever who had lost nearly everything she'd spent the first half of her life trying to achieve and wound up in Hellcat Canyon, subsisting on the basics, telling herself she was content.

Oddly, something else was revising in her, and it wasn't just lust.

She *did* like to be on top, frankly.

And it had been ages since she'd needed to rise to any kind of new challenge.

J. T., in his way, was the biggest challenge she'd ever encountered.

J. T. handed the menus back to the maître d', ordered in rapid-fire French, and the maître d' bowed and departed.

"You been single since your divorce, Britt?"

Damn. She sucked in a quick breath.

Another quick question, and an entirely reasonable one. If she'd been nearly anybody else.

"Pretty much." She inhaled. "That is, yes. Do you miss *Blood Brothers* . . . excitement? Hullabaloo?"

His head went up and he fixed her with a stare.

He was making it very clear that he knew she'd dodged that question.

She felt a pressure in her chest, a frisson of panic that he would simply get tired of trying to coax her out.

And then, for God's sake, she hoped he would give up

and then would get back to what they were clearly very good at, which was banging each other into oblivion, and then he would be gone from her life.

But he answered her question.

"I did at first. Miss all the craziness around *Blood Brothers*, that is. But those years were like someone dropped a bag of cash from an airplane and I had to grab as much as possible of everything thrown my way before it all blew away. And that included roles *and* relationships. So during that time I was so busy grabbing, it was hard to know how much of it I really *enjoyed*. It was only after it settled down, if that makes sense."

"Roles and relationships." She wondered if that was a reference to Rebecca Corday. Five years was a long time for someone like him to be with one person. And their breakup was fairly recent, in relationship terms.

Then again, breaking up was seldom quick and effortless. It was often a long time in the making.

She ought to know.

And John Tennessee McCord was allegedly allergic to the "L" word.

She supposed that was something Rebecca Corday ought to know.

"It's hard to get a perspective on events, and even people, when you're in the thick of them," she said. "And it's hard to know which opportunities are right for you, and which ones you just think you should want."

He quirked a corner of his mouth. "Yeah . . . wanting . . . that's a killer. Recently, I had a shot at a part I wanted more than . . . literally more than any other part in my entire career. I wanted it so much it was nearly physical pain. A script called *Last Call in Purgatory*. Fantastic writing. Set at the end of World War II, about a washed-up formerly brilliant writer who's kind of a lush and the woman he's in love with. I auditioned three times. Anyway, I heard back this week. And . . . I didn't get it."

"Oh, J. T. I'm so sorry."

He shrugged. "It's Hollywood. Anything can happen. But the competition . . . and the *wanting* . . . you can try to be Zen about it. But that letdown is never not a killer."

"I think all that means is you're a competitor. And one thing I learned as a cheerleader is you have to actually learn how to fall in a way that doesn't break anything essential as well as do those backflips."

He took this in thoughtfully. "Backflips . . ." he repeated musingly.

As if he was getting ideas about what they ought to do after dinner.

But she knew he was processing what she'd just said.

She took a deep breath. She could do this. She could give a little something else of herself to him.

"For a little while . . . I gave up a lot of stuff I used to love. It just sort of . . . happened that way. But lately . . . I've started to think that wanting things . . . really, *really* wanting things . . . is how you know you're still alive."

He said . . . absolutely nothing.

She was beginning to understand that J. T. was likely feeling the most and thinking the most when his expression was least readable.

Some errant, fiercely tender impulse swept through her. Because he might be direct, and he might be tough, but something told her she was getting at places he normally kept protected.

And then his mouth turned up at the corner ruefully. And he leaned toward her, across that lit votive candle.

"By that definition, Britt, I'm more alive than any guy on the planet. Because you have no *idea* how I much I want you."

Good God.

He could so easily render her breathless.

She stared at him.

Suddenly they were the only two people on the planet, and neither of them had any purpose or goal or need beyond the physical. And maybe that's all this ever needed to be.

"Feel like proving it?"

"Think we can get dinner to go?"

"I'll get you anything you want, sweetheart."

The maître d' was next to them before J. T. had his hand all the way up in the air to beckon.

CHAPTER 14

Britt deposited her purse and keys on the little table near the front door, and then closed it behind them. And J. T. was officially in her house, which was probably the last thing she would ever have imagined a week ago.

"This your mountain lion?"

J. T. bent down to get a look at Phillip, who had greeted them at the door, and held out the back of his hand. It was bumped by a pink cat nose.

"Yep. Careful, he's vicious."

"*Prrrp!*" Phillip trilled and flung himself on his back beseechingly, then rolled.

"I can see that," J. T. said.

Phillip sprang back up and flung his body at J. T.'s shins and rubbed the length of them.

"Suck-up," she said to her cat and bent down to scratch the back of him while J. T. scratched the front of him.

And then J. T. stood and began wandering through the front room, looking like a big handsome wild animal picking his way through a new habitat.

He paused in front of a photo of Will and smiled. "This your nephew?"

"Yeah. That's Will."

No one could help smiling when looking at Will.

"I have a nephew, too, 'round that age. Hardly ever get to see him."

"That's a shame," she said sincerely.

She imagined it would be awfully hard for ordinary humans to merge into the fast-lane life J. T. lived. Or maybe it was like a carnival ride, and he waved at them each time a rotation of his merry-go-round brought them into view again.

Next he plucked up a deep-orange silk pillow from her sofa, which was a sort of pale shade of olive with a high tufted back. Soft and velvet and unusual, and better yet, a steal from the Goodwill store. It was the one she'd been clutching when she'd watched him in *Agapé*.

He scanned the room, his expression gratifyingly impressed. "You have an amazing eye for color and form."

"Don't I know it."

That was a little Mae West-ish of her, but she was a little tipsy from the excellent wine at the restaurant.

He grinned at that. "Did you make these, too?"

"Um . . . I made the pillows, from thrift-store silk. I refinished the picture frames. I refinished that trunk . . ."

Oh shit!

She realized too late she'd left her sketchbook on the trunk, and she watched him reach for it in what felt like slow motion.

"Oh . . . that's just . . . you don't want to . . . *argh!*"

But he already had it in his hands. He was staring down at it raptly.

And his face was lit with delight.

"Holy crap, this is Glenn Harwood from the Misty Cat!" he guessed. "Only he's a *walrus*. That is freaking brilliant."

"Don't turn the—"

He turned the page.

"And this is Sherrie. She's a lady walrus." He glanced up at her, thoroughly amused. "Are there lady peanuts in here, Britt?"

"No. J. T., I'd rather you didn't—"

He turned another page.

"J. T. . . . I really wasn't ready to—"

"Let me guess . . . this angry bull with the big square face is Truck."

She sighed. "Yeah," she admitted.

"Britt, these are absolutely brilliant." He looked up at her, his face ablaze with a warmth and admiration and surprise. "You don't want me to look at them? But why?"

"I don't want *anyone* to look at them, but since you're already into it . . ."

He forgot to listen to her answer because he was already turning the page. "I don't know who this little minx is."

And it *was* a little minx: slinky and self-satisfied, a little haughty, a little vulnerable.

"Oh . . . that's Kayla Benoit."

"Ah, the lady with the boutique she named after herself." J. T. was amused. "The woman you tried to fling at me as a consolation prize. And the woman she fought with in the street is . . . where is she?"

Britt surrendered and leaned toward him, and paged ahead, right past the horse drawing she didn't want him to see. "Right here. Casey Carson. You may have noticed her in the Misty Cat picking up her lunch or dinner. I made her a lioness. She's kind of fierce and open. A little bit innocent, a little bit not."

He smiled at that description. "I like the bow on top of her head."

"And her hair is *perfect.* She always has the best blowout."

She exhaled the tension she hadn't realized she'd been holding when he laughed.

"Britt, these are amazing. I mean, *really* great. They have so much life and charm. Each drawing practically tells its own story. You ever think about doing a children's book, an animated series, something like that? You've never shown them to anyone?"

"Nope. Well, just my nephew. I guess it's just I . . . only recently started drawing again. Feeling a little delicate about sharing it with anyone. I feel a little weird about sharing them with *you*. Let alone the world."

"Well, a cartoon is a long shot. Best things in life are long shots. And you could make enough money from a book to get, oh, a *1995* Ford Contour."

She laughed.

And then froze mid-laugh. Because now he was paging backward.

No. No no no.

"J. T., would you like to see my bed—"

It was too late. He froze, staring at the dashing horse, wearing jeans and boots and a black T-shirt.

"Holy sh . . . this is me," he stated definitively.

Almost accusingly.

She bit her lip.

He looked up at her. "I'm a . . . *horse*?"

She was never in a million years going to tell him why she'd drawn him as a horse.

She hesitated. "Technically . . . you're a stallion," she confessed faintly.

"Because . . . I'm hung like one?" he guessed on a hush that was all stifled hilarity.

"You're quite adequately hung, but that's not why."

"Adequately *hung*!" he crowed softly, delighted. "Say more dirty things like that to me. I want that on my headstone when I die. 'He was adequately hung.'"

She laughed. "Stop!"

"But why then? Why am I a horse?"

She sighed, gustily. "Do I have to say?"

"Yes," he decided. "You have to."

Another silence.

"It's because . . ."

"What? What's wrong?"

"It's a little embarrassing," she whispered.

He cradled the back of her head in his hand, his fingers dragging softly in the downy hairs there, and she was suddenly incredibly glad for the updo, because her neck was wildly sensitive. If anyone was determined to seduce her, that's where they ought to start.

She lifted her head up to see his eyes, hot and admiring and tender.

Her eyelids went heavy.

"Tell me," he said softly.

"I think horses are very handsome."

He grinned at that. "Great. Go on," he whispered.

"And a little untamed. And majestic. They have dignity and integrity. They're at home outdoors. They *belong* outdoors."

"All good," he murmured. "Were you going to mention anything about how much you love to ride them?"

She lifted her head up and studied him in a heavy-eyed assessing way, as if she was picturing doing just that, and by his expression she could tell that look went straight to his groin like a skillful hand.

He cleared his throat. "I didn't see *you* in there."

That was an interesting point. "I guess I just didn't know what I should be."

"*I* know." He trailed his hand down to her shoulder, snagged the zipper on her dress, and dragged it down, down.

"What's that?" she murmured.

"A wildcat. Because I just *know* you're about to use your teeth and nails to make me wild."

Her laugh evolved into a soft sigh that tapered into a moan when he slipped his hands into her dress and skated them up and down, up and down, softly, softly.

"It's true that I can't promise I'll go easy on you," she murmured against his mouth, when it touched hers. Whisper soft.

His hands, the night, her skin, his lips, hers. They were all of a sultry piece, all indistinguishable from each other, all erotic.

They got lost in long, slow, drugging kisses, and long slow, drugging caresses. Kissing just to be kissing. Touching just to touch.

Suddenly it felt serious and right, and it unnerved her.

Britt finally pulled away and tucked her head beneath his chin. And then she sighed and gave a single little shimmy.

And just like that her dress slid from her into a pool at her ankles.

She was nude.

And he was speechless.

"Damn, Britt." His voice was a rasp.

She took him by the hand. "Show me how you'll do it lying down."

Luckily there wasn't far to go, because the house was little, and so was her bedroom.

She sat down on her bed and pulled him down over her. He practically ripped his lovely shirt off and flung it with violence, as though it was trying to keep him away from her on purpose, across the room, where it settled on a lamp. They were finally skin to skin.

The pleasure of her nipples chafing his bare skin was decadent. She rubbed against him like a cat, and half sighed, half moaned shamelessly, and he hissed in an oath, part endearment, part pleasure. Her fingers followed the seams between the gorgeous etched quadrants of muscle on his chest, and her lips and her tongue and her breath followed her fingers, and she savored the feel of stomach leaping and the hoarse rush of his breath. "Christ. *Britt*." He made her name sound synonymous with *need*. Or *want*.

She drew her tongue all down that seam that divided his ribs into muscle while his hands destroyed Casey's updo and trailed her neck and ears in a way that made her wilder still, and she nipped and kissed all down the ferny trail of hair that vanished into his jeans, and then she dragged her mouth teasingly over the bulge in his jeans, and turned her cheek to rub over it there.

And now he was writhing and arching and attempting to reach his buttons. "Jesus . . . help me, you wench . . ."

She laughed and did the honors with a deft tug, and the buttons all rippled open easily. With some less than graceful but ultimately effective fish-out-of-water thrashing they finally got him out of his jeans and underwear and completely nude and his big, lovely hard cock was hers for the tasting.

But he rolled her over so swiftly she gasped.

It was his turn to show her what he could do with his hands and mouth. Slow, strategic, clever, knowing, relentless. In moments she was enslaved. His thumbs rocking and chafing over her nipples, sending fine bolts of delicious lightning through her, until she was more lust than human. His fingers slid between her thighs and feathered, teasing, over the satiny, sensitive skin there, skating just shy of where she was throbbing like a freaking jungle drum, because he was a bastard and clearly he wanted to hear her cravenly beg.

"J. T. . . . *please* . . . you son of a . . ."

And then he got there and found her hot and wet and she forgave him the torture when he proved he was absolutely maestro with his fingers, and she moaned shamelessly, moving in rhythm with him. "Yes," she affirmed. "Dear God, *yes*."

And then suddenly threaded his fingers through hers and pinned them back and he was over her body, and with one deft knee he had her legs apart and she rose up to lock them around his back.

He thrust in, and moved into her slowly, slowly. His eyes were nearly black and their gazes fused with such intensity, for an instant she literally forgot who was who.

It was clear he was going to try for finesse. He withdrew, and teased both of them by sliding his cock lightly over her wet curls, and she sucked in a long breath from the electric bliss of it, then cursed him for the torture.

And then he was inside her again, and she rose up to take him deeply. He eased back, and then plunged, then eased back, and slowly sank into her again, each time uncovering layers of bliss she really never dreamed existed, each one of those layers building upon the next. Her head thrashed backward and her hips arched up, and she freed her hands from his because she needed to urge him on.

She dragged her fingers over his chest, trailed them over his narrow white hips, slid her palms into the lovely little scoops of muscle on his ass to pull him hard against her. Nipped at his nipples, and dragged her hands down to stroke his balls for the pleasure of watching his eyes go blacker still. And his rhythm got steady and faster and she could feel him everywhere in her body.

"Oh. My. God," she moaned, as she felt the banking of pleasure that promised to be mind-blowing.

"I know, right?" he half rasped, half moaned, both self-congratulatory and awestruck.

"*J. T. . . .*" It was a raw whisper, half laugh, half plea. Jesus.

He unleashed both of them.

Her fingernails dug into his shoulders as his hips drummed. And then his eyes went hot and dazed and she knew he was racing toward his own release as she rose up to meet hers. And when it came it was cataclysmic, a near killing pleasure, bowing her body upward, racking her with wave after wave of indescribable pleasure.

And she wrapped her arms around him and held him when he went still and as his body shook, her name a tattered rasp.

And then he gently laid his head on her chest, his back heaving, and she ran her hands over it, savoring, feeling both conquered and conqueror and unutterably, unaccountably moved.

Britt opened her eyes to dusty golden sunlight pouring through the high window in her bedroom. A shadow pattern of leaves was using J. T.'s smooth back as a canvas. They must have fallen asleep after they'd ravished each other. It was already warm in the little room.

He was a stomach sleeper. So lovely to know these things about a guy. These little intimacies.

She admired how his eyelashes shuddered on his cheeks in his sleep for a time. Smiling slightly.

His eyes popped open. He smiled sleepily. "Hi."

"There's a shadow pattern of leaves on your back. It's very pretty."

"Zat so. There's something pretty in front of me, too."

"Ha."

He sighed happily and rolled over and scooped her into his arms, so that his shoulder was her pillow now.

He dipped his head and kissed her shoulder lingeringly. Right where she'd transformed a round, ugly scar into something beautiful. Something that could be kissed by a beautiful man.

They lay like that for a moment of utter, empty bliss.

And he was quiet for so long, his breathing so steady, she thought he might have dozed off again.

"Britt . . ." he said sleepily, turning to kiss her tattoo again. "You gonna tell me about the guy who did this to you?"

He said it so casually, so naturally, that it took a moment for the words to sink in.

Her heart stopped.

She went absolutely rigid.

He kept his loose hold on her.

She swallowed.

It was a moment before she could speak.

"How did you know what it was?"

"I've seen cigarette burns before. You managed to turn it into something beautiful."

She inhaled a steadying breath.

"Is it so obvious?" Her voice was frayed.

"No, sweetheart. It's not. It's really not. It's just . . . maybe it's just I know more than a little bit about violence. It was my dad's default way of burning off a little of his natural-born misery. Drink, smack us around, repeat. I know what it does to a person. How you go into the world with a chip, or with something to prove, or something to hide. You kind of get to know the signs in other people. But not everyone's going to default to what I just guessed, because not everyone has . . . I guess that kind of lens."

That kind of lens.

She wanted to think about that.

"Am I right?" he asked.

She was quiet for a time. "Yes," she whispered.

And now she wanted to tell him the story she'd never told anyone, not in total, anyway, but she didn't have any kind of narrative prepared.

She took a deep breath. And released it. His hands moved down her back.

"Okay. Like I said, I grew up in your basic middle-class family. We were happy and pretty ordinary, probably, by most people's terms, anyway. We didn't have a lot of money, but neither did anyone else we knew. I was a cheerleader, I got great grades, got a scholarship, went to a great college, got great grades there, too. It was all hunky-dory. I worked my butt off for all of it. And then I met this guy at college . . . he was gorgeous and charming and from a rich family and I fell head over heels. We got married, I got a job writing marketing copy and doing some illustrations; everything was really just perfect. We were both what anyone would call successful. I figured this was my reward for having a plan, and sticking to that plan, and being a good girl. For all the good grades and so forth. I thought it was cause and effect, you know?"

"I know. I get it."

She took a deep breath, and released it. "He only smoked when he was stressed. Which turned out to be a lot, and easily—he wasn't good about handling challenges, because he'd never really had any. I didn't really understand any of this before we got married. We had our first big fight over him smoking and lying about it, actually. Sort of dumb. I teased him about wanting to look cool at his age. But it turned into a fight about other things, and then . . . he *hit* me." Even now it was astonishing to say it out loud. "Just hauled off and hit me in the *face*. It was so surreal, J. T. I can't begin to describe how surreal. I'd taken plenty of falls as a cheerleader and I played other sports and so forth, so it's not like I was a stranger to pain. But no one had *ever* hit me like that before."

J. T.'s entire body was as rigid as a board.

Oddly, her body eased a little. Probably because she'd never said these words out loud to anyone before and carrying them around had required a very particular kind of balance from her.

"I'm pretty quick and strong. But he was a big guy. So what happened next was . . . he . . . somehow he . . . he got hold of my wrist and just held it so hard that I couldn't move. And then he just ground the cigarette into my shoulder. I never in a million years saw it coming. It was almost an out-of-body experience, like I was watching it happen to someone else. The pain was insane."

And her mind knew it was over but her body tensed again, as if it was happening as she spoke.

She felt J. T.'s chest rise as he sucked in a deep breath and let it go, too. As if to steady some wave of emotion.

And neither of them said a word. It was a lot for anyone to take in.

But if anybody could, he could. This much she knew.

"Did you leave him after that?" His voice was abstracted.

She gave a soft humorless laugh. "No. I did all these rationalization gymnastics instead. Because everything else in my life had made sense, and I had to make sense of this, too, you know? I thought . . . could I love part of him and not another part? Could I fix him? Because I felt like . . . doesn't everyone deserve to be loved even if they're flawed? He cried and was so abject and so appalled, and I actually felt sorry for him. It was horrible. And he didn't hit me for a long time after that. But then, he did. Again. And again."

She took a deep breath and he adjusted to hold her closer.

"The fourth time he hit me I was out of there. I went to my sister's house that night and I never looked back. I mean, it's kind of like, you can love a beautiful house next to a nuclear waste site, but ultimately it's a slow death sentence to live there, right? He cried and begged and apologized again but I was at least smarter than that, even if my heart was still a mess. And I'm making a long story really short, but it wasn't easy. None of it. It took a few years to leave him. I never told my family the whole story, but I think they kind of guessed. Especially my sister. I divorced him. And he was so ashamed he never put up a fight."

She had never said these things aloud to anyone. Not in so many words, anyway.

J. T. was as rigid as if he was absorbing the impact of those blows for her, right now.

"What happened to him?"

"He's dead."

"You kill 'im?"

He said this so casually. As if it was a matter of course.

"Car accident. Going too fast around a curve in his BMW. Rolled the car. About two years ago."

"That's a pity. I would have done it for you," he said idly. "It would have been my pleasure. I did all my own stunts, did you know? I know ways."

"Yeah? How would you have done it?"

"Well . . . let's say he was strolling down the street. I would swing down from a ladder . . ."

"Yeah?"

". . . that was dangling from a helicopter . . ."

"Yeah?"

". . . . and get his neck in a scissor lock with my powerful thighs. And just twist it until I heard a crunch."

"Wow. That is *bloodthirsty.* I like it. Although that's much flashier than he deserved."

They were quiet for quite some time, and just listened to a bird singing outside the window.

"Did you stop loving him?"

The question kind of surprised her. Given that he was allegedly allergic to that word.

"Eventually. Yeah. Well before I divorced him, anyway."

They were quiet for a long time. They heard the *scritch, scritch, scritch* of Phillip in his litter box. A homey sound.

She got the sense that J. T. was deciding what to say.

"There was a period of time when I thought my career was tanking. And I didn't . . . er, handle . . . it all that well. To put it mildly."

"Swatting photographers, stuff like that?" she asked. "Asking cops who pull you over if they know who you are?"

He winced. "Yeah. The odds are really not in anyone's favor when it comes to a long, glorious acting career. Kind of like you, I thought at one time my own success had been kind of cause and effect. Like I'd had something to do with it, when really, it was down mostly to luck and timing. Finally I thought . . . What if I never act again? Who will I be? Because that's the guy I'll have to live with the rest of my life. Whoever you are *without* all the window dressing, all the ego, all the stuff you think you need and that you think defines you . . . Well, that's who we *really* are. I didn't much like myself for a while. I had to figure out who I was in order to tolerate being alone. I would say that's the one benefit of at least a little failure," he said dryly.

"That's exactly it," she said, amazed. "That's the word. I felt like a failure. My whole life, I was so invested in being that good girl and I guess I kind of felt I earned all my successes that way. I felt like I let my entire family down, in a way, because I'd fucked up and made a bad choice that I thought was a good choice, and brought that darkness into our happiness. So I ended up questioning everything I'd ever done or thought or felt in light of that one decision to marry Jeff, and in the process it was like I completely lost my moorings. I stopped going to work and I lost my job. And everything fell apart from there."

"And that's how you ended up here, in Hellcat Canyon," he guessed.

She looked up at him then, eyes wide, because it was so on the nose. "One day I put things in my car and packed up Phillip and just drove and drove. I ended up here. I thought for a while it would be just until I figured things out. But the figuring-things-out part of life never seems to end. And I love it here, anyway."

He was quiet a moment.

"Bastard's name was Jeff?" he murmured.

It was, peculiarly, a relief to hear him say it that way: sleepy-voiced, idly. It utterly de-fanged the memory of him.

"Yeah."

She could hear Jet the dog in the throes of his first bark of the morning off in the distance.

"I was doing a stunt one day on a movie set," he said finally. "And it went wrong—there was some miscalculation, and the car hit a ramp at the wrong angle, and it went flying through the air, and it could have been the end of me. And you'd think you'd be scared under those circumstances, right?"

She nodded. She was scared just thinking about it.

"Thing was, while it was happening, I was more surprised than anything else. I felt like a doll being tossed across a room, just that consequential. That two seconds or so up there between the time where there was absolutely nothing I could do and the time my fate would be decided for me, I just had to kind of surrender. But you know, that moment was kind of freeing."

She took this in, and she felt a sort of epiphany trying to break through. "So what you're saying is . . ."

"What I'm saying is, maybe our triumphs and tragedies are not as profound as we think they are, and maybe *we're* not as important as we think we are, and maybe that's okay. Maybe we don't have as much control as we think, and that's okay. Or maybe life is just like . . . say you were traveling a road, and you took a scary wrong turn. Or hit a pothole that trashed your alignment and gave you whiplash. And it's taken you a while to find your way back. So maybe the guy you married doesn't say *anything* fundamental about you. Or even if it does . . . maybe it's something you needed to learn to keep going down the road that was right for you. Maybe it doesn't have to tarnish everything about your past. And maybe it doesn't have to affect your future."

Every bit of this rang so true to her, it was like a light being switched on in a dark place.

And it wasn't like J. T. was the Buddha or some sage. He was just another human who was trying to figure it all out, the same as she was. But he'd just said all the right words in a row. He'd said what she'd thirsted to hear for so long and just didn't know it.

They lay in silence. She listened to his breathing, as soothing as the wind in the leaves outside.

"The worst part was . . ." she whispered. Then she cleared her throat. "I always felt like there must be something fundamentally wrong with me, something soul-deep wrong, if I chose a man like Jeff. I thought only a damaged person would choose another damaged person. I've done my fair share of self-help reading. But I never could shake that feeling."

It was the bone-deep shame that had dogged her for years.

"Well . . ." he said easily. "What kind of man am I?"

She propped herself up on her elbow and looked down at him for some time, studying him like a map.

"Racking up the superlatives?" he guessed dryly.

"You're a good one," she said softly. Definitively.

"And what part of you tells you that?"

She paused again.

"Every part of me."

He smiled a slow smile. "There you go, then," he murmured. "And I haven't known a single part of you to lie yet."

She sighed contentedly and sank back down on her pillow next to him, and stared up at the ceiling of her beloved little cottage. It suddenly seemed brand-new.

He yawned and stretched and slid his arm gently out from beneath her. "I'll go make coffee. Or do you want tea?"

"Coffee today, I think. It's in the freezer. I ground up the beans. You'll see it. French press is on the counter."

He slid out of bed and utterly unselfconsciously and nudely strode toward the kitchen.

And as she drowsily listened to the homey sounds of him clinking around in the kitchen, she thought about what he'd said about lenses.

She was beginning to understand that J. T. was more like her than she ever dreamed: that his early life may have toughened him up, but it had also sort of shaved a fine layer away from whatever protective coating humans usually wore out into the world. So that he saw everything a little more acutely. Felt things that much more strongly.

This, too, was part of why he was a brilliant actor.

And she was now someone who saw beauty and poignance in beat-up chairs and dying plants. Who *physically* suffered when she witnessed someone being hurt and bullied. After Jeff, all the painful poignant things were going to hurt a little bit more from now on. Because she'd been extra tenderized. But the good things, the beautiful things, would feel that much better, too.

She had the kind of lens that allowed her to see J. T. as a person—a real person, with hurts and flaws and vulnerabilities—and not just a series of Google results, right from the beginning.

Maybe that's why she'd been so squirrelly to begin with.

Maybe she'd sensed he'd be able to see her clearly.

When she hadn't yet been really ready to look at herself. She wasn't sure how ready she was now.

"I think your mountain lion wants something to eat," he called.

"His food is in the little cans in the cupboard next to the fridge. His dishes are up next to it."

She listened, lulled, to cupboard doors opening and closing, then heard the little "pop" of a tin being opened.

"Oh, wow, buddy, this stuff is rank," he said frankly to her cat. "You really going to eat that?"

She smiled.

And then she luxuriously stretched all of her limbs at once, as if testing to see whether the sides of her box had really been kicked down.

They had toast and coffee and each other for breakfast, all in the kitchen. Britt had never done it in a chair before, but J. T. couldn't resist untying her robe the same way he'd untied her halter top a few days ago, and he was pleased with the naked woman he found inside, and one thing led to another, and she did get to be on top. Like a cowgirl. Scandalous and thoroughly satisfying.

"Let's go swimming. I know a place," J. T. murmured suddenly. Against her sweaty neck.

"You seem to know a *lot* of places."

He laughed. "Sweetheart, we've only just begun. But this one kind of came with my new house."

So she got into her bikini, a faded red-and-white Hawaiian print number, and they chucked her Kindle and towels and a thermos of iced tea into a big tote, and then he drove them to his new house.

They were quiet on the way. They listened to Wilco on the stereo instead of talking.

He wasn't quite sure why he'd asked for the truth about

her husband, one that he'd already pretty much guessed. Only that he'd somehow known she'd needed to be divested of that secret before she could allow herself to be fully known.

And he wanted to know her. With the same sense of restless hunger and promise he'd felt when he'd looked up at the hills of Hellcat Canyon. The sensation felt oddly like . . . freedom, maybe? When in his experience women had been anything but.

He knew what it was to have your world shattered. It happened when he was eight, when his mom left and at ten, when she died. And he got used to living out various trials and embarrassments in the public eye. It gave a person a sense of perspective. Acting was how he'd escaped or soothed himself from all of that. Becoming a different person for a time was pretty liberating.

Britt was indomitable, he was pretty sure. But she was just beginning to reassemble her life and its new form wasn't entirely ready for the light of day, like her drawings.

He parked his truck in front of his house, dashed inside to collect his things, and rejoined her.

"OK, the trail down can be pretty precarious, but I'm a great navigator. Trust me."

She hesitated. She opened her mouth, about to say, "I can do it on my own," he was pretty sure. Then she clapped it closed. And she finally gave him her hand, and he accepted it like she'd just handed him an Emmy.

He smiled and gripped it fast.

And she allowed him to be her rudder as he led her down the crooked path that traced the river and opened up into the swimming hole a hundred or so yards down.

The pool was bound by a few huge granite rocks, and a nice, big flat one near the narrow beach.

"Ta-da!" he said.

She was gratifyingly impressed. "What a find, J. T.! I've never seen this pool before."

"Found it first day I was here. Followed the sound of the water. Pretty sure I'm hardly Ponce de Leon, but I bet it's ours at least just for today."

They whipped out their towels and flapped them down over the big flat granite rocks that flanked the pool, deposited their tote, then splashed on in.

The chill sucked the air out of him at first. But then it was exhilarating, and they got used to it. And then they frolicked like otters.

"Race you to that rock." He pointed to a big granite boulder jutting out from the beach.

She beat him handily.

"Ha!" She exulted, albeit breathing like a bellows.

"Wench!" he laughed. Both pleased and nonplussed. And high-fived her.

"I'll give you a head start next time, J. T."

He kissed her.

For a long time.

"I almost forgot how much I love to win," she mused when they came up for air.

"I'm sure it'll all come back to you," he teased. "We've established that you like the view from up top."

She laughed and shot away from him like a mermaid.

A half hour later they waded dripping out of the water and stretched out on the rock to get warm. They fished out their e-readers. They read and passed the thermos full of iced tea back and forth, swigging at it like a couple of bums under an overpass. Britt on her stomach with her bikini top untied so the sun could erase any tan lines, J. T. on his back.

J. T. felt as happy to be himself as that rock or that boulder or those trees were to be what they were. Present and purely content and right where he should be.

She chuckled.

He turned to her and smiled. "What are you reading?"

"It's a Susan Elizabeth Phillips book. It's pretty funny. What are you reading?"

"Malcolm Gladwell. *Outliers.* It's good, but I guess I'm not really in the mood for it today."

"Wanna swap? I've read this one before. I like Gladwell and I haven't read that one."

They swapped e-readers and read in companionable quiet for a time, instinctively, almost unconsciously, shifting every now and then to make sure their legs, their hips, some part of them was always touching.

Until the inevitable time came when they wanted all of their parts to be nudely touching.

They hurried back to his house to break in the bed he'd bought at Home Depot.

And not only broke it in, but nearly broke it.

CHAPTER 15

"John Tennessee McCord, are you living in sin with Britt?"

Britt froze over the sink, a dish in one hand, the scrubber in the other, letting the water profligately run. She realized she was holding her breath.

She was washing up the dinner dishes and J. T. was over on Mrs. Morrison's porch, sharing a drink and a chat, which he did pretty much nightly now. And Britt could hear every word.

J. T. didn't answer right away. She heard him take a stalling sip. The ice cubes tinkled.

It was a good question, though, Britt had to admit. What *were* they doing? They talked a lot about nearly everything, they laughed more than she'd laughed in ages, they swam, they watched television with J. T.'s arm slung around her, they read, they hiked, they had lots and lots of sex. There didn't seem to be any point in stopping or discussing the fact that their date of about three weeks ago had never really ended, in the way there really isn't any point in thinking too hard about what your lungs were doing at any given moment. It had just happened. It was that easy.

They didn't go back to Maison Vert, though. By some

tacit agreement they'd decided not to let J. T.'s reality intrude.

"Well?" Mrs. Morrison pressed him.

"Well, I'm just thinking my answer over, in light of your shotgun sitting right there."

"I'm old, and I don't have time for equivocating. Seems to me like a yes or a no would get the question answered."

Good God, to be quite that bold and fearless, Britt thought. When the sands in your proverbial hourglass were running out before your eyes, maybe it was easier to cut to the chase.

She almost hoped he didn't answer.

All she knew was that life with J. T. here made her previous life, by contrast, feel like that chair out there on the porch with the frayed cane back. Like something that was functional and homely and a little broken but could potentially be a work of art. The whole world had paradoxically gotten roomier and brighter by virtue of the addition of a large man crammed into her little house. A large man who, she'd learned, sometimes liked to eat peanut butter straight from the jar with a spoon.

A large man who had never cohabited with Rebecca Corday.

"I think we're just thoroughly enjoying each other's company at the moment in all the ways available to men and women," J. T. finally said.

Wow. *Nice save, J. T.*, she thought dryly.

Mrs. Morrison chuckled and gave her knee a slap. "John Tennessee McCord, you should have been a politician."

"Don't rule it out. In my next career, maybe. If the acting thing goes kaput."

Britt carefully dried the dish and inserted it in the rack so she could hear the next thing they said.

"That was a clever answer, and I like you, John Tennessee McCord, but don't you hurt Britt Langley, J. T."

Britt froze.

How in God's name would a man respond to *that*? By running in the opposite direction, and Britt would hardly blame him if he did. In dreams, the moment you noticed you were dreaming was the moment you woke up, usually.

"You should worry more about me!" J. T. said, after what was likely a nonplussed silence. "See this here bruise on my neck? She's enthusiastic, our Britt."

Britt's jaw dropped.

"*John Tennessee McCord!*" Mrs. Morrison was thoroughly, delightedly scandalized.

She heard something that sounded like a smack—that would be Mrs. Morrison giving him the swat he deserved. J. T. was laughing wickedly.

Britt was scandalized, too, and she realized she was blushing.

But she was also grinning.

He really could charm the birds from the trees, and he could get away with saying things no ordinary human could get away with saying. In part because one of the loveliest things about J. T. was that he generally liked people, and they knew it.

She turned the water off. She drew in a long breath.

He hadn't answered the question. She was actually a little glad.

His phone was on the table. And she would never look at it, but every time an e-mail or a text rolled in, it chimed, and it chimed a lot.

It chimed now.

Speaking of sands in an hourglass, that's what every little chime felt like. She knew he was preparing for things when she was away at work, struggling to write a wedding toast, setting up meetings for *The Rush*, answering e-mails about a big, fancy celebrity wedding that he'd

RSVP'd to ages ago and that had nothing at all to do with her. She'd never expected to be included in that. Nor had he suggested she be included in that.

And then his downtime would come to an end.

He'd left the peanut butter out on her counter. She smiled when she looked at it. But its presence was worrisome. He now had *his own peanut butter* at her house. And she'd bought it for him. Because it made him happy, and making him happy seemed to be what made *her* happy.

It might be peaceful enough between them now, but in Britt's experience, inherent in every peace was a sort of tension. The sort of tension presented by the smooth unbroken surface of a new jar of peanut butter.

The whole *point* of that surface was to shatter it. Which sometimes felt like the fate of any kind of peace.

A couple of days later Britt slipped out of bed around seven a.m. to get ready for work and tiptoed into the living room, leaving J. T. sleeping. He didn't snore, thankfully. But he occasionally murmured, which was funny. "Damn straight," he muttered once.

She showered and flung on some clothes and just opened her laptop to do her first e-mail and news check of the day when Skype began booping and beeping.

She yawned hugely and answered.

She frowned faintly when her sister Lainie's face filled the screen. Lainie's mouth was wide open. So wide, in fact, that Britt could see the fillings in her back molars.

"Hey Laine. Did you mean to call me, or did the cat accidentally walk across the keyboard again?"

In the background was Laine's living room, pleasantly cluttered. She saw one of Will's shoes and an old afghan their grandmother had knitted on the floor.

Laine still didn't move. Not one hair.

"Lainie?" she tapped the screen, a little worried now. Maybe Skype had locked up?

But then Lainie's cat strolled across the room in the background and stopped to sniff Will's shoe.

Laine still didn't move.

"All right, Lainie, what the hell is *wrong* with you?"

"JOHNTENNESSEEMCCORD!"

Lainie clearly had been working up a head of steam in order to shout that.

Britt winced. "Yikes! Why are you *yelling*?"

"You and JOHN TENNESSEE MCCORD, THAT'S WHY!"

Britt wrapped her arms around the monitor as if she could muffle it. "Shhhhhh! What's the matter with you . . . do you mean J. T.?"

Her sister swiveled in her chair and she saw the back of her sister's morning hair, still in its messy sleep-bun. "MITCH!" she bellowed to her husband. "Honey, she calls him J. T.! She already has a pet name for him!"

"Oh, brother. It's not a pet name, it's his *name* name. Wait . . . what's going on? How did *you* know about J. T.?"

"It's on TMZ! Two pictures of you! And him! One of you getting out of a car at a restaurant and you're wearing a white dress, and another of you in a bikini lying next to him on some big rock. TMZ doesn't know who you are, but I do," she said delightedly and ever-so-slightly inanely.

"Lainie, if you don't stop shouting you're going to make all the neighborhood dogs bark." And maybe wake J. T., but she didn't say that. "What are you talking about? We're on TMZ? How did we get on TMZ?"

"Go look."

"I believe you. I will in a second."

Her mind was now whirling, and it was way too early for her mind to be whirling.

How the hell would anyone get pictures of them?

"How on earth did you wind up with John Tennessee McCord, Britt?"

"I won him over with a fart joke."

"SHUT. UP."

Britt laughed. Pretty much the only thing better than J. T. was sharing the news of him with her sister.

"I totally remember that bikini you're wearing in that picture. You got it on sale that day we went to T.J. Maxx around March a few years ago. You look really pretty, Britt. And that white dress is *super* cute."

"Thanks. I got it on sale *plus* I had a coupon, plus I got to use someone else's discount!"

"Score! But how did this *happen*?"

"Okay, the CliffsNotes version is that he's in Hellcat Canyon for work. Speaking of which, I have to get to work, Laine. I'll tell you the rest later. Oh, and don't tell Mom and Dad! Not yet!"

"You and *John Tennessee McCord*." Britt had broken her sister, apparently, and now all she could say were those three words and variations thereof.

"Told you it was nice up here."

Her sister laughed dizzily. But it was clear from her expression that she had a thousand suppressed questions.

Britt showed mercy. "All right. You get one more question."

"Okay, but it's an essay question. And it's this: What is he like?" Her sister had deferred to her wishes and was speaking on a hush now.

Britt hesitated for effect. She crooked her finger for her sister to get closer to the screen.

And then she leaned toward the screen and stage-whispered.

"*So* hot."

Lainie froze again.

And then she made a little whimpering sound.

And then she leaned back blew out a long, satisfied breath. "You always were an overachiever. Way to get back on the horse, Britt." She sounded awed.

"Jeez, Lainie, he's not a horse."

"You sure about that?" J. T. said from the doorway behind her.

Lainie froze again. Her head whipped to and fro on the screen.

"OH MY GOD," she whispered hoarsely. "Who was that? Is that *him*? There? Is he there right now?"

Britt hesitated.

Then she nodded smugly.

Lainie squeaked.

Mitch's face squeezed into the Skype frame. "Tell him I loved *Blood Brothers*! And *Faster than the Speed of Sound*! Tell him I said, 'Daaaamn, Son—'"

Britt clapped her laptop closed.

She turned to look at J. T., who looked sleepy and delicious clothed in nothing but shadows.

"So . . ." she said brightly after a longish silence. "My sister just Skyped."

"Yeah? How is she?"

"She's great."

A funny little silence fell.

"How much did you hear?" she asked resignedly.

"Just the horse part." He smiled faintly. "But I already knew that."

Another uncomfortable little moment beat by.

She ought to say, *You're not* just *a horse to me.*

But that might bring up uncomfortable questions about what he actually was to her, and it was much too early in the morning to have that conversation.

She'd prefer never to have it, actually.

"Okay, then. Well, there's something else you should know," she began carefully.

"I think I know it. I got a congratulatory text from my agent. He thinks you're cute."

He handed Britt his phone, and it was open to the photos.

Britt's heart lurched. There she was with J. T. exiting Maison Vert. They were both smiling, her head turned toward him, his hand possessively on the small of her back just shy of her butt. Nothing said "we're doing it" like that particular pose.

Perfidious maître d' had probably sold them out, even after J. T. had given him a fifty!

But the second photo was much more unnerving.

There she was sprawled on her stomach, the ends of her bikini top trailing against the rock, her knees bent up, her feet crossed. He lay alongside her on his back, one knee up, the other tipped companionably against her calves. Their heads were turned toward each other. They were smiling. It was a breathtaking moment of casual intimacy violated by a telephoto lens.

She didn't think she'd seen any two happier or peaceful-looking people. It was stunning.

It was peculiarly disorienting to watch it from the outside. Because anyone watching that would assume things about how they felt about each other.

And yet the fact that the photo existed at all was deeply creepy.

She gave the calendar on the wall an unconscious flick of a glance. It was July 31.

That wedding in Napa was just two weeks away.

"Gosh. Tell your agent thanks." But her voice was abstracted. And a little thick.

Someone had thought it worth hiking up to that rise to get that photo, and neither one of them had noticed. They looked happy because they were happy in that moment, and they were completely absorbed in each other.

"I'm sorry about this," he said quietly.

"Don't be. I look great in that dress."

He gave a short laugh. But there wasn't much humor in it.

"I thought we were safe swimming there, otherwise I might have been more vigilant. I bet that first photographer followed us here, or was somehow tipped off about the swimming hole. How, I don't know. They're like wasps tracking the scent of meat. They just kind of know."

"Yeah, I don't think anyone in town can afford a telephoto lens. And they see enough of me as it is, in the Misty Cat."

She was trying for a joke.

He smiled tautly.

And the silence was just as taut as that smile.

He drew in a breath. "Britt, I don't want you to have to be part of that zoo. The photographers and sycophants and all that. That stuff is my job. It doesn't have to be part of your world."

"It's okay," she said. After a moment.

She said it automatically, because she hadn't fully thought it through yet. Her impulse was to reassure him. But if she'd said instead, "I don't mind," for instance, it would have implied that she considered herself a part of it already, or that she thought he was inviting her to be a part of it.

And it occurred to her that what he might be saying now is that he never really intended for her to be part of that world in the first place. That she was, indeed, what he was doing in his downtime. She could picture a magazine cover article now: "*French, karate, blondes: what John Tennessee McCord does in his downtime.*"

"Maybe it's just a couple of photos," she suggested. "Maybe it won't turn into any kind of a zoo. Maybe it doesn't have to mean anything."

"Maybe," he said.

Neither of them believed it.

"I have to get to work," she said finally. Quietly.

"I'm going to do some work on the roof over at my house today. See you tonight?"

That "see you tonight" had been implied for weeks now.

The fact that he was saying it injected that first note of caution and uncertainty in their little idyll.

"Sure."

She took a step away toward the door, suddenly eager to run off some of this emotion.

And suddenly he curled her back into his chest and held on to her a moment.

She could feel his heartbeat against her cheek. She clung to him for a moment, too. God, he smelled amazing.

He kissed her temple.

"Tonight," she said into the delicious wall of his chest.

But J. T. was pretty intuitive. He could probably tell she was ruffling her flight feathers, and not just to get out the door to the Misty Cat this morning.

J. T. watched her dart out the door to work and realized he was smiling, which was a reflex when it came to watching Britt.

But then his smile faded, and gave way to the pitch black of his mood and he wasn't quite able to parse out a single reason for it.

He'd been getting texts all morning from friends who were, frankly, simply glad to see him and to find out where he was and wanted to know if they'd see him in about a week at the Nicasio wedding.

From Linda Goldstein (with a flurry of emojis: a thumbs-up, a blonde girl, a heart, and a bikini):

She's pretty, John Tennessee! I hope you're happy!

And then his phone chimed in with another text.

She's cute. Are all the girls like that in Hellcat Canyon?

Effing Franco Francone.

J. T. reflexively, angrily, texted back a photo of his Emmy.

Then, just as he was stuffing his phone back into his pocket, another text chimed in.

BTW, McCord, they cast me in a secondary role in *The Rush*. Three-episode arc. See you in Napa in a week?

Franco again. J. T. went still. Just for an instant an old reflexive gladness kicked in. Because he and Franco really had a blast working together on *Blood Brothers*. The press had loved their relationship. They had, indeed, almost been brothers.

Until Franco accused him of stealing his girl.

And J. T. had knocked him flat in a parking lot.

The press had loved that, too.

"You can't lose her if she really loves you," J. T. had said at the time. Staring down like a conqueror at a flattened Franco, whose nose was bleeding.

It seemed an eternity ago. What a pompous young prick he'd been back then. As if *he* knew anything at all about love.

It occurred to him, however, that he might not have been wrong.

He stared at Franco's text.

And decided not to answer it. Yet.

He forced himself to examine his mood. Stealthy paparazzi photos were a way of life for him. All the women he'd dated before understood implicitly that they were part of the Hollywood ecosystem, the way mosquitoes and barnacles had their role in nature. Rebecca in particular was adept at making that work in her favor.

But Britt was still learning how to feel safe again in the world, and with a man. He'd earned that trust, and he cherished it.

And some asshole had stalked them with a camera.

He had a hunch Britt could actually cope with all of that. She had a competitive streak, after all.

But at the heart of the usual anger was something new: a little, cold shard of something that might be fear.

He'd seen Britt glance at the wall calendar.

As if she was counting the days until he'd be out of there.

She was a bolter. It was a built-in defense.

J. T. suspected all she needed was a reason.

Not only would this never have bothered him before, he would have been the one counting the days. An Advent calendar, so to speak, for relationship escape.

How did a woman who'd begun as a good time turn into three weeks of hot nights entwined under absurdly floral sheets, twilights with a chatty rum-swigging, nonagenarian, cat food in his basket at the grocery store, and a sense that he was finally, after forty years, where he should be?

Something soft wrapped around his ankles. A tail.

He looked down into the benevolent green gaze of Phillip.

He sighed, knelt to pet him for a while.

He could entertain Phillip for an hour at a time by aiming a laser pointer all over the place. Phillip would stalk and pounce and scramble but he never caught it, because it couldn't be caught, of course. It didn't really exist.

J. T. wished he was as simple as Phillip. He probably was, once.

He was starting to think he just couldn't play the same game over and over.

J. T. arrived at his house, happy to have any opportunity to hammer nails into things, because that might just suit his mood. The uneasy shard in his stomach didn't go away.

But when he got out of his truck outside of the house, a new sound was mixed in with the river and squirrels and trees.

Somewhere, someone was already hammering.

Not a swift, steady *tap tap tap* on a nail.

It sounded more like someone was swinging a mallet into a stake or a fence post.

He just listened a moment, as if it was music, and imagined that it was the sound of a spike being driven into the symbolic black heart of paparazzi everywhere.

Or maybe it was the sound of a monumental tack being driven into time itself. So he could hold these past few weeks with Britt in place, to keep them from flying away, to keep them from moving on.

Half wishing he walked around every day like his character in the *Blood Brothers*, one hand on his gun half the time, he moved on silent feet toward the sound and then stopped. Surprised. He had a gun. He just didn't always travel with it.

A few yards down the trail he stopped.

There was the sheriff, swinging a big hammer at a wooden sign, pounding it into the ground near the creek next to that narrow path.

And then he stood back and swiped a hand across his brow.

"Morning, Sheriff."

He got the sense the sheriff had already seen him.

"Morning, McCord." He stood back and let J. T. read the sign.

Anyone caught in this area with a telephoto lens might be mistaken for vermin and shot on sight.

J. T. smiled slowly. "Well."

"I aim to protect and serve," the sheriff said dryly.

"Much obliged, Sheriff."

"Call me Eli."

"You want something cold to drink after that hard labor, Eli?"

"Thanks, but I got some bad guys to catch. Some teenagers were throwing apricots at cars off the overpass."

"Hooligans. Can't have that."

"We caught the guy who took that photo, by the way," Eli told him, moving back up the trail. "Sprained his ankle trying to climb down to get even closer to you and couldn't walk himself out of there. Some kids found him hollering up there later and we had to stretcher the fool out. He ended up in the hospital in Black Oak. I think we scared him sufficiently so he won't be back. And we cited him for trespassing."

"Thanks for that. At least he made his buck." J. T. was ironic.

The sheriff paused near him and they both looked back at that sign and listened to the water. "Those photos pissed me off, too, McCord."

"Yeah," J. T. said grimly. "I felt like I should be able to protect her from that."

"You should be able to just be with her without going through hell."

Something about the way Eli said it made J. T. think *maybe* there was a little subtext there.

J. T. flashed back to that moment at the Misty Cat. And the sheriff's expression as he watched. Glory Greenleaf onstage.

And then he remembered something with startling clarity: the Eternity Oak was carved with the initials ELB + GHG.

"You got that right, Eli," was all he said, quietly.

It was pretty clear love hadn't been kind to Eli Barlow, either. He wondered if he regretted that little visit to the Eternity Oak.

"See you around, McCord." Eli Barlow touched his hat and headed off, back down to the road.

CHAPTER 16

Just like a rock chucked into the river, the photos of J. T. and Britt caused a ripple through all of Hellcat Canyon.

Casey and Kayla were thrilled almost to incoherence to see Britt in a Kayla dress with a Casey hairstyle getting into a truck with movie star on a website that millions of people read.

"You almost look like someone he would really date, Britt!" Kayla told her.

Unfortunately, Britt knew exactly what Kayla meant.

"Gosh, thanks, Kayla. The dress, the makeup. I'm sure that's why the photographer decided to take the picture at all."

And a week went by, and the rhythm of their days mostly resumed. But the conversation J. T. and Britt ought to have but weren't having now ran like a subliminal hum through every word they said to each other, through everything they did. It kept them ever-so-slightly on edge and made every word they said to each other just a little careful, a little more polite than it ought to be.

Sex helped them forget about that. The wanting part didn't go away in the least. It in fact, diversified. In terms of positions and locations.

But Britt was reminded of an old television she'd once had, that developed an odd hum. She'd thought nothing of it, because everything that gets old seems to develop quirks along the way. It went on like that for a year.

Until the day there was a loud "pop" while she was watching a repeat of *Friends* and flames shot out its back.

Deep down inside she knew nothing good could come from unattended hums.

"Surprise me," J. T. said, clapping his Misty Cat menu shut. "Like you did last night."

Last night she'd finally told him about Sherrie and Glenn and the mermaid and the fisherman.

As an actor, he was intrigued. They hadn't quite tried it out because they hadn't worked out the wardrobe, but it had led to some friskiness that left both of them flattened, panting, replete and chock-full of bonhomie this morning.

J. T. had gotten into the habit of stopping in at least once or twice a week during one of her shifts. He always ordered a Glennburger with cheese.

"Surprise, huh? Be careful what you wish for, J. T.," she purred. And she swiveled to take his order up to the counter. She'd decided she was going to bring him a turkey club with spicy mustard, because he liked that, too. She loved knowing the things he liked. God knows he knew the things she liked.

The french fries he'd ordered as a side were up and she whisked them back to him with a smile, and then zipped away again.

It was the lunch rush and the place was packed and in full cheerful conversational roar, and silverware was clinking and Giorgio's spatula was ringing on the grill and Casey Carson was waiting for her to-go order, so when the door opened, no one paid much attention at first.

But when the door didn't close, people looked up.

And conversations winked off, one by one, like bulbs blowing out.

Fully half the jaws in the place froze mid-chew. The rest swung open as if the hinges had snapped.

Every head swiveled toward the door. Every pair of eyes was unblinking and wondering.

And there wasn't a sound except for the sizzle of meat on the grill. It was threatening to be the first time in history Giorgio had burned anything.

Rebecca Corday was like a carnal version of a Disney heroine. The light from the doorway obligingly backlit her flame-colored waves and made the floaty, gossamer peasant top she wore all but transparent. Her brilliant blue eyes were enormous and almost perfectly round. The rest of her appeared to be makeup free, but her great wide pillow of a mouth painted red. She'd been *born* to sell lip gloss.

Her legs were miles long, about the diameter of a thin woman's forearms, and encased in faded jeans.

It was like a gazelle had wandered into a watering hole occupied by lapping wildebeests.

Sherrie gripped Glenn's arm in either excitement or trepidation, and he covered her hand with his as if they were waiting for news of plane crash survivors.

Britt surreptitiously rested her own hand on the counter because the world was dropping out from beneath her, and there were no handholds anywhere.

A ringing started up in her ears.

And when she looked at J. T., her stomach plummeted another fourteen stories, and took her heart with it.

Because he'd frozen.

His face was taut with some indecipherable emotion, equal parts fury and wonder and astonishment, all underlaid by something hard and resolute that she couldn't read at all.

He slowly, slowly, lowered his fork.

He stood and moved in almost dreamlike silence toward Rebecca Corday. The two of them paused in what to onlookers appeared to be a moment of silent communion.

And then they both turned as one and went right out the door.

The first one to speak was Casey. "You could see her boobs right through that thing," she said, sounding more impressed than censorious. "What there was of them."

The next sound was the clang of the spatula on the grill as Giorgio whipped around and turned his burgers in the knick of time.

Little by little, conversations revved into motion again.

But they never really rose above a murmur.

Britt still couldn't move. She literally felt so nauseous she nearly buckled. And she was also so surprised it was very nearly funny. Because it couldn't be real, could it? That couldn't have possibly just happened?

"You know that thing Kayla says she can do with a cherry stem? Tie it in a knot with her tongue?" Britt said faintly to Casey.

"Yeah?"

"I bet Rebecca Corday can do that with her entire body."

She had no idea why this was the first thing out of her mouth after seeing J. T. disappear.

"Yoga," Casey said knowledgeably and solemnly. "She's probably so bendy she can kiss her own butt."

Britt watched that door in numb shock. A great toxic soup of emotions—rage, humiliation, wounded pride, a sick fear—that never ought to mingle were now simmering in her bloodstream. "She's almost *luminescent.* Like she's an alien or fairy." She was incensed by this.

"That's because she'd moisturized and exfoliated and waxed to a fare-thee-well," Casey said pragmatically.

"I hear they do shapes down there now, don't they?" Sherrie mused, turning to Casey as the expert.

"What do you mean, shapes?" Glenn was suspicious.

"They prune it *down there*. Into shapes," Sherrie explained.

It took him a moment.

And then he was aghast.

"What, like how the shrubberies at Disney World are shaped like Pluto and Mickey, that sort of thing?"

"Probably not Disney characters. But you never know with Hollywood." And in Hellcat Canyon, Casey was the one who passed for an expert on Hollywood. Given that she, like Britt's sister, read TMZ the way Mrs. Morrison read her Bible.

"Why would you need to do anything but trim the runway?" Glenn was utterly baffled.

"Fashion," all the women, even Britt, said aloud at once.

That was as cryptic a word as you could say to Glenn.

"I was so much happier when I didn't know that," he muttered. "If young women have that much time on their hands, they should learn a useful skill, like plumbing, or Olympic pole vaulting, or knitting. Or *waitressing*," he said meaningfully.

But not without sympathy. It's just that Glenn always thought that being useful was the cure for anything that ailed you.

Britt numbly shifted herself. She couldn't quite feel her limbs, but they seemed to be doing what they ought to do. She dutifully moved from table to table. She probably wrote down orders. She couldn't remember any of it.

Time ceased to move normally. The afternoon was a desert now. A barren, J. T.-less wasteland.

And when it became clear that he wasn't coming back, Britt started to bump into things. Like a broken toy.

Maybe . . . maybe he'd been expecting Rebecca all along.

It was so counter to everything she thought she knew about the man that her mind all but ejected it violently.

And yet she'd been profoundly wrong about a man once before.

And eventually Glenn cleared away J. T.'s table as if he were cleaning out a deceased loved one's closet.

And instead of excited murmurs and speculation, which is what one would expect after what was probably the most famous movie star in the world had strolled in and then out with another famous movie star, the Misty Cat remained almost funereally quiet, apart from clinks of silverware on the plate. Her tips were a little larger than usual, too.

This tender solicitousness managed to reach in through the numbness. She *was* touched. She knew this was because they had all been rooting for her and J. T. And just a few weeks ago she didn't think anyone gave a whole lot of thought to her at all.

She wondered how many of them anticipated this as the inevitable end.

It was, appropriately enough, like something out of a bad movie.

Her phone rang and she gave a start. And just like that, her heart boomeranged between joy and fury.

It was J. T.

It rang and it rang.

And it rang.

Fury won.

She stabbed it to voice mail.

The sun was cruel to nearly everyone today, high and hot as a blow dryer aimed straight into the face.

Cruel to everyone, that was, except Rebecca. She looked spectacular in any light.

J. T. aggressively pushed his sunglasses onto his face. As far as he was concerned, looking at her head on was like looking into an eclipse.

"What the hell are you doing here? And where's your bodyguard, Rebecca? Aren't you usually flanked by a couple of brutes these days?"

"Hello to you, too, Johnny. You look great! Not even an air kiss? No? Fine. Don't you have a black belt now? Something else you did in your downtime? I told them to stay at home and you'd look after me."

"That was presumptuous as hell."

"When have I been otherwise?"

Fair point.

"How did you know I was at the Misty Cat? And what the hell are you doing here in Hellcat Canyon?"

"I bummed a ride with Sven Markson and we flew into that airfield a few miles up the road. Everyone's starting to head up to Napa." She waved a hand in the general direction. By "everyone" she meant Hollywood royalty and by "bumming a ride" Rebecca of course meant flying in luxury on director Sven Markson's little private Lear jet, which he shared generously with her since her movie, *Better Luck Next Time*, had doubled both his wealth and cachet. "I took a cab in to Hellcat Canyon from there. And by 'a cab' I think I mean '*the* cab' because I'm pretty sure there's only one in this part of the woods. I had to *wait* for it." She sounded astonished. Rebecca never had to wait for anything anymore.

He stared at her blackly until her confident smile wavered.

"No, Rebecca," he explained slowly, as if she were a dull child. "I'm not going to do 'breezy' with you. It's not as cute as you think it is. The last time we spoke was right before you left Cannes with Anthony Underhill. I haven't seen you since. You never returned any of my calls or texts. And if you need your memory refreshed about *why* you dumped me, there are a few hundred articles about it on the internet. I remember in particular 'The Top Ten

Reasons Rebecca Corday is better off without John Tennessee McCord.' So color me baffled about your presence here."

"Oh, God, John. You shouldn't have read them. I didn't." She sounded genuinely pained.

"Bullshit."

"Well, not all of them."

She never could resist reading about herself. She counted on fresh internet mentions the way she counted on water gushing out when she turned on the faucet in the morning. She would be just as shocked if either stopped.

"That one was e-mailed to me. By guess who."

She struggled not to smile. And then she did. That famous smile that could light a theater. "Let me guess. Franco?"

"Who else?"

She laughed. And once upon a time he'd lived to make her laugh, and now it was as charming as the sound of shattering glass.

"Okay, John, as for the rest of why I'm here, I'd rather not talk in the street. Can we go back to your place, wherever that is? It's pretty hot in the sun right here. I saw your truck over there. Can't miss it."

He sighed gustily. "For fuck's sake. Get in the truck."

He stalked over to it without waiting for her and he didn't open the door for her.

She did as ordered, and he peeled away from the curb fast enough to spit gravel behind them.

He was stonily silent.

She watched the scenery. "It's pretty as a movie set, this little town, and—oh, look! My Macy's campaign on all the bus benches!" She gave a little delighted bounce in her seat.

He said nothing.

"So you're going to be like that, Johnny?"

He said nothing.

"I can keep talking even if you don't."

He said nothing.

"Nice country here, even if it's a little hot."

He said nothing.

And finally she shut up.

He turned up the road to his cabin and cut the engine.

"*This* place? It looks like that house made of straw the first little pig made."

He said nothing.

She shot him a look. Rebecca's confidence was iron-clad. He never could intimidate her.

He didn't open her truck door, which was something she wouldn't fail to notice, because J. T. was a gentleman.

And he didn't offer to take her bag—a worrisome bag, because he'd seen it dozens of times before.

It was her favorite overnight bag.

He flipped on the ceiling fan and opened the windows and said nothing to her as she took a look around at his simple furnishings.

"You shopped the Bachelor Pad collection at Ikea?" she sounded amused.

He said nothing. "Okay, talk, Rebecca."

"Well. Are you going to offer me something to drink first, Johnny?"

"I'm afraid if I do you'll be like Persephone and be obliged to stay here for six months out of the year."

Her brow furrowed a little. "Who's Persephone? Is she in the latest Harry Potter movie? It sounds like a phone sex pseudonym, if you ask me."

He stared at her. He honestly wasn't certain whether she was joking.

"Persephone. Daughter of Demeter, the Greek goddess of the spring? She was kidnapped by Hades, taken to the underworld, and because she ate six pomegranate seeds she's obliged to return for six months out of the year, and that's why we have fall and winter."

She furrowed her brow as if he were speaking Sanskrit. "So . . . so you're reading about Persephone for a role?"

He opened his mouth to reply. Then he sighed. To be fair, a really successful acting career didn't often leave anyone much time for reading, or to become otherwise *interesting.*

And her career was stratospheric.

"Green tea? I can throw it over ice."

He belatedly wished he'd pretended he'd forgotten about the green tea. It seems he'd lost the art of game playing. Everything had always been strategy with her. They'd always traded the power back and forth, because he'd known he was Rebecca's weakness.

"Thanks," she said softly. Touched he'd remembered.

He just snorted. He vanished into the kitchen, put the kettle on to boil.

"Does Underhill know you intended to come here?" He didn't look back at her.

Underhill. The man she'd dumped him for in Cannes.

Her ensuing little silence felt planned. And that just made him angrier.

"He may or may not still be my boyfriend."

At one time he would have found this coyness maddeningly irresistible. Because Rebecca was smart the way an animal was smart, and when they'd first met, she'd seen underneath his cocky, effortless charm and magical bone structure to his deep-buried seam of doubt: that because he was a backwoods Tennessee boy and he would never be good enough for her, that he would always have to *earn* her, that he'd won the lottery when she'd thrown her lot in with him.

And boy, did she work that seam skillfully.

Except that he wasn't that guy anymore.

He'd once felt lucky to be with her. He now knew, thanks to Britt, that "happy" and "lucky" weren't synonymous.

Shit! Britt! He scrambled for his phone and called her immediately as the kettle boiled.

She shot him straight to voice mail.

He swore softly.

He turned around suddenly. Rebecca was watching him.

And she didn't disguise her expression fast enough.

And that expression made it very clear that *he'd* always been Rebecca's weakness.

He could think of nothing else that would have brought her all the way here.

Suddenly every muscle in his body felt pulled tight. He turned around again. As he grabbed a cup down from the shelf he rummaged around in his soul for a vestige of that old delicious pain Rebecca's circumspection usually caused. He came up empty. Too much had happened in a year.

He was, quite simply, too old for that crap.

He just wanted to be with one particular woman.

Who had just stabbed his call to voice mail. And he could hardly blame her, given how he'd exited the place. He'd just been so *shocked*.

He sighed. "Yes or no, Rebecca. Does Underhill know you're here?"

He sensed his tone surprised her.

"Not specifically. He knows I'm away on business, but he doesn't know I'm here, and he doesn't know I came to see you."

His temper was going to get the better of him in a minute. Ironically, the kettle was boiling already. As if in sympathy.

"I'm not going to ask it again. How the hell did you know where I was and why are you here?"

She finally stopped playing, fished her phone out of her big butter-soft leather bag and turned it around to show him a text.

> "Looks like J. T. is having a good time in Hellcat Canyon."

With a link.

To TMZ.

And the photos of him and Britt.

Fucking Franco Francone.

"He sure knows how to play you," he said grimly.

Rebecca shrugged.

"So that's the 'how,'" Rebecca said with mock blitheness instead, then reached into her thousand dollar leather bag and plopped what was quite obviously a script on the table.

"This is the 'why.'"

He stared at it.

It was the script for *Last Call in Purgatory.*

He stood motionless amid a great backwash of role lust and yearning and anger and regret.

For a moment he couldn't speak.

"How did you know about this?" he said quietly.

"I heard they turned you down. And all I know is you're perfect for it."

No matter what she'd said and done, she'd always been his champion.

"I am," he agreed cautiously.

"Well, now they want me for it. They want me so much that they'll give me nearly anything I want, including a say in the casting. And what I want . . . is you."

CHAPTER 17

Texts had been chiming in at fairly steady intervals since Britt got home from work.

Britt please we need to talk.

Britt, I'm sorry. I didn't mean to bail just like that. I had to get her out of there. Please text me back.

Tell the mountain lion I said hi.

Tell the azalea I said hi.

Britt . . . please don't shut me out . . .

Where had he found an image of a beseeching man? That one *almost* made her smile.

"J. T. says hi," she told Phillip. Who stretched and yawned, showing the entire pink inside of his mouth, then walked over and flopped into her lap as if he'd been walking hundreds of miles to get to her. She buried her hand in his fur.

It was darkening in the house. And yet she couldn't find the will to get up and turn on a light.

She hadn't moved from the couch since she arrived home from work. She literally felt as though she had the flu. Or like something essential had been scooped out of her, leaving her hollow and uncertain how to walk now.

How had she not been prepared for this feeling?

She finally listened to the voice mails.

"Britt, I swear on everything I hold sacred I didn't know she was coming or how she even knew I was here. Call me back. I'm sorry I left like that. I just . . . my reflex was to get her out of there as fast as possible. Rebecca sews mayhem."

She punched it over to the next message.

"Britt, I don't blame you if you're mad. I fucked up. I can see that now. Let me at least explain. Please call me back."

She couldn't move. He certainly *sounded* sincere. He sounded, in fact, as though he were in actual physical pain.

He was an actor, of course.

So was the world-famous beautiful woman with whom he'd disappeared with this afternoon. Whose giant head and giant sparkly lips were out on the highway.

Britt looked around. Her house, formerly her sanctuary, seemed irrevocably changed now, because she saw J. T. everywhere in it: nude, his lovely little pale butt as he reached up for cups in the cupboard. The new porch railing. In her bedroom, where she had watched him sleep for a little while, his back dappled by the shadowed pattern of leaves and where they had all but set the sheets on fire.

And every inch of her body, of course.

She closed her eyes, but whoop! He was there, too.

In all likelihood he would be in her dreams, too.

She had only herself to blame, of course.

There must be some sort of romance law, like those rules you used to solve geometry proofs. It would read: *the devastation is precisely equivalent to the bliss.*

The joke was on her, she guessed. She'd outsmarted herself. She'd wanted to get back on the horse with J. T. and she'd been wearing lust blinders. She'd reasoned herself into a fling and she hadn't expected to feel much more than sated and triumphant when it was over.

And now . . . now she couldn't isolate one dominant emotion from the great knot of them pulsing in the center of her.

Pain radiated through her whole body.

Her phone was finally quiet.

She didn't know whether to be sorry or grateful he'd given up.

Maybe she could dodge forever the "It was fun while it lasted conversation" until he was gone.

One more text rang in. She lunged for it.

Britt, I'm coming over

She texted back:

DON'T.

It was a brutally satisfying word to type.

Don't.

The air went out of J. T. as surely as if Britt had jammed a pool cue between his ribs.

He couldn't have moved if the roof was caving in.

He sat frozen, feeling half dead. The remnants of a delivered pizza, half veggie, barely eaten, sat on his coffee table next to the script.

He was an actor. Surely he had the skills to keep it together right now. Because Rebecca was watching him and she was the last person in the world he wanted watching him if he was going to fall apart.

Rebecca had once made him feel a lot of things, but devastated was never one of them. And that seemed somehow absolutely significant right now.

"Pizza didn't agree with you?" she asked softly.

He must look like hell if she was concerned. Or felt the need to feign concern.

"Yeah," he said abruptly.

He was savagely hurt in a way he could never quite recall feeling. He had no experience with accommodating this kind of pain. It reverberated through him, and he was as stunned, as if he'd crashed headlong into a wall.

And then the anger began to singe and curl all the other emotions up at the edges.

If he meant *anything* at all to Britt, she should have the common decency to just talk to him.

She was a grown damn woman.

He realized Rebecca was still watching him.

"Why are you still here, Becks?" he said wearily. "Aren't you heading up to Napa?"

"My app tells me there's no room at the only B and B here in town right now. The Angel's Nest? There's only one motel within ten miles of here, and my reconnaissance tells me they sell meth in the parking lot the way crafters sell handmade soap on Venice Beach. I figured we could ride up to Napa together. It's only a couple of hours. You going to kick me out?"

He stared at her.

This was Rebecca. She was always either about presumption or strategy or some combination thereof.

His fault. He should have asked her what her plans were sooner.

And he would have, if he hadn't been worried about Britt calling him back.

Women.

For God's sake. Possessing a penis was nothing but a burden sometimes.

And then, to his amazement, Rebecca laid a soft, persuading hand on his knee.

Or, technically speaking, his upper thigh.

He looked at her hand. He was as surprised as if she'd dropped a scorpion on him rather than a big hint. Her hand, or any other part of her, was absolutely the last thing on his mind at the moment.

And then he slowly looked up at her. His expression must have shown unflattering incredulity.

Her hand flew off immediately.

Her own expression was almost comically amazed.

It was entirely possible no man had ever before turned that expression on Rebecca.

At least he knew now that Rebecca had an agenda within an agenda.

"I'll take the couch. You can have the bed," he told her curtly. "I'll take you as far as San Francisco, but you can find your own way to Napa from there. I am not showing up to that wedding with you. That is final."

They stared each other down.

"Fine," she said, sounding surprisingly neutral.

He exhaled. "And I need some sleep. So if you could just . . ."

He wasn't going to sleep. But he wanted to be alone while he stared at the ceiling. And simmered in confusing feelings.

Another little silence, which was Rebecca deciding whether or not she ought to negotiate.

"Okay then. Good night, Johnny," she said finally.

And she rose like a queen and took herself off to the bathroom to do whatever things were required to preserve her beauty overnight.

He turned out the light and stretched out on the sofa.

Outside, he could hear the deer trotting past.

One of Britt's favorite sounds.

"Britt, honey, will you come here a moment?"

Glenn's voice sounded suspiciously sweet as he beckoned to her from behind the counter about ten minutes after she'd walked in the door of the Misty Cat.

She was only a few minutes late, but she was still rubbing her eyes, which were raw and red and sandy from staring at her ceiling all night instead of sleeping, wired by a sort of unspecific self-righteous fury and that actual physical gut ache that kept her thrashing until she was wound like a burrito in her sheets and Phillip finally stalked off in disgust to sleep elsewhere.

She'd tried to do up her hair in its usual barrette on the way in. From Glenn's expression, she hadn't quite got it right.

"You look like hell," Glenn assessed tactfully.

"You silver-tongued devil. Now I know what Sherrie sees in you."

He snorted. "Mr. McCord paid for his lunch yesterday but he didn't eat it. I'd like you to take this to him. Now. Sherrie and me will manage the lunch rush. You can make up the hours some other day."

He said this briskly and handed a white paper bag to her, fragrant with its load of burger and fries.

She couldn't have been more shocked if Glenn had said to her, "Britt honey, I'd like you to take this here Christian and feed him to the lions."

"But . . . but . . ."

Sherrie was hovering in the kitchen, pretending not to listen. The two of them were in cahoots, she was pretty positive.

"You *saw* what happened yesterday," Britt said. "He walked on out of here the moment he clapped eyes on her and he didn't come back."

"We *all* saw what happened yesterday. He call or text you last night?" Glenn asked her shortly.

Britt was cagily silent.

"Thought he would," Glenn said triumphantly. "He maybe text you more than once?"

She glared sullenly at him.

Glenn was a parent. He could probably not only put up with her evasion all day, he could see right through her.

"What'd he want, Britt?"

"He wanted me to call him or text him back," she finally, begrudgingly, confessed.

"And did you?"

"Of course not."

"Why the hell not?"

"I didn't want to."

Glenn's brows dove in a frown. "And is that all he wanted? He apologize for bailing like that?"

Pride and wounded feelings and fury and a whole soup of other things made her want to lie to Glenn.

Another part of her was curious about what he would say. Because she knew, deep down, both Glenn and Sherrie cared about her.

"He wanted to come over," she confessed. "And yes. He apologized."

Apparently she wasn't going to be allowed to savor martyrdom for even a millisecond.

"Thought so. McCord is a stand-up guy. He cares about you. He fixed your *porch*."

Glenn equated carpentry with character.

"Whose side are you on?" She was pissed now.

"I'm on the side of whatever gets your moping over with fastest, which means you need to talk to him."

"Who says I'm *moping*?"

Glenn snorted as if that didn't even warrant an answer. "Go on, get going. I don't want my food to get cold."

Britt narrowed her eyes at him.

She finally snatched the bag from his hand. "You taught all your kids to swim by throwing them into the pool, didn't you?"

"Worked, too," he said cheerfully. "They all swim like fish."

"Maybe it's because they're all part *mermaid*," she called slyly over her shoulder as she stalked out of the Misty Cat.

"*Mer*—? Sherrie!" he bellowed.

Britt would have trudged, protestingly, all the way to J. T.'s house—it was a fifteen-minute trudge, if she wanted to do it that way—but her conscience got the better of her and there really was no sense in wasting good hot food, so she picked up the pace, and she was just about at that turn in the road when . . .

Fuck.

Her stomach did a swan dive off a cliff.

Rebecca standing out on J. T.'s deck, gazing contemplatively out through the trees, in the manner of a woodland princess. She was clad only in a man's white dress shirt, open to expose most of her clavicle, and it barely covered her butt. Her long, thin white thighs most decidedly did not touch.

Britt pivoted, prepared to head off in the other direction and concoct a lie for Glenn, but she was a bad liar and apparently she had, much to her dismay, a sense of integrity.

It was too late, anyway. Rebecca gave a start when she saw her.

"Oh! Good morning! You're that waitress . . . aren't you?"

She aimed a Klieg light smile at her. All blinding, uniform teeth and sparkly eyes.

Zero actual human friendliness.

Pretty, but a little unnerving. Quite a bit, in fact, like that billboard out on the highway.

And if Rebecca had said nearly *anything* else, Britt might have thrust the white bag at her and bolted in the opposite direction.

But that sentence had the ring of a sword unsheathing. And "that waitress" had been delivered gingerly.

And that's how Britt knew that Rebecca considered her worthy of competition.

Britt's competitive reflexes kicked in.

"I suppose I am 'that waitress.' My name is Britt."

Britt smiled back at her. Her teeth might not look like piano keys, but her father had paid for orthodontia and she had dutifully worn her retainer every night for years.

And two could play the "don't blink" game.

They played it for a few seconds more.

"I'm Rebecca Corday, Britt. You might know me from that billboard out on the highway." She gave a self-deprecating little laugh and a hand flutter in that general direction.

"Oh yeah. I know that billboard. It sure casts a shadow."

Britt thought she detected an eyebrow twitch.

But Rebecca wasn't the highest paid actress in the world for no reason.

"I like your top," Rebecca said brightly, finally. "That's a great color on you. Walmart sure is making some cute clothes these days."

"They sure are," Britt twinkled back at her.

She expected Rebecca meant this as an insult. But it was really the wrong tack to take with her. She could talk for *hours* about her knack for finding a bargain, and she was proud of it *and* the top.

"Are you here because you're looking for John?" Rebecca said, her voice sympathetic. "He's *catnip* to women. They were always tracking him down wherever he lived."

John? She called him John? That seemed all wrong. Very mundane. She wondered if that's why Rebecca did it—an attempt at domesticating him.

"Tennessee" seemed to be so much a part of him that the 'T' at the very least seemed necessary.

"I get the internet, too, Miss Corday," she said evenly. "I've read the stories about him. I know him pretty well. And John called me twelve times yesterday."

This didn't cause even a ripple over Rebecca Corday's beautiful features. But she did go rather still.

And then she tilted her head ever so slightly and studied her.

"Is that so? You must not have called him back," she said. "I can't blame you. Given his history with me."

Damn. Rebecca was smart. Smart in a Dr. Evil sort of way. Britt had once seen a cat toying at a wriggling gopher, trying over and over again to find that one place to administer that killing bite. She was reminded of that right now.

"I just came to bring him the food he ordered," Britt said. Which was technically true.

"Well, he's still asleep. We were up all night. Just like old times."

This came with a misty smile and a picturesque tuck of her glorious hair behind her ear. Then she stretched, and the shirt she was wearing edged up ever so slightly. Revealing the tops of ivory hairless thighs and a peek of something lacy and fuchsia.

Britt averted her eyes.

"He's so *creative* about finding ways to amuse himself when he's away from Hollywood," Rebecca added fondly. "He always did know how to fill his downtime."

"J. T. is pretty resourceful." Britt said this tightly.

But she was losing her grip on her bravado. Because she was new to whatever this nasty little game was, and she hadn't slept at all last night, and Rebecca Corday—Rebecca Freaking Corday, of all the people in the world!—was clearly prepared to duel her to the death.

Rebecca smiled sweetly.

"I confess I was a little astonished by the condition of this cabin he bought. But then, he does love to fix . . . broken things."

WOW.

Bull's-eye.

Britt froze, as astonished as if she'd literally been shot.

Some distant, minuscule part of her was impressed with how accurate and how ruthless that guess had been.

She knew it was a guess. It had to be. If she knew anything at all about J. T., and she thought she did, she couldn't imagine he would ever say a word about her to Rebecca.

But then, she couldn't imagine the J. T. she knew spending five years of his life with this spectacularly beautiful, uniquely horrible woman.

She gawked speechlessly.

Rebecca gave her a slow, sympathetic smile and shrug. The silent implication being, *Sorry kid, but you never had a chance against me.*

"Rebecca, who are you talk . . ."

J. T. wandered out onto the deck.

He was fully clothed. He wasn't buttoning his jeans or mopping his brow or doing anything else that hinted that he might have just been ravished or had ravished Rebecca all night.

That was no definitive proof that he hadn't, however.

His eyes were shadowed and red-rimmed from lack of sleep and her heart both ached and exulted because it was probably her fault.

When she saw him, the last vestiges of her bravado sifted away like so much dust and her knees nearly gave way. Because instantly, the world was in color again.

She realized, with a shock, that he was her favorite person.

But J. T.'s expression was hard and cold. It wasn't an expression he'd ever turned on her before.

If she had to guess, she would have said he was seething.

"Your friend came by with some lunch for you," Rebecca volunteered, sweetly, when it seemed no one would ever speak.

"Delivery. From the Misty Cat." Britt's voice was shaking. She held up the bag, feeling like an idiot. "*Glenn* insisted I bring it," she added pointedly.

"Yeah? Good to know that someone had to force you to come see me, Britt."

Okay, then. He was definitely seething.

And all that did was make Britt even angrier.

His ex-girlfriend was standing behind him in her *panties*, for God's sake.

"Could you give us a minute, Rebecca?" J. T. didn't look at Rebecca at all when he said it.

He addressed this to Britt as if he was afraid she'd dart away if he took his eyes off her.

They stared each other down.

For a moment it looked as though Rebecca intended to stay exactly where she was.

And then she smiled beneficently, pivoted like a model

reaching the end of a runway and glided back into the house, the tail of the shirt fluttering just above her microscopic buttocks.

"And put something on your damn bottom half," he called after her.

If Britt knew Rebecca, and she thought she did, she expected that particular command would be ignored.

Britt handed the white paper bag up to him.

He barely looked at it. He set it aside on the little table.

"Rebecca collects men's dress shirts like pelts. The one she's wearing was never mine," he said shortly.

"Yeah, I knew that. I'm pretty sure there's no such thing as a dress *T*-shirt, anyway."

It was a mild opening shot.

"Why didn't you call me back, Britt?" He lowered his voice.

"Well, because I didn't want to, J. T.," she said tautly.

His stomach tied itself into a trucker's hitch.

They stared each other down for a moment.

"Let's go for a walk. Down by the creek," he said abruptly.

She pivoted and stalked in that direction. He followed her swiftly down the steps and flanked her in a few strides.

He went to reach for her hand, a reflex now. But she kept hers so adamantly close to her sides they might as well have been strapped there with bailing wire, and he felt like an ass.

He holstered his hands in his pockets.

They walked wordlessly a moment, tracing that path to the swimming hole, the last place he could remember being perfectly happy. Back in that brief interlude when he was delusional enough to think his life could be simple. *Nothing* was ever simple when it came to women.

Their feet crunched pebbles and old fallen leaves and pine needles. And he reached up and dragged his finger idly through the leaves of a low-hanging oak, as if it were a pet. Seeking comfort from anywhere.

She skidded a little down the dirt bank toward the river. He didn't offer her his hand again.

And then he stopped.

"Okay, Britt. I tried to tell you about a dozen times that I wasn't expecting her to just show up like that."

"That was pretty clear from that very complicated expression on your face when you saw her."

"Yeah. I just bet it was complicated. Let me ask you something. How complicated is my expression right now?"

They locked glares.

She was a stubborn woman. But he probably had as much right to anger as she did at the moment.

And she was smart enough to know it.

"What *is* she doing here then, J. T.?"

"She brought a script with her—"

"And about five years of shared history, right?"

"Britt—"

"Shared naked history."

"Britt—"

"And Walmart *does* have cute clothes sometimes," she said vehemently.

"Sure, sure," he soothed, startled.

"I think she's a mean person, J. T."

"You're not wrong," he confessed grimly.

"And she *stayed* with you last night."

"There was apparently no place else for her to go. I slept on the *couch*. Britt."

"She wouldn't *fit* on the couch. Her legs are about fourteen miles long. And there's not much of a distance between the couch and your bed anyway, is there, J. T.? Just one or two strides on those long, long legs."

"Should I have sent her to the Shady Eight?"

"Good God, no, she can't stay there," she said, startled. In all seriousness.

"I would have stayed with you, Britt. And left her alone. Except for one word. DON'T."

He was aware of the sound of his breath and hers rushing, rushing. From anger, from fear.

"You just don't seem to get it, J. T. Your ex-girlfriend is on bus benches and magazines and on a freaking billboard. She towers over Hellcat Canyon on that billboard like . . . like . . . that creepy sun baby in the Teletubbies. The whole town saw those pictures of us. And then she just appears, and yesterday I stood there like an ass and watched while everyone in the Misty Cat watched you get up out of your chair and drift on out of there after her, as if she was some kind of human tractor beam."

The image was both unflattering and priceless.

"EX." He growled that word and raked his fingers back through his hair in frustration. "Ex-girlfriend! Rebecca's whole goal in life has always been to take over the world. Her *job* is to tower over highways on billboards. I don't see what that has to do with you and me. And if I wanted to be with her I'd be *with* her, right now, instead of out here having a *great* time arguing with you."

He thought, for a moment, she was almost tempted to smile.

He seized the moment. "I love that you said 'tractor beam.'" He said swiftly, gruffly. He loved all those odd little things she said.

But she didn't smile. "I think she wants *you*, though, J. T."

"That doesn't mean she can *have* me. Rebecca always wants what she thinks other people have. She hunts down happiness like an anthropologist. And I must have looked happy to her in those photos. And I was. I am. Was. Am."

Hell.

Britt quirked the corner of her mouth. "Gosh. Smooth, J. T."

He sighed. "Britt, my reflex was to just get her out of the Misty Cat. I *had* to get her out of there. It was a public service. All those jaws hanging open were bound to catch flies and Giorgio would have burned something and Glenn would have gotten the blame."

He'd hoped for a smile. She was determined not to give him one.

"I'm sorry I went about it so awkwardly. It's just . . . I didn't want her anywhere near you, Britt," he said. "Because I know all too well what she's like. And now . . . so do you."

"She said you were up all night." Her voice was thick now. Her eyes were shining.

Dear God. If Britt cried, his heart would snap in half with a report like a fired 22.

He could just *hear* Rebecca's insinuating voice saying that.

"That's what she does. She messed with your head. We were up most of the night about the *script*. And catching up on people we know, industry news, things like that."

"Sounds like a good time," Britt said. Bitterly.

"Well, it wasn't a *bad* time. It was shop talk with a colleague. The worst part of the night was realizing the woman I've made love to every day for the past three weeks couldn't be bothered to call me back."

Britt went still. He saw the guilt flicker over her features.

He pressed his advantage. "Twelve phone calls and three apologies for something I really had no control over is my limit, Britt. You either believe me or you don't. I'm not going to grovel. And I haven't heard you apologize to me yet."

Her jaw dropped. "You want *me* to apologize to *you*?"

"Common decency and three weeks of hot sex dictates you could have at least answered one of my calls. Do you think I can't possibly have any feelings of my own, because my job is to have pretend ones?"

Damn.

He'd just argued himself right into a corner. Because he knew what the next question would be.

They stared at each other in wary silence now.

"All right, J. T.," she said quietly. "What *are* your real feelings?"

He crammed his hands into his pockets. Closing off, protecting himself.

And he looked at her. Into her shining eyes, with the mauve shadows beneath them. And his chest tightened and he couldn't breathe. And suddenly he was in that car sailing up the ramp and he didn't know how he was going to land or if there was even a ramp and he couldn't do it.

"I like what we have going," he said, finally. Quietly. "I don't want it to end."

He knew immediately it was wholly inadequate.

But then someone else had always written his words for him.

"But wasn't it *always* going to end, J. T.?"

And suddenly his hands iced. "What do you mean?"

"L.A., people like Rebecca, red carpets, movies—*that's* your real life. That's where you belong. Not here Hellcat Canyon. This is . . . the *dream* you're having during your downtime. Only I'm the hobby this time. We both got something out of it."

And it was like she'd literally kicked the foundations out from under him. Inwardly he was flailing. He felt the blood rush from his face.

"My life is wherever the hell I want it to be," he said hoarsely. "And I like it right here, right now."

"I think once you get back among your own kind, you'll probably forget all about that."

But her expression was at odds with her tone. She was saying things, for whatever reason, that she didn't mean.

And then he slowly straightened. And gave a short, bitter laugh.

He knew exactly what she was doing. And why.

"You know . . . it could just as easily be me out there on a billboard, advertising *The Rush* when it airs. Because that's my job, too. And I get that my life can be kind of overwhelming, with the paparazzi and the gossip sites and all of that. The thing is, I don't think that's your issue here at all, Britt."

And now she was nervous. Her own hands were knotting and unknotting in front of her.

"I don't know what you're talking about." Her breath was coming swiftly now.

He delivered the words with slow, deliberate ruthlessness. "Rebecca might be towering over Hellcat Canyon out on the highway. But if you run away now, that means your ex-husband is still towering over your whole damn life. And how can I compete with a dead man?"

Her mouth dropped open. She made an arid little sound. And then:

"How *dare* . . ."

She didn't finish that sentence.

He couldn't seem to stop the words. "If you love being afraid more than you like being with me, then fine. Be afraid. Just don't *lie* about it. You might as well get it over with and just run, because I know that's what you're dying to do right now. Just go."

Her face blanked in shock. "You *son* of a—"

She pivoted. She took two steps.

"Britt—*damn* it—I didn't—just—wait—"

But she was running now.

Her hair was a bright flash through the trees and then she was gone.

He watched, feeling like his heart was a bomb about to go off in his chest.

And then he shoved his hands through his hair. "ARRRGH!"

He stood there, hearing his own pain and frustration multiplied as an echo through the trees.

CHAPTER 18

Finally he stalked back to his house. He froze in front of it.

He'd almost forgotten Rebecca was inside.

And then he sighed resignedly and climbed his own steps as if he were headed for the gallows.

Rebecca was standing in front of his open refrigerator, critiquing the contents, no doubt performing her usual complicated calorie calculus in her head: if she ate three peanuts on the plane, she could maybe have one grape and a slice of turkey, but then she would have to spend thirty minutes on the treadmill or eat nothing for dinner. That kind of math was more exhausting than those thirty minutes on the treadmill.

She didn't turn around. "You're really drinking *beer* these days, John?"

She made it sound like, *You've really been drinking* anti-freeze *these days, John?*

His long, black silence was such a presence it finally made her turn around. She slowly closed the refrigerator door carefully and pressed her back against it.

He could only imagine what she saw on his face, because her eyes went wary.

She studied him, clearly deciding on his approach.

"Oh, come on, Johnny," she said softly, cajoling, teasing, placating. "She's just a waitress. She can't be the *first* waitress you've had."

She made it sound like he'd gone on a trip and forgotten his toothbrush, so he went out and got another one, just for the duration. Everyone was temporary. Rebecca was absolutely certain *she* would always be the prize.

This was Rebecca's way of being sophisticated.

He stared at her in amazement.

"Number One on John Tennessee McCord's Top Ten Things He Doesn't Miss about Rebecca Corday: hearing her use the word *just* to describe people."

That pissed her off. Her complexion swiftly went a blotchy pink.

"Where does Underhill think you are right now, Rebecca?"

She stared at him, probably wondering whether to equivocate.

But then her face crumpled in earnest.

"Oh, Johnny. He's such a . . . Let's just say he'd never punch a photographer, because it would mess up his manicure. I hardly ever laugh with him. He doesn't *get* me. He's not like . . ."

She caught herself.

He knew she was about to say, *He's not like you.*

He heard all this with increasing incredulity.

"So he got on your nerves and he wasn't perfect and you just left because you can't be bothered to work things out? That's what you do? What the hell is *wrong* with everyone when they think they can just fucking *walk away* so easily?"

His voice escalated and escalated and then he sat down hard on the sofa and before he could help himself wrapped his hands across the back of his head and leaned forward and gulped in deep breaths, as if he'd just experienced an abrupt change of altitude.

And then leaned back and closed his eyes. And tried to steady his temper and the beating of his heart.

From the stillness in the room, he figured he'd done what he was certain few men had ever succeeded in doing: he'd shocked Rebecca Corday into silence.

What the hell had just happened? One moment he was happier than he could remember being. The next he was blown sky high and spiraling through the air, falling and falling and falling, falling with the full consciousness of how sickeningly painful the landing would be.

He should have said it. He should have said it.

But Britt had her fears, and he had his. His started with "L."

And the irony was that probably the very thing that allowed them to see each other clearly was the thing that doomed them. They could use each other's wounds to administer killing blows.

His whole body almost rang with shock, as if he'd finally landed after being blown sky high.

"I'm sorry if I scared your friend off."

He opened one eye and then the other and looked at Rebecca balefully. She was now sitting across from him.

Rebecca sounded gentle, even contrite. Somewhat. And she did look concerned, though shot through that concern was a peculiar anxiety. The words "your friend" were purely tactical and so very Rebecca. An attempt to diminish. She seemed incapable of being anything other than strategic.

"Don't flatter yourself, Rebecca," he said, and his voice sounded odd in his own ears. Frayed and dull. "She's not my 'friend,' and you didn't scare her. She scared herself off."

Though he *had* chucked the metaphorical lit match right into that gasoline.

So he supposed he'd helped scare Britt off, too.

He closed his eyes briefly again. He wanted to be alone. But he couldn't just tell her to scram.

"Let's read lines," she suggested softly.

He opened his eyes. He was a grown-ass man, and he'd endured misery before, and he knew surefire ways to at least forget it.

He took a deep breath and looked down at lines he now could have recited in his sleep. But he knew he would automatically deliver them with a subtle difference with an actress of Rebecca's caliber.

Acting had always been his escape. And for a little while, via the magic of someone else's words, he could become someone else.

Someone who for the duration of a script didn't have to feel the burning crater in the center of him that felt like a Britt-ectomy.

J. T. awoke smiling. He stretched and reflexively reached for Britt.

He grabbed air, and caught himself just before he toppled from the sofa onto the floor.

He went motionless, surprised. And then he groaned and flung an arm over his eyes as memory and awareness sifted in.

It was the day after a major skirmish and smoke was still rising from the battlefield.

He kicked off the sheet he'd dragged over his body, then swiftly, sloppily folded it up, and padded into the kitchen to make himself a cup of coffee. He wanted to get out of here before Rebecca woke up. His body, fit though it was, thought he was nuts to be spending more than one night on his hastily purchased Home Depot sofa, and he stretched and his spine cracked.

He paused to peek in on her, because she'd left the bedroom door ajar. He knew that was an invitation but he quite simply didn't care. She was sleeping like she always had, with her long limbs flung out like an invasive kudzu vine, trying to grab all she could even in sleep. She was wearing an eye mask, even though it was black dark at night here in the woods. She'd taken the liberty of stripping off his pillowcase and replacing it with a silk one to protect her famous head of hair, lest a single one of the strands break. She had a shampoo contract now, too.

J. T. knew aaaaaaall too well the staggering minutiae that went into maintaining Rebecca Corday. He knew a twinge of sympathy. But that was her trip, not his.

He closed his eyes as if he could make her vanish that way.

Opened them again and damn it, there she was.

He backed away and reflexively reached down to pet Phillip. But he wasn't at Britt's house, which was where Phillip was.

And a fresh tide of fury and regret and disbelief washed in. He didn't want to text Rebecca and run the risk of waking her up. He scrawled a note on the back of the pizza receipt and affixed it to the refrigerator with the bottle-opener magnet.

I have a meeting with the location manager for The Rush. Back before noon.

And he bolted from the house. Getting back to work was what he needed, because he needed to do something he was good at, and relationships clearly weren't it.

Two days without sleep combined with righteous indignation and savage hurt paradoxically made Britt feel almost euphoric. It was like anesthesia. Or maybe one of those drugs people took at raves to make themselves really happy and affectionate and carefree.

Not that she'd ever taken one. She'd only heard. Probably Greta over at the New Age store would know.

She breezed into work only a few minutes late and seized her order pad, and Sherrie swooped her into a bosomy hug before Britt could back out of it. She squeezed her for a time while Britt endured it stoically.

Glenn and Giorgio were behind the grill watching this carefully.

"Oh, honey. You look like you didn't sleep at all, and not in a good way. How did your conversation with J. T. go?"

"Oh, that? Him? Yeah, we decided it's over," she said brightly.

A look of alarm ping-ponged between Sherrie and Glenn.

There was a cautious pause. "Are you sure you're fit for work? You look a little . . ."

She really must look terrible. It was *very* unlike Sherrie to be diplomatic.

"I'm fine. I mean, the thing reached its natural conclusion. We talked about it. It was just one of those things." She gave a great shrug with one shoulder. "We had fun, it's done. Ha ha! That *totally* rhymed."

Three parallel lines of concern etched themselves deeply into Sherrie's forehead. "You are a *bad* liar. Have you looked in a mirror today? Did you sleep at *all* last night?"

Britt laughed merrily, and a little too loudly. "I can't remember, but I'm fine, honestly. I have my health. I have my friends. I really don't care what he does or who he does it with or where he does it or what he . . . yeah."

She'd lost track of her prepositions. And the question. And the sentence.

She *might* actually be a little bit tired.

"Hmm. Where is Rebecca Corday?" Sherrie asked carefully.

"At his house. And on a billboard out on the highway. She took great pains to tell me that, too."

Sherrie hissed in a long breath as if someone had stepped hard on a sore toe.

And Britt needed to pivot away from that expression of sympathy lest it cut her in two.

She accepted two hot plates from Giorgio and frisked over to a customer, and turned a smile on the diner that had them leaning back in shock at its brilliant ferocity.

Yep, she was *fine*.

J. T. returned from his meeting with the location manager in a marginally better mood, because *The Rush* was going to be exactly the kind of work he loved: gritty, real, intense, nuanced. He'd be proud of it, no matter how many viewers they managed to capture. They'd do some more walking of the Hellcat Canyon and surrounding hills and peaks in the days ahead, planning scenes, and he liked playing a pivotal role in that. He already had more meetings in his calendar. Filming wouldn't start in earnest for a couple of months, some of it here in Gold Country, some of it in Los Angeles.

For the first time in weeks he wished he could hurry up time. Clearly he sucked at downtime.

He pulled up in front of his house just before noon, suddenly wondering whether he was hallucinating from lack of sleep.

Because a shiny blue Porsche was parked on the side road. In his spot.

He pulled the truck in behind it and stared, oddly jarred.

He realized it was the first Porsche he'd seen in all of Hellcat Canyon.

And then he suddenly knew exactly who it belonged to.

He got out and slammed the door of his truck, took the steps two at a time and let himself into his house.

"What the actual *fu* . . ."

Franco Francone was sitting on his couch, arms flung over the back of it, beer in his hand, grinning and looking right at home.

He also looked unforgivably, blackly amused.

The silence was tense.

"You gave him one of my *beers*?" J. T. said to Rebecca, finally.

This made Franco laugh.

"Why, Johnny? Are you worried he's going to be like Per . . . per . . . the woman who went to hell you told me about?" Rebecca asked.

"Persephone?" he and Franco said at the same time.

Franco shot him a secret half smile.

Because Franco naturally got the joke and thought it was funny.

Franco had gone to Harvard. He was educated up to his eyeballs. Basically the opposite of J. T.

But both he and J. T. were readers of everything.

They couldn't be more opposite on paper, but there had been dozens of reasons the two of them had clicked as friends.

Franco had been with Rebecca for about four months when Rebecca, in inimitable Rebecca fashion, had decided she wanted J. T., the bigger star, the hotter guy, at least in Hollywood commodity terms, and J. T. had leaped at the chance.

Franco had never really forgiven J. T. for this. Not all the way, anyway. It was more about the one-upmanship than the girl, J. T. suspected. Franco couldn't stand to lose any more than J. T. could.

Then again, J. T. wasn't sure if he'd ever really forgiven himself.

He suspected that, over the years, Franco had figured

out that J. T. had done him a favor when it came to "stealing" Rebecca from him. Not that he'd ever admit that.

"What is it with you two?" Rebecca groused. "Are you sure it's masculine to know that sort of thing? The Persephone nonsense?"

She was trying to make it sound like teasing but it emerged as peevish.

"I bet you every penny I got Sir Anthony Underhill knows who Persephone is, Rebecca. Which should be all the answer you need," J. T. said.

Franco laughed at that.

Rebecca, truthfully, looked more relaxed than she probably should, given the presence of two former lovers, one of whom had slightly bloodied the other over her. Then again, drama was her medium, the way the sea was the medium for saltwater fish.

"What the hell *are* you doing here, Franco?" J. T. asked.

"An old school friend of mine owns a winery about thirty miles up the road and I was heading up this way for Nicasio's wedding anyway, so I thought I'd come check this area out and surprise you. And *who* should open the door but Rebecca. You should have *seen* the look on her face. For that matter, you should see the look on yours right now."

"How did you know where I was living?" He was pretty sure he already knew the answer to that.

"I just asked the nice lady at the Angel's Nest, where I thought I'd try to get a room, and she just assumed we were 'blood brothers' in real life." He put "blood brothers" in air quotes. "Told me you bought the 'old Greenleaf place.'" He put the "old Greenleaf place" in air quotes, too. "Told me about all the hiking trails and the Eternity Oak. That sounds like one scary damn tree, by the way. She hasn't watched our show, but she sure Googled it. We had a great chat. She's a hoot."

J. T. sighed. He really wasn't going to hold it against Rosemary, who couldn't in a million years fathom the dynamic between the three people in this room. She quite simply wouldn't have time for it. The people in this town, most of them anyway, were frankly too nice and too decent and too busy to imagine such useless complexity.

"See anything interesting on the way into town, Franco?" Rebecca asked slyly.

"Of course," he indulged. "Saw your billboard out there on the highway, Rebecca," Franco said, taking a sip of his beer. "Nothing scarier than a twenty-foot-tall Rebecca Corday."

She laughed, clearly thoroughly pleased.

"So what's going on here, kids? Is this the resurrection of Rebeccasee?" Franco looked from one to the other. "Gonna go carve your initials on the Eternity Oak, be bound together forever?"

J. T. and Rebecca remained silent.

"Underhill know you're here, Becks?" Franco tried.

More silence.

"Tennessee would just kick Underhill's ass if he showed up. Isn't that right, J. T.?" said the guy who got his ass kicked by J. T.

"Oh, sure," J. T. said easily. "If he took a swing at me. But I can kick it fancier than ever now. I have a black belt."

Franco could fight well enough but he was just too damn lazy to go through all that trouble to get a black belt. And that was one of the main differences between them. J. T. had always tried harder. At everything. And he was always willing to be meaner, like a cornered wild animal.

But Franco was slyer.

"Where's the pretty woman in those TMZ photos, J. T.? You have her stashed here somewhere, too? Was she happy to meet a big star like Rebecca?"

That was some fine slyness right there.

"That woman is none of your business, Francone."

He'd slapped those words down like a guillotine.

Damn.

Franco was smart and J. T. had been a little too quick on the draw there.

Franco studied him, musingly.

J. T. met his gaze unblinkingly. Staring a threat.

"She's a waitress at the Misty Cat Cavern in downtown Hellcat Canyon," Rebecca supplied blithely into the silence, although her voice sounded a little strained. "I met her. But J. T. won't tell me anything else about her."

"That . . ." Franco mused, "*is* interesting."

Franco knew J. T. pretty well.

"Let's all go down to the Misty Cat and show everyone we're friends," Rebecca said suddenly. "I could use a bite to eat."

By *bite* she literally meant a bite. It was about all she would eat.

Unless she took a bite out of Britt, which was what J. T. was worried about.

And by *everyone* she apparently meant the world. Rebecca assumed the entire world was documenting and interpreting her every move.

She wasn't far wrong.

"Worst. Idea. Ever," J. T. said unequivocally. "And I've already eaten. Eat something here before you head out, Becks. There's celery in the bin."

Franco yawned and stretched. "I'm pretty hungry. While you two are thinking about it, I think I'll just go down to the Misty Cat and get my own table."

He stood and grabbed his keys and was out the door in a flash.

Bastard.

"You should open with 'I have a Porsche,' Franco," J. T. shouted after him. "She'll love that."

Fuck, fuck, *fuck*. He froze indecisively, staring after Franco.

There was no hope for it. He swiped at the bowl where he usually tossed his truck keys.

It was empty.

"Where the hell are my keys?"

"Right here." Rebecca dangled them. "Let's go get some brunch, J. T."

He nearly groaned. Rebecca was a liability. He could hardly abandon the highest paid actress in the world, both because of the script, and because, like it or not, he had manners.

But J. T.'s reflex was to be wherever Britt was.

He snatched the keys from Rebecca and bolted out the door, and she followed him.

Franco walked into the Misty Cat Cavern grinning as though walking into the Misty Cat Cavern was the best thing that had ever happened to him. And paused in the doorway, as if all the bemused diners who paused to stare at him were red-carpet photographers.

He'd never been subtle or shy about making an entrance.

Sherrie froze where she was hovering near the grill.

And then a smile split her face and she all but skated over to him across the clean linoleum floor.

She blasted him with her usual warmth and welcome. "Oh, my *goodness*, you're Mr. Franco Francone! You must be in town to visit Mr. McCord! Gosh, I hope you'll sign a menu for my little granddaughter. She's *such* a fan of your show. As am I, hon."

"I am, indeed, Franco Francone. McCord speaks very highly of this establishment. And to whom do I have the *extreme* pleasure of speaking?"

"Well, I'm Sherrie Harwood, and the pleasure is all

mine, Mr. Francone. My husband, Glenn, and I own this fine establishment. If you come with me we'll give you our best table." She winked, given that the tables were all Formica, approximately thirty years old, and came in two sizes. It was pretty much a table democracy at the Misty Cat.

She got him settled in and waylaid Britt, who was darting across the room with two plates in her arms.

"You got yourself another famous handsome customer, Britt. Friend of J. T.'s."

Britt paused and looked in the direction of Sherrie's chin nudge.

Boy, Sherrie wasn't kidding about the handsome part. Francone was in jeans and a white button-down shirt. He was unequivocally gorgeous, with waving black hair, deep-set melting-chocolate eyes, and cheekbones so artfully chiseled they wouldn't look out of place in the Louvre.

She wondered if Rebecca had collected one of *his* shirts.

"You don't have to go wait on him, Britt," Sherrie whispered. "If it's too . . . you know . . ."

"That man is *not* J. T. I'll be just fine. "

Britt was distantly aware that every time she heard the name *J. T.,* it was like a tiny mallet was driving a tiny tack into her heart.

"Ookaaay," Sherrie said dubiously. "But if—"

But Britt had dropped off her orders with a pair of diners and zipped over to Franco's table.

"I'm Britt," she said briskly. "I'll be your server. What can we get started for you?"

"Well, hello Britt. I'm Franco Francone," he said to Britt. "Maybe you've seen *Blood Brothers*?"

He clapped his menu shut, leaning back, and smiled at her as if *she* was the best thing to happen to him all day and was positive he was the best thing to ever happen to *her.* She could imagine this pretty effectively captivated a large portion of the female population.

She, of course, only knew Franco Francone as one of the stars of the "Controversy" section of J. T.'s Wikipedia page.

"So I'm told by every single person in this place, Mr. Francone, and if they didn't tell me, all those heads craning in your direction might be a hint. Forgive me, but I never did watch your show. What can I get for you?"

"J. T. said I should open with 'I have a Porsche.' which must mean that won't impress you in the least. Because he's not going to give me any kind of advantage with someone as gorgeous as you."

J. T. Tap. A little spike right into her heart.

She was immune to Franco Francone, though.

Well, mostly.

"Isn't that cute, Mr. Francone. I'm guessing he knows you pretty well." She said this ironically.

She realized too late that Sherrie may have had a point. She might not actually be equal to a conversation that featured the name *J. T.* She could feel herself weakening. As if she was actually losing blood with every mention of his name.

"What impresses you, Britt?" Franco asked.

"Customers who eat fast and leave big tips."

He laughed. "J. T. and I are friends. And I get the sense that you're loyal, Britt, which is a great quality. Maybe my favorite quality in a person. But right now you're being loyal to a guy who's probably negotiating a reunion with his ex-girlfriend. And I hate to say it, but Rebecca always gets what she wants."

He said this almost apologetically. But grimly, too.

He must have seen something in her expression then, because he leaned back suddenly.

"Whoa," he said. "You're even scarier than Rebecca when you're mad."

"You're a bit confused, Mr. Francone," she said smoothly. "I frankly don't care about any of that or either of them. I do care about what you might want for breakfast."

"Good to hear. Want to go for a ride in my Porsche after breakfast?"

"I'm not a golden retriever, Mr. Francone. A *car* ride doesn't excite me. What can I get for you?"

"Then let me take you to dinner. Because I already like you. And I think you're stunning. J. T. always did have a flawless eye for singular beauty. No wonder he was so closemouthed about you."

Singular? She almost snorted. "Everyone likes me, Mr. Francone. Being likeable is a minimum requirement of my job. I'm aware I have a certain appeal. And I'm not certain I like *you*."

He was smiling at her in earnest now, a real smile. "You will be by the end of dinner."

And for a mad millisecond she wavered. She suspected an evening with him would be entertaining, or at least yield a story to tell later, if nothing else.

"It might make J. T. *su*-ffer," he wheedled on a singsong.

It was the wrong thing to say.

She wasn't like him. She wasn't like any of them, probably J. T. included.

And she'd already done her part to make J. T. suffer; of that she was pretty sure, and that could be part of her anger this morning.

She was really pretty bloody angry at herself.

"I don't play games, Mr. Francone. It's boring and chickenshit and the eggs Benedict are the special today. What can I get for you?"

Franco was looking at her with some astonishment.

"I'll have the eggs Benedict," he said humbly.

"Good choice, Mr. Francone."

She pivoted sharply and found herself eye level with a T-shirt-clad wall of a chest.

She looked abruptly up into a pair of blue eyes rimmed in red and shadowed in mauve. Little did she know, it was a bit like looking in a mirror.

Her heart felt like it literally did a backflip.

For a second neither of them spoke.

She was afraid to breathe, because she might inhale the scent of him, and that was her aphrodisiac, and she'd probably melt into a tired puddle on the floor.

"His real name is Ed, you know. Not Franco. Ed *O'Malley*. He's Irish," J. T. finally said.

That was quite the non sequitur.

Franco shot J. T. a dirty look.

"Is it?" Britt said sweetly. "It suits him. Handsome and exotic. We can't all have three names to choose from. Sometimes you just have to make one up."

Franco was grinning at this. "You heard the lady, J. T. It suits me. Handsome and exotic."

And suddenly, like the back peeling off a decal, Rebecca Corday appeared from behind J. T.

Britt was badly startled. Rebecca had probably been turned sidewise, Britt thought. The woman was about as thin as a dime when in profile.

Rebecca slinked into the chair across from Franco, plucked up the menu and fanned it open in her long fingers. Light bounced from her flawless manicure.

J. T. remained standing.

He'd actually *brought* that woman back into the Misty Cat?

"This is a rare occasion, Britt," Franco told her. "Rebecca eats only every couple of weeks. Like a boa constrictor."

"Ha ha." Rebecca didn't look the least bit amused.

"We're all out of mice today." Brit said this as politely as possible. Suddenly it felt like a hot little fist had taken up residence behind her eyes. "I can go see how we're fixed for rats, however."

And here she and J. T. locked eyes in a gaze so hard, steely, and complex it could have supported a rush-hour commute.

"I'm not hungry," he said. Though she hadn't asked him what he wanted.

He didn't sit down. Even when Franco pushed a chair out for him with his foot.

Rebecca was studying Britt and J. T. very closely. As if she thought Britt intended to mount J. T. right here at the table. She remembered what J. T. had said about Rebecca hunting down happiness like an anthropologist. It looked as though she wished she had a magnifying glass to help her study what J. T. saw in Britt.

If Rebecca came at her, Britt thought she might be able to swiftly tie Rebecca's skinny limbs into a knot and immobilize her.

Rebecca put the menu down. "I'll have the veggie burger." She smiled brightly.

Britt tore her eyes away from J. T.'s. And it almost literally felt like tearing, that was how reluctant they were to leave him.

"I'm sorry . . . Miss Corday, is it?" Britt said. It was petty. But it felt really good to say it.

Rebecca's smile congealed.

"Could you please point out the veggie burger on the menu?" Britt knew damn well there wasn't one.

Rebecca's smile became more fixed and she tilted her head. "I'm sure you all could whip something up like that, *caaan't* you?" She was all dazzling, melting sweetness and the inflection was very "pretty please?"

"Rebecca . . ." J. T.'s voice was a slow, ground-out threat. "Pick something else."

It was like he hadn't even spoken.

"If you would be so kind as to go and ask your cook . . . Britt, right?" Rebecca's voice was velvet and her eyes were flints. "Tell him it's for me. Tell him he might have seen my billboard out on the highway."

She and Rebecca smiled at each other in a silent yet beaming showdown of mutual loathing.

"All right," Britt said pleasantly, finally. "I'll just go do that."

She was looking forward to it.

She whipped around so fast the breeze she created almost yanked the menu out of Rebecca's hands and stalked over to Giorgio.

Sherrie grabbed her by the elbow and halted her. "I'll say it again. You don't have to wait on them, Britt," she said slowly. It was just shy of a command. "I'm not sure you should be allowed near sharp implements today."

"I said I don't care," she said a little too loudly.

Sherrie's eyes went wide.

"Oh, my gosh, Sherrie. I'm so, so sorry, I don't know how that happened. I mean, I don't care," she said, in her new serene voice. She seemed to have lost the ability to modulate volume or tone. "It's not a problem. Besides . . . I could take her."

This she muttered so blackly that Giorgio surreptitiously slid his knife block a little further out of reach.

"Atta girl," Glenn said. Glenn clearly thought suffering built character.

Sherrie shot him a quelling look, and he shrugged. "My money's on Britt. I think she can take that skinny thing, too. And J. T. doesn't look too delighted to be in her company."

J. T. was almost comically glowering. If he were a cartoon, a fluffy black cloud would be parked right over his head.

But he finally lowered himself into a chair across from Franco, aware, probably, that he was more conspicuous standing than sitting.

"It will be over soon enough," Britt said. "They'll be gone. Everything comes to an end eventually, right? Everything in life is ephemeral, right? *Tempus fugit?*"

This earned her three concerned frowns, one each from Sherrie, Glenn, and Giorgio.

She ignored them and handed over Franco's tag. "Giorgio, Mr. Francone would like the eggs Benedict, and Ms. Corday would like a veggie burger."

And then she waited with held-breath glee for the anticipated response from Giorgio.

He didn't disappoint. He uttered his first and possibly final complete sentence of the day.

And Britt whooshed back to the table, smiling as though he'd handed her a pearl.

"Ms. Corday, I asked Giorgio about the veggie burger," she said politely.

"What did he say?"

"Are you seriously fucking kidding me."

Rebecca froze. And then she turned two colors, white then red, both of them furious. "*I* . . . what . . . you . . ."

Britt patiently recited, "He said, 'Are you seriously fu—'"

"I heard you," Rebecca said testily.

"You did ask her, Rebecca," J. T. said. Both J. T. and Franco were wide-eyed with glee and holding their breath.

"Giorgio is a little bit temperamental," Britt said serenely. "All artists are. You're welcome to choose something else."

They stared at each other.

"I think I'll choose to eat somewhere else," Rebecca said tersely.

"*Excellent* choice," Britt purred, wondering why Rebecca Corday didn't employ professional tasters like a despot king who feared poisoning. She was so thoroughly unpleasant.

Rebecca slipped out of her chair and stalked out of the Misty Cat, leaving a trail of wide eyes in her wake.

And Britt watched her go and was reminded that oh yes, indeed, she did love to win.

The sudden absolute silence made Franco look up from his phone, which is where he'd retreated while this was going on. Probably this nastiness was all par for the course in Hollywood.

"*You* and Becks can go," he said to J. T. "I'm sticking around for my eggs Benedict."

J. T. ignored him. "Britt," J. T. said with what sounded like extreme patience "May I have a word?"

She balked. And then: "I can give you one minute. I have a job to do."

He'd already scoped out a nook on the other side of the counter behind the row of napkin holders and he beckoned her over here.

"I want you to know that I didn't want to bring her in here, Britt. I would never do that. It was *not* my idea."

"That's okay, J. T.," she said serenely. "Bring her anywhere you want. I don't care what you do or who you do it with. Go wherever you want. Do whatever you want."

He frowned. "What's the matter with your voice? You drink your breakfast?"

She sucked in an impatient breath. "What *are* you doing here?"

"I followed Franco in here because he was . . . determined to meet you. And I know him pretty well. "

"God. The two of you are children."

"Yep," J. T. admitted grimly.

"You should know he asked me out," she added.

J. T. whirled on Franco. "Bastard, I *knew*—"

Franco was scrolling through his e-mails on his phone and leisurely chewing an English muffin Sherrie had apparently just brought to him. He must have felt the waves of heat from J. T.'s glare. He looked up and gave a little wave.

She was aware that pretty much everyone in the diner was watching them, if not overtly, then covertly, in the reflections in the sides of napkin holders and the backs of spoons and the like.

"I'm not going to go out with him. I don't want to go out with him. Do you really think I'm that fickle? Do you really think I can just be *had* that easily by any gorgeous man?" She was aware her voice was rising.

He closed his eyes briefly. He drew in a breath that made it sound like he was trying to suck patience from the air. "No," he said, evenly. "No, sweetheart. I know you can't just be had. For God's sake." His voice almost cracked there. "I know how lucky I've been."

Oh, God. That word. It threatened to burn away the lovely, numbing righteous fog of anger.

"Then *why* did you follow Franco here?" Her voice was threatening to crack.

He pushed his hair out of his eyes. Struggling, again, for words.

"I guess my instinct was just . . . from the moment I saw you, Britt, right here at the Misty Cat . . . to fight off all other contenders. And to just . . . be wherever you are."

He began to blur before her eyes. Because she was about to cry.

"Britt . . ." he said urgently, softly. Stepping toward her. "Sweet—"

"*Don't* call me sweetheart." She swiped viciously at her traitorous eyes.

He went still. As if she'd shoved a knife right in.

And she saw something hard and resolute pass over his features.

Before they went carefully neutral.

"I'm leaving for Napa for Nicasio's wedding this afternoon. I'll be gone for a few days."

"I know," she said. "Back to your world."

She could have sworn he was counting to ten silently in his head before he spoke.

"There's only one world, Britt. Some of us live in all of it instead of one tiny corner of it."

That was quite the swipe.

"The three of you should have a *wonderful* time," she said with a sort of savage sweetness. "I have to go, J. T."

"For a run?" he said brutally.

She growled and whipped around again and stalked back to the grill.

CHAPTER 19

An hour later Britt was hurling her purse onto her sofa and plopping herself down in front of her laptop. She glared at the wall for a moment, and absently bent to pet Phillip for a while.

And then she almost reflexively called her sister.

Laine answered right away. Her familiar face filled the screen.

"Are you okay, Bip? Shouldn't you be working right now?"

"Glenn sent me home."

"Yikes. Because of your eye infection?"

"What the—my *eye* infection?"

"Remember when you used that five-year-old mascara when you shouldn't have and got an infection and your eye swelled shut and was all oozy? That's kind of what you look like right now."

Maybe she should have looked in the mirror before she called Laine.

Glenn had sent her home out of pity and told her to sleep the rest of the day. She could pick up a night shift to make up the hours.

"Wow. That's pretty bad. I haven't looked in the mirror yet today. "

And then a lightbulb appeared to go on in Laine's head. Her eyes went wide.

"Oh, shit. You've been crying. What *happened*?"

She paused.

"It's over with J. T."

Laine literally clapped her hands to her face. "Nooooo! *Whyyyyyy?*"

"We had a big fight. And he told me to just go." Which was technically true, but it left out a whole lot of stuff. What she wanted right now was sympathy and vindication.

"Oh, Bippy. I'm so sorry. I thought it might be just a fling, but look at you! You're clearly torn up. Are you . . . were you . . . in *love* with him?"

"In *love* with him?" she spat scornfully. "Don't be ridiculous! He can go to hell!"

"But are you in *love* with him?"

"I don't care what he does! Or *who* he does it to! Or when he does it!"

"Soooo . . . in other words, you're in love with him."

Britt moaned and dropped her face into her hands. "I didn't *know* I was until it was over," Britt all but wailed. "Or maybe I did and just didn't want to think about it because I was scared of what would happen next."

The sex had been all crashing cymbals and crescendos, it nearly obscured the reason for it: the humble, intimate little offerings of a broken house in the woods surrounded by blue-eyed Mary's, a fixed porch, a half-dead azalea. One soul striving to be worthy of another. Longing to give to each other what they needed most. A coded way of saying, "I *know* you. Your happiness is mine."

They'd been falling in love from the moment he'd walked into the Misty Cat.

Although J. T. likely didn't know it, wouldn't say it, and probably didn't believe it. And she didn't know how on earth that would ever change.

"Did you tell him you were in in love with him? Is that what ended it?" Laine wanted to know.

"No," she said sullenly. "Of course I didn't say that. How stupid would *that* be?"

"Yeah, love is *super* dumb," Laine mocked. Albeit gently.

Britt snorted.

Her sister's brow furrowed. "But you have to catch me up, Bip. Is that what the argument was about? The fact that he's not in love with *you*? You know he's supposedly never said that word to anyone."

"I've read the articles, too," Britt said testily. "All he said was, and I quote, 'I like what we have. I don't want it to end.'"

"Well, who wouldn't like no-strings sex! I think that's man-speak for I don't want to think about the future ever and don't make me talk about my feelings but I want to keep doing you until I don't want to anymore."

"*Right?*" Britt lapped up the vindication. "And while we were arguing about this outside his house, you know who was inside?"

"Who?"

She paused strategically. "Rebecca Corday."

Laine's mouth dropped open. "Hold the phone! Rebecca *freaking* Corday? His *ex*?"

"Yeah," she said. "She just showed up out of the blue yesterday and she spent the night at his *house*."

Laine was frozen. She was clearly impressed with the awfulness of this. "Whoa. That's pretty bad."

"*Right?*"

"She's going to that wedding in Napa, too. Is she his date?"

Holy shit. That was a horrible thought.

"I don't know," Britt whispered. "He said he was going alone so . . . I don't think so."

"But . . . wait, Bip. Hasn't he been staying with you? Where were you when she was staying the night at his house?"

She hesitated. "At my house."

Damn.

Laine was pretty smart and she knew Britt all too well. She'd pick up on that hesitation.

Laine tipped her head and studied Britt in silence.

And then:

"Were you being pigheaded, Bip?" she said suspiciously.

"Way to be supportive, Lainie."

"But you are. You're pigheaded. I mean, it's a good thing, too. You never quit. You also weren't always the best at bending. Or admitting when you were wrong. *Super* obnoxious quality, by the way."

Britt opened her mouth. A dry squeak of indignation emerged.

"I have a hunch you're being pigheaded somewhere in this situation. I think you're leaving a bunch of stuff out. Did he *invite* her to stay with him?"

"No, she just showed up out of the blue with a script of a movie that she wants J. T. for, and she's on her way to Napa, but—"

"Did he apologize to you for the unscheduled interruption in your, I dunno, fling? Affair? Sex-a-thon?"

She hesitated. "Yes."

"Did he try to explain what she was doing there?"

"Yes."

"Do you believe him?"

She hesitated. "Mostly," Britt hedged. "Okay, I think I do."

"Pigheaded," Laine said triumphantly.

Maybe it had been a mistake to call Laine.

"But she's his ex. And how the hell can I compete with Rebecca Corday, Laine?"

Laine, the celebrity lover, was clearly struggling with this concept, too. "Frankly, I don't know how you could *resist* competing with her, because that's who you are. Is that what you and J. T. were fighting about? Do you think he wants her back?"

"He says no. But I mean, she is who she is. There's a freaking billboard of her on the highway right here. And I think she wants *him* back. She's dangling a part he really, really wants. And Franco Francone says—"

Laine held up her hand. "Tell me you did not just say the name *Franco Francone* in that offhand fashion."

"He showed up in Hellcat Canyon, too, and he said Rebecca always gets what she wants. He has a little experience with her, as I'm sure you know."

Now Laine's eyes were narrowed. "*Franco Francone?* I'm starting to think you're making all of this up."

"I swear I'm not! Franco's a bit player in this story, so pay attention, Laine."

"Fine. Okay, think of all the exes *you'd* never want back, Britt. Do you think J. T. would play you? Or is he a good guy?"

Britt drew in a breath. J. T., the porch fixer, the cat feeder, red hot lover, the tender, funny honest guy—

"Yeah," she said thickly. "He's a good guy."

Totally inadequate words to describe J. T.

"Then . . . I mean . . . okay, what's *really* bugging you, Bip?"

Nervousness made Britt's fingertips go icy. She felt like a tree forced to suddenly grow a new branch. There was no precedent in their relationship for what she wanted to say to Laine. But she needed to say it because she wanted to hear what Laine had to say.

She cleared her throat. "When we were arguing he said . . ." She pulled in a fortifying breath. ". . . he said he didn't think Rebecca was the problem. He said I was looking for a convenient excuse. To run. Because . . . because you know . . ." She swallowed. And then she got the words out with admirable steadiness. ". . . because of . . . Jeff. What happened with Jeff."

Laine went still.

Her breath seemed to be held.

"Are you?" Laine said tentatively, her voice a near whisper, so gently. And Laine was never gentle with her. It was like she was trying not to spook a forest creature. "Looking for an excuse to run?"

Britt swiped at tears that were now streaming. "I don't know. Maybe? Probably, yeah. It's hard, Laine. It's been hard. Being scared is not *normal* for me."

"I know, Bip. You were always fearless. The bravest person I know."

"I'm starting to wonder, though, Laine, about my definition of brave. I was able to talk myself into this thing with J. T. to begin with because I knew he wouldn't be around for long. And now it's like . . . if I catch a whiff of pain I want to head it off at the pass. I want to get *it* before it gets me. And this feels like the most scared I've ever been, somehow. More scared than with Jeff."

Laine took this in thoughtfully.

"I think I get it," Laine said after a moment. "But I think maybe fear as a *concept* is your enemy. Not J. T. And maybe you're this scared because he means that much to you."

Britt liked the sound of this. But she had no idea what to do about it.

Laine inhaled and swiped her hands over her face in frustration. "*Argh.* I hate it when you cry."

"Me, too!" Britt said.

They both laughed sniffly laughs, and Laine swiped tears out of her eyes.

They were quiet together again.

"I have to say, though, that it sounds like J. T. knows you pretty well. Do you think he's hurting, too?"

"Maybe," she said begrudgingly. "Probably," she allowed a second later, more faintly, and guiltily, because the idea of him hurting brought with it a fresh wave of pain. "His mom died when he was ten. I'm beginning to think we're both bad pickers when it comes to relationships. He picked someone who'd bail on him again."

"Poor J. T." Laine almost whispered this.

"And you know what he said? He said his impulse was to be wherever I was."

"Oh my God." Laine's hand went up to her mouth. "That is about the sweetest thing I ever heard, Britt."

"I know. He said it while Rebecca Corday waited for him outside the diner."

Laine sighed in great resignation. "Have to tell you, I don't know what to make of that. I wouldn't want to be him right now, that's for sure. I like things to be pretty simple. His life sounds like it's never *not* complicated."

"He says I can either believe him or not about Rebecca."

Laine snorted. "Easy for him to say."

"Yeah, well. I think once he's back in his own milieu at that wedding in Napa he'll realize he's just been in a sort of dream world here. So as of now . . . the thing with us . . . pretty sure it's over."

Saying these words aloud felt like flagellating herself. And to give Laine a chance to dismiss them as hogwash.

Laine was thoughtfully quiet while Britt sniffled.

And then Laine sighed. "I don't know what to tell you, except . . . you'll probably survive."

Britt was silent. "Wow. That is one stirring speech, Patton."

"Listen to me." Laine was a little pissed off. "Britt, you're really freaking smart, but you're so proud and you shut people out when you're hurt and scared and sometimes you *need* a little outside perspective. Not everything is in your control and life is not a test that comes with a Scantron and a number-two pencil. It's okay to feel a whole bunch of feelings. All that means is you *have feelings*. Feelings are good. Remember in cheerleading practice? You kind of just learn how to fall. And falling gets easier every time. You survived Jeff. You'll survive this. Maybe you have to fall over and over again in order to master it. Maybe that's all life is. Maybe that's all this is."

Britt was astonished.

"That's a much better speech," she allowed after a moment.

And Laine actually sounded a little like J. T., but Britt wasn't going to tell her that.

Laine laughed.

"I don't want you to be hurt or scared, Bippy. It kills me. But I also don't want you to think this is the end of the world. And if you really do love him, maybe you should try to get him back. I've never known you to run away from a challenge, and I can't imagine you can't take Rebecca Corday with one hand tied behind your back, blindfolded."

"I totally could."

"But if you're still too scared, then maybe that's something you just have to wait out. Maybe you're not ready. And if it's really over, you'll probably survive to get back up on another horse one day. That's all I'm sayin'." She swiveled her head and bellowed, "MUFFIN!"

Britt gave a start.

"Crap! Gotta go, Britt! The cat is tearing around the house. I think he has a dingleberry. I have to grab him before he gets up on our comforter. Love you! Alley-oop!"

The screen went black.

Britt couldn't bring herself to say Alley-oop back. She didn't feel like she had the right anymore.

CHAPTER 20

A brilliant scarlet-and-purple sunset hung like bunting over a scene out of a fairy tale—or out of a Hollywood movie. Same difference this time, J. T. thought. And this particular movie had a cast of hundreds. Fairy lights twinkled in the trees surrounding them; laughing, lounging, cuddling guests clustered at tables covered in white umbrellas that bloomed like little toadstools all over the sprawling green Napa grounds. The ones who weren't at the tables were dancing or doing deals or mingling or drinking way, way too much or possibly sleeping with someone they shouldn't in one of the myriad guest cottages.

Speaking of drinking too much, Rebecca was out on the dance floor and she was drunker than he'd ever seen her. She was wearing an astonishing purple dress, very short at the hem, high in the front, scooped so low in the back the teensiest hint of butt cleavage showed. He wouldn't be surprised if half the men in the place were walking around with involuntary boners thanks to that dress.

He'd asked her to take the wheel of his truck and drive the whole way from Hellcat Canyon to San Francisco, where he'd left her to find her own way to Napa. And on that drive his wedding toast finally poured out of him. He was suddenly fucking Shakespeare. And he'd tapped it all into a draft e-mail to himself in his phone.

Rebecca wasn't happy about that at all.

And now J. T., after a lot of aggressive and mostly agreeable socializing, had finally found a spot alone at a table on the outskirts of the party. He wanted to be alone.

Guests kept finding him anyway, to pay homage.

Clyde Gordimer, an actor, said, "J. T., my man, that wedding toast . . ." He mimed a knife to the heart. "You're setting the bar too high for the rest of us."

"Ah, c'mon, Gordimer. You never met a bar you didn't love."

Gordimer laughed and fist-bumped him and strolled on.

A few minutes later, the esteemed multi-Oscared actress Dame Naomi Nivens knelt next to him and said on a hush, "J. T., I want you to know . . . that toast . . ." She clasped her hands. "The stuff of legends. If only all men thought the way you do."

"Maybe they do," J. T. told her, "and they just can't say it."

She nodded as if he was a sage and drifted off again.

The thing was, most people who knew both him and Rebecca knew that toast couldn't possibly have had anything to do with her.

Which, he suspected, was why Rebecca was drinking like a fish.

J. T. stood again and wove swiftly through the crowd to seek out a waiter and another glass of champagne. On the way he ran smack into Franco.

Who was actually with *Missy Van Cleve.*

How she'd gotten her own invite to one of the most exclusive, security-enmeshed weddings he'd ever attended, was beyond J. T., given that there was no way she was Franco's plus one. She was wearing a champagne-colored lace minidress, and, if J. T. had to guess, no underwear.

"I think you know each other," Franco said.

"Tenssesseee!" Missy was drunk. And delighted to see him.

J. T. stared at Franco for a long, incredulous time.

"What?" Franco demanded.

"For the love of *God*, man." J. T. was genuinely pained. "Really? Come on, *Edward*. Even I know you're better than this. Grow. The Fuck. Up."

He sighed gustily and took himself off back to his table.

He might be a little drunk, too.

"'Bye, Tenseeseesee!" Missy waved after him.'

He settled in again, and looked toward the bride and groom's table, smiling. They gave off their own light, those two. You couldn't help but look at them, any more than you could help but look at the moon.

And he got out his phone and flipped through to that photo of him and Britt lying on beach towels on a rock, their knees touching. Yearning tightened his gut. He'd once been that happy. He hadn't really known it. He was unconsciously seeking his own light when he looked at that photo.

Someone swiftly took the chair next to him. He looked up and he managed to get his features under control instantly.

"J. T."

"Good to see you, Phil."

Phil, as in Phil Zahn, the director of *Last Call in Purgatory*. Vigorous, a little plump, balding, eyes like lasers. Good guy and scary smart.

J. T. produced a welcoming smile, even as the words *Last Call in Purgatory* conjured such simultaneous shame and lust it was almost Pavlovian.

"Boy, your toast was a real hanky-soaker, J. T. My wife had to redo her mascara twice."

"Gratifying," J. T. said with a small smile.

"I always knew you had it in you. Listen, I know the producers shot you down in the end, J. T., but I know Al told you I want you however I can get you, J. T. Don't tell my wife. Ha ha. But when Rebecca said she wanted you to read with her for *Last Call in Purgatory,* well, funny how things change. You two have never been on film together and the publicity would be a wet dream for them. So I guess we'll see you at the studio at around one this Wednesday. And I have a favor to ask."

"Name it."

"My son-in-law is head of cardiology at the Placer County Children's Hospital. I was hoping you and Rebecca would film a PSA for them, since Hellcat Canyon is so close. That's where you've been, right? Sven Markson has put his jet at your disposal, and Rebecca told him to pick the two of you up at that little airfield outside Hellcat Canyon on Tuesday."

J. T.'s smile felt like it was going to crack. He'd love to do that PSA under *any* other conditions. He did *not* want to haul Rebecca back with him to Hellcat Canyon.

He was booked solid with lunches and dinners in San Francisco tomorrow with various friends and colleagues. At least he'd have a mostly Rebecca-free day tomorrow.

"Happy to do it. Honored to be asked," is what he told Zahn.

Phil gave him a back thump and a smile. "My wife wants to get home, so I'm outta here. Nice wedding, huh? Congrats again on that toast."

Home sounded good to J. T., too.

Wherever the hell that was now.

As if she'd heard her name, Rebecca, who had finally strolled off the dance floor, plopped down next to him, and laid her head on his shoulder. "Hi, Johnny."

He stiffened, and stretched for his drink on the table. Her head slid off gracelessly and she nearly toppled from her chair. She righted herself with a little uncharacteristic flailing.

"Enjoying yourself, Becks?" he said ironically. "Thanks for volunteering me for that PSA."

"You are SO welcome." She was too drunk to catch the irony. "Hey, J. T.? I'm ready to get back to my cottage. Will you walk me? It's getting dark and Gordon Papadakis is getting handsy out there on the dance floor. I'm afraid he plans to follow me."

J. T. stared at her. Hell.

J. T. He knew that "Wanna walk me?" for what it was. But Rebecca was who she was, and she was hammered, and he knew it probably wouldn't be safe for her to get to her cottage on her own.

So it was quite a long moment before he answered.

And then he sighed. His manners wouldn't allow him to do otherwise.

"All right. I'll walk you."

They stood. She leaned against him tipsily, struggling a bit in her towering Jimmy Choos, as they wandered the serpentine stone path that wound through the cabins, the night air velvety on the bare parts of his skin, and loneliness was practically a train whistle through his soul.

Loneliness, he decided, was a beautiful night in the company of the wrong person.

"Why so sad, Johnny?" she asked.

"Who says I'm sad?" He was surprised.

Surprised that it showed, actually. And surprised that she'd noticed.

"You're just quiet. You usually try to make me laugh. Make me laugh, Johnny."

"I don't take orders, Becks. You know that."

He said nothing else. He'd rather be alone with his thoughts of another woman than with Rebecca Corday in the flesh.

He might be the only man in the universe who would.

Fortunately it was a shortish, if dimly lit, walk.

"That was a really remarkable toast today, Johnny."

"Yep," he said shortly.

"I had no idea you knew all those things about that word you're so scared of."

"I just learned 'em," he said curtly. He suspected she knew that.

And Rebecca finally stopped walking.

"This your cottage, Becks? I'll watch you get in."

She turned to face him.

"I can make you happier," she murmured. She startled him by toppling forward and burying her face in his neck and inhaling as though she'd been missing his smell.

And then she turned her head and slid her big, pillowy billboard-worthy lips landed on his.

He was astounded. He turned his face away from her swiftly and put a hand out to keep her from toppling forward when he did that.

And he put his hands in his pockets, as if tucking them away for the night. Making his point.

They stared at each other in the dark.

"Good night, Rebecca," he said firmly.

This wholesale rejection seemed to have startled her into some semblance of sobriety.

She stared at him, wide-eyed. Then her eyes narrowed.

Because she then spun with surprising grace.

And flung her door open and closed it behind her with something like a slam.

He heaved another sigh. *Women.*

He strolled along the path back the way he came, hands in his pockets, and took the turn that would lead him back to his own cottage, a healthy distance away from hers.

He stopped abruptly.

Propped in front of one of the cottage doors was a sad

orchid in a pot. Its petals were browning. It looked just about ready to give up the ghost.

He stood in front of it for a while, as if it were a shrine.

Britt was just about to turn out her light for the evening when she heard a text chime into her phone.

Her heart leaped and she seized the phone.

It was a picture of a half-dead orchid.

Thinking of you.

Damn him. Damn him. Because she was now both laughing and crying.

She stared at it. Willing it to yield more in the way of information.

She couldn't quite decide how to reply. Or whether she should at all.

She mulled, staring out at the night, imagining him standing there, feeling alone in that crowd, alone enough to text her.

Finally, she scrolled through her emojis.

And found one of a little blue flower.

And that's what she texted back.

Hopefully he would see it as an apology. Or an olive branch.

She fell asleep holding her phone as if it were his hand, and a little crack opened up in all her fear and anger, just big enough to allow a little ray of hope to shine in.

A few hours later she woke with a start when it vibrated with an incoming text.

She stirred sleepily and glanced down eagerly.

It was from her sister.

Britt's stomach turned to ice when she read it.

I'm here if you need me, Bippy.

With a link.
To TMZ.

REBECASSEE REDUX!

John Tennessee McCord and Rebecca Corday were seen canoodling at Director Felix Nicasio's wedding in Napa this weekend while her lover of a year, Sir Anthony Underhill, films overseas, oblivious.

Good buddy Franco Francone confirms it. "They seem to be really happy together."

No.

Shit. Shit shit shit shit shit.

That son of a *bitch.*

Franco had actually given them a *quote*?

J. T. was incandescent with anger. Of course someone had managed to take photos, even though the photographers had all signed confidentiality agreements and the wedding guests were Hollywood royalty and had nothing to gain from a photo like that. Paparazzi, like mosquitoes, really could manage to squeak in anywhere. Some waiter or staff member had been bribed, probably.

There he was with Rebecca's head resting dreamily on his shoulder, as if she had every right to be there. Of course she looked dreamy. She never stopped acting, and she never stopped looking beautiful.

A split second before he'd all but flicked her off like an insect.

Worse was the second photo: the two of them, talking outside Rebecca's guest cottage, Rebecca leaning into him, as though she'd just been kissed senseless.

When he was really trying to set her drunken self back up on her feet.

Two moments that meant less than nothing to him, but taken out of context were elevated to profundity. J. T. sat down hard on the hotel bed and dropped his head into his hands and growled savagely.

Then he stood up and paced the room.

Everyone he knew would see those photos. And while the Hollywood community at large knew the drill and would take it with a grain of salt, except for maybe Sir Anthony Underhill—poor sap, his publicist was probably fielding a lot of phone calls this morning.

Britt would see those photos.

And if she was squirrelly before . . . well, that was nothing compared to how she'd feel now.

And in truth, he couldn't blame her.

Because there was no way he'd insult her with a flurry of "I can explain!" texts. At a certain point he just sounded like a guy crying wolf. She wasn't that stupid.

But he also couldn't bear sending her texts that were ignored. It *really* wasn't fun the first time.

He stared at his phone.

At the blue flower she'd given him that had sent his heart skyrocketing.

She probably felt like an ass for sending it now, and he wouldn't blame her.

He vented by sending Franco a one-word text:

Asshole.

With a link to that website.

He got a text back immediately.

I thought you and Becks were working it out.

He frowned. Was Franco being a jerk, or was he actually contrite?

He texted back.

No.

Franco texted back.

Sorry man. Worried about a particular other woman seeing it?

He stared at that a moment, wondering again whether Franco was being a jerk.

Or being a friend.

With Franco, half the time the two were synonymous.

He sat there, paralyzed with fury and panic.

Three seconds later he got another text from Franco.

If she really loves you, you can't lose her.

Wow.

Franco must have waited *years* for a chance to say that. It was almost cinematically timed. He might be Irish, but he could hold a grudge like a mafioso.

Thing was . . . J. T. might not have actually been wrong when he'd said it the first time.

Maybe he wasn't entirely clueless after all.

And if these photos shot straight to hell whatever remaining chance with Britt he had, so be it.

And he might be out of his mind. But like he'd told Britt about his truck, he didn't like to give up on things.

Maybe he should remind her she'd said the very same thing.

"This is not what I ordered," Casey said firmly, pushing away a Glennburger with cheese and bacon.

Britt had heard this sentence quite a bit all day.

"Oh, Casey, I'm so sorry."

She'd been saying *that* sentence a lot all day, too.

Britt snatched up the plate so quickly the pickle wedge rolled off the edge and thumped onto the table. As if it, too, were scrambling to get away from her.

Who knew misery came in such wide and surprising varieties and had infinite strata?

Those two photos on TMZ were all but stamped on her corneas, and it was like she was trying to see around them as she moved about the restaurant.

Just when she'd told her sister J. T. was a good guy, too.

So much for that. It was almost *hilarious* how wrong she'd been.

He might be the only guy in the world who'd drunk-texted a dying orchid to a woman.

And she might be the only woman in the world stupid enough to fall for it.

The other possibility, of course, was that she might have driven him right into the clutches of Rebecca Corday with her . . . what was the word Laine used—ah, yes: pigheadedness.

All possibilities were awful.

J. T. had made her feel like a fool, whether or not he knew he was being photographed.

She was just pivoting to dart back to the grill with the botched order in her hands when Casey clamped her hand on her arm and held her fast.

"Britt." She stared somberly into her face. Like someone about to issue a blood vow.

Britt was alarmed. "What?" she asked on a hush. "What is it?"

Casey hesitated for strategic effect.

"We are going to get drunk."

"Come again?"

"You're coming over to my house tonight, I'm going to

make margaritas, and we're going to get drunk, because that's what you need."

"Listen to her, Britt," Sherrie said, whizzing by to fetch back to the kitchen another order Britt got wrong.

Ah, hell. They were probably right.

Alcohol wouldn't kill her feelings for J. T. stone-cold dead. But it might give her a merciful reprieve from them. There would be plenty of time to feel terrible later.

Giorgio was glowering at her. She mouthed "sorry" at him.

He shook his head to and fro mournfully. As if he'd known from the moment John Tennessee McCord walked into the Misty Cat that his flawless grill coordination, the poetry of his days, would be shattered.

CHAPTER 21

Like any responsible citizen who planned to get drunk on a weeknight, Britt took the bus as close as she could get to Casey's house. To add insult to injury, she was required to sit on the bus bench featuring Rebecca Corday trailing a scarf from her flawlessly manicured fingertips. But it really enhanced her drinking mood.

She brought the now fully recovered coleus plant with her. She knew, somehow, that Casey would take good care of it. She would at least make sure that the leaves were regularly trimmed.

Britt hadn't drunk a little too much with a girlfriend in ages.

She wondered if she'd lost her knack.

Casey's house was a white cottage about twice the size of Britt's house. Its green shutters matched the tidy lawn, which, like the shrubs, was clipped ruthlessly short, as befitted the yard of a hairstylist and waxer.

She nearly crashed into a long tubular wind chime dangling from the front porch and rang the bell.

Which only made her think of J. T., who had nearly been brained by one at the Angel's Nest.

She could hear the promising sound of a blender through the door.

She waited it out. Then rang again.

Casey flung the door open. A big pitcher of something frothy and pink was in her hand and a shaggy yellow dog panted knee-level.

"I'm so glad you came, Britt! I thought we'd go sit in here. My roommate is working tonight so we have the place to ourselves."

"Oh, good! I . . . I brought you a plant, Casey."

Casey beamed and scooped it into the crook of her free arm.

"Gosh, that is awfully sweet of you, Britt. It's beautiful! Let's just bring it in here with us. It'll like the kind of light we get in the kitchen."

She led Britt through a hall painted a very stylish glossy orange. The walls were decorated with framed inspirational messages in striking modern fonts: "Imagine"; "An eye for an eye will only make the whole world blind"; "Give Peace a Chance." She suspected they were more aspirations than credos, given Casey's own mythology.

Her living room was clean lined and tidy and contemporary and bright, and she'd managed to blend turquoise and orange in her upholstery and accessories in a way that didn't singe Britt's corneas.

She settled at the vintage blue retro Formica table in the kitchen while Casey pulled down glasses the size of goldfish bowls and poured the drinks.

They sat for a moment of shy silence, sipping. Britt had forgotten how delicious margaritas were. They'd sucked half of their glasses down before anyone spoke.

"So are we going to talk about the elephant in the room? Initials J and T?" Casey wanted to know.

"Him?" Britt snorted. "I don't care about *him*."

"Of course you don't," Casey soothed.

"He can do anyone or anything he wants. We were just having a little fun. S'over now."

"Of course you were! Of course it is!"

"He can, in fact, fuck himself." Wow, two sips in and her psyche was liberated.

"He probably can!" Casey encouraged. "Speaking of which, I'm just going to come right out and ask it," Casey said finally. "You don't have to answer . . . you can tell me to mind my own beeswax and I swear on everything I hold dear that I won't tell a soul . . . but was he *good*? Be honest."

Britt took another hearty gulp. She wanted to be *mean*, not honest.

"Okay. Think of the best thing you ever saw . . . ever tasted . . . ever did . . ."

"Yeah?" Casey encouraged breathlessly.

". . . ever felt . . . ever smelled . . ."

"Yeah?"

"And multiply it by a million."

They let that assertion ring alone for a moment.

"Daaaaamn," Casey whispered.

Alas, apparently alcohol ultimately was truth serum.

"But I don't care about him at *all*!" Britt added hurriedly.

"Of course you don't," Casey soothed. "And can I tell you something, Britt? He kind of scares me."

Britt gave a short laugh. "Gosh, I didn't think anything scared you, Casey. You know, he's actually a lovely person. Who has a great laugh and wears reading glasses and looks like a fallen angel when he sleeps."

Britt blinked. That was some florid blather. That margarita was a fast worker.

Casey was apparently arrested by the tipsy poetry of this, because her eyes went dreamy.

She took another sip. She was beginning to think Casey was right about getting drunk. Feelings were for the birds! She would feel her feelings later!

"I have to confess, I like my guys big and dumb and sweet. And hot. Not look-into-the-sun hot, though. I'm more comfortable when I can manage them. Which is why Truck was my type."

"Was . . . or is?" Britt teased slyly.

Casey actually slowly blushed. And looked faintly distressed.

So Britt didn't bug her about that anymore.

She took another sip. They were quiet a moment. The big yellow dog panted companionably under the table. And licked Britt's ankle, and she giggled.

"Is it hard to talk about J. T.?" Casey sounded tentative. "Sorry if it is. It just seems like you need to."

"Honestly, I don't even know how to talk about how I feel right now. You saw those photos. And you saw what happened at the Misty Cat when Rebecca Corday walked in the first time. Half the town did."

"It was like the only giraffe at the zoo finally got a mate."

"Thanks. Thanks for that."

"You're prettier than she is."

Britt snorted.

"*As* pretty. In a different way. Pretty without needing to wax or trim a thing."

This was about the highest compliment Casey could give a person, and Britt was quite touched.

"You're pretty, too," Britt told her.

"I know," Casey said placidly. "And you know, I get afraid of things, Britt. I do. I get afraid I won't find anyone to settle down with and have kids before it's too late. Because that hasn't quite worked out for me. I get afraid something will happen to my house, like a big tree falling on it. But I went to Greta at the New Age store and she told me how to feng shui the place for protection."

"Can't hurt!"

"That's what I said!" Casey said.

They sipped a moment in silent solidarity.

"Do you remember that fight I had in the street with Kayla? About Truck," Casey ventured.

"Casey, I think you have to assume that fight has passed into legend. They'll probably start teaching it in school around here, along with Sutter's Mill and Fort Sumter."

She sighed. "Well, I'm not proud of that. My mama tried to raise a lady. And I do know how to behave. But Kayla started it. You know what she said? 'You're *never* going to find someone.' Kayla and I go way back to when we were little girls. She *really* knows how to hurt me. It's funny, because I think that's her biggest worry, too—that she won't find anybody. And that's how we ended up fighting. Anyway, if I have any sort of credo it's this: I always fight back."

Britt was uncertain about the wisdom of this credo.

"You're not a believer in passive resistance? Turning the other cheek?" she tried.

"Oh, you mean like Gandhi and all that? The thing is, passively resisting Kayla would have gotten me snatched bald-headed that day. Turning the other cheek would have gotten that one slapped, too. Sometimes you just have to wade on in there and flail a bit and hope for the best," she said placidly, and tipped the pitcher into Britt's margarita glass.

Britt took a healthy sip. "This is the *best* margarita I've ever had." The more she drank, the easier it went down, too. Casey wobbled to her feet and pressed the button on the blender to ensure they wouldn't run out.

She wondered if Casey's last sentence ought to be her philosophy, too: wade on in there and flail a bit.

"If you're going to fight, you might as well *try* to win, right?" Casey settled into the chair opposite her and clinked her glass against hers. "Even if it isn't pretty. And if you can't win, sometimes revenge is sweet."

"But knowing when you can't win is part of it all, too, probably. Or when *not* fighting is kind of the only way you *can* win."

Casey was quiet a moment.

"Oh, sweetie," she said finally, gently.

Which was the first time Britt realized that everyone really did believe she'd lost J. T. forever.

She supposed it was touching that everybody cared.

It was a peculiar emotional position to occupy. To know that when the truth of it settled in for good, that when he was gone and stayed gone, or was underfoot in Hellcat Canyon alongside Rebecca Corday, that the townspeople had her back, like a lot of busybody feather pillows.

"You're so smart, Britt," Casey said suddenly. "You're the bomb, you really are. I always wanted to be your friend, but I didn't think I was smart enough. I felt shy."

"You were *shy*? I'm sorry, I didn't mean to say it like that. *I* was shy. I always admired how bold you are, Casey. You're so cool."

They had clearly already reached the affectionate phase of inebriation. They beamed at each other.

Casey linked her fingers into a little hammock and propped her chin on them and gazed at her.

"What is Rebecca Corday like?"

"Shurprisingly . . ." Britt mused, then stopped, surprised that she'd already lost control of her s's. "She's kind of a bitch."

"I *knew* it," Casey said with calm satisfaction. "Probably because she's hungry all the time. More margarita?"

"Hit me," Britt said.

Casey had to work the next day, but she claimed hangovers made her move more slowly and only improved the precision of her haircuts. So they drank about two entire pitchers, all told, before they decided they ought to get Britt to the bus stop before the buses stopped running.

Britt pointed at things all the way to the bus stop and narrated as if they were on a nature walk.

"The stars are so beautiful. They remind me of J. T."

"That tree is so beautiful. It reminds me of J. T."

"The night shmells so nice. So does J. T."

"The whole wide world reminds me of J. T."

They arrived at the bus stop.

"There's fucking Rebecca Corday on the bus bench," Britt said darkly. "She reminds me of J. T."

Casey was surprisingly patient through all of this.

Together they paused to stare at their mutual nemesis.

This bench featured the ad of Rebecca Corday clutching a purse, leaping with the unbridled joy of being beautiful, wealthy, doable, ubiquitous, and probably currently within touching range, if not doing range, of J. T. McCord.

"She looks like a bunny like that, don't you think, Casey? Holding that purse, getting ready to jump?"

Casey tipped her head. "I don't see it."

Britt fished about in her purse and came out with the heavy-duty Sharpie she used to letter signs for Gary.

"Here, let me show you."

She looked about to make sure no cars were coming.

She carefully drew ears, long adorable oblong ears, one of them with a little bend, on top of Rebecca Corday's head. She added an extravagantly fluffy tail to her butt. With a few strokes of the pen she turned the purse into a basket full of eggs. She finished it off with fuzzy freckled cheeks and whiskers and buckteeth.

She stood back with a spokesmodel flourish. "*See?*"

Casey was in awe. "*Omigosh!* You're totally right! That's so cute! I didn't know you could *draw*. You're the bomb, Britt."

"No, you're the bomb!"

"You are!"

That went on for a while.

"Hey, I have an idea! You have to make *me* a bunny, Britt."

"I don't know if I can."

"I have all the same parts as Rebecca, right? I have a face."

Britt assessed her shrewdly by the light of the streetlight. "Okay, okay! Great idea! I *will*. Sit down."

Casey sat down hard on the bench, and Britt zoomed her face in close to Casey's to study her new canvas.

Britt decided to start with little freckled cheeks and whiskers.

Casey giggled.

"Shhh," Britt said. "Hold still. You're wiggling. Wiggling and giggling."

"But I have to. That's what they do. Bunnies wiggle." She wiggled her nose up and down.

They erupted into such a storm of giggles that Casey fell off the bench.

"Whoop!" Britt seized her arm and hauled her back up onto it. "Okay, shhh, shhhh. Sheriously. Sheriously. Hold still."

"Okay. Okay."

Britt went to work on drawing little oblong ears over Casey's eyebrows. She meticulously—especially for someone so full of margaritas—colored in a little black nose.

"That tickles. I might sneeze."

"Shhhh. Don't. We're almost done."

She finished off the whiskers. And then leaned back.

"OH. MY. GOSH. OHMYGOSH. You are so CUTE, Casey!"

"Yay!" Casey exulted. "Cuter than Rebecca?"

"*So* much cuter. Wait—let me finish that one whisker!"

"No, YOU'RE cuter." She nudged Britt so hard she was on her way off the bus bench. She flailed out for Casey, who snatched her upright just in time.

"But Britt . . . Britt . . . I need to tell you something."

Casey seized Britt's hands in hers and earnestly gripped them. Her expression was suddenly mournful and deadly earnest.

Which was hilarious because she was now a bunny.

"What? You can tell me anything, Casey."

"Okay. I want you not to feel sad. It's just . . ." She lowered her voice to a whisper. "I love your hair. But Rebecca Corday . . . has super great hair. I want to play with it. I want to braid it and blow it dry."

Britt laughed. "That's okay. I think her hair is pretty, too. Know what else I *hate* that has really cool foofy hair? I'll whisper it to you."

She leaned toward Casey and did just that, right into her ear.

Casey sat bolt upright. She was utterly motionless a moment.

And then a slow evil smile spread all over her face.

"I have an idea," Casey said.

Britt struggled awake to the sound of her phone ringing and ringing and ringing. Whose ringtone was "White Rabbit"? When had that happened?

She fumbled for it with some effort and slid the call to answer.

She tried to say, "Hello."

It came out, "Unnh."

"BRITT! Oh my God, you finally answered! You alive? I was so worried! You didn't wake up when I texted." It was Casey, and she was whispering. *Stage*-whispering. Her roommate must be home.

"What time is it?"

"Does it matter? It's your day off. But yeah, it's almost eight a.m. I have a very, very important question."

"Okay," Britt managed.

"What happened last night?"

"Umm . . . we drank margaritas and then . . ."

She stopped.

It worried her very much that she didn't know how to finish that sentence.

"I have whiskers on my face," Casey hissed.

"Happens when you get older," Britt mumbled. "Just wax them."

"BUNNY whiskers. And ears over my eyebrows. I have a freaking BUNNY FACE."

She was managing to be hysterical while whispering, which was really quite a feat.

Britt lay as still as possible. Good God. Who was playing bongos outside at this hour?

It took her what felt like another minute to realize the pounding was coming from inside her own head. It was the Margarita Marching Band.

"BRITT! Are you there? Are you alive? Are you okay?" Casey was now shouting in a whisper.

"I'm just trying to . . . I mean, we drank margaritas, Casey, we didn't take peyote or lick any psychedelic toads, so I don't know why you're seeing a bunny face in the mirror. Unless you did when I wasn't looking? Or after we got home? Wait . . . how *did* we get home?"

Her clothes were still on. She ran an experimental hand over her body, and all her limbs were present and accounted for. She inhaled.

She smelled like strawberries.

But her head and her stomach were playing a really nasty duet.

"I called Kayla and she took you home. No. Britt, I have SHARPIE whiskers. Black ones. I have a SHARPIE nose and eyelashes, too, and ears that sort of rise up over my eyebrows. Like a BUNNY. I. AM. A. BUNNY."

Silence.

And through the sludge of her hangover the memories began to reassemble.

"Oh . . . oh crap," she whispered in horror. "I remember now . . . at the bus bench . . . You asked me to turn you into a bunny . . . because you thought the bunny on the bus bench was cute. And so we bunnified Rebecca Corday . . . and then . . . and then . . ."

The silence on the other end told her Casey was remembering all of this, too, and everything else they'd done, with equal horror.

In light of all they'd accomplished last night, every bit of it illegal, one part of it kind of dangerous, it really was kind of a miracle they'd gotten home in one piece.

"You kept wiggling your nose when I was drawing . . . and then you fell off the bench laughing while I was working on it." Her memory was sludgy. Forming words felt like trudging through a swamp and they were all still a little slurry.

"Well, I guess that explains that one long whisker that zips right up to my ear. And that bruise on my hip." Casey was sounding a little more pragmatic now.

Britt was utterly silent. If she laughed, which she wanted to do, her head would explode.

"Do you know what's *really* weird, Britt?" Casey said this on a hush.

As if there was anything weirder than this.

"What?"

"I look really good this way." Casey's voice was suffused with stifled hysterical laughter. "You're really talented."

Britt started to laugh, then moaned. "Don't. Don't laugh. Don't make me laugh. I can't laugh. My head hurts."

"Shit shit shit. I have to go to work *right now.* And do hair. As a BUNNY FACE."

"Can't your assistant take your clients today? Or at least until you get the ink off?"

"She's is home with the baby. She's taking her to the doc because she was running a little temp. I told her yesterday I'd take *her* clients. All the waxing and stuff."

Britt started laughing again and stopped when she was reminded of how much that hurt. "Good luck, Bunny Face." She hung up the phone.

CHAPTER 22

"Gosh, how many T-shirts do you own, now, Johnny? I think you might be working on a fetish."

"Sixteen."

"Does this country remind you of the Tennessee backwoods? Doesn't it seem sort of inevitable that you'd wind up with simple folk again?"

"Nope."

The relatively short ride back from Napa with Rebecca was *deeply* uncomfortable.

He was purposely giving Rebecca deadpan one-word answers to these barbs, which he knew was simply making her crazier.

They were both pissy, for entirely different reasons. Rebecca had kissed him, and he'd rebuffed her, and she was seething. Their peers at the wedding had congratulated him over and over on the profundity of a beautiful wedding toast that Rebecca knew had nothing to do with her. And the whole world had seen pictures of the two of them that made their relationship look like the opposite of the icy, tense atmosphere inside the cab of his truck.

The two of them were old hands at being awkwardly photographed. And they ought to have been reading lines or discussing the *Last Call in Purgatory* script.

Instead, the silence between them was practically louder than the radio.

Which he kept turning up and Rebecca kept turning down.

Relief swept through him when the familiar exit signs began appearing.

Rebecca had decided she was going to get a blow-out before they visited the children's hospital to film the spot. He could get rid of her for at least an hour, maybe more.

And then her giant head began to swell into view on the billboard on the highway.

And suddenly she shot to an erect position like a prairie dog popping out of its burrow.

"Johnny. Oh, no. Oh, Jesus. There's . . . something wrong. " Her voice was urgent and dumbstruck

His head jerked toward her. "What's going on? You okay?"

"No," she said, her voice strange, and about to escalate into hysteria. "No I am not okay at all. Look at my billboard. LOOK AT IT. My billboard! Pull over!"

He slowed down.

He slowed down a little more.

And then he pulled over to the side of the road.

They both stared, utterly arrested.

For different reasons.

There was Rebecca, all right, the way Rebecca always wanted to be: larger than life, high above everyone else, isolated in all that white space like a work of art on a museum wall. Her giant sparkly raspberry lips were still pursed, blowing her dandelion.

But in all that impactful white space someone had drawn a huge and surprisingly detailed . . .

Yeah, it was a clown.

An extraordinarily skillfully rendered, really vivid clown.

He was wearing puffy checked pants and long curly-toed shoes, and great luscious fluffy shocks of hair billowed out from the sides of his mostly bald head. And he was bent over at the waist, his gaze aimed lasciviously out onto the highway drivers.

His butt was high in the air and aimed right at Rebecca's pursed lips.

"What. The Effing. Hell. Is. That." Rebecca could barely get the words out through a jaw tight as a vise.

"It's a clown," J. T. explained mildly. "It looks like you're kissing a clown's butt."

It was so funny it was practically a religious experience. He almost floated out of his body.

"I CAN SEE THAT."

He let a heartbeat's worth of silence get by.

"Good-looking clown," he said mildly.

Her head whipped toward him. Lightning was practically shooting from her eyes.

He knew instinctively that the milder he was, the more incensed Rebecca would get and the funnier it would get.

He was comprised of total happiness.

"It's fucking INSULTING."

"It's just a clown butt, Rebecca. You've probably kissed worse things," he said. Mildly.

Rebecca was probably about to launch from her body, too. For other reasons completely. She was magnificent when in a temper. And horrible.

On the one hand, landing national ad campaigns and having your face on billboards and bus benches could be viewed as an impressive achievement.

On the other hand . . . clown butt.

It was an epic struggle, but he could not keep the smile from spreading over his face. As big as any grin sported by a circus clown anywhere.

Rebecca saw it and she clamped her mouth shut, mute with fury.

He was pretty sure he knew exactly who'd drawn that clown.

How she'd done it was a little worrisome. That wasn't an easy climb.

Why she'd done it . . . well, this was the first time he'd ever felt peculiarly heartened by vandalism.

If Britt wanted to deface his ex-girlfriend's advertisements, surely it was due to an excess of passion.

And maybe . . . just maybe . . . it meant that she cared. Even in spite of those photos.

Either that, or she had completely lost her marbles.

His thoughts were on her as he cruised through town with funeral-procession speed so they could inspect the bus benches. Rebecca's thunderous face and whitely tight lips were aimed out the window, her arms wrapped around her torso like battle armor.

On one bench, Rebecca bounding with a purse had been transformed into a bunny. A really competent, charming bunny, with a full complement of whiskers and a pair of buckteeth. The purse had been transformed into a basket.

"*Buck. Teeth?*" Rebecca hissed.

On the next one, the one where she was performing a Julie Andrews twirl and trailing a scarf, the scarf had been transformed into what appeared to be a boa constrictor, which was devouring her arm. Rebecca's mouth had been turned into a little "O" of distress and she appeared to be trying to shake it off. The boa was wearing a big smile.

Rebecca muttered something unintelligible that ended with a furious, "atrocity."

The last bench was the coup de grâce, though. The one where her head was tilted back and she was aiming an ecstatic smile upward.

She hadn't been transformed into anything.

But the artist had given her a single, huge, erupting zit.

Rebecca made a low, feral sound in her throat. Like a cornered badger.

J. T. pulled up in front of the Truth and Beauty. "Here we are!" he said cheerfully. "You'll feel better after you've had a blow-out."

She flounced out of the truck and slammed the door so hard it should have caused an earthquake in the next county.

And he sat still for a moment, thinking furiously.

The funny part, the sweet part, the part that all but broke his heart right then and there: that Britt couldn't even be truly mean when she was trying to be mean.

All of those pictures were adorable.

He hesitated.

And then, for God's sake, even if he waded into the face of her cold rage and rejection, he just had to know if she was okay.

He performed an illegal U-turn in the middle of the street and headed up to Britt's house.

Britt finally, tentatively, slid one foot out from under the covers and put it on the floor. And the cool floor against her bare foot felt so good to her sore head, she just lay there like that for an indeterminate number of minutes.

She got the rest of her body up in cautious increments in a similar fashion, and inched across the floor with shuffling steps, as if she were carrying a live grenade, careful not to jostle her head or her stomach. She made it to the kitchen and discovered about two inches of old, cold coffee left in yesterday's pot. She dumped it in a cup with shaking hands and put it in the microwave.

Feeding Phillip about did her in. She gagged at least four times when his little column of meat slithered out of the can and splooped onto his dish.

And then she took the coffee outside and very, very carefully, in tenderly careful increments, stretched out on a lawn chair.

The morning sun was on her toes, and she was pretty certain that lying motionless like that was all she was fit for today.

That was how J. T. found her about fifteen minutes later.

She'd closed her eyes for a little while, and she was never certain whether she fell asleep again.

But when she opened them, J. T. standing over her, peering down.

She stared at him for what seemed like an inordinately long time.

Her heart leaped up like a puppy.

And then it crash-landed when she remembered he was the reason she had a vicious hangover.

"Did you spend the *night* out here, Britt?" He touched her arm as if to test whether it was clammy. He sounded worried.

"No," she said. "I just got here."

She said it as though she'd been traveling with a passport for days.

He settled back against the railing to study her. His face was a veritable lantern of suppressed glee all shot through with concern.

"So you're back from Napa."

"Yeah."

"Have fun?" she managed the faintest hint of acid.

"A modest amount," he said, matching her irony.

He was a big boy. He could do his own dirty work and bring the photos up.

He hesitated a beat, and then:

"So . . . what about you? You do anything . . . I dunno, *fun* . . . last night, Britt?"

Uh-oh.

She thought her answer through for what felt like quite some time. "Went out with a friend."

Her voice sounded dreamy. She'd forgotten how thoroughly alcohol savaged every single one of your senses. She wanted to speak quietly so as not to jar her head.

"Mmm. Friend, huh?"

"Casey."

"Ah, Casey. What did you ladies do?"

Another little delay while her brain searched out the word.

"Drank," she whispered.

He stifled a laugh. "You don't say."

She had nothing to say to that, really.

"You know . . . as I was driving back into town from Napa this morning . . . I saw a lot of new artwork."

Oh. Crap.

"And since I know how you like to transform things, I thought you might be interested to hear how some of the Hellcat Canyon's public art has been, shall we say, transformed."

She remembered he played a cop on *Blood Brothers.* He knew how to interrogate a suspect. He could just corner her into the truth with these innocent little comments.

She remained silent. You can't incriminate yourself if you don't talk. She'd learned that from cop shows, too.

The intent of this long, long silence was clearly to shred her nerves to pieces.

"I just have one very pressing question, Britt."

"Okay," she whispered.

He paused strategically.

"Why a clown?"

It took her a long while to answer.

Finally she decided she didn't have it in her to attempt a defense.

"Fun." Her voice was a shamed, resigned hush. It was almost peaceful to surrender to truth this way.

"Fun?" His voice was peculiarly taut.

"Fun to draw. All the curves." She got her hand up in the air to demonstrate. "Their big balloony pants and curvy shoes and . . . and . . . their . . . foofy hair and . . ."

She faltered when she risked a look up and saw his expression.

His face was peculiarly brilliant and tense, and his eyes appeared to be watering, as if he was holding in a sneeze.

"And?" he prompted on a hush. Like some hybrid of a prosecutor in court and a child hearing the best bedtime story ever.

"And . . . I love animals. But I hate clowns."

She confessed this in the shamed, whispered monotone she recognized from that part in crime dramas when the perp breaks down and confesses.

There was a silence.

"Britt." He sounded as though he was strangling. "I'm going to step off the porch a moment so I don't hurt your head."

A few moments later from a distance away, she heard him smack the oak tree with his hand as he roared with laughter. She heard flapping as he frightened off a few roosting birds.

Flapping, she recalled, was one of his favorite sounds.

"Oh, that's so sweet," she murmured. "You're so thoughtful."

He really was. The bastard really was.

He was a nice person. A nice person who had canoodled with his ex at a wedding in photos the whole effing world could see.

He returned a moment later, apparently having got all of that out of his system.

"I guess you decided you were ready to show your artwork to the world. You sure did it with a bang."

"Guess so," she said, with faint irony since she didn't have the energy or brain cells to debate that.

"The one with the zit. That was pure evil genius."

"I know. Her skin is so pretty."

She covered her eyes with her arm and heaved a sigh. She would make a terrible criminal if this was how easily she confessed to things.

Her new credo, she decided, was, "Margaritas are not the answer."

She should get that printed up for Casey to hang on her living-room wall.

"Could you stand right there and block the sun again, J. T.? It's not my friend this morning."

He shifted to the right obligingly.

And they were quiet again. That blue jay who liked to harass Phillip let fly with a series of squawks.

"I'm not proud of it, J. T.," she said finally. "It just kind of . . . happened."

"Well, we all do things we're not necessarily proud of."

"You're the expert," she muttered.

He didn't rise to that bait.

He was just quiet, but it was the sort of quiet of someone who has something on their mind.

"Casey's my friend now," she said, idly. After a moment. "We call each other and everything."

She could feel him smiling. "Your friend is a delinquent."

She smiled slowly and faintly. "I know."

They were quiet together, and even when he wasn't saying anything it was just lovely to have him sitting there even though he was peculiarly the greatest source of happiness and the greatest source of pain she'd ever known, greater than a cigarette ground into her skin. She didn't know why he'd come.

"Any more where that came from?" He pointed to her coffee.

She passed her cup to him.

He took a sip. Then winced mightily. "This is yesterday's."

"Yep."

"Had any aspirin yet?"

"Nope."

"I'll go make more coffee. Don't move."

"Couldn't if I tried."

He was gone for what felt like quite a while, and then he returned with a cold rag and a pillow, which he punched to cloud-softness and folded neatly. He lifted her head as tenderly as if it were spun glass and slid it beneath.

He handed her a little glass of water and a pill. She took them with incriminating pen-stained fingers.

Then he went back inside and puttered about in the house, probably making the coffee. She heard him talking to Phillip like he was an old friend. She smiled. That was how her house was supposed to sound.

And then her heart hurt horribly because it was never going to sound like that again.

He returned.

"Feeling a little better?"

"Yes."

But actually, no.

"Good. I came to tell you something."

And all of a sudden she was rethinking the need to hurl, because her stomach violently knotted.

It would just be her luck if the last image he took away of her was her retching over the side of the deck.

"Britt . . . those photos on TMZ? . . . I take it you saw them . . ."

He took her absolute held-breath torturous silence as an affirmative.

"I know how this is going to sound . . ."

She kept her breath held.

"But it's not what they look like."

"*Wow*," she managed. A scorn-laden whisper.

Several seconds later.

"There weren't even supposed to be any photographs *taken* there. Some asshole paparazzi managed to get in anyway. TMZ had it totally wrong. And Franco was way out of line to give them a quote. Rebecca and I are *not* back together, and we never will be."

It was hard to rejoice at these words. Let alone believe them.

The photos had been branded on her soul since yesterday.

"If you're wondering how it looked to *me*," she managed to coat her languid hungover voice in irony, "it looked like Rebecca had her head dreamily on your shoulder and it looked like you liked it. And it looked like you'd just been kissing in some kind of dark alley."

It was the longest sentence she'd managed today. Each word of it felt she was calling up ground glass from her very depths.

He went still.

He took a long breath. "Okay . . . I know you don't want to hear this but just try . . . *try* to imagine all the split seconds of your life you would hate to have freeze-framed. Imagine, for instance, a photo of Truck's hand on your ass while you're smiling. Because *I* saw that moment at the Misty Cat, and I saw the moment after that. Imagine everything you've ever done, your entire life as a whole, broken down into split-second fragments of time, each of them photographable. Now imagine them without context. Imagine a photographer watching you like a *fucking hawk* looking for a moment that means a payday for him. I basically shrugged Rebecca off my shoulder, but you didn't see *that* photo. Becks was drunk and she asked me to walk her back to her room. It was dark. It wouldn't have mattered who she was, Britt, I wouldn't have let her walk there on her own. Maybe I should have looked for someone else to walk her, but she is who she is now, for better or worse. There aren't a whole lot of people she can trust. I am who I am, and I couldn't just let her go alone. I did not kiss her. She did try to kiss me."

A little murderous spike of jealousy pierced her hangover over that last sentence.

God. For better or worse, she knew this was true: he wasn't going to let Rebecca Corday wobble drunkenly off to her room alone.

He wouldn't be J. T. if he'd done that, no matter how she loathed thinking about it.

It all *sounded* true.

But it didn't make the photos any less painful.

"Where is she now?" Britt managed.

"I just dropped her off at the Truth and Beauty to get a blow-out."

Britt froze.

And then she tried to sit up. "Oh, God. Oh God, no."

Rebecca was going to walk into the Truth and Beauty and see that Casey had a *bunny face*.

It was the funniest, most horrifying thing she could imagine.

"Britt, honey, you need something to hurl into?" J. T. was on his feet and poised to grab a flowerpot.

"No . . . I'm . . . just . . . thinking about bunny faces."

Casey, Britt was pretty sure, could handle herself.

And then what he'd just said about Rebecca fully penetrated.

"J. T. . . ." she said slowly. "*Why* is Rebecca still here with you?"

He pushed his hair back in both hands, a wholly frustrated, resigned gesture. He knew she wasn't going to like what he said.

"We were both approached at the wedding and asked to do a promotional spot for the Placer County Children's Hospital. How could I say no to that? It's in Black Oak. We're going to fly to Los Angeles from the airfield here. It seemed childish to tell her to rent her own car to get there. Especially since, last I heard, you didn't care what I did or who I did it with."

She *had* said that.

That shut her up.

"You got something to tell me, Britt? Want to reverse your position on that?" His voice was a little harder now. "I notice you didn't decorate any other advertisements around town. Just the Rebecca Corday ones."

Just a few short days ago that suggestion that she reverse position would have resulted in the two of them riffing on the types of positions she was best at, reverse as in cowgirl being one of them, and then giving a few of them a shot.

It seemed an eternity ago. Time ought to be measured in emotion rather than hours or days, Britt thought. Two happies ago. A misery and a half from now. Like that.

She didn't speak.

"Did it ever occur to you, Britt, that I don't have a roadmap for whatever this is, either?"

Britt was silent and a cold spot settled into her already roiling stomach.

None of this was what she needed to hear in order to forgive him.

The next silence was long and grim.

When he finally spoke again, he sounded drained.

"There's still nothing going on with me and Rebecca. But I can't keep saying that over and over. And I get why it's scary for you. I get why the timing of Rebecca showing up is weird. I can't put a force field around myself. But I feel like I can't do or say the right thing here, Britt. And I'm pretty sure it wouldn't matter *what* I said or did."

She didn't say anything for a time.

There *was* one thing he could say. All she needed was three words. She somehow knew she could handle the craziness, the uncertainty, the *everything* about his life. If it was laid down over an unshakeable foundation of those words. The ones he feared most.

"Why *are* you here, J. T.?"

She managed to say it quietly and evenly. But her heart had begun to hammer.

It was his turn to go silent.

"I couldn't go to Los Angeles without . . . without seeing you. I saw the billboard and the benches and . . . I was worried about you, Britt."

She suddenly felt unutterably weary.

That was that, then. A welfare check, so to speak.

Or at least that was all he was going to cop to.

"I don't need you, J. T. I'll be just fine without you. You can just go."

The silence that followed seemed oddly absolute.

The kind, she imagined, that would follow when the earth finally topped turning.

She looked at him.

He was holding himself utterly still. His features had an almost waxy stillness, as if he'd utterly vacated his body. The light had gone out of him.

As if he was the one suffering with a brute of a hangover, and trying not to jostle it.

"Well, then," he said. His voice was a little frayed, too. "I guess that's what I needed to know."

He pushed away from the railing he'd repaired.

He looked down at her and she looked up at him.

And then he bent and he pressed his lips to her forehead, where ten minutes ago it had hurt the worst.

She closed her eyes.

Now all the pain was in the middle of her chest. Her heart felt like charred ruins.

And oddly it felt like she was the one who'd lit the match.

There was some kind of brick clogging her throat. She didn't say anything else.

His lips lingered there. She was half certain he'd leave a brand.

But he finally stepped back.

His eyes were closed. But he opened them again right away.

"Sweetheart, I won't grovel. And I won't be back."

And then he was gone.

CHAPTER 23

She lay still for a long, long time because she didn't want to move yet.

She was vaguely aware she was lingering out there in order to savor the last of his presence, like an echo.

Somewhere through her hungover hurt she had the vague sense that she'd done something horrible to J. T. Possibly something worse than he'd done to her.

She'd been her best self with him, and somehow the threat of losing him had turned her into her worst self.

But look at what he'd given her, in the process. A community who cared about her. Actual friends. A revived libido. A clear willingness to display her art in public again. A refreshed lust for competition. A renewed respect for the dangers of alcohol.

It was all good, and all because of him. But she thought she'd trade all of it plus a kidney if she could only turn back time to two weeks ago, and stop it right there.

She finally stirred when her phone rang. She could move without throwing up now, she found out, so she went into the house and answered it.

It was Casey.

"Oh my God, Britt, Rebecca Corday came into the Truth and Beauty today! I nearly had kittens!"

One day she would tell Casey that she'd drawn her as a lioness. One day, possibly even soon, she'd show her the drawing she'd made. Casey would like it even more than the bunny face, she was pretty sure.

"Yeah? What did you tell her about your Bunny Face?"

"I told her I passed out on the bus bench and the same vandal did to me what they did to her. And we commiserated over it."

Britt didn't think she'd ever laugh again, but she laughed then. Just a little. "I knew you could handle it. You're the bomb, Casey."

"No, you're the bomb."

"I think I'm too old to drink like that now, though, Casey."

"That's okay. We can go the movies and do other things that adult women are supposed to do. We can quilt."

Britt smiled faintly and then the smile died.

"He's gone, Casey."

Casey was quiet a moment. "Oh, sweetie."

Another silence, rich with sympathy.

"We'll talk about it later, when we're both all the way sober."

"Okay," Britt said in a near whisper.

There was a brief little silence.

"Did you get to blow-dry her hair?" Britt said finally.

"I did. I was surprised. It's kind of thin. She probably doesn't eat enough."

"Once a week. Like a boa constrictor."

Casey snickered.

They ended the call.

Bip, I know you think he's a dog, but you HAVE got to see this!!!!!!!!! It has three million hits already. P.S. The dead azalea? That is so you.

Brit roused herself from the fetal-position slumber she'd tipped into a few hours after she'd last talked to Casey, awakened by the chime of her sister's text and startled by the staggering number of exclamation points.

Should she even bother?

But she clicked the YouTube link anyway. Really, how much worse could it get?

Her heart gave a swift hard jump when she saw the title.

"John Tennessee McCord's Toast at Felix Nicasio's wedding."

It was one of those illicit videos filmed by someone who annoyingly held their cell phone vertically.

But the still was of J. T., holding up a glass. He looked so handsome in a tux her head went light. He seemed both utterly at home up there, with hundreds of eyes on him, and a little diffident.

And speaking of painful, her heart was slamming away in her chest.

She held her breath. Said a silent prayer.

Then exhaled and pressed play.

Whoever had recorded it had clearly hit record when he was already a few words into the toast.

"Most of us sitting here, we're in the business of fantasy and illusion," J. T. was saying. "So many things about our lives are outsized. We show up on billboards. On the big screen. In millions of living rooms weekly. Someone else writes beautiful or moving or funny words for us, and they're accompanied by huge sweeping scores or hip soundtracks so that we and the audience know how and when and what to feel. So sometimes it's hard to know whether what we've got is love . . . or publicity."

This was greeted by scattered nervous laughter.

"Because real life isn't like the movies. Real life doesn't have crisply crafted story or character arcs or big crescendos. The love scenes aren't choreographed. Sometimes it just flows forward more or less uneventfully, with intermittent explosions or grace notes. And we can't always wrap everything up and make everything better with a big theatrical gesture."

"You tell 'em, Tessnesseese!" Some drunken female shouted.

This was greeted by a chorus of shushes.

"In real life, it's hard to know if love is what you're in. For a few reasons. First, well, we aren't handed a script that we can read cover to cover that tell us that yep, that's love, all right. And secondly . . . well, maybe your life up to that point has been a grittier sort of art-house movie or horror flick. So maybe you've never been in that kind of movie before and don't recognize the genre." More laughter and some murmurs here. And Britt's heart squeezed like a painful little fist, thinking of the kind of movie J. T. had grown up in. "And thirdly . . . well, I think the reason we refer to it as 'in love' is because when you're in it, you occupy it the way you occupy your own skin. Or the way you occupy a little house, maybe with a picket fence and a formerly broken porch, with one other person. When you're *in* something, you can't always see clearly that you are."

He had that audience in thrall.

Britt had stopped breathing.

He looked up, and then she could have sworn he looked her straight in the eyes.

"And movie love, like our outsized lives, is big: big moments, big declarations, hopefully, big grosses." He paused, grinning, when the audience laughed. "But in real life it's the little things. Maybe it's peanut butter in the house because she knows you like it. You bring her a half-dead azalea because you know she'll love it better than roses and you want to see the look on her face when you hand it to her. And it's in the silences. In how you enjoy everyday things more, like reading, because she's reading next to you."

Someone was audibly weeping now. Britt could hear it.

Or maybe that was her. She sniffed and swiped at her eyes.

"Felix—and I don't think he'll mind if I tell you this now, because he's done locked his woman *down*—" They all laughed. "He was a wreck shortly after he first started dating Michelle. We all know he's a guy's guy, a bachelor in that old-fashioned, groovy sense . . . and we all saw that he was just laid low by her. He wanted to know, 'J. T., how do *I* know I'm in love?' And I wasn't much help to him then, and I do apologize, Felix. You've punished me enough for being useless then by making me make this damn toast." Lots of laughter here and a few enthusiastic hoots.

It settled down, and J. T. got somber. "But I feel like I have a duty to Felix and Michelle and everyone here. Because if you're wondering, gentlemen, if what you're *in* is love, I might be able to help."

He paused. The silence all but echoed. Not even the clink of a glass or chink of silverware.

"When whatever you're feeling is so huge that it's tempting to want to call it other big words, like fear or awe, and it's so *easy*, easy as breathing, that you think you can't possibly have earned the right to be that happy, and so hard it can drive a proud man to his knees, where he will beg for forgiveness, for another chance, for rights to the remote . . ." Laughter greeted this. "It might be love."

"And it might be the 'L' word," he continued, "if you want to suddenly be a better person than you ever have been in order to be worthy of her, and you don't even know where to start. This is how, by the way, I think the world becomes a better place. We want to be better for the people we love."

"Preach it!" someone shouted. Britt thought it sounded like Franco, and it was awfully close to the mic.

"And it might be the 'L' word if you don't want to say that word out loud, because calling it only one thing feels almost inadequate, a disservice to the actual condition, because it's actually a million feelings."

"Oh my God," Britt murmured, her hands on her face. Tears poured down through her fingers. "Oh, J. T."

"You will feel needed. Absolutely essential. Not because of your fine face and projected grosses"—he paused for the laugh he'd anticipated—"but because you are what turns the movie of her life from black-and-white to color. By some miracle, you are lucky enough to be precisely what makes her life better, even if you don't always make her life easier. And you will finally feel at home, which is less about a place than about where she is."

"Oh . . ." Britt breathed.

And with a few words born of fear and anger and wounded pride, she'd told him she didn't need him. That he didn't belong here. What had she *done*?

"It will make you feel stronger than you've ever been, and weaker than you've ever been. And you somehow realize that weakness is in fact a strength you didn't know you had.

"The hard part, the irony, is that sometimes you don't know what you've got until you experience the world without her in it. When you're with her, it's like the first time anyone anywhere saw a movie in color. You never knew the world contained such brilliance, such music. Without her, the world is suddenly two-dimensional and black-and-white and soundless and there are no subtitles."

The wedding guests were dead quiet. Moved unto speechlessness, remembering, perhaps, or reviewing their own loves.

"And I think the surefire way of knowing? Nothing,

nothing, not even jumping a stunt car through a hoop of fire, scares you more than the notion that she might not love you back."

He paused. He took a steadying breath.

"And so . . . maybe you don't say it."

He cleared his throat and looked down. You could have heard a pin drop.

Britt could have sworn everybody in the tent was frozen.

She was frozen.

She held her breath, and rooted for him to say the next words.

She thought maybe he couldn't finish.

He finally lifted his head again.

When he spoke again, his voice was a little gravelly. "I submit to you: You're not really brave, gentlemen, until you say that word to the person you love, and are prepared for the consequences of her answer. It might be the hardest and best thing you ever do. Even if you crash and burn. But *don't*, don't let that opportunity get away from you. It will end you."

Britt was pretty sure all the rustling she heard in the background was caused by tissues plucked from pockets or shirt sleeves being dashed against eyes.

"I know it was a long road for Felix and Michelle. Some of us know their story a little better than others. And my brothers and sisters, Felix is ultimately a brave man, which is why he's sitting up there right now, grinning like an idiot and is he . . . yep, he's crying, too! Check it out, I made Felix Nicasio cry!" Laughter and whoops greeted this. ". . . next to a woman he probably feels he doesn't deserve, and most of us agree. I jest, I jest. You got lucky, too, Michelle, y' hear, and I know you'll take care of each other."

"I will, J. T.," Michelle said, sounding quite sniffly. Felix handed her a handkerchief.

"So raise your glass to Felix and Michelle, who make each other, and us, and the world, better, because they love each other. May the movie of their life be an unforgettable triumph, like every movie we've all been in, according to our publicity."

A great roar greeted this, laughter and cheers and thundering applause. And the cell phone recording it tumbled to the ground and stopped recording as whoever illicitly recorded it clearly got carried away and dropped it in the act of applauding.

Tears poured unchecked down Britt's face. Obscuring everything, which was kind of ironic, given that everything was suddenly clear.

Sometimes you were the stunt driver, aiming for that flaming hoop, and soaring triumphantly through the air.

And sometimes you were the ramp that launched the driver into triumph.

Britt intended to be J. T.'s ramp.

It was so much easier to be brave when she could be brave for someone she loved. All she had to do was make it possible for him to say what he wanted and needed to say to her.

Her only fear now was that she had forever blown it.

It was almost midnight when she finally decided to call Casey.

She held her breath as the phone rang and rang.

Casey answered, and actually sounded alert. "Britt!"

"I'm so sorry to call so late . . . Casey . . . what are you doing right now besides trying to sleep?"

"I was awake! Oh my God, Britt, did you see J. T.'s video?" She was sniffling, too. He'd made all the women in the world cry, it seemed. *That's my man*, Britt thought proudly.

"I did see it. And this is about J. T. I need your help.

Are you up for Round Two? I screwed up big-time, and I need to make it right before it's too late. It might already be too late."

Casey was more than game once she heard Britt's plan. Thank God for friends who were delinquents. "I'll be right over," she said, absolutely thrilled.

Britt ended the call and stared at her phone. She was nervous as hell, and her palms were sweating, and she'd never felt more alive.

Sometimes love was in the quiet moments. But sometimes, like in the movies, a grand gesture was called for to really get your point across.

She took a deep breath and looked at herself in the mirror. "Alley-oop, Britt."

J. T. locked his house door and stood back to stare at it. He'd loved this house, but suddenly it felt like a movie set, unreal, without Britt in his life. Maybe he'd sell the place when they were done filming Hellcat Canyon location shots.

Something tumbled toward him and knocked into his boot. He picked up an old horse-chestnut husk, blown from one of the thousands of trees in the hills here.

That's just how he felt. Empty and exhausted.

Rebecca was really quiet. And she'd been really quiet all night, too. Her mood was both taut and pensive and it was unfamiliar to J. T., but he patently didn't care what she was thinking.

At the moment, he wanted to get away from the scene of where he'd been happiest, because it was like a taunt. Rebecca chucked her bag into the front seat, and he chucked his overnight bag in after it, and in the cool gray early light he maneuvered his truck onto the road. Past the river. Past the vista point that looked out over the canyon where he and Britt had found a new use for his truck. Back through town. Past the turnoff to Britt's house. Past the redecorated bus benches and the Misty Cat. He could have sworn he saw a movement in the upstairs window there, even though it was too early for anyone to be in.

And finally out onto the highway.

All in utter silence.

They had the road completely to themselves at this time of day. That billboard was visible in the distance, and it was entirely white. But Rebecca had clearly vanished from it. Efficient of them to take the clown version down so quickly. J. T. thought it was kind of a shame.

But . . .

Wait.

He squinted. He'd thought the billboard was all white, but was there writing on it?

"Guess they took my ruined billboard down," she finally said with some satisfaction. "They should have a new one up pretty soon. Same ad."

They got a little closer. J. T. stepped on the brake and slowed to a crawl.

It looked as though a fresh layer of white butcher paper had been slapped up over the entire thing.

He slowed down even more.

"Hey . . . doesn't that say 'J. T.?'" Rebecca was confused.

He nearly drove off the road.

He got a grip on the steering wheel in time and carefully pulled over to the shoulder and cut the engine instantly.

He froze, staring at the billboard.

DEAR J. T.,

I LIED. I NEED YOU.

Below it was a drawing of a huge and exceptionally attractive chicken, with fluffy, elegant plumage and meticulously rendered feet. Next to it was an adorable donkey, its ass pointed toward the highway, its head peering coyly over its shoulder.

The word *Me* was written above them in big, bold blocky letters. And two arrows ran from that word: one pointed at the chicken, the other at the ass.

"John." Rebecca was sure awake now. "What the hell? You just scared me to death."

"Shush," he said so abruptly she actually recoiled.

And then he sucked in a long, long breath.

Sighed out all that air.

And yanked the keys from the ignition and tossed them in her lap.

"Here."

She stared at them as if he'd handed her a snake.

"What's the matter with you? Can't you drive? Are you having a stroke?"

"I'll get a flight out of Sacramento or San Francisco into L.A. tonight or tomorrow. No matter what, I'll get there somehow and I'll meet you at the studio. I'd take you back to town and see if we could get you another ride, but if you don't drive yourself to the airfield now you're going to miss your flight."

"You mean our flight."

"I mean *your* flight."

"John, for God's sake, what's going on?"

"I'm going back to Hellcat Canyon. Something I have to do. I have feet. I'll walk there."

"It's that waitre—"

He stopped her with a look like a hard, cold wall.

"These seats have just been Armor-Alled, Rebecca. All I have to do is open the door and give you just a little nudge and you'll shoot out like a watermelon seed. And so help me God, if you call her 'that waitress' again, that's what I'll do. And I'll leave you on the side of the road. Britt. Her name is Britt."

She drew in a breath and sighed it out. "I'm sorry."

"Good."

"You know why I do it."

"Yep."

"I shouldn't do it."

"Nope."

She smiled an uncertain tight smile. "I always liked you best when you called me on my B.S."

"That's because you're perverse, Rebecca."

"It's just that . . . you're . . . special, J. T. There's no one like you." She said this almost pleadingly.

Rebecca was actually trying to be sincere.

"Yeah. I'm a prize."

They were silent a moment.

He looked into her beautiful eyes and felt only impatience.

She swallowed. "That speech at the wedding . . . it was about her, wasn't it?"

"Yep," he said shortly.

Rebecca leaned back against the seat. She sighed. "Look," she said softly. "I want to lay it on the line right now. I know I blew it, Johnny. I confess I had an ulterior motive when I came here—I thought maybe we could talk about starting again. I couldn't *bear* seeing you with someone else, and that's when I knew how wrong I'd been. What we had was unforgettable and . . . I should have tried harder. I shouldn't have bailed. We just have to—"

"Here's the deal, Becks. I don't love you."

He saw her take that like a blow.

He was in too much of a rush to feel too sorry.

"The best thing you ever did was dump me in Cannes, and for that I owe you a debt of gratitude. We are simply never going to happen that way ever again. That's a fact. There will be no discussion. Are you hearing me?"

She stared at him in mute shock.

"I'm sorry to say it that way. I just needed to get it said and fast. Because God knows I don't want you to miss your jet."

She was staring at him, apparently frozen in shock. She'd gone white.

"Come on. You don't actually love me either, do you?" he demanded softly.

She gave a short, incredulous laugh. And then all at once, her big round blue eye were brimming with tears.

She gave her head a sharp toss and she sniffed, her nose already going pink.

Which is how he knew the tears were real.

She probably did love him. Or thought she did. He sincerely doubted she really knew.

He sighed. No matter what, he couldn't relish hurting her.

"I'm going to do you the favor of assuming you can be a rational, detached professional when it comes to me, and that's based on no evidence whatsoever, and you'll tell them I was held up and y'all will wait for me to get there. But if not, I'm okay with that, too. You can tell them that John Tennessee McCord hasn't changed one bit, and he's the unreliable ass of ten years ago. Your call. We can make a great movie and I think you know it. When it comes right down to it, caring about that kind of thing is what we have in common. And that's about it. But right now, all I care about is Britt. And I never liked it when you called me Johnny."

He had a sense he was bludgeoning her with the words, but primarily it was because she was unaccustomed to unvarnished honesty. No one except him had ever told her the truth about anything, particularly herself.

"Bastard." The word lacked oomph. She'd said it to him too many times. He'd heard it too many times.

"They should probably invent a new word for me," he sympathized.

She jerked her gaze from his. And she stared stonily out through the windshield. Her jaw was taut.

There were a dozen things he could have said in the following silence. But only one thing seemed important right now, and she was just waking up and feeding the cat, and putting the coffee on and maybe watering the plants . . . and damn, but he wanted to be there. For every little thing.

"Leave the truck in the airfield parking lot, Rebecca, and hand the keys off to the guy at the front desk, tell him I'll be along for them later. Or you can just set the truck on fire when you get out of it, if that's what you feel you need to do. I'm insured up the wahoo."

He'd miss that truck, if she did that. But sometimes it was good to know when to let go.

He slid out and shut the door hard behind him and started walking. Quickly.

He didn't look back.

Not even a few moments later, when he heard the motor start or felt the spit of gravel against his calves as she roared off toward the airport.

He hadn't been walking for very long along the highway when a big silver truck slowed down next to him.

He glanced over.

Aw, hell's teeth.

Truck Donegal's big square handsome face was hanging out the window. "Where's your truck, McCord?"

"Long story."

He said nothing else. But his entire body was tense as a compressed spring. Prepared for anything Truck might want to throw down.

They regarded each other unblinkingly.

"Hop in," Truck said finally, neutrally, and surprisingly mildly. "I'll take you back to town."

J. T. hesitated. He'd look like an ass, or worse, a chicken, if he refused.

He sighed.

Truck unlocked the door. And J. T. went around to the passenger side and got in.

The inside turned out to be spotless and polished. A little air purifier in the shape of a pine tree hung from the rearview mirror. The guy took good care of his truck.

This was a guy with pride, in general.

And a guy with pride would really suffer over not being able to find work for more than a year.

They drove in absolute silence for about two minutes.

And then J. T. smelled something . . . unusual. "What's that smell? It smells *great* in here."

Truck cleared his throat. "Got me a catering gig. A little wedding down in Lightning Forks. That's why I had to set out early."

J. T. turned around. On the little seat behind them several trays were indeed covered in Saran Wrap and heaped with things.

Many of them on sticks.

"Is that . . . chicken *satay*?"

Truck kept his eyes on the road as he took the little curving exit into town.

"I Googled it," Truck admitted, not looking at J. T. "And it actually sounded pretty tasty. So I got me some chicken and I made some. And it turned out great. And I made some other stuff I read about when I read about the satay. And that turned out great, too. Turns out I have kind of a knack for this stuff." He said this with a sort of mild, bemused pride. "And I've been cooking a lot of stuff since. To make a long story short . . . Kayla Benoit—

you know, from the dress shop in town?—is hooking me up with weddings and baby showers."

J. T. was astounded.

A slow smile spread over his face. "*Daaaaamn*, Truck."

The guy swiveled his head and grinned at him.

J. T. was a little worried about what might go down between Casey and Kayla now, though.

They drove in silence for a moment.

"McCord, I owe you an apology for—"

"I appreciate the gesture Truck, but it's Britt you owe the apology to."

"You're right. I'll apologize to her, too."

J. T. nodded.

And to his surprise, once he was in town, Truck, without asking, took the turn up the road to Britt's house.

And he idled the engine a few houses down from hers.

"How'd you . . ." J. T. began.

But probably everyone in town knew.

Truck smiled at him again, with something very like sympathy.

"Go get 'er, McCord."

CHAPTER 24

He saw the back of her first. She was watering the plants. And he just hung back and watched, and soaked up the scene. He noticed the coleus was gone, which meant she must have adopted it out, but now she had another patient, something with big, broad shiny green leaves that had some brown spots.

"You're all doing *great*," he heard her murmur.

His heart squeezed.

She put the watering can down and turned and gave a start when she saw him.

And then Britt's heart, formerly charred and withered, sprang back to full blossoming glory.

J. T. was wearing, shockingly enough, jeans and a black T-shirt. And he was holding a tray covered in plastic wrap.

They stared at each other in silence.

"Hi," she said. Her voice was awfully faint. More an exhale than a word.

"Hi," he said. His voice was a little on the gruff side.

They didn't say anything else for a time.

"I brought some chicken satay." He settled it carefully on the little table on her porch.

"Oh," she said. "Thanks."

Apparently this conversation was going to be catered.

Her heart was jackhammering away in her chest, overjoyed at its resurrection.

"So . . ." He inhaled. He sounded nervous, too. "Got your message. The one out on the highway."

Her face was hot now. "Okay."

"That was a pretty brave thing for a chicken to do."

She smiled tentatively. "I was sober when I did it, too."

"By the way, I don't really think you're a chicken, Britt."

"But you were right, J. T. About me running. About me . . . looking for an excuse to run."

He nodded shortly. A tense little silence passed.

"Britt . . . what did you mean when you wrote, 'I need you'?"

"What I meant was . . ." She drew in a breath. "I lied when I said I didn't need you." And then the words came in a rush. "I'm so sorry. I know it was a horrible thing to say and I was lashing out because I was hurt and my pride was hurt and . . . *everything* hurt. And I lied when I said I'd be just fine without you. I have never felt so happy, or safe, or cared for, than I have with you. And I have . . ." she swallowed. "Oh God, I have felt half dead without you. And not just because of the hangover."

Light surged into his face, brilliant and joyous.

But then he went still again. Cautious.

"Britt, I'm going to talk for a while now. Do you want to sit down?"

She welcomed that suggestion. Her knees were weak anyway.

She sank onto her patio lounge chair.

He came up the steps slowly, as if he was afraid she might dart off, and he leaned against the now sturdily repaired railing.

She could hear him breathing in the still of the morning. He seemed to be rallying his thoughts.

"When I was a kid back in Tennessee . . ." He cleared

his throat. "When I was a kid back in Tennessee, I got through tough days because I could dream of better things. And I *got* those better things. And I learned I didn't want everything that came my way. It took being really unhappy to learn what happiness is."

He stopped to check the impact of this on Brit.

"Okay," she said softly, encouragingly.

"I'm going to fly to L.A. tomorrow and read for that part unless my agent tells me that's out of the question. It's Hollywood. Anything can happen. If and when it finally shows up in the theaters, it could be a musical starring Neil Patrick Harris and the Muppets, for all we know. And even though I'll be filming *The Rush* for a while come fall, and I don't know whether I'll get *this* part, there might very well be other movies. And I will go away for a few months and maybe kiss other women as part of what I do for a paycheck and people may say or print untrue things about me. I might even kiss another guy if the part is good enough. That's my life. It's a crazy life. But dreams are like that, surreal and fragmented and unpredictable. And being a part of that life . . . that might not be something you want. I wouldn't blame you. But before you say anything . . ."

He paused a moment here.

He was a little blurry, and she swiped at her eyes. And she couldn't speak if she tried.

". . . I guess what I'm saying is that because of all of this I consider myself some authority on dreams. You're smart, Britt, but you were wrong about one thing. The part with us? That's not the dream. We're the *real* part. *We're* the only thing that matters. The other stuff is the hurricane. You and me, we're the *eye* of the hurricane. And you know . . . you know how your lungs just know to breathe in and breathe out? It's like that with us. I breathe in, you breathe out. I don't know how else to say it. I need you, Britt. When we don't fight it . . . you and I . . . we just *know.* We just work."

He dropped his forehead into his hands briefly and then pushed his hair back, and sighed, and it tapered into a short, wondering laugh. "I am so in love with you."

His voice broke ever so slightly.

She could hear him breathing.

Or maybe it was her breathing.

All she knew for certain was that she had to get to him. She stood very, very slowly.

She crossed the porch to him, and looped her arms around his neck and pressed her cheek against his cool, stubbly morning cheek and pressed her body against his, and his arms wrapped around her slowly, and then tightened.

"I *love* you," he repeated fiercely. Claiming his right to that word for the first time. "And I will always do *everything* in my power to make sure you feel safe."

"I love you, too, J. T. So much," she whispered in his ear. "I'm not going anywhere, unless you want me to come with you. I can do crazy, I can do quiet. Knowing us, it'll be both. But Hellcat Canyon is *our* home."

His shoulders moved in a huge, satisfied sigh. He held on to her tight, and she held on to him.

And she breathed in and he breathed out.

They had been kissing passionately for five or ten minutes when *Taking Care of Business* erupted from J. T.'s phone.

"Gotta take this," he told her apologetically. He kept one arm looped around her as he answered the call. "Hey Al."

"Rebecca's dropped out of the running. So that's the end of that," Al said briskly.

J. T. quickly pressed the phone to his chest and whispered, "Rebecca's dropped out." He'd told Britt about his truck. She'd told him about the toast video, because he miraculously hadn't heard about it yet, and it actually made him blush.

But Al was still talking. J. T. raised the phone back to his ear.

"But it seems the producers saw that toast video from Nicasio's wedding. It's closing in on five million hits, you romantic son of a bitch. And they realize that you're catnip to millions of women. They want you to fly in and read with Tara Gonzales instead. So it's all about you, now, and they just have to cast the other lead. Check your e-mail for your flight numbers and boarding passes. We'll have a car pick you up in about four hours."

Tara Gonzales. Another big star, a fine actress, a smoldering brunette with a body like sin. She would be amazing in that role, too. She had a husband and three adorable kids and no history whatsoever with J. T.

J. T. smiled slowly. "Sounds great, Al."

"I'll take you to lunch while we're there."

"Natch," J. T. said, and ended the call.

He stared at Britt in utter bemusement.

"Your expression says you have some amazing news," Britt prompted.

"So . . . like I said, Rebecca dropped out. But because of that video of the toast, and all the publicity around it, they want me to test with Tara Gonzales tomorrow. The part is mine. Now it's all about me."

She gave a short, amazed laugh. "Tara Gonzales? That troll?" she teased. "Actually, I love her."

"So does her husband." He kissed her.

"Wanna come with me? We'd be back in a couple of days," he murmured, when they came up for air.

She touched his face. "You go do this. It'd leave Sherrie and Glenn in the lurch if I do. Next time. I promise. I'll be fine, J. T., I swear. I'll miss you, but I can't wait to see you in this movie. And to buy a dress at Kayla's boutique for the premiere."

He studied her face as if to ascertain the absolute truth of this. Checking to see if she was, indeed, okay.

She loved him. She knew *he* loved *her*.

She knew pretty much what she'd just signed up for.

And she did trust him, and that was the honest-to-God truth.

But J. T.'s expression was a little somber. He was pensive about something.

"What do you want to do for four hours?" Britt asked him.

And then his eyes took on a portentous gleam. Some kind of lightbulb had just clicked on in his head.

She was pretty sure she knew the answer. She hoped, anyway.

But it was his turn to surprise her. "I think we should go for a hike."

Once or twice a week, when they could get away alone, Glenn and Sherrie took a long hike in the cool of the evening, if it did cool down in the evening, which was no guarantee.

Their favorite hike was Full Moon Falls, because they could stop by the Eternity Oak to admire their initials. Glenn had carved them there with absolute unswerving conviction when the two of them were still in high school.

The scar was old and bold, and the tree, they liked to think, bore it proudly.

They stopped before it like a shrine.

And then Sherrie gasped. "Oh, my goodness. Look, honey. Brand-new initials up there on that branch. You can see they've just been carved. It's a little raw."

They moved in for a closer look.

BEL + JTM
2016

"Well, I'll . . . be . . . damned," she breathed. "That's our Britt and John Tennessee McCord."

Glenn whistled long and low. "Hooo-ly *smokes*."

Sherrie stood on her toes and touched the newly carved initials gently, as if they were delicate and alive.

John Tennessee McCord had done it neatly and precisely, but then, he had carpentry skills.

"Glenn, you know how I always get goose bumps when something feels right?" Sherrie held out her arm to show him that she was covered in them.

"Sure. Like I got when I first laid eyes on you."

She was the only one who knew how romantic and tenderhearted her husband was. He was forever saying things like that to her.

She smiled and looped her arm in his, and they moved on up the trail.

"You think Britt and J. T. will have a Hellcat Canyon wedding pretty soon?" she asked.

"Hope so. With that whole Hollywood crowd, sure would be good for business."

Romantic and tenderhearted and *practical*.

"That right there, Glenn. What you said. *That's* why I love you."

Later that night, from his gate at the Sacramento airport, J. T. texted a photo to Franco Francone.

For once, it wasn't his Emmy.

Instead, when Franco clicked it open, he saw Britt and J. T. standing right beneath their freshly carved initials on the Eternity Oak. J. T.'s arms were wrapped around her and her head was leaning back against his chest. They were wearing huge smiles.

She really loves me.

is what it said.

Franco, who was never going to tell J. T. that he was the one who'd recorded and posted that wedding toast video on YouTube, texted back

Good.

Next month, don't miss these exciting new love stories only from Avon Books

Chasing Lady Amelia by Maya Rodale

Lady Amelia is fed up with being a proper lady and wishes to explore London, so one night she escapes . . . and finds herself in the company of wickedly tempting rake Alistair Finlay-Jones. Inevitably they end up falling in love and making love. When Amelia finds out that Alistair has been ordered to marry her, he must woo her and win back the now-angry American girl.

Under the Wire by HelenKay Dimon

When Reid Armstrong learns that his former fiancée has disappeared on a top-secret science expedition, he rushes to her rescue. Second chances don't come often and he needs to prove his worth to Cara Layne or die trying. Cara can't trust anyone, least of all Reid. Even if his skills get them out alive, he's a heartache waiting to strike twice. Yet being in close proximity proves their connection burns hotter than ever.

Drive You Wild by Jennifer Bernard

With his good looks, hitting records, and played-for-the-fans arrogance, Kilby Catfish left-fielder Trevor Stark makes women lose their minds and men lose their cool. But every time the major league team comes calling, Trevor keeps himself in the tiny Texas town. *Why* is heart-tuggingly top secret. Until the team owner's daughter comes to Kilby . . . trying everything up her sexy sleeve to make Trevor talk.

Discover great authors, exclusive offers, and more at hc.com.

REL 0616

At Avon Books, we know your passion for romance—once you finish one of our novels, you find yourself wanting more.

May we tempt you with . . .

- **Excerpts** from our upcoming releases.
- Entertaining **extras,** including authors' personal photo albums and book lists.
- Behind-the-scenes **scoop** on your favorite characters and series.
- **Sweepstakes** for the chance to win free books, romantic getaways, and other fun prizes.
- Writing **tips** from our authors and editors.
- **Blog** with our authors and find out why they love to write romance.
- **Exclusive content** that's not contained within the pages of our novels.

Join us at
www.avonbooks.com

An Imprint of Harper Collins*Publishers*
www.avonromance.com

Available wherever books are sold or please call 1-800-331-3761 to order.

FTH 1013

Give in to your Impulses!

These unforgettable stories only take a second to buy and give you hours of reading pleasure!

Go to ***www.AvonImpulse.com*** and see what we have to offer.

Available wherever e-books are sold.

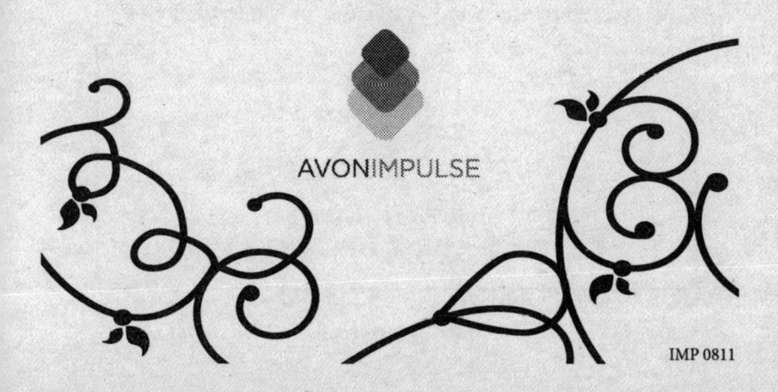

IMP 0811

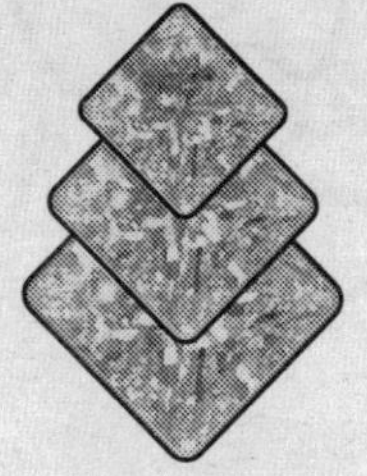

AVONBOOKS

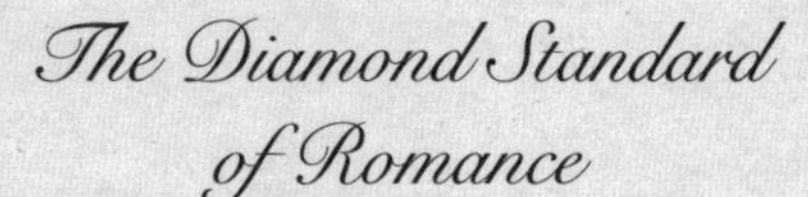

Visit AVONROMANCE.COM

Come celebrate 75 years of Avon Books
as each month we look toward the future
and celebrate the past!

Join us online for more information about our
75th anniversary e-book promotions,
author events and reader activities.
A full year of new voices and classic stories.
All created by the very best writers of romantic fiction.

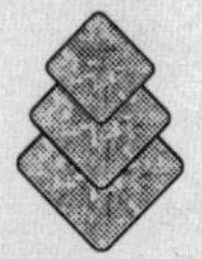

Diamonds Always
Sparkle, Shimmer, and Shine!